JOHN BUNYAN (1628–88) was born at Elstow, near Bedford, the eldest son of a tinker. His schooling was slight. In 1644 he was mustered in the Parliamentarian army and stationed at Newport Pagnell. During the early 1650s he underwent the prolonged spiritual crisis he later graphically recorded in one of the classics of Puritan spirituality, *Grace Abounding to the Chief of Sinners* (1666). Following his conversion he joined the Bedford Baptist church, and the congregation quickly recognized his gift for preaching. This led, in 1656, to the beginning of a literary career in the course of which he would publish some sixty works of controversial, expository and practical divinity, marked by an uncompromising zeal, a trenchant directness of style, and a particular concern for the spiritual welfare of common people. During the twelve-year imprisonment for nonconformity which followed the Restoration (1660–72), writing became the chief means by which to fulfil his vocation. It was not, however, until the publication in 1678 of *The Pilgrim's Progress* that his genius declared itself. The imaginative persuasiveness and realistic authenticity of this allegory have earned for it an unprecedentedly extensive readership and for its author his unique place in literary history. It was followed in 1680 by its sequel, *The Life and Death of Mr. Badman*, by the elaborate multi-level allegory *The Holy War* in 1682, and by Part II of *The Pilgrim's Progress* in 1684, works which substantiate Bunyan's claim to be the founder of the English novel.

JOHN STACHNIEWSKI was Senior Lecturer in the Department of English and American Studies at the University of Manchester. He is the author of *The Persecutory Imagination: English Puritanism and the Literature of Religious Despair* (1991). He died in September, 1996, at the age of 42.

ANITA PACHECO teaches in the Department of English at the University of Hull. She is the author of articles on Aphra Behn and the editor of *Early Women Writers: 1600–1720* in the *Longman Critical Readers* series (1997).

OXFORD WORLD'S CLASSICS

*For almost 100 years Oxford World's Classics have brought
readers closer to the world's great literature. Now with over 700
titles—from the 4,000-year-old myths of Mesopotamia to the
twentieth century's greatest novels—the series makes available
lesser-known as well as celebrated writing.*

*The pocket-sized hardbacks of the early years contained
introductions by Virginia Woolf, T. S. Eliot, Graham Greene,
and other literary figures which enriched the experience of reading.
Today the series is recognized for its fine scholarship and
reliability in texts that span world literature, drama and poetry,
religion, philosophy and politics. Each edition includes perceptive
commentary and essential background information to meet the
changing needs of readers.*

OXFORD WORLD'S CLASSICS

JOHN BUNYAN

Grace Abounding

with Other Spiritual Autobiographies

Edited with an Introduction and Notes by
JOHN STACHNIEWSKI

with

ANITA PACHECO

Oxford   New York

OXFORD UNIVERSITY PRESS

1998

Oxford University Press, Great Clarendon Street, Oxford OX2 6DP

Oxford New York

Athens Auckland Bangkok Bogota Bombay Buenos Aires
Calcutta Cape Town Dar es Salaam Delhi Florence Hong Kong Istanbul
Karachi Kuala Lumpur Madras Madrid Melbourne Mexico City
Nairobi Paris Singapore Taipei Tokyo Toronto Warsaw

and associated companies in
Berlin Ibadan

Oxford is a trade mark of Oxford University Press

Editorial matter © Anita Pacheco and Joanna Stachniewski 1998

First published as an Oxford World's Classics paperback 1998

British Library Cataloguing in Publication Data
Data available

Library of Congress Cataloging in Publication Data
Bunyan, John, 1628–1688.
[Grace abounding to the chief of sinners]
Grace abounding with other autobiographies/John Bunyan; edited with
an introduction and notes by John Stachniewski with Anita Pacheco.
(Oxford world's classics)
Includes bibliographical references (p.).
Contents: Grace abounding/John Bunyan—A relation of the imprisonment of
Mr. John Bunyan-–Confessions/Richard Norwood—A short history of the life of
John Crook—The lost sheep found/Lawrence Clarkson—The narrative of the persecution
of Agnes Beaumont—Appendix: Radical and nonconformist groups in seventeenth-century England.
1. Bunyan, John, 1628–1688. 2. Authors, English—Early modern, 1500–1700—
Biography. 3. Puritans—England—Biography. 4. Norwood, Richard, 1590?–1675.
5. Crook, John, 1617–1699. 6. Claxton, Laurence, 1615–1667. 7. Beaumont, Agnes,
d. 1720. 8. Christian biography. 9. Spiritual life. I. Stachniewski, John. II. Pacheco,
Anita. III. Title. IV. Series: Oxford world's classics (Oxford University Press)
PR3329.G1 1998 274.2'07'0922—dc21 97–41682
[B]
ISBN 0-19-282132-6

1 3 5 7 9 10 8 6 4 2

Typeset by Best-set Typesetter Ltd., Hong Kong
Printed in Great Britain by
Caledonian International Book Manufacturing Ltd.
Glasgow

For Jeannie and Adam

CONTENTS

Introduction   ix

Note on the Texts   xliv

Select Bibliography   xlvii

A Chronology of John Bunyan and his Times   l

Abbreviations   liv

GRACE ABOUNDING   I
  John Bunyan

A RELATION OF THE IMPRISONMENT OF
MR. JOHN BUNYAN   95

CONFESSIONS   123
  Richard Norwood

A SHORT HISTORY OF THE LIFE OF
JOHN CROOK   157

THE LOST SHEEP FOUND   171
  Lawrence Clarkson

THE NARRATIVE OF THE PERSECUTION OF
AGNES BEAUMONT   191

Appendix: Radical and Nonconformist   225
  Groups in Seventeenth-Century England

Explanatory Notes   229

INTRODUCTION

BUNYAN'S spiritual autobiography has elicited contradictory responses. Some critics lay it on the couch and ask it to speak of its neurotic symptoms. Others disparage its claim to veracity (Bunyan declared in the Preface that he would '*lay down the thing as it was*'), suggesting that it subordinates recollection to its pastoral purposes, or that it exaggerates its mental drama as a form of sectarian self-promotion. This edition presents *Grace Abounding* alongside four other autobiographical texts which help to illuminate the nuances of feeling and meaning embedded in Bunyan's writing. In this context, *Grace Abounding* appears neither an idiosyncratic, obsessional production nor a declaration of credentials much influenced by its anticipated reception, but a richly exemplary text emerging from a shared cultural experience.

Bunyan was born in 1628 near Elstow, a village just over a mile from Bedford. His family had declined from their status of small-holders in the sixteenth century; his father Thomas worked as a brazier or tinker. In the 1630s, Bunyan attended a local school, but his education was short-lived: he soon left to follow his father's trade. The Civil War broke out in 1642, and in November of 1644 Bunyan joined the Parliamentary army, either voluntarily or by conscription in a county levy.

The collapse of censorship during the civil war years produced, in Christopher Hill's words, 'a great overturning, questioning, revaluing of everything in England':

Groups like the Levellers, Diggers, and Fifth Monarchists offered new political solutions (and in the case of the Diggers, new economic solutions too). The various sects—Baptists, Quakers, Muggletonians—offered new religious solutions. Other groups asked sceptical questions about all the institutions and beliefs of their society—Seekers, Ranters, the Diggers too.[1]

Bunyan probably saw little or no active service during his two and a half year spell in the Parliamentary army, but we can safely assume some degree of exposure to this climate of religious and political

[1] *WTUD* 14.

radicalism. He would in all likelihood have heard radical puritan preachers during this period, and come into contact, from 1645, with detachments of the New Model Army, in which radical ideas were rife. *Grace Abounding* records Bunyan's encounter in 1650 with the 'cursed' antinomian principles of the Ranters (p. 16) as well as his later theological disputes with the Quakers (p. 36).

When his regiment was demobilized in July 1647, Bunyan returned to Elstow, resumed his trade as a tinker, and married the first of his two wives at some point in 1648–9. The intense spiritual crises which occupy the bulk of *Grace Abounding* spanned the years 1649–55. They led eventually, after his decisive encounter with the poor women of Bedford, 'sitting at a door in the Sun, and talking about the things of God', to his introduction to the open communion Bedford Baptists. He was baptized and registered as a member of this congregation in 1655. Over the next few years he built up a reputation as a preacher, engaged in public disputation with Quakers, and published various theological works: the anti-Quaker polemic, *Some Gospel Truths Opened* (1656); *A Few Sighs from Hell or the Groans of a Damned Soul* (1658), an urgent and menacing evangelical sermon which excoriates the rich; and, in 1659, *The Doctrine of the Law and Grace Unfolded*, his fullest statement of his essential theology, in which his autobiography is briefly adumbrated.

Hard on the heels of the Restoration, Bunyan was arrested in a barn in the village of Lower Samsell, where he was conducting a meeting (in November 1660). He was charged, under an Elizabethan statute of 1593, with refusal to attend services of the established church and with 'calling together the people' and preaching to unlawful meetings and 'conventicles'. Some members of radical sects, Fifth Monarchists especially, were involved in plots to overthrow monarchy once more and restore a republic.[2] Partly out of suspicion and partly out of vindictiveness, the authorities bore down hard on nonconformist leaders, whether or not they dissociated themselves from such activities. Nonconformity was itself taken as evidence of disloyalty and treacherous intent. Bunyan was tried by a bench of ex-Royalists who had suffered severe penalties in the Interregnum. Three months after his imprisonment in Bedford county jail, attempts were made to persuade him to accept terms for

[2] See Keeble, 28.

his release; but as this would have meant undertaking not to preach, which would have gone against what he took to be God's command, Bunyan could not comply.

Bunyan was eventually released in 1672, as a result of Charles II's Declaration of Indulgence. He had helped to maintain his family by making shoelaces. He had also written and published various works, including *Grace Abounding*, and had probably already embarked on his most famous work, *The Pilgrim's Progress* (1678).

Experimental Calvinism and spiritual autobiography

This brief biographical sketch has largely overlooked the aspect of Bunyan's life which is perhaps most crucial for an understanding of *Grace Abounding*: the religious culture into which he was born. The Reformation, which triumphed (precariously) in England from the accession of Elizabeth I, brought to the lives of English people a set of Protestant beliefs whose dominant inspiration was the Genevan theocrat John Calvin. The most influential of these (though not the one Calvin himself would have wanted to stress) was a strong form of predestination, which was as explicit about the assignation of damnation (reprobation) to the majority of mankind, before their creation, as it was about the salvation (election) of the chosen few. This is known in retrospect as 'double predestination'. The doctrine derived logically from Calvin's emphasis on the absolute sovereignty of God: God was all-powerful and perfectly just, while human beings were wholly impotent and corrupt. Calvin would allow no fudging of this, such as the substitution of divine foresight for actual divine ordination of all that happened in the world. To allow human beings any freedom of choice would be to derogate from God's sovereignty and qualify human depravity. Not being able, in theory at least, to *do* anything to improve their chances of salvation, people were thus driven to an often anguished introspection aimed at establishing whether they were members of the 'elect', whether they were the recipients of 'saving faith' or 'saving grace'.

They were helped in, or held to, this endeavour by a pastoral ministry which, both in pulpit and print, concentrated attention on what were called the 'signs' of election and reprobation. The most influential English Calvinist was William Perkins, who in 1589 published *A Treatise Tending unto a Declaration whether a Man Be in the Estate of Damnation or in the Estate of Grace*. As church historian R. T. Kendall says, it 'inaugurated a new era in English theology'.[3] The preachers for whom the quest for signs was a central preoccupation tended to be those known as 'puritans'; and the form of Calvinism such an emphasis promoted was 'experimental'—based, that is, on the evidence of experience. The individual Christian's life, and mental states, should exhibit conformity to a pattern of elect experience. William Perkins (and after him Bunyan himself) even drew a map of the phases through which the elect should pass, counterparted by the progress of the reprobate to hell. The elect would receive an 'Effectual calling', which would be followed by 'Justification', 'Sanctification', and eventual 'Glorification', while the reprobate would either receive 'No calling' at all or 'a calling not effectual', followed by 'a yeelding to Gods calling', 'Relapse', 'Fulness of sin', and 'Damnation'.[4]

   The Bible was of course the claimed source of the theology (Bunyan's *Mapp*, mentioned above, is made up of biblical quotations), but it is probably truer to say that the theology determined a reading practice which turned the Bible itself into the ultimate book of signs: it was sifted for its binary application to the reader's own life. The Old Testament provided 'types', or metaphoric foreshadowings, of New Testament events; and both Testaments could do the same for the personal experiences of the reader. Bunyan's most protracted anguish involves feared identification with both Cain, who sold his birthright, and Judas, who directly sold Christ. He seeks to differentiate his circumstances from theirs and associate himself instead with Peter, a type of the forgiven traitor. It was a compulsive reading practice which led, as is evident not just from Bunyan but from the likes of the semi-literate Agnes Beaumont, to extensive memorization of the Bible. Bible verses, usually taken from the King James translation, occasionally from the Geneva, were woven into the fabric of consciousness, helping to construct identity. Bunyan's *Pilgrim's Progress* is presented similarly as a book of signs in which intimate and anxious engagement, self-identification, is encouraged:

   [3] R. T. Kendall, *Calvin and English Calvinism to 1649* (Oxford, 1979), 1.
   [4] Perkins's 'Table' is prefixed to his *Works* (Cambridge, 1603). Bunyan's *Mapp* can be found in Offor vol. iii. Both are reproduced in Stachniewski, 164–5 and 196–7. Perkins's Table is in turn derived from Calvin's successor in Geneva, Theodore Beza. In the quote from Perkins spelling has been partially modernized.

'*Would'st read thy self, and read thou know'st not what* | *And yet know whether thou are blest or not,* | *By reading the same lines? O then come hither,* | *And lay my Book, thy Head and Heart together*'.[5] *Grace Abounding* relives the experimental religion of an individual who wishes to regard the testimony he gives, and the very act of scrupulous self-reading, as constituting the evidence, the signs, of his election.

These cultural conditions of authorship must adjust our expectations of autobiography. The introspection which gives us, in the seventeenth century, virtually the first inward-looking autobiographies is impelled by this quest for assurance. Bunyan's mother, for example, is never mentioned, although she dies when he is 16. Nothing is said either about his father's rapid remarriage. His father only appears for his spiritual failures: not being aware of the typological meaning of the Israelites as the chosen people; not having taught him to speak without swearing. The only evidentiary contributions that Bunyan's wife (either wife) can make to his life as recorded here is to provide him with two religious books inherited from her father; and to be the occasion of his sceptical plea to God to end her premature contractions, which results in severe divine punishment eighteen months later. There is too, it should not be overlooked, the very moving account Bunyan gives of his distress at forced abandonment of his family when in prison (*GA* 89–90).

As well as producing what would in other circumstances be startling autobiographical omissions, it might be said (it certainly has been said[6]) that the aim of exhibiting conformity to an elect paradigm distorts what the autobiography *does* contain. The fact is that all autobiography distorts the past; it is a narrative of experience which is both subject to all sorts of pressures in the writer's present and reliant on the reprises of reprises (and misprisions of misprisions) which layer memory. In this case, however, it should be recognized that, unlike say an autobiography in which personal vanity is bound to have its say, the pressure towards truth-telling is also strong. Bunyan was lumbered with the belief that God was the true author of the story he was trying to write, and that if he falsified it,

---

[5] *The Pilgrim's Progress*, ed. N. H. Keeble (Oxford, 1984), 7. All references to *The Pilgrim's Progress* will be to this edition.

[6] See examples in Stachniewski, 129–31.

by laying claim to spiritual experiences or certainties he did not really have, this would expose him as a hypocrite—not one of the elect after all.

If, as some commentators suggest, puritans' lives 'fell under their gaze into the pattern [of election] set by Paul'[7] and expounded from the pulpit, we would have been spared, or denied, the gruelling oscillations between hope and despair (with the pendulum sticking for whole years in despair) which mark Bunyan's record and give it its psychological intensity. The doubleness of predestination produced a doubleness of vision: the paradigm of reprobation (as explicit as that of election, and statistically much more probable) was always an influential possibility. The Independent divine Thomas Goodwin likened sign-hunting to perspective paintings which looked at from one side exhibited a devil, from the other an angel or beautiful woman: 'So some have lookt over their hearts by signes at one time, and have to their thinking found nothing but hypocrisie, unbelief, hardnesse, self-seeking; but not long after examining their hearts again by the same signes they have espied the image of God drawn fairely upon the table of their hearts.'[8] In the end, only one of the paradigms could discover itself to be true for any one life. So there was a constant pressure to nag at the contradictory evidence, to keep experience under daily review; to try to argue anxiety away, certainly, but without evading the apparent grounds of anxiety. Fear of rejection, on the one hand, and fear of hypocrisy, on the other, disciplines the writing. Intellectual honesty is forced on Bunyan, though the intellect is hemmed in by what will seem to most modern readers the most peculiar premisses.

There is, it is true, a narrative attempt to make the elect reading supervene as the objective story, dissolving the fears of reprobation as subjective and delusory. But that framing of the experience as a document certifying election (comparable to the 'Roll' Christian acquires on his journey and is required to submit at the Heavenly Gate) does not eclipse the record of despair which fills most of its pages. Nor does Bunyan pretend to have left radical anxieties about his spiritual state behind—as his present-tense confessions in the Conclusion demonstrate. It is the unflinching excavation of the

---

[7] William Haller, *The Rise of Puritanism* (New York, 1938), 91.
[8] *Childe of Light Walking in Darknes* (1636), 193.

abject which gives *Grace Abounding* its literary value: the unparalleled moment-by-moment precision with which, through terse metaphor and recaptured logic, it takes the reader down into that experience of knotted feeling. Bunyan is certainly also surprised by joy, but the joy at its most intense is not Wordsworthian: it is the emotional reflex of sudden release from strangulating anxiety and despair.

Young Bunyan's religion in its social milieu

The religious culture into which Bunyan was born did not exist in a vacuum. It battened on to existing social conditions, and its meanings varied with them. The credibility of the Calvinist doctrine of predestination was enhanced by the disturbing unpredictability of human lives in a society whose agrarian economy was undergoing transformation and whose competitive laws of commerce were too new to be rationally apprehended. Larger forces than human will seemed overwhelmingly to determine human destinies. We have seen that Bunyan's family was, like countless others, at the sharp end of these changes. Owning land in the sixteenth century, and thus enjoying respectable smallholder status, the Bunyans had been forced into sale and were reduced to lowly, artisanal work as tinkers by the time of John Bunyan's birth. This is the social background against which his crisis of identity becomes more understandable.

The belief that a few were chosen, through no merit of their own, and the majority excluded, matched observation, but it also implied Bunyan's own exclusion. This inference drew support from the cultural habits that accreted to social stratification. So, for example, he was from early childhood a habitual swearer. It was a form of compensatory emphasis, giving his speech a swaggering authority denied to it by his 'inconsiderable' social status. But when he was rebuked for this on one occasion, his crestfallen response revealed the brittleness of his defiance (*GA* 11–12). Swearing was against the law;[9] so too, from 1644, was playing sports on Sundays.

Here again the young Bunyan found himself on the disreputable side of a social divide. Sports on the village green had once been

---

[9] Legislation was stiffened by an Act which came into operation on 1 Aug. 1650; but prior to that, an Act of 1624 remained in force (*Statutes of the Realm* 12 vols. (London, 1810–28), vol. iv, pt. 2, 1229–30).

viewed as harmless pastime for the lower orders. But they had become politicized. When Charles I and Archbishop Laud reissued James I's *Book of Sports* in 1633, actively encouraging Sunday sports, they did so as an act of defiance of puritan sabbatarianism. The culture of puritanism was, as they saw it, dividing communities and fomenting greater social and political consciousness among the common people. Game-playing expressed the kind of peasant innocence and unvarying repetition on which the old order saw its stability to rest. But the puritan ascendancy in Parliament led, by the time of Bunyan's adolescence, to legislation proscribing Sunday sports. Now they too identified the riff-raff, signifying illiteracy, idleness, and presumed reprobation.

Literacy, too, was a dividing agent.[10] Bunyan's parents, laudably, sent him to school; but it was a half-hearted business for the tinker boy: as we have seen, he soon abandoned it, presumably realizing that such education as he could obtain would not lift him socially. He returned to game-playing, and took up his father's calling.

In ways such as these the young Bunyan's irredeemable social baseness—'of that rank that is meanest, and most despised of all the families in the Land' (p. 6)—was confirmed. So far as this world was concerned there was no prospect of a reversal. To gain respectability he tried religious devotion, but while he enjoyed the surprised approbation of fellow villagers, his heart was not in it. He was inwardly unconvinced by his pious chatter. His adulation of the clergy and its paraphernalia at Elstow Abbey was a form of self-prostration, by which he eventually felt humiliated.

The strength of Bunyan's feelings of being got at is apparent in episodes such as the voice from heaven when he was playing cat (p. 10), or his fears that God would crush him with the huge bells in the Bell Tower, or by collapsing the tower itself (pp. 13–14). Bell-ringing on Sundays, except to call people to church, was another parliamentary proscription; and it reflected puritan opposition to all recreational ringing.[11] It is noteworthy that Bunyan had these feelings of persecution before he encountered the Bedford Independent church which was to draw him fully into the experimental Calvinist

---

[10] See Keith Wrightson, *English Society 1580–1680* (London, 1982), 220–1.

[11] Parliamentary Ordinance of 8 Apr. 1644 (*Acts and Ordinances of the Interregnum 1642–1660*, ed. and collected by C. H. Firth and R. S. Rait (repr. Holmes Beach, Fla., 1972), 420–2).

thought-world. The belief in a providence which frequently expressed God's anger through dramatic events was very widely held. But it was puritans who tended to collect and disseminate examples with lugubrious fascination.

The difference in the religion Bunyan encounters in the poor Bedford women is that it inverts the class presumptions which were built in, consciously or not, to its expression through the state church, whether episcopalian or presbyterian. They are poor and yet emancipated, reborn into a new world in which they are not to be 'reckoned' among their neighbours. The usual standards of social measurement no longer apply. In fact social lowliness seems to make it easier for them to accept their 'miserable state by nature' in the theological sense, to embrace the idea that all human claims are 'filthy', and thus to be joyously responsive to the divine grace which saves them from their wretchedness (p. 14). This powerful social ingredient in the appeal to Bunyan comes through much of his writing—in his first sermon-treatise, *A Few Sighs from Hell* (1658), for example, in which the impervious rich get a roasting, or in *The Pilgrim's Progress*, where, we are nudged by a marginal note at Vanity Fair, '*Sins are all Lords and Great ones*' (p. 77). The rich have more reason to be attached to the things of this world, to be 'carnal'. The new world to which Bunyan is now desperate to gain access is above all else actualized by a new language: it is the consuming language of experimental Calvinism, based on the reciprocal exchange of spiritual experiences. It is this language community, equalized by shared interior spirituality, that achieves separateness from the values and reckonings of the familiar social world.

It was much easier, however, for Bunyan to recognize this escape route than to avail himself of it. And again a significant part of the explanation for this seems to be social. He has the greatest difficulty in being convinced that he can be a recipient of God's mercy because of the extent to which he is prone to feelings of exclusion. There was already a conception lodged in his mind of this all-powerful being who had always been represented to him as the highest authority in his society, validating its structures and laws. 'I did flie from his face,' Bunyan confesses in edition 5, 'that is, my mind and spirit fled before him, by reason of his highness, I could not endure' (p. 48). The self-suggesting metaphor which keeps recurring to express Bunyan's despair—and which *The Pilgrim's Progress* develops into a picture in the Slough of Dispond—is 'sinking'. Bunyan's family had been sinking to their 'low' position (p. 6). He is easily assailed by the conviction that he is sinking to hell.

The deep and protracted despair into which Bunyan is felled by momentary mental assent to the insistent inner voice's mysterious command '*Sell Christ*' registers the entanglement of religious feeling with social predicament in a more pointed way. The text Bunyan sets against this dire temptation, as an ultimate damage-limiting consolation, is Lev. 25: 23: '*For the land shall not be sold for ever, for the Land is mine*' (p. 39). The equation of selling Christ with the sale of land can be sanctioned by typological practice; but it is also highly suggestive of the fall from social grace of Bunyan's own one-time farming family. The context of the Leviticus quotation concerns the redemption of the land of any Jewish brother who 'has waxen poor' and sold to wealthier neighbours. He and his kin should be given the opportunity to redeem their property; and if they are unable to do so, it will eventually revert to their ownership in the year of the Jubilee (which signified to Bunyan the Day of Judgment). Bunyan's forefathers had sold the family land. There was no possibility, in material reality, of redeeming it. This horror seems to have been transposed into a spiritual formulation: 'what have I disinherited my poor Soul of!' (p. 52) For a long time Bunyan holds the anguished belief that God has chosen this sin for him because it is the notorious unforgivable sin (see note to *GA* 31, below), and it thus plays out the reprobate destiny assigned to him. The text that haunts him, as the ineluctable biblical type of his sin, is the one dooming the reprobate Esau to futile remorse after selling his birthright (the land, of course, which passes to Jacob). It takes Bunyan over two years to come through his anguish. It is difficult to believe that the material counterpart of this sense of exclusion and irreparable loss was not an enabling condition of its extremity.

Regeneration in Grace Abounding *and* The Pilgrim's Progress

The conversion process is the primary subject-matter of both *Grace Abounding* and *The Pilgrim's Progress*—and it is a process, a halting one, rather than a single event. In fact the 'regeneration' of the believer was a more familiar concept to the preachers of the time. Attempts have been made to divide up Bunyan's autobiographical narrative into neat developmental segments (for example by Beatrice Batson[12]), but Bunyan does not signal these. It is extremely difficult to say when Bunyan is converted. This was defined as the reception of 'saving faith' and 'saving grace'. Certainly there are euphoric experiences of triumphant certainty, but these are always at risk of retakes, subject to self-directed charges of subjectivism and to the evacuation of all spiritual sense. Even in the Conclusion to the work Bunyan confesses to atheist thoughts: 'when this temptation comes, it . . . removeth the foundation from under me'. His most blessed divine visitations are rendered meaningless. These disclosures, impressive in their candour, do not, as critics often do on Bunyan's behalf, consign the disturbing experiences to the safety of the past. The present-tense confessions survive revisions of the text right up to Bunyan's death.

Bunyan keeps faith with this instability in *The Pilgrim's Progress* in which Christian's entering the Wicket-Gate, encountering the Cross, and finding himself relieved of his burden—an identifiable moment of conversion—does not prevent complete losses of faith much later on: the Giant Despair episode and even the River of Death. On the other hand, it is probably useful to keep in mind the broadly conceived sequence of Christian experience as described by Paul (and accented by divines such as Perkins): conviction, vocation, justification, sanctification, and glorification. The Christian, convicted of deep sinfulness, is called by God—that is, has an acute sense of a personal summons. Emptied of all self-confidence, he or she gratefully seizes the free gift of God's grace, apprehending justification by the innocent death of Christ (he pays the penalty for sin on his or her behalf). Sanctification is the gradual process by which the righteousness of Christ, imputed by God to the penitent sinner, actualizes itself through the purifying influence of the Holy Spirit, mediated by the Bible, in the Christian's life—making him or her the

---

[12] E. Beatrice Batson, *John Bunyan: Allegory and Imagination* (London, 1984), 13–14. Anne Hawkins points to the need scholars seem to have of a crisis conversion event to help them structure the narrative. Hawkins prefers a process of 'conversion, relapse and reconversion' (p. 268), and picks out the vision of golden seals (*G.A* 37) and the victory of the promise of grace in the battle of the texts (p. 61). But this is perhaps also over-structuring, underrating both the instability of all Bunyan's moments of assurance and the intimidatory theology which could construe relapse as evidence that conversion had been temporary and inauthentic. See Anne Hawkins, 'The Double-Conversion in Bunyan's *Grace Abounding*', *Philological Quarterly*, 61 (1982), 259–76.

saint ultimately fit for heaven. Glorification is the after-death experience of heavenly glory (of which there could be visionary anticipations—''Twas glorious to me to see his exaltation' (p. 66)). As with Freud's phases of childhood development, it would be naive to conceive of these categories as simply sequential: they are inter-penetrating.

There are points at which *Grace Abounding* and *The Pilgrim's Progress* diverge as well as important coherences between them. It is often suggested (for example, Sharrock, 138–9, *PP* 375; Hill, 72) that the Wicket-Gate can be compared to the gap in the wall of Bunyan's dream (which he had shortly after encountering the poor women in Bedford), through which he has immense difficulty passing (*GA* 18–19). Both derive from the same biblical source ('Enter ye in at the strait gate' (Matt. 7: 13)). Yet there is a sharp difference between Bunyan's own desperate struggle to get his body through and the ease with which Christian is admitted (*PP* 21). Getting to the gate is the troubled journey the allegory focuses on. Besides, Bunyan has a long way to go before he receives a call; the dream, unfulfilled in reality, leaves him 'in a forlorn and sad condition' (*GA* 19). He spends a year scouring the Bible for reassuring words that came to him, eventually finding them in an apocryphal book. Disappointed but partly comforted, he still recalls (at p. 23) his continuing anguish that he has not been called. Recovery from this state is assisted by the ministry of John Gifford, the pastor chosen by the founding members of the Bedford Independent church.

It is only now that Bunyan experiences 'an evidence for Heaven, with many golden Seals thereon, all hanging in my sight' (p. 37), counterparting the 'Roll with a Seal upon it' (*PP* 31) which Christian receives just after entering the Wicket-Gate and shedding his burden. Even this is put in question by edition 5 which inserts 'as I thought' after 'evidence', presumably because Bunyan is about to run into the most devastating period of despair of his salvation. Of course Christian's seizure by Giant Despair (*PP* 93–7) also occurs far into the narrative. Both *Grace Abounding* and *The Pilgrim's Progress* distinguish between the objective fact of evidence of salvation and the states of mind Christians can succumb to. In the allegory this works very satisfactorily since it is possible to objectify the evidence in the form of a certificate. Christian can lose it, forget about it, but in the end he can also hand it in. In literal reality, however, things were more difficult. Bunyan, as he thought, was vouchsafed golden seals, as on a legal document, guaranteeing his place in heaven; but this visionary apprehension was hardly likely to remain with him permanently, and turns out to be evanescent.

The term Bunyan sometimes uses for the subjective spiritual state is 'frame' (*GA* 11, 32, 74). But to call it subjective is in a way misleading because the assured frame of mind was supposed to be the internalization of something objective. Bunyan had to muster belief in an objective validation. Recovery from despair at 'selling Christ' requires his recognition that it was 'not my good frame of Heart that made my Righteousness better, nor yet my bad frame that made my Righteousness worse' (pp. 65–6). He must distinguish between his 'frames', or mood-governed perspectives on his spiritual status, and the objective fact of Christ's righteousness which is freely imputed to him. This is comparable to the distinction between Christian's doubts and despair, which are temporary and subjective, and his possession of a concrete certificate of assurance, and, in the Giant Despair episode, a material key. The trouble was that the negative, reprobate frame seemed objective while it was being experienced. *Grace Abounding* powerfully expresses the feeling of being taken captive by a state of mind ('this kind of despair did so possess my Soul' (p. 11)) which seeded the later Giant Despair episode.

Equally, however, the two works share the portrayal of emancipation as arbitrary, effected miraculously by an outside force. Christian, suicidally depressed in Doubting Castle, 'as one half amazed' suddenly discovers 'a *Key* in my bosom called *Promise*' (*PP* 96) (i.e. the written gospel promises of forgiveness and salvation); while for Bunyan himself, 'suddenly this sentence fell upon my Soul, *Thy righteousness is in Heaven*' (*GA* 65). Release is as from prison: 'Now did my chains fall off my Legs indeed (p. 66). So powerful is the feeling of emancipation that the preceding misery can seem absurd (as it does for Christian when he escapes from Doubting Castle); but mood, or frame, can be all-enveloping, blocking access to an opposite state of mind.

Alter egos in Grace Abounding *and* The Pilgrim's Progress

One of the most striking affinities between the two works is the use of alter egos to establish and reinforce identity as a member of the elect. This process is more uninhibited in the allegory where no real person is involved. But the rudiment of the procedure can be seen in encounters in *Grace Abounding*, both negative and positive.

Rejection of his best friend Harry, 'to whom my heart before was knit more than to any other' (*GA* 15), helps to mark Bunyan's own spiritual progress. The same process occurs with the 'religious intimate Companion' who adopts the 'cursed principles' of the Ranters: he became 'as great a stranger as I had been before a familiar' (p. 16). The process of self-definition is furthered by discriminating rejection of other human beings—a process which is amplified (from Obstinate and Pliable on) into a structuring principle in *The Pilgrim's Progress*.

Even the devil can contribute to self-definition. One consistent direction of revision of *Grace Abounding* is minor enlargements of the devil's role. For example, after the words 'Yet, said I, I will pray' (p. 57), edition 5 adds: ''Tis no boot, says he. Yet said I, I will pray'. The doubting, mistrustful self is palmed off on the devil, whose speaking part is slightly elaborated in a number of places.

But Bunyan can also see himself as the negative exemplum in ways that cross-refer with *The Pilgrim's Progress*. There is a facile glibness in his early attempts at religious devotion which is picked up to characterize Talkative and Ignorance. When he encounters the poor Bedford women: 'I drew near to hear what they said; for I was now a brisk talker also my self in the matters of Religion' (*GA* 14). There is a paradox here, for on the one hand 'brisk talker' is obviously disparaging. Ignorance is described as 'a very brisk lad' (*PP* 101). Yet on the other it is the talk of the Bedford women that attracts, at the same time as it reproves Bunyan. Talkative is found out because while he likes to talk of godly things there is no evidence of more than talk (*PP* 82).

While the young Bunyan similarly approaches the women because of his interest in talk, he differs from Talkative by acknowledging that the Bedford women 'were far above out of my reach'. Most impressive to him was their talk of a new birth (shortly to be allegorized, or literalized, in his wish-fulfilling dream) about which he knew nothing. Distinctive language use—'the Language of *Canaan*' (*PP* 74)—was an important means, for sectaries, of establishing their collective sense of separate identity. Bunyan felt the women 'spake as if joy did make them speak' and that they were 'as if they had

found a new world, as if they were people that dwelt alone' (*GA* 14).
This sense of a new world superimposed on the existing one is given
full expression in *The Pilgrim's Progress*, the contours of which are
at once familiar and transfigured by membership of the Christian
community.

Community and preaching

Despite the intense solitariness inhabited by most of Bunyan's
autobiography, the role of the Christian community—the Bedford
Independent church—is critical in securing his spiritual confidence
and releasing his gifts. In fact the two are probably very closely
related. From his first spiritual breakthrough, when the words '*My
love*' take hold of him, his impulse is to communicate what he has
experienced, even if it means preaching to the crows. He intimates
the writing of the autobiography, and its purpose: 'wherefore I said
in my Soul with much gladness, Well, I would I had a pen and ink
here, I would write this down before I go any further, for surely I
will not forget *this*, forty years hence; but alas! within less then forty
days I began to question all again' (*GA* 28). Writing would stabilize
his experience, provide the kind of objectivity which might act as a
bulwark against terrifying despair when the positive thoughts and
emotions faded. But the urge to speak of his emancipation was
equally strong: 'I longed for the company of some of Gods people,
that I might have imparted unto them what God had shewed me'
(p. 75).

Telling the saints (Bedford Independent church members) of his
spiritual experiences, giving his testimony to a group of formally
appointed church members, was for the Bedford church a condition
of Bunyan's, and anyone else's, membership. We may assume that
it was a briefer version of the testimony represented by *Grace
Abounding* itself that gained him admittance (see pp. 71–2). Finally
certified, like Christian with his Roll, Bunyan appears very quickly
to have been urged to speak to meetings of the faithful, and not long
after that (1656) to preach in public. His suffering was a rite of
passage; it gained him acceptance and respect.

The very intensity of what Bunyan underwent fortified his belief
in the absolute primacy of spiritual experience and enabled him to
speak publicly with impassioned conviction. When he preached, he

XXIV

felt himself 'wrapt up in the glory of this excellent work' (p. 80). 'Now before I go any further,' he addressed the reader of *The Doctrine of Law and Grace Unfolded* (1659), 'I must needs speak a word from my own experience of the things of Christ . . .' (*MW* ii. 156). Lacking the educational qualifications of the ordained clergy, who sneered at 'mechanick' preachers, Bunyan relied on his own spiritual experience to authorize and authenticate his ministry. The compulsive quest for assurance had, in fact, gained him an education: he knew the Bible inside out, and had developed, in the desperate and strenuous arguments he had with himself, the interpretative and argumentative skills which enabled him to dispute with Quakers and later, more impressively, with his socially harangu-ing but theologically less literate persecutors. Now at last he had found a more effective means than swearing to 'make my words have authority' (*GA* 12).

But Bunyan could also preach about salvation with a frightening urgency. Elation at coming through the struggle with despair was evidently short-lived. Not long after being received into fellowship with the saints, Bunyan is again assailed by blasphemous urges and now, too, by malicious thoughts towards fellow communicants at the Lord's Supper. These assaults, prompted no doubt by fears about his own genuineness which the Lord's Supper focused, continue for three-quarters of a year (pp. 71–2). Such experiences inform Bunyan's early preaching: 'Now this part of my work [preaching of "the curse of God by the Law"] I fulfilled with great sence; for the terrours of the Law, and guilt for my transgressions, lay heavy on my Conscience' (p. 78).

It was not uncommon for autobiographers to conclude their narratives with an account of their call to a preaching ministry (John Crook is one of many Quaker examples).[13] It was in Bunyan's case a strong way of affirming his integration into the Christian com-munity and shifting emphasis away from personal doubts. His mode of address in the Preface expresses confidence in his subject posi-tion, that of a minister speaking to his spiritual children. He even aligns himself with the Apostle Paul, his entire title a neat reprise of Paul's words, also from prison, to Timothy: 'And the grace of our Lord was exceeding abundant with faith and love which is in Christ

---

[13] See Watkins, 61–2.

Jesus. This is a faithful saying, and worthy of all acceptation, that Christ Jesus came into the world to save sinners; of whom I am chief' (1 Tim. 1: 14–15). He too lays claim to being the '*Chief of Sinners*', a claim to intensity of conviction rather than competitive pre-eminence.

Bunyan's first word, '*Children*', goes beyond Paul, in fact, in affirming his own status. Paul generally uses 'brethren', except in the individual case of 'son' Timothy whom he sees as spiritually begotten by him.[14] Bunyan's work is 'dedicated to those whom God hath counted him worthy to beget to Faith', a metaphor of paternity which is derived from Paul (1 Cor. 4: 15) but which forms the basis of his address throughout. In the light of his struggles to be reconciled to God the Father, and his apparent dissatisfaction with his own father, this achievement of the paternal role, spiritual as well as natural,[15] seems profoundly satisfying. Preaching gave him the satisfaction of the approbation not just of those who urged him to it but of those who attributed their salvation to him: 'those who thus were touched, would love me, and have a peculiar respect for me' (p. 77). It was moreover a calling. He was 'more particularly called forth' (p. 76). In accordance with Paul's instruction 'let every man abide in the same calling wherein he was called' (1 Cor. 7: 20) and example (he was a tentmaker), Bunyan remained in his manual-labour calling of tinker. But the calling to the ministry of the Gospel, first revealing and then releasing his talents, gives him that sense of being swept along by a greater power which does much to consolidate his faith: 'as if an Angel of God had stood by at my back to encourage me' (p. 79).

Imprisonment

Bunyan's narration concludes with twenty-two paragraphs about his imprisonment. It is perfunctory about his arrest and trial (p. 87), concentrating instead, as befits the generic undertaking, on the spiritual

[14] For exceptions, see Margaret Thickstun ('The Preface to *Grace Abounding* as Pauline Epistle', *Notes and Queries*, 230 (1985), 180–2), who sees Bunyan's parental relation as modelled on Paul.

[15] As a natural father Bunyan seems to have had mixed success: his eldest son, John, took to 'drunkenness, card-playing, stoolball', and dancing round the maypole (Hill, 270; Patricia Bell, 'John Bunyan and Bedfordshire', in *The John Bunyan Lectures, 1978* (Bedfordshire Education Service), 35–6).

effects of his imprisonment. Again we find that spiritual desertions, as when he contemplates possible execution, can recur. But most of this *Account of the Authors Imprisonment* is movingly courageous and modestly confident.

Most moving, however, is the wrenching description of forced separation from his wife and children (her stepchildren): it is 'as the pulling the flesh the bones'; he thought of himself 'as a man who was pulling down his house upon the head of his Wife and Children'. (p. 90) Yet the strength of feeling conveyed helps to measure the level of commitment to the faith that kept Bunyan in prison for twelve years—longer than any other religious dissident in the period of the Great Persecution (1660–72), though many died from prison diseases. Readers of *The Pilgrim's Progress* often click their tongues at Christian stuffing his fingers in his ears, as he leaves the City of Destruction, to deafen himself to his family's entreaties. But it might be asked what we would think of him had he *not* done this. Since they want no part of his expedition, he can only proceed by doggedly blocking thoughts of them.

Imprisonment, though a dire predicament, paradoxically supports the positive reinforcement provided by the call to preaching. 'I never,' Bunyan avows, 'had in all my life so great an inlet into the Word of God as now' (*GA* 87). The pattern of adversity followed by illumination is emboldened, with the advantage, psychically, that much of the adversity is unambiguously inflicted by those hostile to God's truth. Although his (social and material) place and (social and material) state could not now be lower in the world's estimation, material lowness has become spiritual height: he is best placed to rely entirely on spiritual sustenance. 'I never knew,' he proclaims, 'what it was for God to stand by me at all turns, and at every offer of Satan, &c. as I have found him since I came in hither' (p. 88).

On Bunyan's then understanding of the law, persistent refusal to conform (the course to which he was irrevocably committed) could lead to his execution. He vividly imagines the scene: 'so possessed with the thought of death, that oft I was as if I was on the Ladder, with the Rope about my neck' (p. 91). Finally, though, he is consoled by the reminder that 'it was for the Word and Way of God that I was in this condition'. Like a small child, entrusting itself to its parents by leaping into their arms in deep water, he will 'leap off the Ladder even blindfold into Eternitie, sink or swim, come heaven, come hell;

Lord Jesus, if thou wilt catch me, do; I will venture for thy Name' (p. 92).

A Relation of the Imprisonment of Mr. John Bunyan

This text is not, of course, a part of *Grace Abounding*. It is a document—made up of five reports or letters from the imprisoned Bunyan to the church—about his arrest, prosecution, and imprisonment; unpublishable in the time when it was written. The manuscript of *A Relation of My Imprisonment* was in the hands of Bunyan's descendants until 1765, when it was first published. Detailed and dramatic in its record of Bunyan's exchanges with his interrogators, it no doubt served as moral reinforcement, in 1661, for his intimidated congregation. Time and again Bunyan is able to use his superior biblical knowledge to floor his socially superior opponents. Also inspiring to the faithful would be Bunyan's record of his wife Elizabeth's spirited attempts to have his case reconsidered at the midsummer assizes. She rounds magnificently on those, at the Swan Inn where she seeks out the judges, who mutter that he is a tinker: 'Yes, said she, and because he is a Tinker, and a poor man; therefore he is despised, and cannot have justice' (p. 119).

While Bunyan's resilience and fortitude in custody are deeply impressive, and while it is apparent that this physical persecution, as for Agnes Beaumont, took the edge off the psychic persecution to which he remained prone, it is important to remember the terror to which he was subjected. A mumbled remark he half heard as he left his interrogators, in response to his statement of resolution, intensified his fears that he would be executed. Twelve Aylesbury Baptists who persisted in refusing to conform were sentenced to death, though the sentence was not carried out.[16] It is only hindsight that can make Bunyan's fear seem improbable.

Grace Abounding *and the Other Autobiographies*

As is evident from Bunyan's Preface, the habitual practice of remembering and narratizing their spiritual experience, especially the process of conversion, was a puritan imperative. It was the evidence

[16] See Keeble, 45.

of salvation which was the condition of salvation: the elect had to possess 'assurance'. Christian and Faithful exhibit, in *The Pilgrim's Progress*, the way in which the trading of experience was also the bonding agency of the puritan community. Spiritual autobiographies, of which hundreds are extant from the seventeenth century,[17] therefore emerge naturally as a literary excrescence of a much wider cultural practice. The texts included here show something of the range of experience which could develop from the same puritan matrix, which, whatever it later becomes, begins as experimental Calvinism. It provided the means by which a sense of self was constructed, and the incentive to explore states of mind with an introspective rigour and historical tenacity which, with the lone exception of Augustine's *Confessions*, was unprecedented in literature.

Richard Norwood, 'Confessions' (written 1639–40)

Richard Norwood's 'Confessions', unpublished until this century (and which is here abridged to one-third its full length), gives us a private record of the ways in which Calvinist and puritan language and culture shaped a sense of identity from early childhood. It shows how intertwined were available vocabularies for self-understanding and the social processes to which an early seventeenth-century youth could be subjected. How the young Norwood (born 1590) understands his early schooling, his running away to sea, his journey to Rome, his addiction to masturbation, or his feelings of inferiority are all permeated by the Calvinist-puritan paradigms of election and reprobation, divine grace and inescapably corrupt human nature. Norwood's memoir predates most spiritual autobiographies (the genre was to flourish in the 1650s), so he cannot be accused of writing to a generic formula; it gives us rather the categories through which experience was, from the first, lived and understood. Norwood's testimony, from the turn of the seventeenth century, exemplifies articulately the ideological claustrophobia which puritan-Calvinist modes of thought could impose. Bunyan's mental conflicts develop from the same premises: he too gives the impression, for much of his narrative, of a caged mind.

[17] See the Appendix in Watkins for a bibliography of those published before 1725. Watkins points out, however, that most of the spiritual autobiographies were published for the first time in the nineteenth century.

The parallel between Bunyan and Norwood is made more interesting by the fact that, for both, religious sensibility was bound up with circumstances of family decline. Norwood's father was a gentleman farmer who, like many farmers in the late sixteenth century, suffered losses, forcing the family to move more than once. This results in Richard's humiliating withdrawal from grammar school and apprenticeship to a London fishmonger. The combination of unfamiliar market forces, competitive individualism, and the continuing influence of patronage which characterized this period seems to have resonated early in Norwood's life with the Calvinist doctrine of a happy few chosen arbitrarily by an all-powerful God. So, when he loses a scholarship to stay on at the grammar school to a fellow pupil (whose father turns out to be the school patron's steward), exclusion from the education which might have secured his future produces not so much resentment of an injustice as rueful confirmation of his own sinful nature.

This episode is one of many instances in Norwood's narrative in which the pervading feeling is one of rejection. He makes the sad observation of his 17-year-old self that 'I was always (to my remembrance) convinced in my thoughts that I was in an evil estate'. The good opinion of people who know him produces an inward scepticism, a sense of discrepancy between that opinion and his misgivings about himself which only strengthens a lonely self-consciousness. Sensitivity to the often repeated fact that his father is 'much decayed in his estate', along with the severe punitive treatment he received as a child, merge into the Calvinist idea of pre-assigned identities.

Norwood illustrates well how elect identity was not something people could wish on themselves. This is not merely a matter of reminding ourselves of the arbitrariness of what Calvin himself called *decretum horribilis* (of reprobation). It was impossible, by wanting them however desperately, to acquire the emotional responses which were consistent with election. These emotional responses were, arguably, not so much effects of personality or expressions of moral character as the product of social structures. For example, one of the signs of election, frequently reiterated, was contentment and faithfulness in one's calling. Yet it is unsurprising, given his background and the aspirations encouraged by his education, that Norwood cannot feel contented with the destiny of fishmonger, or able to remain faithful to it. Having disobeyed that injunction (along with marriage the most important area in which parental choice should be respected[18]), he is further enmeshed in a guilty sense of himself. Yet, as his attempt at reconciliation with his father and his visit to a cleric reveal, he is unable to find a credible avenue of penitent conduct. He is driven into a posture of rebellion, the psychic cost of which is enormous. His father stalks his nightmares, 'always greivously angry with me'. Norwood's feelings about God are an extrapolation of these social circumstances, of which he was conceived to be the real source.

A deterrent to conversion for Norwood is the Calvinist doctrine of 'perseverance': the elect, once converted, could not fall away. The fearful distance Norwood keeps from God is partly motivated by the anticipation of relapse. This would then expose him as the recipient of a 'calling not effectual' or a 'temporary conversion'. Not long after his conversion experience at the age of 26, when he seems to win through to a perception of God as benevolent, he falls into just this trap: suspecting that he has been seduced into laying claim to a converted state in which he is unable to persevere; that God 'had thus lifted me up to make my fall the more terrible'. His underlying distrust both of God and of his own status seems to make the claim to reconciliation a fatal mistake.

Like Bunyan, Norwood finds his mind taken over by blasphemies. They are a natural lashing out, from a level beyond conscious control, against an authoritarian deity who appears intent on rejecting and punishing him for ever; and yet, in a vicious circle, by evidencing corrupt nature, they provide further signs of that intent. The seeming unavoidability of these blasphemous thoughts threatens to confirm the despair that a reprobate destiny is playing itself out.

Like Bunyan and John Crook, Norwood often needs to invoke the devil in order to offload the states of mind which belonged to the reprobate. And yet Norwood's record shows how terrifyingly real that figment could come to seem. After sharing Norwood's nightmare world, it is harder to discount Bunyan's reports of, for example, the devil tugging his clothes when at prayer, as some kind of dramatic embellishment. The psychological intensities seem to

---

[18] See, for example, William Perkins, *Christian Oeconomie: Or a Short Survey of the Right Manner of Erecting and Ordering a Familie, according to the Scripture*, trans. T. Pickering (1609), 147.

have been such that they produced objective correlatives, or at least hallucinations which even retrospect cannot uncouple from reality.

Norwood's autobiography is, like Bunyan's, a recapitulation of narratives which are always forming themselves in his mind. On one version, a version which often possesses his mind, everything that happens illustrates and develops the life of a reprobate. He easily infers a malevolent providence. God, after all, hated the reprobate, and his persecution of them was unremitting. Hence the plausibility of his dark suspicion that God has lured him into a fake conversion. Such thoughts were perfectly logical in view of the paradigms of election and reprobation which kept effacing each other. Bunyan is no less logical (no more paranoid) when he suspects that he has succumbed to the one unpardonable sin because he is subject to a reprobate rather than an elect providence (*GA* 43–4). Double providence is the outworking, the mechanism, of double predestination. Norwood's review of his life, like Bunyan's, seeks assurance, without falsification, that an elect paradigm can accommodate the evidence of experience, can impose its providential and thus narrative shape upon it. This is no easy task when, as he admits, 'my heart was deeply and dangerously poisoned and forestalled with a . . . harsh conceipt of God and of his ways, which I can very hardly shake off unto this day'. Bunyan too speaks of the conditioning effects of a long-term sense of divine persecution: 'because my former frights and anguish were very sore and deep, therefore it did oft befall me still as it befalleth those that have been scared with fire' (*GA* 65). Neither Norwood nor Bunyan writes from a transcendent authorial plateau: the autobiography is itself a stabilizing gesture.

To the extent that Norwood does develop, and write from, a position of relative assurance, this relates to his absorption by his calling, as surveyor of the Bermuda Islands and as a teacher of mathematics. His earlier wish to 'settle my self I cared not in how mean a calling so might have the favor of God and turn away his displeasure' had been unrealistic; his unsettled state continued to be expressed by his Wanderlust. He can only begin to 'settle my self', in faith as in life, when the favour of God seems to express itself in progress with his studies and the more dignified employment it gradually brings him. The pattern is again similar to Bunyan, who gains in assurance as he becomes integrated into the Bedford separatist community and supplements his (continued) calling as tinker with the new and satisfying one of preacher.

A Short History of the Life of John Crook (1706)

John Crook was a prominent figure amongst the Quakers with whom Bunyan fiercely disputed. To Bunyan Quakers were heretics; they were also the sect with which Baptists were in keenest proselytizing rivalry. But we will not have a sympathetic understanding of their culture, infinitely more remote from ours than their local subcultures were from each other, by looking at their polemical differences (which Bunyan outlines in *Grace Abounding* (p. 36) from his point of view); we must first seek to inhabit their shared subjectivity.

Crook's formative spiritual experiences were remarkably similar to Bunyan's. Even his language is remarkably similar. He gives a classic statement of what can now be best called 'subjectification' in the puritan-dominated London of the 1630s: the process, that is, by which the mind is captured by, made subject to, the experimental Calvinist culture, so that the sense of self frames itself unavoidably in its terms. He is hooked on sign-hunting, which at once obliges him to lay claim to the signs of salvation and precipitates him into horror at his hypocrisy in doing so. He has the sense of providential persecution, expecting dire punishment. Like many of the spiritual autobiographers, he feels strongly lured to suicide. Like both Norwood (pp. 151–2) and Bunyan (*GA* 51), he is locked into interiority ('bore [my condition] secretly in my own Bosom, few knowing how it was with me') by the terror of having a reprobate self-diagnosis confirmed.

Crook shares with Bunyan a tendency to conceptualize, and linguistically register, his experience as passive—'tossed up and down, from Hope to Despair'. He too has the impression of being called in a sermon. His troubled mind has already been trained on certain common preoccupations, so that he is ripe for this sense of personal summons—what Louis Althusser calls 'interpellation'—as the man who 'feared the Lord, and yet walked in Darkness'. The sense of the invisible hand of God at work is enhanced by the arbitrariness of Crook's own decision-making: he had that morning metaphorically dropped his staff on the ground (something Clarkson does literally (p. 183)) to tell him which way to go. It is a paradox that the more

lost, disorientated, a person feels, the stronger the potential app
of the idea that the most random decisions are actually foreordained
by a higher power. Experiences of such a call replicate each other—
Norwood has a similar one (p. 152)—suggesting that the puritan
preachers had honed the technique. And as for Bunyan the experience of rapt conviction is soon lost, 'so that I questioned all that ever
I had at any time given me to refresh me, as being but a Delusion,
and no Truth in it'.

The elusiveness of the spiritual experiences intensifies the fear of
inauthenticity, which in turn increases psychological dependence on
the puritan culture. If the experiences can be shared and repeated,
their reality status becomes enhanced. Anxious mutual interrogations (he 'would often, as I had occasion, be enquiring of Professors
how it was with them') give rise to intimacies ('communicating
our Experiences each to other') which reinforce the sense of distinctive community Bunyan first recognizes in the poor Bedford
women (*GA* 14).

Even Crook's reaction to the Ranters closely resembles Bunyan's,
and is revealing of the shared cultural and political conditions to
which both were responding. The rigours of experimental Calvinism
tempt Crook to 'a slighting of my former Strictness': perhaps the
Ranters were right that sin and its dire consequences were merely
received notions, without reasonable basis. It is disconcerting that
those who had been 'as Religious as my self' have succumbed to
such beliefs. However, the 'Sense and deep Impression . . . both of
great Troubles (in being delivered from them all) and sweet
Consolation . . . did stick upon me so, as to keep me from' them.
Bunyan too is disorientated ('unable to judge'). Yet despite the fact
that the Ranters' profession of spiritual immunity to sin is 'suitable
to my flesh', he remains captive, like Crook, to the impressions
already made on him: God 'kept me in the fear of his name, and did
not suffer me to accept of such cursed principles' (*GA* 16).

While Crook's puritanized superego, like Bunyan's, inhibits him
from joining with the Ranters, it is clear that the promise of release
from the anxiety over salvation is an important part of the appeal to
him of the Quaker evangelist William Dewsbury, who entered
Bedfordshire in 1654: 'Such Words passed from him, as implied the
miserable Life of such, who notwithstanding their Religious Duties
or Performances, had not Peace and Quietness in their Spirits'.

The anxiety over salvation has widened into a sense of disorientation which the breakdown of structures of authority brings in its train. The discrediting not only of Episcopal but also of Presbyterian authority through the 1640s has led to a free-for-all which seems to Crook to cut away all firm ground from under him. Quakerism offers a logical answer: if no external authority can be relied on, then the source of stability, of 'lasting peace', must be internal: 'God within' (p. 169).

Crook differs from Bunyan in his belief that all people have in themselves the source of potential divine illumination, so he speaks for example of 'openings'—when the inner light discovers itself. Unlike Clarkson, who sees each change of opinion as a rejection of something false, Crook does not disparage his previous puritan experience but sees it as contributing to his illumination. Bunyan could not take so relaxed a view of religious differences as Crook. His confidence in the reality and efficacy of the dissenting culture relied on belief in the Bible (which to Crook was merely 'the best outward Rule in the World' (*Life*, 49)) as a stable source of supreme authority. He also needed to believe in divine grace as the arbitrary gift of an authoritarian God, emphatically coming from outside himself, in order to counter the quailing subjective feelings which had accreted within a social structure which arbitrarily demeaned and excluded him. Bunyan's apprehension of the separateness of the divine Christ, and the transfer of credit (imputed righteousness) that enables psychologically, is what most marks his faith off from the inner light emphasis of the Quakers.

Yet there is much also that links them, including Crook's section titled '*How I came by my Ministry*' (*Life*, 39–45). Both men drag themselves to preaching in the most despondent moods; both are elated with inspiration while preaching; both return to their gloom the instant they stop (compare *Life*, 49 with *GA* 78). Crook's daily request to God is that 'his blessed Truth may be preached through' the Holy Spirit, and that 'neither Wit nor Parts, outward Learning nor Gifts, Persons nor Forms, may ever be set or esteemed above it'. Both authors lack the recognized educational preparation and have to invoke their own experience of a call to authorize their ministry. Both find themselves vehicles of a spiritual power, recipients of gifts of understanding and expression which work inwardly to inspire them.

Lawrence Clarkson, The Lost Sheep Found (1660)

Bunyan habitually bracketed Ranters and Quakers. But then he too could be stigmatized as a Ranter.[19] Perceptions depended on how far down the subjectivist track of spiritual liberty one had travelled. Even Lawrence Clarkson, who leaves the most explicit record of Ranter activities and belief (though *The Lost Sheep Found* was written ten years after the events, from the eccentric standpoint of a follower of the 'prophet' John Reeve), emerges from the same cultural matrix.

Lawrence Clarkson is best remembered as a Ranter or as a Muggletonian; yet he too came under the sway of the puritan ministry. His record of his spiritual pilgrimage through seven religions tells us as much about a shared culture as about fringe extravagances. Again it is striking how the young Clarkson is first drawn to puritan culture. What seems to be an assertion of independence actually delivers him into the sign-hunting fever and psychological tyranny of experimental Calvinism. Such is the pressure to evince the gifts of the spirit which won acceptance in the puritan community that he fakes extempore prayer, having prepared it in advance—and then breaks off humiliatingly when he forgets his lines. The terror of hypocrisy then grips him too. As episcopacy falls into popular disrepute, he pursues his quest for assurance in London, making daily visits to such nonconformist (Presbyterian) eminences as Edward Calamy and Thomas Case. Now he reads the forbidding works of Thomas Hooker (which had titles like *The Soules Humiliation* (1637)), 'which so tormented my soul, that I thought it unpossible to be saved'.

In this state of masochistic dependence on the Presbyterian pastoral ministry Clarkson is drawn into the Civil War. Like so many others he soon comes to see Presbyterian as new priest writ large, and transfers his allegiance to ascendant Independency. Presbyterians too fetishize set forms in the mandated *Directory of Worship*, and they too make tyrannical demands, such as compulsory tithes.

The Commonwealth's Christian utopianism inherent in the Independent concept of autonomous 'gathered churches'—the belief, that is, that the light of Scripture would unite all in

---

[19] See Edward Fowler, *Dirt Wipt off* (1672), 40.

fundamentals—released the creative spirit of people like Lawrence Clarkson. The dialectic between experience and holy writ generated a wide variety of new beliefs, but they tended to share similar directions. The breakdown of the traditional authority of church and state represented by bishop and king, followed by the failure of the Presbyterians to command national support for their alternative version of a disciplinary society (a nationwide hierarchy of courts presided over by a consistory of ministers), led to an exhilarated sense among some of the ruled, towards the end of the 1640s, that institutional authority and its laws had become redundant. The Christian community of visible saints (those who had given testimony of their conversion) was regulated by inner imperatives derived from Scripture.

But the inference from the fissuring of state-and-church authority could be bolder than this. It could produce the antinomian position that those who live by grace are above the moral law, even that God himself is immanent in them. This position divided into a more and less conservative version. The more conservative, which Clarkson encounters among certain Baptists, merely gives added emphasis to the most fundamental tenet of Protestantism, that salvation is by faith alone (solifidianism). Possessors of faith, or grace, it was maintained, have been freed from the bondage of the law of Moses by the internal operation of the Holy Spirit guiding them in the way of righteousness, without need of coercion. By giving this belief unqualified emphasis it was possible to escape the 'legal' spirit to which Bunyan was accused of still being a slave. But it continued to be assumed that the result, the fruits of the spirit, would be moral and lawful conduct, as essentially handed down in the Ten Commandments.

The more radical version of the doctrine, however, held that true spiritual liberty consists in serene transcendence of the law of Moses, which can best be attested by committing what were regarded as 'sins' without any feeling of guilt: 'there was no man could be free'd from sin, till he had acted that so called sin, as no sin'.[20] This is the Ranter position to which Lawrence Clarkson had moved, around the period 1649–50, when his publication, *A Single Eye All Light, No Darkness* (1650), drew the attentions of a parliamentary committee—

---

[20] *A Single Eye All Light, No Darkness* (1650), 14.

and helped to trigger the Blasphemy Act directed against Ranters and people with similar beliefs in August 1650.[21] The moral holiday was over. Unlike Bunyan, Clarkson seems to have been able to renounce his latest beliefs in order to secure his release from prison.

In the end it might be said that while some Ranter writings transmit real exhilaration and intellectual excitement, as well as (in some) a fitful vision of social justice, there was a desperate naivety, or perhaps an ultimate flippancy, in their wholesale rejection of traditional structures of authority. In her autobiography, the Baptist Jane Turner attributes the appeal of antinomian ideas to the giddy sense of freedom that followed the breakdown of ecclesiastical authority: 'having been a long time in darkness and ignorance, under the Bishops and Presbyterian yokes, they were generally weak in Judgement, though (it may be) strong in affection, and so the more easily deceived; like children ready to catch up anything that hath a glorious appearance'.[22] She was probably right: which is to say, given the actual distribution of economic, social, and political power, this bid for freedom from inherited ideological disciplines was self-deceiving. That may be why Bunyan's writing seems more imaginatively adequate to his epoch. It takes the measure of antagonistic forces and helps to establish a counter-culture of dissent which, though retaining an authoritarian God, a strict code of obedience to law, and a concept of humanity as acted upon rather than autonomously acting, actually proved viable for centuries. Ranters, on the other hand, have even suffered the indignity of being denied any real historical existence. J. C. Davis's *Fear, Myth and History: The Ranters and the Historians* (Cambridge, 1986), which argues that the Ranter scare was a bogey which has served political conveniences (both old and new), has been hotly contested; yet some weight must be given to as curious and prolix a contemporary commentator as Richard Baxter, who averred that Ranters were 'so few and of so short continuance that I never saw one of them'.[23]

[21] *An Act Against Several Atheistical, Blasphemous and Execrable Opinions Derogatory to the Honor of God, and Destructive to Human Society. Parliamentary Proceedings* ii (1650), 979–84: 9 Aug. 1650.

[22] Jane Turner, *Choice Experiences* (1653), 49–51.

[23] Quoted by Davis, in 'Debate, Fear, Myth and Furore: Reappraising the Ranters', *Past and Present* (1993), 205. For opposed views, see the other contributions to this

Before reaching Ranterism's heady deconstruction of Protestant religion Clarkson becomes involved, from 1645 on, in the more secular strand of the radicalism released by the wars and the decisive role in them of the New Model Army. His first extant publication, *A Generall Charge* (1647), contains elements of an intelligent scepticism about the Leveller programme, urging consciousness-raising amongst the English populace as a precondition of effective political change. The habits of servility—a kind of self-enslavement—are, he recognizes, deeply ingrained. Clarkson writes in the name of what he calls 'Experienced Reason' (p. 25), which suggests a fusion of the 'experimental' epistemology learned from Calvinism with a new secularizing thrust. Gerrard Winstanley, the Digger leader who, in the spring of 1649, instituted a practical demonstration of communist living at St George's Hill, was to favour the substitution of 'Reason' for 'God'. Clarkson appears to have attempted a practical implementation of his combined spiritual and political radicalism by joining the Digger colony. But Winstanley was angered by the disruption of communal living caused by Ranter libertinism. He considered Ranters to be 'self-ended',[24] the very opposite of the principle of Reason (which always looks to the betterment of mankind); and the last thing he needed was sexual scandal to add fuel to the fires of the hostile men of property.

Clarkson, presumably in retaliation in *The Lost Sheep Found*, reports that he 'made it appear to Gerrard Winstanley' that there was 'a self-love and vain-glory nursed in his heart', and construes 'Reason' as the reverse of Winstanley's meaning: 'Reason was naturally enclined to love it self above any other, and to gather to it self what riches and honor it could'. For Clarkson, reason leads to disillusionment. Each move to a new faith (there are seven in *The Lost Sheep Found*) is prompted by the discovery of scriptural contradiction of the previous position; but in the end it is, he concludes, the Bible itself which is self-contradictory. This produces a blanket scepticism and atheism, which, rather than acting as a new source of evangelical zeal, curdles to cynicism. The concluding phase of

debate in *Past and Present*, and Christopher Hill's review in *History Workshop Journal*, 24 (1987).

[24] Gerrard Winstanley, *Works*, ed. G. Sabine (New York, 1941), 539. See also pp. 399–403: *A Vindication of Those Whose Endeavors is Only to Make the Earth a Common Treasury, Called Diggers.*

Clarkson's pilgrimage is an explicit flight from Reason to the unabashed, enthusiastic, anti-rational Faith which was to become, after Clarkson's own failure to establish himself as Reeve's successor, Muggletonianism. Reason, the opening to *The Lost Sheep Found* makes clear, is lord of the devil's kingdom.

The final pull on Clarkson, then, is not the atheism which is, in a sense, the logical outcome of his *via negativa*. There is no developed enlightenment or sceptical philosophy to take either the affective or the intellectual place of Protestant spirituality. Atheism is no more sustainable for him than it was for Bunyan. The puritan matrix prevails, even in the generic associations on which *Lost Sheep* relies. It presents itself as yet another book of signs, and takes both the egotism and the cruelty which were tendencies in puritanism to almost parodic extremes: Clarkson is, the title-page announces, 'the onely true converted Messenger of Christ Jesus, Creator of Heaven and Earth'; his pilgrimage ends not only with his own salvation but with the damnation of virtually everyone else: 'notwithstanding all his former Transgressions, and breach of his Fathers Commands, he is received in an eternal Favor, and all the righteous and wicked Sons that he hath left behinde, reserved for eternal misery'.

'The Narrative of the Persecution of Agnes Beaumont'

Agnes Beaumont's narrative of events leading up to and following the death in February 1674 of her farming father John Beaumont—an account of domestic persecution for her faith, and then of her public trial in a coroner's court on a malicious charge of parricide (which also implicated Bunyan)—is very different from the spiritual autobiographies of all sectarian colours. Rather than a spiritual history, it is a vivid snapshot of the most traumatic passage of a young woman's life. It is fascinating for many reasons: its glimpses of seventeenth-century provincial domesticity, especially the position of women, of the role of gossip in village life, of the social tensions associated with religious dissent, to name a few. But it also complements the other autobiographies because, although based on an episode rather than an interior history, it exhibits the *mentalité* with which puritans inhabited seventeenth-century social structures. Autobiographies like Bunyan's and Norwood's do have significant social backgrounds which can help us to understand the

foregrounded interior life. Agnes Beaumont's narrative further
adjusts perspective, grounding puritan habits of sense-making in a
social world which dramatically tests them.

We see in the 21-year-old Agnes Beaumont[25] (who became a
member, inscribed by Bunyan's hand, of a sister congregation of the
Bedford church at Galimgay in 1672) how, in a qualified way, puritanism could empower women in humble circumstances. What looks
like an absolute paternal dominion, extending to such matters as
permitting the child to attend religious meetings, is, in Beaumont's
mind, subject to the higher authority of a divine providence in whose
power she shares through prayer: 'And I found at last by Experience
that the only way to prevail with my father to let me go to a meeting
was to pray hard to god before hand to make him willing'. The mental
habits of experimental Calvinism relativize paternal authority,
enabling her, when the crisis arises, to hold out against her father's
will with remarkable doughtiness. Saying this should not seem to
detract, however, from the intimidating power of the father of a
single woman, whose livelihood depended on him, both alive and
dead. That power was buttressed and legitimated in many ways. Even
the language in which a woman had to understand herself could
conspire against her. The moment of capitulation to her father, in
the tense farmyard scene, is in response to his ultimatum, which
addresses her as 'Hussif'. Two opposed meanings, 'housewife' and
'hussy', were available: either *OED* 1: the mistress of a household;
a thrifty woman; or *OED* 3: a woman of low or improper behaviour.
John Beaumont appears to offer his daughter the choice of meanings: either be disowned as an immoral woman or take the keys,
symbol of housewifely duty, and remain bound by it.

Yet even in her eventual surrender Beaumont holds a power in
reserve which is almost sinister. John Beaumont had told her that 'I
should never Come within his doors Again, unless I would promise
him Never to go to a meeting Again as long as he lived'. When she
finally agrees, the terms are heavily reiterated in a way that suggests
that he has invited his own providential death: '*Well father*, said I, *I
will promise yow that I will never go to a meeting; Again, as long as yow
live, without your Consent*; not thinking what doler and misery I

---

[25] The Parish Register records Beaumont's birth at Edworth on 1 Sept. 1652. Her
memorial stone in the Tilehouse Street Meeting in Hitchin makes her 68 at her death
in 1720.

brought upon my self in so Doing.' Beaumont appears to be thinking of the torments of guilt she is bringing on herself, the pattern
resembling Bunyan's consent to 'Sell Christ'. But there is also a
sense in which the dolour and misery can be attached to her father's
death. The magic of providence ensures, by exploiting her reiterated
qualification, that Beaumont is not kept from her spiritual
obligations.

In the face of persecution the puritan's inner resources were most
potently displayed. In the highly intimidating circumstances of her
trial, when her life is at stake, Agnes Beaumont has the 'faith
And Courage' to 'look my Accuser in the face with boldness'. The
psychic energies of self-accusation, which had resulted from her
eventual capitulation to her father, are with relief redirected into
righteous defence against wrongful accusation and persecution by
external enemies. Powerful sources of intimidation—gender, class,
and status in a hierarchical and authoritarian society—could melt
before a fierce sense of righteousness. Comparably, it is with a note
of triumph that Bunyan answers the slanders against him: 'My Foes
have mist their mark in this their shooting at me. I am not the man'
(*GA* 86).

Both Bunyan and Beaumont rest their assurance on biblical texts
which, in circumstances of persecution, lose any troubling ambiguity. In prison, a text whose reversibility troubled Bunyan when suffering feelings of inner persecution ('we know all things shall work
together for good to them that love God' (p. 105; compare *GA* 43–4)
can be adduced with triumphant certainty; it has become unambiguously fortifying. Agnes Beaumont also avails herself of it.

A question naturally arises as to how far Beaumont is indebted in
her writing to the influence of Bunyan, and to *Grace Abounding*
in particular. Certainly there are distinguishing characteristics
of Bunyan's idiolect which find their way into Beaumont's style of
reportage, and, it appears, into her actual mode of experience.
Sometimes this looks like direct responsiveness to *Grace Abounding*.
For example, Bunyan in his Preface exhorts his congregation in these
words: '*Have you forgot the Close, the Milk-house, the Stable, the Barn,
and the like, where God did visit your Soul?*' Beaumont dutifully
records: 'And, the Lord knowest it, their was scarce a Corner in the
house, or Barns, or Cowhousen, or Stable, or Closes, under the
hegges, or in the wood, but I was made to pour out my soul to god'.

Yet it sounds genuine enough. For more indirect indebtedness, take this sentence: 'So then I stood a while at the window silent, and that Consideration Came into my mind, *How if I should Come at last when the door is shut and Jesus Christ should say to me, "Depart from me I know you not"'*. Not only are the connective phrases familiar from Bunyan ('that Consideration Came into my mind'; '*How if*'); the specific horror of being shut out is also strong in *Grace Abounding* (the wall in his dream, the gate of the city of refuge, as well as biblical texts which he feared 'shut me out') and may well have conditioned Agnes Beaumont's sensitivity to this seizure by the allegorical or spiritual meaning of her immediate physical experience. Biblical texts play as forceful a role for Beaumont as for Bunyan in providing ways of making sense of experiences as they occur. Beaumont's texts are usually slightly inaccurate, and without book references, suggesting both their memorial possession (for the period of crisis when, excluded from her home, she is without her Bible) and her attitude to the Bible as a sea of floating signifiers waiting for personal meanings to attach themselves to.

There are other similarities to Bunyan—the use of interior dialogue for example, which gains further dramatic immediacy. But Beaumont, uneducated though she appears to be, has dramatic narrative resources of her own too, notably proleptic devices. The dream of the fallen apple tree (her father's death), the suggestive texts such as the one about trial by fire (female parricides were burnt at the stake), are cryptic early warnings, having the joint function of knitting the narrative with anticipation and fulfilment and of suggesting, at least retrospectively, a providential control which is consolingly intimated to the believer. They may also insinuate a claim to prophetic gifts, with which women in the Civil War sects had often been associated.[26]

At the age of 50 Beaumont married a landowning gentleman, Thomas Warren, who left her half his estate on his death five years later. The next year, 1708, she married Samuel Story, a prosperous and pious fishmonger. The high point of her life, however, for which she became celebrated among nonconformists in the latter half of

[26] See e.g. Keith Thomas, 'Women and the Civil War Sects', *Past and Present*, 13 (1958), repr. in Trevor Aston (ed.), *Crisis in Europe 1560–1660* (London, 1965); and Nigel Smith, *Perfection Proclaimed: Language and Literature in English Radical Religion 1640–1660* (Oxford, 1989), 45–53.

the eighteenth century,[27] was the sequence of events in early 1674 which thrust her into a position of antagonism to the venerable authority of a father, and defence of her life in a court of law. Puritanism provided an alternative source of authority which removed this young woman from the domestic confinement in which her parent's power was absolute. Without any compromise of her love for her father (which would have exposed her to scandal), she is sustained by her communally consolidated faith in an overruling power to face her persecution with fierce integrity—'to look my Accuser in the face with boldness'.

[27] Her tale was published in 1760 in a collection of narratives titled *An Abstract of the Gracious Dealings of God with Several Eminent Christians in their Conversions and Sufferings*. There were ten editions up to 1842. It was published separately as a cheap tract in 1801.

NOTE ON THE TEXTS

Grace Abounding

Six editions of *Grace Abounding* (first edition 1666) were published in Bunyan's lifetime. Of these, the undated third (?1674) and the fifth (1680) contain substantial additions. There are no extant copies of the second and fourth editions. The sixth edition (1688) makes no changes of any significance, though it does introduce some errors; appearing in the year of Bunyan's death, it may well not have been overseen by him. The three significant editions, 1, 3, and 5, pose a problem for the modern editor.

The fact that this is an autobiography provides a strong reason for favouring edition 1. It was written closest to the time of the recorded experience, and even if the emotional involvement of this first text can produce distortion as well as immediacy, there is a kind of authenticity in this too. (For example, Bunyan appears to exaggerate his poverty in a misleading phrase which he later amends, p. 9.) The colloquialism of Bunyan's language tends to be smoothed in subsequent revisions, which again can be regarded as a loss. Perhaps most importantly, there is a claustrophobic intensity in the original text, trapping the reader in the desperate logic which is relentlessly pursued from paragraph to paragraph. Added paragraphs tend to digress. Added phrases and sentences tend to repeat (often anticipating), or to moralize (with adverbs such as 'desperately'), what is already there. The effect is again one of dilution of the original reading experience. I have wanted to make that experience available to the modern reader.

On the other hand, the passages added in editions 3 and 5 often contain fascinating material: for example, Bunyan's glancing reference to his period as a soldier in the parliamentary army, his recorded encounter with Ranter ideas and followers, and his rebuttal of slanders against him. They cannot be ignored, or relegated to an appendix where they would make no consecutive sense. Yet it is in the interest of an informed response to these passages, too, that they be easily identified. Particular pressures exerted themselves on Bunyan at the times of revision which a reader should be allowed to consider.

To follow edition 1 when available but bundle in with it the added bits would be to produce a text of the autobiography which the author never approved. And editorial eclecticism—favouring local readings from different editions—would further elevate the editor's judgement over the author's.

What I have therefore done is to follow edition 1, but to include, in brackets and indented, all new paragraphs, or substantial additions to paragraphs, from editions 3 and 5. Curly brackets [ ] signify 3 and square brackets [ ] signify 5. Square brackets are also used for paragraph numbers as they appear in edition 5 (and in Roger Sharrock's well-known edition (Oxford University Press, 1962)); these accompany the edition 1 numbers throughout. I have judged that it would clutter the text too much, and defeat the aim of making edition 1 available to the reader, were I to include in brackets the briefer addenda supplied by the later editions. Where something significant is added in a phrase, I draw attention to this in a note. Of course, other minds might find significance in other phrases, but this is a necessary loss if the other aims of the edition are to be achieved.

This is the first modern edition which follows the original editions consistently in spelling and in punctuation. That is to say, I have followed edition 1 except in the added sections, where I have followed 3 for those first appearing in 3, and 5 for those first appearing in 5. Seventeenth-century punctuation differs from modern, but it is not, in Bunyan's (or his printer's) case, an obstacle to reading. Commas in particular normally indicate the rhetorical phrasing of sentences, and actually facilitate reading. On the very rare occasion that the placement of a comma instead of a stop can trip the reader, I have made the silent alteration—as I have corrected any indisputable misprints.

There are unique copies of editions 3 and 5: the former in the Pierpont Morgan Library, New York, the latter in Bedford Public Library. I have collated the copy of edition 1 in the British Library (which has a corrected state of gathering B) and that in the Pierpont Morgan Library (which has a corrected state of gathering A). I have also examined copies of edition 6 in Bedford and in the University of Manchester John Rylands Library. I am grateful to the staff at these libraries. I have a special debt of gratitude to Mrs Inge Dupont, Head of Reader Services at the Pierpont Morgan Library, for her very generous and scrupulous assistance.

The Other Texts

The editions and manuscripts followed for the other texts are unproblematic. *A Relation of the Imprisonment of Mr John Bunyan* was first published in 1765, from Bunyan's manuscript. Richard Norwood's 'Confessions' were first published in a modern-spelling edition, *The Journal of Richard Norwood, Surveyor of Bermuda*, ed. W. F. Craven and W. B. Hayward (New York, 1945), which I mention because it was sometimes a useful aid in deciphering the manuscript. The manuscript is in the Bermuda Archives. *A Short History of the Life of John Crook* was published posthumously in 1706. There was only one edition of Lawrence Clarkson's *The Lost Sheep Found*, in 1660. 'The Narrative of the Persecution of Agnes Beaumont' was first published by Samuel James in 1760, with other narratives, under the title *An Abstract of the Gracious Dealings of God. With several Eminent Christians, Their Conversions and Sufferings.* My text is taken in full from the early transcript (or perhaps Beaumont's own script) in the British Library, BM MS Egerton 2414. Improvement of the punctuation and some modernization of the spelling have been necessary to aid comprehension. I have included, from the other transcript, Egerton 2128, the short passages of uncertain authenticity which it adds as a postscript.

SELECT BIBLIOGRAPHY

Primary texts

Camden, Vera J. (ed.), *The Narrative of the Persecutions of Agnes Beaumont* (East Lansing, Mich., 1992).

Church Book of Bunyan Meeting 1650–1821, facsimile edn. Introd. G. B. Harrison (London, 1928).

Myers, William (ed.), *Restoration and Revolution: Political, Social and Religious Writings 1660–1700* (London, 1986) (extracts from Agnes Beaumont's 'Narrative').

Sharrock, Roger (gen. ed.), *The Miscellaneous Works of John Bunyan*, 12 vols (Oxford, 1976–90).

Smith, Nigel (ed.), *A Collection of Ranter Writings from the 17th Century* (London, 1983).

Tibbutt, H. G. (ed.), 'Minutes of the First Independent Church (now Bunyan Meeting) at Bedford 1656–1766', *Publications of the Bedfordshire Historical Record Society*, 55 (1976).

Critical studies of Grace Abounding

Beal, Rebecca S., '*Grace Abounding to the Chief of Sinners*: John Bunyan's Pauline Epistle', *Studies in English Literature*, 21 (1981), 147–60.

Bell, Robert, 'Metamorphoses of Spiritual Autobiography', *English Literary History*, 44 (1977), 108–26.

Camden, Vera J., 'Blasphemy and the Problem of the Self in *Grace Abounding*', *Bunyan Studies*, 1 No. 2 (1989), 5–19.

Carlton, Peter J., 'Bunyan: Language, Convention, Authority', *English Literary History*, 51 (1984), 17–32.

Corns, Tom, 'Bunyan's *Grace Abounding* and the Dynamics of Restoration Nonconformity', in Neil Rhode (ed.), *History, Language, and the Politics of English Renaissance Prose* (Binghampton, forthcoming).

Hawkins, Anne, 'The Double-Conversion in Bunyan's *Grace Abounding*', *Philological Quarterly*, 61 (1982), 259–76.

Mandel, B. J., 'Bunyan and the Autobiographer's Artistic Purpose', *Criticism*, 10 (1968), 225–43.

Stranahan, Brainerd, 'Bunyan's Special Talent: Biblical Texts as "Events" in *Grace Abounding* and *The Pilgrim's Progress*', *English Literary Renaissance*, 11 (1981), 329–43.

Thickstun, Margaret, 'The Preface to *Grace Abounding* as Pauline Epistle', *Notes and Queries* 230 (1985), 180–2.

Watson, Melvin R., 'The Drama of *Grace Abounding*', *English Studies*, 46 (1965), 471–82.

Critical studies of seventeenth-century autobiography

Caldwell, Patricia, *The Puritan Conversion Narrative* (Cambridge, 1983).

Damrosch, Leopold Jr., *God's Plot and Man's Stories* (Chicago, 1985).

Delany, Paul, *British Autobiography in the Seventeenth Century* (London, 1969).

Ebner, Dean, *Autobiography in Seventeenth-Century England* (The Hague, 1971).

Sharrock, Roger, 'Spiritual Autobiography in *The Pilgrim's Progress*', *Review of English Studies*, 24 (1948), 102–20.

Starr, G. A., *Defoe and Spiritual Autobiography* (Princeton, NJ, 1965).

John Bunyan: his life, works, and cultural milieu

Brown, John, *John Bunyan: His Life, Times and Work* (1885; rev. edn. London, 1928).

Forrest, James F., and Greaves, Richard L., *John Bunyan: A Reference Guide* (Boston, 1982).

Greaves, Richard L., *John Bunyan* (Abingdon, 1969).

—— *John Bunyan and English Nonconformity* (London, 1992).

Harrison, G. B., *John Bunyan: A Study in Personality* (London, 1928).

Hill, Christopher, *A Turbulent, Seditious, and Factious People: John Bunyan and His Church* (Oxford, 1988).

Laurence, Anne, Owens, W. R., and Sim, Stuart (eds.), *John Bunyan and His England, 1628–88* (London, 1990).

Lindsay, Jack, *John Bunyan: Maker of Myths* (1937; repr. New York, 1969).

Tindall, William Y., *John Bunyan: Mechanick Preacher* (New York, 1934).

Seventeenth-century Protestantism

Cragg, G. R., *Puritanism in the Period of the Great Persecution 1660–1688* (Cambridge, 1957).

Greaves, Richard L., *Deliver Us from Evil: The Radical Underground in Britain 1660–1663* (Oxford, 1986).

—— (ed.), *Triumph over Silence: Women in Protestant History* (Westport, Conn., 1986).

—— and Zaller, R. (eds.), *A Biographical Dictionary of British Radicals in the Seventeenth Century*, 3 vols. (Brighton, 1982–4).

Hill, Christopher, *The World Turned Upside Down* (London, 1972; repr. Harmondsworth, 1975).

Keeble, N. H., *The Literary Culture of Nonconformity in Later Seventeenth-Century England* (Leicester, 1987).

McGregor, J. F., and Reay, B., *Radical Religion in the English Revolution* (Oxford, 1984).

Stachniewski, John, *The Persecutory Imagination: English Puritanism and the Literature of Religious Despair* (Oxford, 1991).

Tibbutt, H. G., 'John Crook, 1617–1699: A Bedfordshire Quaker', *Publications of the Bedfordshire Historical Record Society*, 25 (1947), 110–28.

Watkins, Owen C., *The Puritan Experience* (London, 1972).

White, B. R., *The English Baptists of the Seventeenth Century* (London, 1983).

A CHRONOLOGY OF
JOHN BUNYAN AND HIS TIMES

1628   John Bunyan is born (baptized 30 November), the eldest of three children of Thomas Bunyan (1603–76) and Margaret Bentley (1603–44), his second wife (married 23 May 1627).

1629–40   Personal Rule of Charles I.

1630s   Bunyan attends a local school, though he soon leaves to take up his father's trade as brazier or tinker.

1633   William Laud appointed Archbishop of Canterbury.

1639   First Bishops' War with Scotland.

1640   Second Bishops' War. Opening of Long Parliament. Archbishop Laud impeached.

1641   Censorship breaks down. 'Root and Branch' Bill introduced. Irish Rebellion. Grand Remonstrance presented to the King.

1642–6   First Civil War.

1642   Suspension of episcopacy.

1643   Assembly of Divines opens. Solemn League and Covenant with (Presbyterian) Scots.

1644   Bunyan's mother, and his sister, Margaret, die (in June and July). In November, Bunyan joins the parliamentary army. 'Tender consciences' resolution passed by Commons.

1645   Execution of Archbishop Laud. Formation of New Model Army. Parliamentary victory at the Battle of Naseby. Ordinances for Directory of Worship and Presbyterian Church Government. Bunyan's father marries his third wife, Anne.

1647   Putney debates. Bunyan returns to Elstow on the demobilization of his regiment on 21 July.

1648/9   Second Civil War. Pride's Purge. Bunyan marries his first wife (name unknown).

1649–55   The period of prolonged spiritual crisis recounted in *Grace Abounding*.

1649   Trial and execution of Charles I. The Commonwealth is proclaimed. Suppression of Levellers.

1650   Suppression of Diggers. Compulsory attendance at parish church is abolished. Blasphemy Act. Suppression of Ranters. Bunyan's daughter, Mary, is born blind (baptized 20 July); three other children follow. Bunyan is introduced to the open communion Bedford Baptists and comes under the influence of their pastor, John Gifford. He encounters Ranter ideas.

1653   Cromwell dissolves the Rump of the Long Parliament. Bedford
          Corporation presents the living of St John's in Bedford to John
          Gifford; the congregation becomes part of Cromwell's loose
          state church.

1653–8   Protectorate of Oliver Cromwell.

1654 (?) Bunyan encounters Quakers.

1655   Bunyan is baptized and registered as a member of Gifford's
          Independent church at Bedford. He begins to 'speak a word
          of Exhortation' at meetings of believers, and soon graduates to
          preaching to the unconverted. John Gifford dies, and is suc-
          ceeded as pastor by John Burton.

1656   Bunyan disputes publicly with Quakers, and publishes the
          resulting polemic, *Some Gospel-Truths Opened*.

1657   Cromwell rejects offer of crown. Establishment of the Second
          Protectorate.

1658   Death of Oliver Cromwell (September); his son Richard suc-
          ceeds him. Bunyan's wife dies. He publishes *A Few Sighs from
          Hell or the Groans of a Damned Soul*. He is indicted for preach-
          ing at the local assizes.

1659   Richard Cromwell abdicates. The Long Parliament and repub-
          lic are restored. Bunyan marries his second wife, Elizabeth,
          who gives birth to three children. He publishes *The Doctrine
          of the Law and Grace Unfolded*. He is by now a reputed
          preacher.

1660   Monck's army marches to London. The Long Parliament is
          dissolved. Monarchy, under Charles II, the House of Lords,
          and episcopacy are restored. Trial and execution of regicides.
          Bunyan is arrested (in November) for holding a conventicle (an
          illegal religious meeting). Elizabeth, 'smayed at the news', has
          their first baby prematurely, so that it dies. John Burton dies. Not
          tolerated by the episcopal authorities, the Bedford church
          becomes 'separatist', or 'nonconformist', and meets in secret for
          the period of 'The Great Persecution' (until 1672).

1661   The Fifth Monarchist, Thomas Venner, leads a small armed
          rising in London. Election of Cavalier Parliament. Bunyan is
          sentenced in January to three months' imprisonment in Bedford
          jail, but as his release depends on his undertaking not to preach,
          this commences a prison term of twelve years.

1661–5   New penal legislation is enacted, known as the Clarendon Code,
          under which nonconformists are persecuted. The episcopal
          Church of England is formally re-established by the Act of
          Uniformity (1662).

1661–72   Bunyan makes shoelaces to support his family, and writes—
          publishing first the poem *Profitable Meditations* (1661).

1662   The Quaker Act identifies Quakers as a particular target of per-
          secution. Charles II's First Declaration of Indulgence is over-
          ruled by Parliament. Refusal to conform under the Act of
          Uniformity results in ejection of over 1,800 clergy. Bunyan pub-
          lishes *I Will Pray with the Spirit*, an attack on the (restored) Book
          of Common Prayer.

1663   Bunyan publishes a conduct manual, *Christian Behaviour*, and a
          second long poem, *Prison Meditations*. Samuel Fenn and John
          Whiteman are elected pastors of the Bedford church.

1664   First Conventicle Act.

1665   Five Mile Act. Bunyan publishes a millenarian treatise, *The Holy
          City*.

1666   Bunyan publishes *Grace Abounding*. He is released from prison
          for a few months, but rearrested for continuing to preach.

1670   Second Conventicle Act promotes harsher persecution.

1671   Bunyan probably writes *The Heavenly Footman* (published
          posthumously) and is sparked, in doing so, to embark on *The
          Pilgrim's Progress*.

1672   Charles II's Second Declaration of Indulgence. Following John
          Whiteman's death, Bunyan is elected pastor of the Bedford con-
          gregation in January. He is released from prison in March. In
          May he obtains a licence to preach under Charles II's Second
          Declaration of Indulgence. Bunyan publishes *A Defence of the
          Doctrine of Justification by Faith*, an attack on the Anglican
          Edward Fowler's *Design of Christianity* (1671). His reputation as
          a preacher grows steadily, extending to London.

1673   Parliament forces withdrawal of Declaration of Indulgence.
          Persecution is renewed. Bunyan publishes controversial views on
          baptism in *Differences in Judgment about Water-Baptism no Bar to
          Communion*.

1674   Bunyan publishes *Peaceable Principles and True* in response to
          attacks by Baptists Thomas Paul and Henry Danvers. This is the
          probable date of the enlarged third edition of *Grace Abounding*.
          It is rumoured by local enemies that Bunyan helped to poison
          the father of his supposed mistress, Agnes Beaumont. Agnes
          Beaumont is cleared of murder by a coroner's jury.

1676   Bunyan's father dies.

1676–7   Bunyan is again imprisoned (December to June).

1678   Bunyan publishes *The Pilgrim's Progress*.

1679   Cavalier Parliament is dissolved. Licensing Act expires and censorship lapses.

1679–81 Three Parliaments pass 'Exclusion' Bills to prevent Catholic James Duke of York's succession to the throne.

1680   Bunyan publishes *The Life and Death of Mr Badman*, and the further enlarged fifth edition of *Grace Abounding*, including rebuttal of slanders. (The new passages may have appeared in the fourth edition (date unknown).)

1681–5 Charles II rules without Parliament. Persecution of dissenters intensifies.

1682   Bunyan publishes *The Holy War*.

1683   The Rye House Plot leads to the execution of leading Whigs. Corporations are purged.

1684   Bunyan publishes *Seasonable Counsel, or Advice to Sufferers* and *The Pilgrim's Progress . . . The Second Part*.

1685   Death of Charles II and accession of James II. Failure of Monmouth's rising. Bunyan conveys his property to his wife, seeking to protect his family from possible penal effects of the 'Tory Revenge' (which persisted into James II's reign) for nonconformist involvement in the Exclusion Crisis.

1687   James II's First Declaration of Indulgence. Bunyan refuses a position in Bedford administration under the government of James II.

1688   James II's Second Declaration of Indulgence. James II escapes to France as William of Orange lands at Torbay. Bunyan contracts a fever after a mounted journey in rain to London from Reading (where he had been on pastoral business, seeking to reconcile a father and son). He dies two weeks later on 31 August, and is buried in Bunhill Fields, Finsbury, on 3 September.

1689   William and Mary are proclaimed King and Queen. Act of Toleration passed.

ABBREVIATIONS

BDBR	Greaves, Richard L., and Zaller, R. (eds.), *A Biographical Dictionary of British Radicals in the Seventeenth Century*. 3 vols. (Brighton, 1982–4).
Beek	von Beek, Marinus, *An Enquiry into Puritan Vocabulary* (Groningen, 1969).
Brown	Brown, John, *John Bunyan: His Life, Times and Work* (1885; rev. edn., London, 1928).
Church Book	*The Church Book of Bunyan Meeting 1650–1821*, facsimile edn., Introd. G. B. Harrison (London, 1928).
Hill	Hill, Christopher, *A Turbulent, Seditious, and Factious People: John Bunyan and His Church* (Oxford, 1988).
Keeble	Keeble, N. H., *The Literary Culture of Nonconformity in Later Seventeenth-Century England* (Leicester, 1987).
Laurence	Laurence, Anne, Owens, W. R., and Sim, Stuart (eds.) *John Bunyan and His England, 1628–88* (London, 1990).
Lindsay	Lindsay, Jack, *John Bunyan: Maker of Myths* (1937; repr. New York, 1969).
McGregor	McGregor, J. F., and Reay, B., *Radical Religion in the English Revolution* (Oxford, 1984).
MW	*The Miscellaneous Works of John Bunyan*, gen. ed. Roger Sharrock, 12 vols. (Oxford, 1976–90).
OED	*Oxford English Dictionary*.
Offor	Bunyan, John, *Works*, ed. George Offor, 3 vols. (Glasgow, 1854).
Sharrock	Bunyan, John, *Grace Abounding to the Chief of Sinners*, ed. Roger Sharrock (Oxford, 1962).
Smith	Smith, Nigel (ed.), *A Collection of Ranter Writings from the 17th Century* (London, 1983).
Stachniewski	Stachniewski, John, *The Persecutory Imagination: English Puritanism and the Literature of Religious Despair* (Oxford, 1991).
PP	Bunyan, John, *The Pilgrim's Progress*, ed. N. H. Keeble (Oxford, 1984).
Tibbutt	'Minutes of the First Independent Church (now Bunyan Meeting) at Bedford, 1656–1766', ed. H. G. Tibbutt, *Publications of the Bedfordshire Historical Record Society*, 55 (1976).

Tindall   Tindall, W. Y., *John Bunyan, Mechanick Preacher* (New York, 1934).

Watkins   Watkins, Owen C., *The Puritan Experience* (London, 1972).

WTUD   Hill, Christopher, *The World Turned Upside Down* (London, 1972; repr. Harmondsworth, 1975).

GRACE ABOUNDING

John Bunyan

A PREFACE:

Or brief Account of the publishing of this Work:

Written by the Author thereof, and dedicated to those whom God hath counted him worthy to beget to Faith, by his Ministry in the Word.

*C*Hildren, *Grace be with you,* Amen. *I being taken from you in pres-ence,** and so tied up, that I cannot perform that duty that from God doth lie upon me, to you-ward, for your further edifying** and building up in Faith and Holiness,* &c. *Yet that you may see my Soul hath fatherly care and desire after your spiritual and everlasting welfare; I now once again, as from the top of* Shenir *and* Hermon, *so from* the Lions Dens, *and from the Mountains of the Leopards,* (Song 4. 8.) *do look yet after you all, greatly longing to see your safe arrival into* THE *desired Haven.*

*I thank God upon every Remembrance of you,** and rejoyce even while I stick between the Teeth of the Lions in the Wilderness,** at the grace, and mercy, and knowledge of Christ our Saviour, which God hath bestowed upon you, with abundance of Faith and Love. Your hungerings and thirstings also after further acquaintance with the Father in his Son; your tenderness of Heart, your trembling at sin, your sober and holy deportment also, before both God and men, is great refreshment to me: For you are my glory and joy,* 1 Thes. 2. 20.*

I have sent you here enclosed a drop of that honey, that I have taken out of the Carcase of a Lyon, Judg. 14. 5, 6, 7, 8. *I have eaten thereof my self also, and am much refreshed thereby. (Temptations when we meet them at first, are as the Lyon that roared upon* Sampson: *but if we over-come them, the next time we see them, we shall finde a Nest of Honey within them.) The Philistians understand me not.** It is a Relation of the work of God upon my own Soul, even from the very first, till now; wherein you may perceive my castings down, and raisings up: for he woundeth, and his hands make whole.** It is written in the Scripture,* Isai.

38. 19. The father to the children shall make known the truth of God. *Yea, it was for this reason I lay so long at* Sinai,* (Deut. 4. 10, 11.) *to see the fire, and the cloud, and the darkness,* that I might fear the Lord all the days of my life upon earth, and tell of his wondrous works to my children, *Psal.* 78. 3, 4, 5.

Moses, Numb. 33. 1, 2. *writ of the Journeyings of the children of* Israel *from* Egypt *to the Land of* Canaan; *and commanded also, that they did remember their forty years travel in the wilderness.** Thou shalt remember all the way which the Lord thy God led thee these forty years in the wilderness, to humble thee, and to prove thee, and to know what was in thine heart, whether thou wouldst keep his commandments or no, *Deut.* 8. 2, 3. *Wherefore this I have endeavoured to do; and not onely so, but to publish it also; that, if God will, others may be put in remembrance of what he hath done for their Souls, by reading his work upon me.*

It is profitable for Christians to be often calling to mind the very beginnings of Grace with their Souls. It is a night to be much observed to the Lord, for bringing them out from the land of Egypt. This is that night of the Lord to be observed of all the children of Israel in their generations, *Exod.* 12. 42. My God, *saith David,* Psal. 42. 6. my soul is cast down within me; but I will remember thee from the land of Jordan, and of the Hermonites, from the hill Mizar.* *He remembred also the Lyon and the Bear, when he went to fight with the Giant of* Gath, 1 Sam. 17. 36, 37.

It was Pauls *accustomed manner,* Acts 22. *and that when tried for his life,* Acts 24. *even to open before his Judges the manner of his Conversion: He would think of that day and that hour, in the which he first did meet with Grace: for he found it support unto him. When God had brought the children of* Israel *thorow the* Red Sea, *far into the wilderness; yet they must turn quite about thither again, to remember the drowning of their enemies there,* Num. 14. 25. *for though they sang his praise before, yet they soon forgat his works,* Psal. 106. 12, 13.

In this Discourse of mine, you may see much; much, I say, of the Grace of God towards me: I thank God I can count it much; for it was above my sins, and Satans temptations too. I can remember my fears, and doubts, and sad moneths, with comfort; they are as the head of Goliah *in my hand: there was nothing to* David *like* Goliahs *sword, even that sword that should have been sheathed in his bowels; for the very sight and remembrance of that, did preach forth Gods Deliverance to him. O the*

*remembrance of my great sins, of my great temptations, and of my great
fears of perishing for ever! They bring fresh into my mind, the remembrance of my great help, my great support from Heaven, and the great
grace that God extended to such a wretch as I.*

*My dear Children, call to mind the former days, the years of ancient
times; remember also your songs in the night, and commune with your
own heart,* Psal. 77. 5, 6, 7, 8, 9, 10, 11, 12. *Yea, look diligently, and
leave no corner therein unsearched, for there is treasure hid, even the treasure of your first and second experience of the grace of* God *toward you.
Remember, I say, the Word that first laid hold upon you; remember your
terrours of conscience, and fear of death and hell: remember also your
tears and prayers to* God; *yea, how you sighed under every hedge for
mercy. Have you never a Hill Mizar to remember? Have you forgot the
Close, the Milk-house, the Stable, the Barn, and the like, where* God *did
visit your Soul? Remember also the Word, the Word, I say, upon which
the Lord hath caused you to hope:* If you have sinned against light, if
you are tempted to blaspheme, if you are down in despair, if you think*
God *fights against you, or if heaven is hid from your eyes; remember
'twas thus with your Father,* but out of them all the Lord delivered
me.**

*I could have enlarged much in this my discourse of my temptations and
troubles for sin, as also of the merciful kindness and working of* God *with
my Soul: I could also have stept into a stile much higher then this in
which I have here discoursed, and could have adorned all things more
then here I have seemed to do: but I dare not:* God *did not play in convincing of me;* the* Devil *did not play in tempting of me;* neither did I
play when I sunk as into a bottomless pit,* when the pangs of hell caught
hold upon me:* wherefore I may not play in my relating of them,* but
be plain and simple, and lay down the thing as it was: He that liketh it,
let him receive it; and he that does not, let him produce a better. Farewel.*

My dear Children,
The Milk and Honey is beyond this Wilderness: God be merciful to
you, and grant you be not slothful to go in to possess the Land.*

Jo. Bunyan.

GRACE
Abounding to the chief of Sinners:*
OR,
A Brief Relation
Of the exceeding mercy of God
in Christ, to his poor Servant
John Bunyan.

1. [1.] In this my relation of the merciful working of God upon my Soul, it will not be amiss, if in the first place I do in a few words give you a hint of my pedegree, and manner of bringing up; that thereby the goodness and bounty of God towards me, may be the more advanced and magnified before the sons of men.

2. [2.] For my descent then, it was, as is well known by many, of a low and inconsiderable generation; my fathers house being of that rank that is meanest, and most despised of all the families in the Land.* Wherefore I have not here, as others, to boast of Noble blood, or of a High-born state according to the flesh: though all things considered, I magnifie the Heavenly Majesty, for that by this door he brought me into this world, to partake of the Grace and Life that is in Christ by the Gospel.

3. [3.] But yet notwithstanding the meanness and inconsiderableness of my Parents, it pleased God to put it into their heart, to put me to School,* to learn both to Read and Write; the which I also attained, according to the rate of other poor mens children, though to my shame I confess, I did soon loose that little I learnt, and that even almost utterly, and that long before the Lord did work his gracious work of conversion upon my Soul.

4. [4.] As for my own natural* life, for the time that I was without God in the world, it was, indeed, according to the course of this world, and the spirit that now worketh in the children of disobedience: [Eph. 2. 2, 3.] it was my delight to be taken captive by the Devil *at his will*, [2 Tim. 2. 26] being filled with all unrighteousness; the which did also so strongly work, and put forth it self, both in my heart and life, and that from a childe, that I had but few Equals,

(especially considering my years, which were tender, being few) both for cursing, swearing, lying and blaspheming the holy Name of God.

5. [5.] Yea, so setled and rooted was I in these things, that they became as a second Nature to me; the which, as I also have with soberness considered since, did so offend the Lord, that even in my childhood he did scare and affright me with fearful dreams, and did terrifie me with dreadful visions. For often, after I had spent this and the other day in sin, I have in my bed been greatly afflicted, while asleep, with the apprehensions of Devils, and wicked spirits, who still,* as I then thought, laboured to draw me away with them; of which I could never be rid. [6.] Also I should at these years be greatly afflicted and troubled with the thoughts of the day of Judgement, and that both night and day, and should tremble at the thoughts of the fearful torments of Hell-fire; still fearing that it would be my lot to be found at last amongst those Devils and Hellish Fiends, who are there bound down with the chains and bonds of eternal darkness.*

6. [7.] These things, I say, when I was but a childe,* did so distress my Soul, that when in the midst of my many sports and childish vanities, amidst my vain companions, I was often much cast down and afflicted in my mind therewith; yet could I not let go my sins: yea, I was so overcome with despair of life and heaven, that then I should often wish, either that there had been no Hell, or that I had been a Devil; supposing they were onely tormentors; that if it must needs be, that I indeed went thither, I might be rather a tormentor, then tormented my self.

7. [8.] A while after, these terrible dreams did leave me, which also I soon forgot; for my pleasures did quickly cut off the remembrance of them, as if they had never been: wherefore with more greediness, according to the strength of Nature, I did still let loose the reins to my lusts, and delighted in all transgression against the Law of God: so that until I came to the state of marriage, I was the very ringleader of all the Youth that kept me company, into all manner of vice and ungodliness.

8. [9.] Yea, such prevalency had the lusts and fruits of the flesh, in this poor Soul of mine, that had not a miracle of precious grace prevented,* I had not onely perished by the stroke of eternal Justice, but had also laid my self open even to the stroke of those Laws, which bring some to disgrace and open shame before the face of the world.*

9. [10.] In these days the thoughts of Religion was very grievous to me; I could neither endure it my self, nor that any other should: so that when I have but seen some read in those books that concerned Christian piety, it would be as it were a prison to me. *Then I said unto God, Depart from me, for I desire not the knowledge of thy ways*, Job 21. 14, 15. I was now void of all good consideration; Heaven and Hell were both out of sight and minde; and as for Saving and Damning, they were least in my thoughts. *O Lord, thou knowest my life, and my ways were not hid from thee.**

10. [11.] Yet this I well remember, that though I could my self sin with greatest delight and ease, and also take pleasure in the vileness of my companions; yet even then, if I have at any time seen wicked things by those that professed goodness, it would make my spirit tremble. As once above all the rest, when I was in my heighth of vanity, yet hearing one to swear that was reckoned for a religious man, it had so great a stroke upon my spirit, as it made my heart to ake.

[[12.] But God did not utterly leave me, but followed me still, not now with convictions, but Judgements,* yet such as were mixt with mercy. For once I fell into a crick of the Sea, and hardly escaped drowning: another time I fell out of a Boat into *Bedford* River,* but mercy yet preserved me alive:* Besides, another time being in the field, with one of my companions, it chanced that an Adder passed over the High way, so I having a stick in mine hand, struck her over the back, and having stounded* her, I forced open her mouth with my stick, and plucked her sting out with my fingers, by which act had not God been mercifull to me, I might by my desperateness have brought my self to mine end.

[13.] This also I have taken notice of with thanksgiving; When I was a Souldier,* I with others were drawn out to go to such a place to besiege it, but when I was just ready to go, one of the company desired to go in my room, to which when I had consented he took my place, and coming to the siege, as he stood Sentinel, he was shot into the head with a Musket bullet and died.

[14.] Here, as I said, were Judgements, and Mercy, but neither of them did awaken my soul to Righteousness, wherefore I sinned still, and grew more and more rebellious against God, and careless of mine own Salvation.]

11. [15.] Presently after this, I changed my condition into a married state; and my mercy was, to light upon a Wife whose Father

was counted godly: this Woman and I, though we came together as poor as poor might be, (not having so much* as a Dish or Spoon betwixt us both) yet this she had for her part, *The Plain Mans Path-way to Heaven*, and *The Practice of Piety*,* which her Father had left her when he died. In these two Books I should sometimes read with her, wherein I also found some things that were somewhat pleasing to me: (but all this while I met with no conviction.) She also would be often telling of me what a godly man* her Father was, and how he would reprove and correct Vice,* both in his house and amongst his neighbours; what a strict and holy life he lived in his day, both in word and deed.

12. [16.] Wherefore these books, with this relation, though they did not reach my heart to awaken* it about my sad and sinful state, yet they did beget within me some desires to Religion: so that, because I knew no better, I fell in very eagerly with the Religion of the times, to wit, to go to Church twice a day, and that too with the foremost, and there should very devoutly both say and sing as others did; yet retaining my wicked life: but withal, I was so over-run with a spirit of superstition, that I adored, and that with great devotion, even all things (both the High-place, Priest, Clerk, Vestments, Service, and what else) belonging to the Church;* counting all things holy that were therein contained; and especially the Priest and Clerk most happy, and without doubt greatly blessed, because they were the Servants, as I then thought, of God, and were principal in the holy Temple, to do his work therein.

13. [17.] This conceit* grew so strong in little time upon my spirit., that had I but seen a Priest, (though never so sordid and debauched in his life) I should find my spirit fall under him, reverence him, and knit unto him; yea, I thought for the love I did bear unto them, (supposing they were the Ministers of my God) I could have layn down at their feet, and have been trampled upon by them; their Name, their Garb, and Work, did so intoxicate and bewitch me.

14. [18.] After I had been thus for some considerable time, another thought came into my mind, and that was, Whether we were of the *Israelites* or no: for finding in the Scriptures that they were once the peculiar People of God; thought I, if I were one of this race, my Soul must needs be happy. Now again I found within me a great longing to be resolved about this question, but could not tell how I

should: at last, I asked my father of it, who told me, *No, we were not*: wherefore then I fell in my spirit, as to the hopes of that, and so remained.

15. [19.] But all this while I was not sensible of the danger and evil of sin; I was kept from considering that sin would damn me, what Religion soever I followed, unless I was found in Christ: nay, I never thought of him, nor whether there was one or no. Thus man, while blind, doth wander, but wearieth himself with vanity: for he knoweth not the way to the City of God, *Eccles*. 10. 15.

16. [20.] But one day (amongst all the Sermons our Parson made) his subject was to treat of the Sabbath day, and of the evil of breaking that, either with labour, sports, or otherwise:* (now I was one that took much delight in all manner of vice, and especially that was the Day that I did solace my self therewith) Wherefore I fell in my conscience under his Sermon, thinking and believing that he made that Sermon on purpose to shew me my evil-doing;* and at that time I felt what guilt was, though never before, that I can remember; but then I was for the present greatly loaden therewith, and so went home when the Sermon was ended, with a great burden on my spirit.

17. [21.] This for that instant did cut* the sinews of my delights, and did imbitter my former pleasures to me: but behold, it lasted not; for before I had well dined, the trouble began to go off my minde, and my heart returned to its old course: but Oh how glad was I, that this trouble was gone from me, and that the fire was put out! Wherefore when I had satisfied nature with my food, I shook the Sermon out of my mind, and to my old custom of sports and gaming I returned with great delight.

18. [22.] But the same day, as I was in the midst of a game at Cat,** and having struck it one blow from the hole; just as I was about to strike it the second time, a voice did suddenly dart from Heaven into my Soul, which said, *Wilt thou leave thy sins, and go to Heaven? or have thy sins, and go to Hell?* At this I was put to an exceeding maze; wherefore leaving my Cat upon the ground, I looked up to Heaven, and was as if I had with the eyes of my understanding, seen the Lord Jesus looking down upon me, as being very hotly displeased with me, and as if he did severely threaten me with some grievous punishment for these, and other my ungodly practices.

19. [23.] I had no sooner thus conceived in my mind, but suddenly

this conclusion was fastned on my spirit, (for the former hint did set my sins again before my face) *That I had been a great and grievous Sinner, and that it was now too too late for me to look after Heaven, for Christ would not forgive me, nor pardon my transgressions*. Then I fell to musing upon this also; and while I was thinking on it, and fearing lest it should be so, I felt my heart sink in despair, concluding it was too late; and therefore I resolved in my mind, I would go on in sin:* for thought I, if the case be thus, my state is surely miserable; miserable, if I leave my sins; and but miserable, if I follow them: I can but be damned; and if it must be so, I had as good be damned for many sins, as to be damned for few.

20. [24.] Thus I stood in the midst of my play, before all that then were present; but yet I told them nothing: but, I say, I having made this conclusion, I returned to my sport again;* and I well remember, that presently this kind of despair did so possess my Soul, that I was perswaded I could never attain to other comfort then what I should get in sin; for Heaven was gone already, so that on that I must not think: wherefore I found within me a great desire to take my fill of sin, still studdying what sin was yet to be committed, that I might taste the sweetness of it; and I made as much haste as I could to fill my belly with its delicates, lest I should die before I had my desire; for that I feared greatly. In these things, I protest before *God*, I lye not, neither do I feign this form of speech: these were really, strongly, and with all my heart, my desires; *the good Lord, whose mercy is unsearchable, forgive me my transgressions*.

21. [25.] (And I am very confident that this temptation of the Devil is more usual amongst poor creatures then many are aware of, even to over-run their spirits with a scurvie and seared frame of heart,* and benumming of conscience: which frame, he stilly and slyly supplyeth with such despair, that though not much guilt attendeth the Soul, yet they continually have a secret conclusion within them, that there is no hopes for them; *for they have loved sins*, Jer. 2. 25. & 18. 12.)*

22. [26.] Now therefore I went on in sin with great greediness of mind, still grudging that I could not be so satisfied with it as I would: this did continue with me about a moneth, or more. But one day as I was standing at a Neighbours Shop-window, and there cursing and swearing, and playing the Mad-man after my wonted manner, there

sate within the woman of the house, and heard me; who though she also was a very loose and ungodly Wretch, yet protested that I swore and cursed at that most fearful rate, that she was made to tremble to hear me: And told me further, *That I was the ungodliest Fellow for swearing that ever she heard in all her life; and that I by thus doing, was able to spoile all the Youth in a whole Town, if they came but in my company.*

23. [27.] At this reproof I was silenced, and put to secret shame; and that too, as I thought, before the God of Heaven: wherefore while I there stood, and hanging down my head, I wished with all my heart that I might be a little childe again, that my Father might learn me to speak without this wicked way of swearing:* for thought I, I am so accustomed to it, that it is but in vain for me to think of a reformation, for I thought it could never be.

24. [28.] But how it came to pass I know not, I did from this time forward so leave my swearing, that it was a great wonder to my self to observe it; and whereas before I knew not how to speak unless I put an Oath before, and another behind, to make my words have authority, now I could speak better, and with more pleasantness then ever I could before: all this while I knew not Jesus Christ, neither did I leave my sports and play.

25. [29.] But quickly after this, I fell in company with one poor man, that made profession of Religion; who, as I then thought, did talk pleasantly of the Scriptures, and of the matters of Religion: wherefore falling into some love and liking to what he said, I betook me to my Bible, and began to take great pleasure in reading, but especially with the historical part thereof: for, as for *Pauls* Epistles,* and Scriptures of that nature, I could not away with them, being as yet but ignorant either of the corruptions of my nature, or of the want and worth of Jesus Christ to save me.

26. [30.] Wherefore I fell to some outward Reformation, both in my words and life, and did set the Commandments before me for my way to Heaven: which Commandments I also did strive to keep; and, as I thought, did keep them pretty well sometimes, and then I should have comfort; yet now and then should break one, and so afflict my Conscience; but then I should repent, and say I was sorry for it, and promise God to do better next time, and there get help again.*

27. [31.] Thus I continued about a year, all which time our Neighbours did take me to be a very godly man, a new and religious man, and did marvel much to see such a great and famous alteration in my life and manners; and indeed so it was, though yet I knew not Christ, nor Grace, nor Faith, nor Hope; and truly as I have well seen since, had I then died, my state had been most fearful: well, this I say, continued about a twelve-month, or more.

[32. But, I say, my Neighbours were amazed at this my great Conversion, from prodigious prophaneness, to something like a moral life;* And truly so they well might, for this my Conversion was as great, as for *Tom* of *Bedlam** to become a sober man. Now therefore they began to praise, to commend, and speak well of me, both to my face and behind my back. Now I was, as they said, become godly; now I was become a right honest man. But, oh! When I understood that these were their words and opinions of me, it pleased me mighty well. For though as yet I was nothing but a poor painted Hypocrite, yet I loved to be talked of, as one that was truly Godly. I was proud of my Godliness; and I did, all I did, either to be seen of, or to be well spoken of by men. And thus I continued for about a twelvemonth or more.]

[33. Now you must know, that before this, I had taken much delight in ringing, but my Conscience beginning to be tender: I thought that such a practice was but vain, and therefore forced my self to leave it, yet my mind hanckered,* wherefore I should go to the steeple house* and look on. But I thought this did not become Religion neither, yet I forced my self and would look on still; but quickly after, I began to think how if one of the Bells should fall; then I chose to stand under a main Beam that lay over thwart the Steeple from side to side, thinking there I might stand sure: But then I should think again, should the Bell fall with a swing, it might first hit the Wall, and then rebounding upon me, might kill me for all this Beam; this made me stand in the Steeple door, and now thought I, I am safe enough, for if a Bell should then fall, I can slip out behind these thick Walls, and so be preserved notwithstanding: [34.] So after this, I would yet go to see them ring, but would not go further than the Steeple door, but then it came into my head, how if the Steeple it self should fall, and this thought, (it may fall for ought I know) would, when I stood and looked on, continually so shake my mind, that I durst not stand at the Steeple door any longer, but was forced to fly for fear it should fall upon my head.

[35.] Another thing was my dancing, I was a full year before I could quite leave it; but all this while when I thought I kept this or that Commandment, or did by word or deed any thing that I thought were good, I had great peace in my Conscience, and should think with my self, God cannot chuse but be now pleased with me, yea, to relate it in mine own way, I thought no man in *England* could please God better than I.

[36.] But poor Wretch as I was, I was all this while ignorant of Jesus Christ, and going about to establish my own righteousness, had perished therein, had not God in mercy shewed me more of my state by nature.]

28. [37.] But upon a day, the good Providence of God did cast me to *Bedford*, to work on my calling; and in one of the streets of that town, I came where there was three or four poor women sitting at a door in the Sun, and talking about the things of God; and being now willing to hear them discourse, I drew near to hear what they said; for I was now a brisk talker also my self in the matters of Religion: but now I may say, *I heard, but I understood not*, for they were far above out of my reach, for their talk was about a new birth, the work of God on their hearts, also how they were convinced of their miserable state by nature:* they talked how God had visited their souls with his love in the Lord Jesus, and with what words and promises they had been refreshed, comforted, and supported against the temptations of the Devil; moreover, they reasoned of the suggestions and temptations of Satan in particular, and told to each other by which they had been afflicted, and how they were born up under his assaults: they also discoursed of their own wretchedness of heart, of their unbelief, and did contemn, slight and abhor their own righteousness, as filthy, and insufficient to do them any good.*

29. [38.] And me thought they spake as if joy did make them speak: they spake with such pleasantness of Scripture language, and with such appearance of grace in all they said, that they were to me as if they had found a new world, as if they were people that dwelt alone, and were not to be reckoned amongst their Neighbours. [Num. 23. 9.]

30. [39.] At this I felt my own heart began to shake, as mistrust-

ing my condition to be naught; for I saw that in all my thoughts about Religion and Salvation, the New birth did never enter into my mind, neither knew I the comfort of the Word and Promise, nor the deceitfulness and treachery of my own wicked heart. As for secret thoughts, I took no notice of them; neither did I understand what Satans temptations were, nor how they were to be withstood and resisted, &c.

31. [40.] Thus therefore when I had heard and considered what they said, I left them, and went about my employment again: but their talk and discourse went with me, also my heart would tarry with them, for I was greatly affected with their words, both because by them I was convinced that I wanted the true tokens* of a truly godly man, and also because by them I was convinced of the happy and blessed condition of him that was such a one.

32. [41.] Therefore I should often make it my business to be going again and again into the company of these poor people; for I could not stay away; and the more I went amongst them, the more I did question my condition; and, as still I do remember, presently I found two things within me, at which I did sometimes marvel, (especially considering what a blind, ignorant, sordid, and ungodly Wretch but just before I was) the one was, a very great softness and tenderness of heart, which caused me to fall under the conviction of what by Scripture they asserted; and the other was, a great bending in my mind to a continual meditating on them, and on all other good things which at any time I heard or read of.

33. [42.] My mind was now so turned, that it lay like a Horseleach at the vein, still crying out, *Give, give*; [Prov. 30. 15.] yea, it was so fixed on Eternity, and on the things about the Kingdome of Heaven, that is, so far as I knew, though as yet *God* knows, I knew but little, that neither pleasures nor profits, nor perswasions, nor threats, could loosen it, or make it let go its hold; and, though I may speak it with shame, yet it is in very deed a certain truth, it would then have been as difficult for me to have taken my mind from heaven to earth, as I have found it often since to get it again from earth to heaven.

[43. One thing I may not omit, there was a young man in our Town, to whom my heart before was knit more than to any other, but he being a most wicked Creature for cursing and swearing, and whoring, I shook him off and forsook his company; but about a quarter of a year after I had left him, I met him in a certain Lane, and asked him how he did; he after his old swearing and mad way, answered, he was well. But *Harry*, said I, why do you swear and curse thus? What will become of you if you die in this condition? He answered me in a great chafe, *What would the Devil do for company if it were not for such as I am?*

44. About this time, I met with some *Ranters** books, that were put forth by some of our Country men; which Books were also highly in esteem by several old Professors: some of these I read, but was not able to make a Judgement about them; wherefore, as I read in them, and thought upon them, (feeling myself unable to judge) I should betake my self to hearty prayer, in this manner; *O Lord, I am a fool, and not able to know the Truth from Errour; Lord leave me not to my own blindness, either to approve of, or condemn this Doctrine; if it be of God, let me not despise it; if it be of the Devil, let me not embrace it. Lord, I lay my Soul in this matter, only at thy foot, let me not be deceived, I humbly beseech thee.* I had one religious intimate Companion all this while, and that was the poor man that I spoke of before; but about this time he also turned a most devilish *Ranter*, and gave himself up to all manner of filthiness, especially Uncleanness; he would also deny that there was a God, Angel or Spirit, and would laugh at all exhortations to sobriety: when I laboured to rebuke his wickedness, he would laugh the more, and pretend that he had gone through all Religions, and could never light on the right till now,* he told me also that in little time I should see all Professors* turn to the ways of the Ranters: Wherefore abominating those cursed principles, I left his company forth with, and became to him as great a stranger as I had been before a familiar.

[45.] Neither was this man onely a temptation to me, but my calling lying in the countrey, I happened to light into several peoples company; who though strict in Religion formerly, yet was also swept away by these Ranters. These would also talk with me of their ways, and condemn me as legal and dark,* pretending that they onely had attained to perfection that could do what they would and not sin. O these temptations were suitable to my flesh, I being but a young man and my nature in its prime, but God who had as I hope designed me for better things, kept me in the fear of his name, and did not suffer me to accept of such cursed principles. And blessed be God who put it in my heart to cry to him to be kept and directed, still distrusting mine own Wisdom, for I have since seen even the effect of that prayer in his preserving me, not onely from Ranting Errors, but from those also that have sprung up since. The Bible was precious to me in those days.]

34. [46.] And now me thought I began to look into the Bible with new eyes, and read as I never did before; and especially the Epistles of the Apostle *Paul** were sweet and pleasant to me: and indeed I was then never out of the Bible, either by reading or meditation, still crying out to *God*, that I might know the truth, and way to heaven and glory.

35. [47.] And as I went on and read, I lighted on that passage, *To one is given by the Spirit the word of wisdom, to another the word of knowledge by the same Spirit, and to another Faith, &c.* 1 Cor. 12. And though, as I have since seen, that by this Scripture the holy Ghost intends, in special, things extraordinary, yet on me it did then fasten with conviction, that I did want things ordinary, even that understanding and wisdome that other Christians had. On this word I mused, and could not tell what to do,* for I feared it shut me out of all the blessings that other good people had given them of *God*: but I was loath to conclude I had no Faith in my soul: for if I do so, thought I, then I shall count my self a very Cast-away* indeed.

36. [48.] No, said I with myself, though I am convinced that I am an ignorant Sot, and that I want those blessed gifts of knowledge and understanding that other good people have, yet at a venture I will conclude I am not altogether faithless, though I know not what Faith is. For it was shewed me, and that too (as I have since seen) by Satan, That those who conclude themselves in a faithless state, have neither rest nor quiet in their Souls; and I was loath to fall quite into despair.*

37. [49.] Wherefore by this suggestion, I was for a while made afraid to see my want of Faith; but God would not suffer me thus to undo and destroy my *Soul*, but did continually against this my blinde and sad conclusion, create still within me such suppositions, That I might in this deceive my self; that I could not rest content until I did now come to some certain knowledge whether I had Faith or no; this always running in my mind, *But how if you want Faith indeed? But how can you tell you have Faith?*

38. [50.] So that though I endeavoured at the first to look over the

business of Faith, yet in a little time, I better considering the matter, was willing to put myself upon the tryal, whether I had Faith or no. But alas, poor Wretch! so ignorant and brutish was I, that I knew to this day no more how to do it, than I know how to begin and accomplish that rare and curious piece of Art, which I never yet saw nor considered.

39. [51.] Wherefore while I was thus considering, and being put to my plunge* about it (for you must know that as yet I had in this matter broken my mind to no man, onely did hear and consider) the Tempter came in with this delusion, That there was no way for me to know I had Faith, but by trying to work some miracle, urging those *Scriptures* that seem to look that way, for the inforcing and strengthening his Temptation. Nay, one day as I was betwixt *Elstow* and *Bedford*, the temptation was hot upon me to try if I had Faith by doing of some miracle; which miracle at that time was this, I must say to the puddles that were in the horse pads, *Be dry*; and to the dry places, *Be you the puddles*:* and truly one time I was a going to say so indeed; but just as I was about to speak, this thought came into my minde, *But go under yonder Hedge, and pray first, that God would make you able*: but when I had concluded to pray, this came hot upon me, That if I prayed and came again and tried to do it, and yet did nothing notwithstanding, then besure I had no Faith, but was a Cast-away and lost: Nay, thought I, if it be so, I will never try yet, but will stay a little longer.

40. [52.] So I continued at a great loss: for I thought if they onely had Faith which could do such wonderful things, then I concluded that for the present I neither had it, nor yet for time to come were ever like to have it. Thus I was tossed betwixt the Devil and my own ignorance, and so perplexed, especially at some times, that I could not tell what to doe.

41. [53.] About this time, the state and happiness of these poor people at *Bedford* was thus in a Dream or Vision represented to me:* I saw as if they were set on the Sunny side of some high Mountain, there refreshing themselves with the pleasant beams of the Sun, while I was shivering and shrinking in the cold, afflicted with frost, snow, and dark clouds; methought also betwixt me and them I saw a wall that did compass about this Mountain; now thorow this wall, my Soul did greatly desire to pass, concluding that if I could, I would

goe even into the very midst of them, and there also comfort myself with the heat of their Sun.

42. [54.] About this wall I thought myself to goe again and again, still prying as I went, to see if I could find some way or passage by which I might enter therein, but none could I find for some time: at the last I saw as it were a narrow gap, like a little door-way in the wall, thorow which I attempted to pass: but the passage being very straight, and narrow, I made many offers to get in, but all in vain, even untill I was well nigh quite beat out by striving to get in: at last with great striving, me thought I at first did get in my head, & after that by a side-ling striving, my shoulders, and my whole body; then was I exceeding glad, and went and sat down in the midst of them, and so was comforted with the light and heat of their Sun.*

43. [55.] Now this Mountain and Wall, &c. was thus made out to me; the Mountain signified the Church of the living God; the Sun that shone thereon, the comfortable shining of his mercifull face on them that were therein: the wall I thought was the Word that did make separation between the Christians and the world: and the gap which was in this wall, I thought was Jesus Christ, who is the way to God the Father. [*Joh. 14. 6. Mat. 7. 14.*] But for as much as the passage was wonderful narrow, even so narrow, that I could not but with great difficulty, enter in thereat; it shewed me, that none could enter into life but those that were in down-right earnest, and unless also they left this wicked world behind them; for here was only roome for Body and Soul, but not for Body and Soul, and Sin.

44. [56.] This resemblance abode upon my spirit many dayes, all which time I saw my self in a forlorn and sad condition, but yet was provoked to a vehement hunger, and desire to be one of that number that did sit in this Sun-shine: now also I should pray where ever I was, whether at home or abroad, in house or field, and should also often with lifting up of heart, sing that of the fifty first Psalm, *O Lord, consider my distress:** for as yet I knew not where I was.

45. [57.] Neither as yet could I attain to any comfortable perswasion that I had Faith in Christ, but instead of having satisfaction, here I began to find my Soul to be assaulted with fresh doubts about my future happiness, especially with such as these, Whether I was elected; but how if the day of grace should now be past and gone?*

46. [58.] By these two temptations I was very much afflicted and disquieted; sometimes by one, and sometimes by the other of them. And first, to speak of that about my questioning my election, I found at this time that though I was in a flame to find the way to Heaven and Glory, and though nothing could beat me off from this, yet this question did so offend and discourage me, that I was, especially at sometimes, as if the very strength of my body also had been taken away by the force and power thereof. This Scripture also did seem to me to trample upon all my desires, *It is neither in him that willeth, nor in him that runneth, but in God that sheweth mercy*, Rom. 9. [16.]

47. [59.] With this Scripture I could not tell what to do, for I evidently saw that unless the great God of his infinite grace and bounty, had voluntarily chosen me to be a vessel of mercy,* though I should desire, and long, and labour untill my heart did break, no good could come of it. Therefore this would still stick with me, How can you tell you are Elected? and what if you should not? how then?

48. [60.] O Lord, thought I, what if I should not indeed? it may be you are not, said the Tempter: it may be so indeed, thought I. Why then, said Satan, you had as good leave off, and strive no further; for if indeed you should not be Elected and chosen of God, there is no talke of your being saved: *For it is neither in him that willeth, nor in him that runneth, but in God that sheweth mercy.*

49. [61.] By these things I was driven to my wits end, not knowing what to say, or how to answer these temptations, (indeed I little thought that Satan had thus assaulted me, but that rather it was my own prudence thus to start the question) for that the Elect only attained eternal life, that I without scruple did heartily close withall: but that my self was one of them, there lay all the question.*

50. [62.] Thus therefore for several dayes I was greatly assaulted and perplexed, and was often, when I have been walking, ready to sink where I went* with faintness in my mind: but one day, after I had been so many weeks oppressed and cast down therewith, as I was now quite giving up the Ghost of all my hopes of ever attaining life, that sentence fell with weight upon my spirit, *Look at the generations of old, and see, did ever any trust in God and were confounded?*

51. [63.] At which I was greatly lightened, and encouraged in my Soul; for thus at that very instant it was expounded to me: *Begin at the beginning of Genesis, and read to the end of the Revelations, and see* *if you can find that there was any that ever trusted in the Lord, and was Confounded.* So coming home, I presently went to my Bible to see if I could find that saying, not doubting but to find it presently, for it was so fresh, and with such strength and comfort on my spirit, that I was as if it talked with me.

52. [64.] Well, I looked, but I found it not, only it abode upon me: then I did aske first this good man, and then another, if they knew where it was; but they knew no such place: at this I wondered that such a sentence should so suddenly and with such comfort, and strength seize and abide upon my heart, and yet that none could find it, (for I doubted not but it was in holy Scripture.)

53. [65.] Thus I continued above a year, and could not find the place, but at last, casting my eye into the Apocrypha-Books, I found it in *Ecclesiasticus* [2. 10]; this at the first did somewhat daunt me, but because by this time I had got more experience of the love and kindness of God, it troubled me the less; especially when I considered, that though it was not in those Texts that we call holy and Canonical, yet forasmuch as this sentence was the sum and substance of many of the promises,* it was my duty to take the comfort of it, and I bless God for that word, for it was of God to me: that word doth still at times shine before my face.

54. [66.] After this, that other doubt did come with strength upon me, *But how if the day of grace should be past and gone?* how if you have over-stood the time of mercy? Now I remember that one day as I was walking into the Country, I was much in the thoughts of this, But how if the day of grace be past? and to aggravate my trouble, the Tempter presented to my mind those good people of *Bedford*, and suggested thus unto me, That these being converted already, they were all that God would save in those parts,* & that I came too late, for these had got the blessing before I came.

55. [67.] Now was I in great distress, thinking in very deed that this might well be so: wherefore I went up and down bemoaning my sad condition, counting myself* far worse then a thousand fools, for standing off thus long, and spending so many years in sin as I have done; still crying out, Oh that I had turned sooner! Oh that I had turned seven years agoe; it made me also angry with my self, to think that I should have no more wit but to trifle away my time till my Soul and Heaven were lost.

56. [68.] But when I had been long vexed with this fear, and was

scarce able to take one step more, just about the same place where I received my other encouragement, these words broke in upon my mind, *Compell them to come in, that my house may be filled, and yet there is roome*, Luke 14. 22, 23. These words, but especially them, *And yet there is roome*, were sweet words to me; for truly I thought that by them I saw there was place enough in Heaven for me, and moreover, that when the Lord Jesus did speak these words, he then did think of me, and that he knowing the time would come that I should be afflicted with fear, that there was no place left for me in his bosome, did before speak this word, and leave it upon record, that I might find help thereby against this vile temptation.

57. [69.] In the light and encouragement of this word, I went a pretty while, and the comfort was the more, when I thought that the Lord Jesus should think on me so long agoe, and that he should speak them words on purpose for my sake, for I did then think verily, that he did on purpose speak them to encourage me withall.

[[70.] But I was not without my temptations to go back again; temptations, I say, both from Satan, mine own heart, and carnal acquaintance; but I thank God, these were outweighed by that sound sense of death, and of the Day of Judgment, which abode, as it were continually in my view. I should often also think on *Nebuchadnezzar*, of whom it is said, *He had given him all the Kingdoms of the Earth*, Dan. 5. 18, 19. Yet thought I, if this great man had all his Portion in this World, one hour in Hell Fire would make him forget all. Which consideration was a great help to me.

71. I was also made about this time to see something concerning the Beasts that *Moses* counted clean and unclean. I thought those Beasts were types of men; the clean types of them that were the People of God; but the unclean types of such as were the children of the wicked One. Now I read, that the clean beasts chewed the Cud; that is, thought I, they shew us we must feed upon the Word of God: they also parted the Hoof, I thought that signified, we must part, if we would be saved, with the ways of ungodly men. And also, in further reading about them, I found, that though we did chew the Cud as the Hare; yet if we walked with Claws like a Dog, or if we did part the Hoof like the Swine, yet if we did not chew the Cud as the Sheep, we were still for all that, but unclean: for I thought the Hare to be a type of those that talk of the Word,

yet walk in ways of sin; and that the Swine was like him that parteth with his outward Pollutions, but still wanteth the Word of Faith, without which there could be no way of Salvation, let a man be never so devout, *Deut.* 14.]

58. [71. cont.] After this, I found by reading the word, that those that must be glorified with Christ in another world *Must be called by him here*. Called to the partaking of a share in his word and righteousness, and to the comforts & first-fruits of his Spirit, and to a peculiar interest in all those Heavenly things, which do indeed fore-fit the Soul for that rest and house of glory which is in Heaven above.

59. [72.] Here again I was at a very great stand, not knowing what to doe, fearing I was not called; for thought I, if I be not called, what then can doe me good?* But oh how I now loved those words that spake of a *Christians calling*! as when the Lord said to one, *Follow me*; and to another, *Come after me*, and oh thought I, that he would say so to me too! how gladly would I run after him.

60. [73.]* I cannot now express with what longings and breakings in my Soul, I cryed to Christ to call me. Thus I continued for a time all on a flame to be converted to Jesus Christ, and did also see at that day such glory in a converted state, that I could not be contented without a share therein. Gold! could it have been gotten for Gold, what could I have given for it! had I had a whole world, it had all gone ten thousand times over, for this, that my Soul might have been in a converted state.

61. [74.] How lovely now was every one in my eyes, that I thought to be converted men and women? they shone, they walked like a people that carried the broad Seal of Heaven about them. Oh I saw the lot was fallen to them in pleasant places, and they had a goodly heritage.* [*Psal.* 16.] But that which made me sick, was that of Christ, in Mark, *He went up into a Mountain, and called to him whom he would, and they came unto him*, Mark 3. 13.

62. [75.] This Scripture made me faint and fear, yet it kindled fire in my Soul. That which made me fear, was this, lest Christ should have no liking to me, for he called *whom he would*. But oh the glory that I saw in that condition, did still so engage my heart, that I could seldome read of any that Christ did call, but I presently wished, Would I had been in their cloaths, would I had been born *Peter*, would I had been born *John*, or would I had been by, and had heard

him when he called them, how would I have cryed, O Lord, call me also! but oh I feared he would not call me.

63. [76.] And truly the Lord let me goe thus many months together, and shewed me nothing, either that I was already, or should be called hereafter. But at last, after much time spent, and many groans to God, that I might be made partaker of the holy and heavenly calling, that word came in upon me, *I will cleanse their blood that I have not cleansed, for the Lord dwelleth in Zion.* Joel 3. 21. These words I thought were sent to encourage me to wait still upon God, and signified unto me, that if I were not already, yet time might come I might be in truth converted unto Christ.

64. [77.] About this time I began to break my mind to those poor people in *Bedford,* and to tell them my condition: which, when they had heard, they told *Mr. Gifford** of me, who himself also took occasion to talke with me, and was willing to be well perswaded of me, though I think but from little grounds; but he invited me to his house, where I should hear him confer with others about the dealings of God with the Soul: from all which I still received more conviction, and from that time began to see something of the vanity and inward wretchedness of my wicked heart, for as yet I knew no great matter therein, but *now* it began to be discovered unto me, and also to worke at that rate for wickedness as it never did before. Now I evidently found, that lusts and corruptions would strongly put forth themselves within me, in wicked thoughts and desires, which I did not regard before: my desires also for heaven and life began to fail; I found also, that whereas before my Soul was full of longings after God, now my heart began to hanker after every foolish vanity; yea, my heart would not be moved to mind that that was good, it began to be careless, both of my Soul and Heaven; it would now continually hang back both to, and in every duty, and was as a clog* on the leg of a Bird to hinder her from flying.

65. [78.] Nay, thought I, now I grow worse and worse, now am I further from conversion then ever I was before; wherefore, I began to sink* greatly in my Soul, and began to entertain such discouragement in my heart, as laid me as low as Hell. If now I should have burned at a stake, I could not believe that Christ had love for me. Alas, I could neither hear him, nor see him, nor feel him, nor savor any of his things: I was driven as with a Tempest, my heart would be unclean, the *Cananites* would dwell in the Land.

66. [79.] Sometimes I would tell my condition to the people of God; which when they heard, they would pity me, and would tell me of the Promises; but they had as good have told me that I must reach the Sun with my finger, as have bidden me receive or relie upon the Promise, and as soon I should have done it; all my sence and feeling was against me, and I saw I had a heart that would sin, and lay under a Law that would condemn.

67. [80.] (These things have often made me think of that Child which the Father brought to Christ, *Who while he was yet a coming to him, was thrown down by the Devil, and also so rent and torn by him, that he lay and wallowed foaming*:) Luke 9. 42. Mark 9. 20.

68. [81.] Further, in these dayes I should find my heart to shut itself up against the Lord, and against his holy Word, I have found my unbelief to set as it were the shoulder to the door to keep him out, and that too, even then when I have with many a bitter sigh cried, Good Lord break it open; *Lord break these gates of brass, and cut these bars of iron asunder.* [Psa. 107. 16.] Yet that Word would sometime create in my heart a peaceable pause, *I girded thee, though thou hast not known me* [Isa. 45. 5.].

69. [82.] But all this while, as to the act of sinning, I never was more tender then now;* I durst not take a pin or a stick, though but so big as a straw; for my conscience now was sore, and would smart at every touch: I could not now tell how to speak my words for fear I should mis-place them: O how gingerly did I then go, in all I did or said! I found my self as on a miry bog, that shook if I did but stir, and as there left both of God and Christ, and the Spirit, and all good things.

[83. But I observe, though I was such a great sinner before conversion, yet God never much charged the guilt of the sins of my Ignorance upon me, only he shewed me I was lost if I had not Christ because I had been a sinner. I saw that I wanted a perfect righteousnes to present me without fault before God and that this righteousness was no where to be found but in the person of Jesus Christ.

84. But my Original and inward pollution, that, that was my plague and my affliction, that I saw at a dreadful rate all ways putting forth it selfe within me, that I had the guilt of to amazement; by reason of that, I was more loathsom in mine own eyes then was a toad, and I thought I was so in Gods eyes too; sin and

corruption, I said, would as naturally bubble out of my heart, as water would bubble out of a fountain. I thought now that every one had a better heart then I had; I could have changed heart with any body, I thought, none but the Devil himself could equalize me for inward wickednes and pollution of minde. I fell therfore at the sight of mine own vileness, deeply into dispair, for I concluded that this condition that I was in, Could not stand with a state of Grace, sure thought I, I am forsaken of God, sure I am given up, to the Devil, and to a reprobate mind,* and thus I continued a long while, even for some years together.

85. While I was thus afflicted with the fears of my own damnation, there were two things would make me wonder; the one was, when I saw old people hunting after the things of this life, as if they should live here alwayes; the other was, when I found Professors much distressed and cast down when they met with outward losses, as of Husband, Wife, Child, &c. Lord, thought I, what a doe is here about such little things as these?* what seeking after carnal things by some, and what grief in others for the loss of them! if they so much labour after, and spend so many tears for the things of this present life; how am I to be bemoaned, pitied and prayed for! my Soul is dying, my soul is damning. Were my Soul but in a good condition, and were I but sure of it, ah, how rich should I esteem my self, though blest but with Bread and Water: I should count those but small afflictions, and should bear them as little burdens. *A wounded Spirit who can bear?*⌉

70. [86.] And though I was thus troubled and tossed and afflicted with the sight and sence and terrour of my own wickedness, yet I was afraid to let this sence and sight go quite off my minde: for I found that unless guilt of conscience was taken off the right way,* that is, by the Blood of Christ, a man grew rather worse for the loss of his trouble of minde, than better. Wherefore if my guilt lay hard upon me, then I should cry that the Blood of Christ might take it off: and if it was going off without it (for the sence of sin would be sometimes as if it would die, and go quite away) then I would also strive to fetch it upon my heart again, by bringing the punishment for sin in Hell-fire upon my Spirit; and should cry, *Lord, let it not go off my heart but the right way, but by the Blood of Christ, and by the application of thy mercy thorow him to my Soul*; for that Scripture lay much upon me, *Without shedding of Blood there is no Remission*,

Heb. 9. 22. And that which made me the more afraid of this, was, Because I had seen some, who though when they were under Wounds of Conscience, then they would cry and pray, but they seeking rather present Ease from their Trouble, then Pardon for their Sin, cared not how they lost their guilt, so they got it out of their minde; and, therefore having got it off the wrong way, it was not sanctified unto them, but they grew harder and blinder, and more wicked after their trouble.* This made me afraid, and made me cry to God, that it might not be so with me.

71. [87.] And now was I sorry that God had made me a man, for I feared I was a reprobate: I counted man, as unconverted, the most doleful of all the Creatures: Thus being afflicted and tossed about by my sad condition, I counted my self alone, and above the most of men unblest.

 [88. Yea, I thought it impossible that ever I should attain to so much goodness of heart, as to thank God that he had made me a man. Man Indeed, is the most noble, by creation, of all the creatures in the visible World, but by sin he had made himself the most ignoble. The beasts, birds, fishes, &c. I blessed their condition, for they had not a sinful nature, they were not obnoxious to the wrath of God, they were not to go to Hell fire after death: I could therefore a* rejoyced; had my condition been as any of theirs.*]

[89.] In this condition I went a great while, but when comforting time was come, I heard one preach a sermon upon those words in the *Song*, (*Song*. 4. 1.) *Behold thou art fair, my Love, behold thou art fair*; but at that time he made these two words, *My Love*, his chief and subject matter; from which after he had a little opened the text, he observed these several conclusions: 1. *That the Church, and so every saved Soul, is Christs Love, when loveless*: 2. *Christs Love without a cause*: 3. *Christs Love, when hated of the world*: 4. *Christs Love when under temptation and under dissertion*:* 5. *Christs Love from first to last*.

72. [90.] But I got nothing by what he said at present, only when he came to the application of the fourth particular, this was the word he said, *If it be so that the saved Soul is Christs Love, when under temptation and dissertion; then poor tempted Soul, when thou art assaulted and afflicted with temptation, and the hidings of Gods Face, yet think on these two words,* MY LOVE, *still.*

73. [91.] So as I was a going home, these words came again into

my thoughts, and I well remember as they came in, I said thus in my heart, What shall I get by thinking on these two words? this thought had no sooner passed thorow my heart, but the words began thus to kindle in my Spirit, *Thou art my Love, thou art my Love*, twenty times together; and still as they ran thus in my minde, they waxed stronger and warmer, and began to make me look up;* but being as yet between hope and fear, I still replied in my heart, *But is it true too? but is it true?* at which that sentence fell in upon me, *He wist not that it was true which was done unto him of the Angel*, Act. 12. 9.

74. [92.] Then I began to give place to the Word, which with power did over and over make this joyful sound within my Soul, *Thou art my Love, thou art my Love, and nothing shall separate thee from my love*; and with that *Rom.* 8. 39.* came into my minde. Now was my heart filled full of comfort and hope, and now I could believe that my sins should be forgiven me;

[yea I was now so taken with the love and mercy of God, that I remember, I could not tell how to contain till I got home; I thought I could have spoken of his Love and have told of his mercy to me, even to the very Crows that sat upon the plow'd lands before me, had they been capable to have understood me,]

wherefore I said in my Soul with much gladness, Well, I would I had a pen and ink here, I would write this down before I go any further, for surely I will not forget *this*, forty years hence; but alas! within less then forty days I began to question all again.

75. [93.] Yet still at times, I was helped to believe that it was a true manifestation of Grace unto my Soul, though I had lost much of the life and savour of it. Now about a week or fortnight after this, I was much followed by this Scripture, *Simon, Simon, behold, Satan hath desired to have you*, Luk. 22. 31. and sometimes it would sound so loud within me, yea, and as it were call so strongly after me, that once above all the rest, I turned my head over my shoulder, thinking verily that some man had behind me called to me, being at a great distance.

[me thought he called so loud, it came as I have thought since to have stirred me up to prayer and to watchfulness. It came to acquaint me that a cloud and storm was coming down upon me, but I understood it not. [94.] Also as I remember, that time as it called to me so loud, it was the last time that it sounded in mine ears, but methinks I hear still with what a loud voice these words

Simon, Simon sounded in my ears. I thought verily, as I have told you, that some body had called after me that was half a mile behind me; and although that was not my name, yet it made me suddenly look behind me, believing that he that called so loud meant me.]

76. [95.] But so foolish was I, and ignorant, that I knew not the reason for this sound, (which as I did both see and feel soon after, was sent from heaven as an alarm to awaken me to provide for what was coming) onely it would make me muse, and wonder in my minde to think what should be the reason that this Scripture, and that at this rate, so often and so loud, should still be sounding and ratling in mine ears. But, as I said before, I soon after perceived the end of God therein.

77. [96.] For about the space of a month after, a very great storm came down upon me, which handled me twenty times worse then all I had met with before: it came stealing upon me, now by one piece, then by another; first all my comfort was taken from me, then darkness seized upon me; after which whole flouds of Blasphemies, both against God, Christ, and the Scriptures, was poured upon my spirit, to my great confusion and astonishment.* These blasphemous thoughts were such as also stirred up questions in me against the very *being* of God, and of his onely beloved Son; as whether there were in truth a God or Christ, or no? and whether the holy Scriptures were not rather a Fable and cunning Story, then the holy and pure Word of God?

78. [97.] The Tempter would also much assault me with this: How can you tell but that the Turks had as good Scriptures to prove their *Mahomet* the Saviour, as we have to prove our *Jesus* is; and could I think that so many ten thousands in so many Countreys and Kingdoms, should be without the knowledge of the right way to Heaven (if there were indeed a Heaven) and that we onely, who live but in a corner of the Earth, should alone be blessed therewith? Every one doth think his own Religion rightest, both *Jews*, and *Moors*, and *Pagans*; and how if all our Faith, and Christ, and Scriptures, should be but a think-so too?

79. [98.] Sometime I have endeavoured to argue against these suggestions, and to set some of the Sentences of blessed *Paul* against them; but alas! I quickly felt when I thus did, such arguings as these would return again upon me; Though we made so great a matter of

Paul, and of his words, yet how could I tell but that in very deed, he, being a subtile and cunning man, might give himself up to deceive with strong delusions, and also take both that pains and travel to undo and destroy his fellows.

80. [99.] These suggestions (with many other which at this time I may not, nor dare not utter, neither by word nor pen) did make such a seizure upon my spirit, and did so over-weigh my heart, both with their number, continuance, and fiery force, that I felt as if there were nothing else but these from morning to night within me, and as though indeed there could be room for nothing else; and also concluded that God had in very wrath to my Soul given me up unto them, to be carried away with them, as with a mighty whirlwind.

81. [100.] Onely by the distaste that they gave unto my spirit, I felt there was something in me that refused to embrace them: but this consideration I then onely had, when God gave me leave to swallow my spittle,* otherwise the noise, and strength, and force of these temptations would drown and overflow, and as it were bury all such thoughts, or the remembrance of any such thing. While I was in this temptation, I should find often my mind suddenly put upon it, to curse and swear, or to speak some grievous thing of *God*, or *Christ* his *Son*, and of the *Scriptures*.

82. [101.] Now I thought surely I am possessed of the Devil; at other times again I thought I should be bereft of my wits, for instead of lauding and magnifying of *God* the *Lord* with others, if I have but heard him spoken of, presently some most horrible blasphemous thought or other would blot out of my heart against him. So that whether I did think that God was, or again did think there were no such thing; no love, nor peace, nor gracious disposition could I feel within me.

83. [102.] These things did sink me into very deep despair, for I concluded that such things could not possibly be found amongst them that loved God. I often, when these temptations have been with force upon me, did compare my self in the case of such a Child whom some Gypsie hath by force took up under her apron, and is carrying from Friend and Country; kick sometimes I did, and also scream and cry; but yet I was as bound in the wings of the temptation, and the wind would carry me away. I thought also of *Saul*, and of the evil spirit that did possess him, and did greatly fear that my condition was the same with that of his. [1 Sam. 16. 14.]

84. [103.] In these days, when I have heard others talk of what was the sin against the Holy *Ghost*,* then would the Tempter so provoke me to desire to sin that sin, that I was as if I could not, must not, neither should be quiet until I had committed that; now no sin would serve but that: if it were to be committed by speaking of such a word, then I have been as if my mouth would have spoken that word whether I would or no; and in so strong a measure was this temptation upon me, that often I have been ready to clap my hand under my chin, to hold my mouth from opening; and to that end also I have had thoughts at other times to leap with my head downward into some Muckhil-hole or other, to keep my mouth from speaking.

85. [104.] Now I blessed the condition of the Dogge and Toad,* and counted the estate of every thing that *God* had made, far better then this dreadfull state of mine, and such as my companions was: yea, gladly would I have been in the condition of Dog or Horse, for I knew they had no Soul to perish under the everlasting weights of Hell for sin, as mine was like to do: Nay, and though I saw this, felt this, and was broken to pieces with it, yet that which added to my sorrow, was, that I could not finde that with all my Soul I did desire deliverance. That Scripture also did tear and rend my Soul in the midst of these distractions, *The wicked are like the troubled Sea which cannot rest, whose waters cast up mire and dirt: There is no peace to the wicked, saith my God,* Isa. 57. 20. 21.

[105. And now my heart was at times exceeding hard;* if I would have given a thousand pound for a tear, I could not shed one, no nor sometimes scarce desire to shed one. I was much dejected to think that this would be my lot! I saw some could mourn and lament their sin, and others again could rejoyce and bless God for Christ, and others again could quiet talk of, and with gladness remember the Word of God, while I only was in the storm or tempest. This much sunk me, I thought my condition was alone,* I should therefore much bewail my hard hap, but get out of, or get rid of these things I could not.]

86. [106.] While this temptation lasted, which was about a year, I could attend upon none of the Ordinances of *God*,* but with sore and great affliction; yea, then was I most distressed with blasphemies: if I have been hearing the Word, then uncleanness, blasphemies, and despair, would hold me as Captive there; if I have been reading, then

sometimes I had sudden thoughts to question all I read; sometimes again my mind would be so strangely snatched away, and possessed with other things, that I have neither known, nor regarded, nor remembred so much as the sentence that but now I have read.

87. [107.] In prayer also, I have been greatly troubled at this time: sometimes I have thought I should see the Devil, nay, thought I have felt him behind me pull my cloaths:* he would be also continually at me in the time of prayer, to have done, break off, make haste, you have prayed enough, and stay no longer: still drawing my minde away. Sometimes also he would cast in such wicked thoughts as these, that I must pray to him, or for him: I have thought sometimes of that, *Fall down*, or, *If thou wilt fall down and worship me.* [Mat. 4. 9.]

88. [108.] Also when because I have had wandering thoughts in the time of this duty, I have laboured to compose my mind, and fix it upon God; then with great force hath the Tempter laboured to distract me and confound me, and to turn away my mind, by presenting to my heart and fancy the form of a Bush, a Bull, a Besom,* or the like, as if I should pray to those; to these also he would at some times (especially) so hold my mind, that I was as if I could think of nothing else, or pray to nothing else but to these, or such as they.

89. [109.] Yet at times I should have some strong and heart-affecting apprehensions of God, and the reality of the truth of his Gospel: but oh how would my heart at such times put forth it self with unexpressable groanings!* my whole Soul was then in every word; I should cry with pangs after *God*, that he would be merciful to me; but then I should be daunted again with such conceits as these, I should think that *God* did mock at these my prayers, saying, and that in the audience of the holy Angels, This poor simple Wretch doth hanker after me, as if I had nothing to do with my mercy, but to bestow it on such as he: alas poor fool! how art thou deceived, it is not for such as thee to have favour with the Highest.

90. [110.] Then hath the Tempter come upon me also with such discouragements as these: You are very hot for mercy, but I will cool you; this frame shall not last alwayes; many have been as hot as you for a spirt,* but I have quench'd their Zeal (and with this such and such who were fallen off, would be set before mine eyes) then I should be afraid that I should do so too: but, thought I, I am glad

this comes into my minde; well, I will watch and take what heed I can: Though you do, said Satan, I shall be too hard for you, I will cool you insensibly, by degrees, by little and little; what care I, saith he, though I be seven years in chilling your heart, if I can do it at last; continual rocking will lull a crying Child asleep: I will ply it close, but I will have my end accomplished: though you be burning hot at present, yet if I can pull you from this fire, I shall have you cold before it be long. [111.] These things brought me into great straights; for as I at present could not find my self fit for present death, so I thought to live long would make me yet more unfit; for time would make me forget all, and wear even the remembrance of the evil of sin, the worth of Heaven, and the need I had of the Blood of Christ to wash me, both out of mind and thought: But I thank Christ Jesus, these things did not at present make me slack my crying, but rather did put me more upon it (*like her who met with the Adulterer*, Deut. 22. 25.); in which dayes that was a good word to me, after I had suffered these things a while, *I am perswaded that neither death nor life*, &c. *shall separate us from the love of God which is in Christ Jesus*, Rom. 8. 38. And now I hoped long life should not destroy me, nor make me miss of Heaven.

91. [112.] Yet I had some supports in this temptation, though they were then all questioned by me: That in the third of *Jeremiah*, at the first, was something to me, and so was the consideration of the fifth verse of that Chapter; that though we have spoken and done evil things as we could,* yet we should cry unto *God, My Father, thou art the Guide of my youth*, and should return unto him.

92. [113.] I had also once a sweet glance from that in 2 *Cor.* 5. 21. *For he hath made him to be sin for us, who knew no sin, that he might be made the righteousness of God in him.* I remember also that one day, as I was sitting in a Neighbours House, and there very sad at the consideration of my many blasphemies; and as I was saying in my mind, What ground have I to think that I, who have been so vile and abominable, should ever inherit eternal life; that word came suddenly upon me, *What shall we say to these things? If God be for us, who can be against us?* Rom. 8. 31. That also was an help unto me, *Because I live, you shall live also*, Joh. 14. 19. But these were but hints, touches, and short visits, though very sweet when present, onely they lasted not; *but like to Peters Sheet, of a sudden were caught up from me to Heaven again*, Act. 10. 16.

93. [114.] But afterwards the Lord did more fully and graciously discover himself unto me, and indeed did quite not onely deliver me from the guilt that by these things was laid upon my Conscience, but also from the very filth thereof, for the temptation was removed, and I was put into my right mind again, as other Christians were.

94. [115.] I remember that one day, as I was travelling into the Countrey, and musing on the wickedness and blasphemy of my heart, and considering of the enmity that was in me to God, that Scripture came in my mind, *He hath made peace by the blood of his Cross*, Col. 1. 20. by which I was made to see both again, and again, and again, that day, that *God* and my Soul were friends by this blood; yea, I saw that the *justice* of *God* and my *sinful* Soul, could imbrace and kiss each other through this blood: this was a good day to me, I hope I shall not forget it.*

95. [116.] At another time, as I was set by the fire in my house, and musing on my wretchedness, the Lord made that also a precious word unto me, *For as much then as the children are partakers of flesh and blood, he also himself likewise took part of the same, that through death he might destroy him that had the power of death, that is the Devil: and deliver those who through the fear of death were all their life time subject to bondage*, Heb. 2. 14, 15. I thought that the glory of these words was then so weighty on me, that I was both once and twice ready to swoon as I sat, yet not with grief and trouble, but with sollid joy and peace.

96. [117.] At this time also I sat under the Ministry of holy Mr. *Gifford*, whose Doctrine, by Gods grace, was much for my stability. This man made it much his business to deliver the People of God from all those false and unsound rests* that by Nature we are prone to take and make to our Souls; he pressed us to take special heed, that we took not up any truth upon trust, as from this or that or another man or men, but to cry mightily to God, that he would convince us of the reality thereof, and set us down therein by his own Spirit in the holy Word; for, said he, if you do otherwise, when temptations come, if strongly, you not having received them with evidence from Heaven, will find you want that help and strength now to resist, as once you thought you had.

97. [118.] This was as seasonable to my Soul, as the former and latter rain in their season;* for I had found, and that by sad experience, the truth of these his words. (For I had felt, *no man can say*,

especially when tempted of the Devil, *that Jesus Christ is Lord, but by the holy Ghost.** Wherefore I found my Soul thorow Grace very apt to drink in this Doctrine, and to incline to pray to God that in nothing that pertained to Gods glory and my own eternal happiness, he would suffer me to be without the confirmation thereof from Heaven; for now I saw clearly there was an exceeding difference betwixt the notions of flesh and blood, and the Revelations of God in Heaven, also a great difference between that faith that is fained, and according to man's wisdom, and that which comes by a man being born thereto of God, *Mat.* 16. 15, 16. 1 *John* 5. 1.

98. [119.] But oh! now, how was my Soul led from truth to truth by God! even from the birth and Cradle of the Son of God, to his ascention and second coming from Heaven to judge the World.

99. [120.] Truly I then found upon this account the great God was very Good unto me, for to my remembrance there was not any thing that I then cried to God to make known and reveal unto me, but he was pleased to do it for me, I mean not one part of the Gospel of the Lord Jesus, but I was orderly led into it; me thought I saw with great evidence, from the relation of the four Evangelists, the wonderful work of God in giving Jesus Christ to save us, from his conception and birth, even to his second coming to judgement: me thought I was as if I had seen him born, as if I had seen him grow up, as if I had seen him walk thorow this world, from the Cradle to his Cross, to which also when he came, I saw how gently he gave himself to be hanged and nailed on it for my sins and wicked doings; also as I was musing on this his progress, that droped on my Spirit, *He was ordained for the slaughter*, 1 Pet. 1. 19, 20.

100. [121.] When I have considered also the truth of his resurrection, and have remembred that word, *touch me not Mary*, &c., I have seen, as if he leaped at the Graves mouth, for joy that he was risen again, and had got the conquest over our dreadful foes, *John* 20. 17. I have also in the Spirit seen him a man on the right hand of God the Father for me, and have seen the manner of his comming from Heaven to judge the world with glory, and have been confirmed in these things by these Scriptures following, *Acts* 1. 9, 10. *Acts.* 7. 56. *Acts.* 10. 42. *Heb.* 7. 24 *Heb.* 8. 38. *Rev.* 1. 18. 1 *Thes.* 4. 17, 18. [122.] Once I was much troubled to know whether the Lord Jesus was both Man as well as God, and God as well as Man; and truly in those dayes, let men say what they would, unless I had it with

evidence from Heaven, all was as nothing to me, I counted not my self set down in any truth of God; well, I was much troubled about this point, and could not tell how to be resolved: at last, that in the fift of the *Revelations* came into my mind, *And I beheld, and lo, in the midst of the Throne, and of the four Beasts, and in the midst of the Elders stood a Lamb*; in the midst of the Throne, there is his God-head, in the midst of the Elders, there is his man hood; but O me thought this did glister, it was a goodly touch and gave me sweet satisfaction; that other Scripture also did help me much in this, *To us a Child is born, to us a Son is given; and the government shall be upon his shoulder, and his Name shall be called Wonderful, Counsellor, the Mighty God, the Everlasting Father, the Prince of Peace, &c.* Isa. 9. 6.

101. [123.] Also besides these teachings of God in his Word, the Lord made use of two things to confirm me in these things, the one was the errors of the *Quakers*,* and the other was the guilt of sin; for as the *Quakers* did oppose his Truth, as God did the more confirm me in it, by leading me into the Scriptures that did wonderfully maintain it.

[124.* The errors that this people then maintained were: 1. That the Holy Scriptures were not the Word of God. 2. That every man in the World had the Spirit of Christ, Grace, Faith, &c. 3. That Christ Jesus as crucified and dying sixteen Hundred years ago, did not satisfie divine Justice for the sins of his People. 4. That Christ his flesh and blood was within the Saints. 5. That the Bodies of the good and bad that are buried in the Church-yards shall not arise again. 6. That the Resurrection is past with good Men already. 7. That that Man Jesus that was Crucified between two Thieves on mount *Calvary*, in the land of *Canaan* by *Jerusalem* was not ascended up above the Starry Heavens. 8. That he should not, even the same Jesus that died by the hand of the *Jews*, come again at the last day, and as man, judge all nations &c.

125. Many more vile and abominable things were in those days fomented by them, by which I was driven to a more narrow search of the Scripture, and was through their light and testimony not only enlightened but greatly confirmed and comforted in the truth;]

and as I said, the guilt of sin did help me much, for still as that would come upon me, the blood of Christ did take it off again, and again, and again, and that too, sweetly, according to the Scriptures; O Friends, cry to God to reveal Jesus Christ unto you, *there is none teacheth like him.*

102. [126.] It would be too long for me here to stay, to tell you in particular how God did set me down in all the things of Christ, and how he did, that he might so do, lead me into his words, yea and also how he did open them unto me, make them shine before me, and cause them to dwell with me, talk with me,* and comfort me over and over, both of his own being, and the being of his Son, and Spirit, and Word, and Gospel.

103. [127.] Onely this, as I said before, I will say unto you again, that in general he was pleased to take this course with me, first to suffer me to be afflicted with temptation concerning them, and then reveal them to me; as sometimes, I should lie under great guilt for sin, even crushed to the ground therewith, and then the Lord would shew me the death of Christ, yea and so sprinkle my Conscience with his Blood, that I should find, and that before I was aware, that in that Conscience, where but just now did reign and rage the Law, even there would rest and abide the Peace and Love of *God* thorow Christ.

104. [128.] Now had I an evidence for Heaven, with many golden Seals thereon, all hanging in my sight;* now could I remember this manifestation, and the other discovery of grace with comfort; and should often long and desire that the last day were come, that I might for ever be inflamed with the sight, and joy, and communion of him, whose Head was crowned with Thorns, whose Face was spit on, and Body broken, and Soul made an offering for my sins: for whereas before I lay continually trembling at the mouth of Hell; now me thought I was got so far therefrom, that I could not, when I looked back, scarce discern it; and O thought I, that I were fourscore years old now, that I might die quickly, that my soul might be gone to rest.

[129. But before I had got thus far out of these my temptations, I did greatly long to see some ancient Godly man's Experience, who had writ some hundred of years before I was born; for, for those who had writ in our days, I thought (but I desire them now to pardon me) that they had Writ only that which others felt, or else had, thorow the strength of their Wits and Parts, studied to answer such Objections as they perceived others were perplexed with, without going down themselves into the deep.* Well, after many longings in my mind, the God in whose hand are all our days, did cast into my hand (one day) a book of *Martin Luther*, his Comment on the *Galathians*,* so old that it was ready to fall piece from piece, if I did but turn it over. Now I was pleased much that such an old Book had fallen into my hand; the which, when I had but a little way perused, I found my condition in his experience, so largely and profoundly handled, as if his Book had been written out of my heart; this made me marvel: for thus thought I, this man could not know any thing of the state of Christians now, but must needs write and speak the Experience of former days. [130.] Besides, he doth most gravely also in that Book debate of the rise of these temptations, namely Blasphemy, Desperation, and the like, shewing that the Law of *Moses*, as well as the Devil, Death, and Hell, hath a very great hand therein; the which at first was very strange to me, but by considering and watching, I found it so indeed. But of Particulars here, I intend nothing, only this methinks I must let fall before all men, I do prefer this Book of Mr. *Luther* upon the *Galathians*, (excepting the Holy Bible) before all the Books that ever I have seen, as most fit for a wounded Conscience.*

131. And now I found, as I thought, that I loved Christ dearly. O me thought my Soul cleaved unto him, my affections cleave* unto him. I felt love to him as hot as fire, and now, as *Job* said, I thought I should die in my nest;* but I did quickly find, that my great love was but little, and that I, who had, as I thought, such burning love to Jesus Christ, could let him go again for a very trifle. God can tell how to abase us; and can hide pride from Man. Quickly after this my love was tried to purpose.]

105. [132.] But after the Lord had in this manner thus graciously delivered me from this great and sore temptation, and had set me down so sweetly in the Faith of his holy gospel, and had given me such strong consolation and blessed evidence from heaven touching my interest in his love through Christ; the Tempter came upon me again, and that with a more grievous and dreadful temptation then before.

106. [133.] And that was to sell and part with this most blessed Christ, to exchange him for the things of this life; for any thing: the temptation lay upon me for the space of a year, and did follow me so

continually, that I was not rid of it one day in a month, no not some-times one hour in many dayes together, unless I was asleep.

107. [134.] And though, in my judgement, I was perswaded, that those who were once effectually in Christ (as I hoped, through his grace, I had seen my self) could never lose him for ever* (*For the land shall not be sold for ever, for the Land is mine*, saith *God*, Levit. 25. 23.*) yet it was a continual vexation to me, to think that I should have so much as one such thought within me against a Christ, a Jesus, that had done for me as he had done.

108. [135.] But it was neither my dislike of the thought, nor yet any desire and endeavour to resist it, that in the least did shake or abate the continuation or force and strength thereof; for it did alwayes in almost whatever I thought, intermix it self therewith, in such sort that I could neither eat my food, stoop for a pin, chop a stick, or cast mine eye to look on this or that, but still the tempta-tion would come, *Sell Christ for this, or sell Christ for that.*

109. [136.] Sometimes it would run in my thoughts not so little as a hundred times together, Sell him, sell him, sell him; against which, I may say, for whole hours together I have been forced to stand as continually leaning and forcing my spirit against it, lest haply before I were aware, some wicked thought might arise in my heart that might consent thereto; and sometimes also the Tempter would make me believe I had consented to it, then should I be as tortured on a Rack for whole dayes together.

110. [137.] This temptation did put me to such scares lest I should at some times, I say, consent thereto, and be overcome therewith, that by the very force of my mind in labouring to gainsay and resist this wickedness, my very Body also would be put into action or motion, by way of pushing or thrusting;* still answering, as fast as the destroyer said, *Sell him*; I will not, I will not, I will not, I will not, no not for thousands, thousands, thousands of worlds; thus reck-oning lest I should in the midst of these assaults set too low a vallue of him, even until I scarce well knew where I was, or how to be com-posed again.

[138. At these seasons he would not let me eat my food at quiet, but forsooth, when I was set at the Table at my meat, I must go hence to pray, I must leave my food now, just now, so counterfeit holy would this Divel be. When I was thus tempted, I should say in my self, *Now I am at meat, let me make an end*: No said he,

I must do it now, or I should displease God,* and despise Christ. Wherefore I was much afflicted with these things: and because of the sinfulness of my nature (imagining that these things were impulses from God) I should deny to do it as if I denyed God; and then should I be as guilty because I did not obey a temptation of the Devil, as if I had broken the Law of God indeed.]

111. [139.] But to be brief, one morning as I did lie in my Bed, I was, as at other times, most fiercely assaulted with this temptation, *to sell and part with Christ*; the wicked suggestion still running in my mind, *sell him, sell him, sell him, sell him*, as fast as a man could speak; against which also in my mind, as at other times I answered, No, no, not for thousands, thousands, thousands, at least twenty times together; but at last, after much striving, even until I was almost out of breath, I felt this thought pass through my heart, *Let him go if he will!* and I thought also that I felt my heart consent thereto.

112. [140.] Now was the battel won, and down fell I, as a Bird that is shot from the top of a Tree, into great guilt and fearful despair; thus getting out of my Bed, I went moping into the field, but God knows with as heavy a heart as mortal man, I think, could bear; where for the space of two hours, I was like a man bereft of life, and as now past all recovery, and bound over to eternal punishment.

113. [141.] And withal, that Scripture did seize upon my Soul, *Or profane person, as Esau, who for one morsel of meat sold his Birth-right; for you know how that afterwards when he would have inherited the blessing, he was rejected, for he found no place of repentance, though he sought it carefully with tears*, Heb. 12. 16, 17.*

[142. Now was I as one bound, I felt myself shut up unto the Judgment to come; nothing now for two years together would abide with me, but damnation and an expectation of damnation. I say, nothing now would abide with me but this, save some few moments for relief, as in the sequel you will see.]

114. [143.] These words were to my Soul like Fetters of Brass of my Legs, in the continual sound of which I went for several months together. But about ten or eleven a Clock one day, as I was walking under a Hedge, full of sorrow and guilt God knows, and bemoaning my self for this hard hap, that such a thought should arise within me, suddenly this sentence bolted in upon me, *The Blood of Christ remits all guilt*; at this I made a stand in my Spirit: with that, this word took hold upon me, *The Blood of Jesus Christ his Son cleanseth us from all*

sin [1 John 1. 7.]: [144] now I began to conceive peace in my Soul, and methought I saw as if the Tempter did lear* and steal away from me, as being ashamed of what he had done. At the same time also I had my sin and the Blood of Christ thus represented to me, That my sin when compared to the Blood of Christ, was no more to it, than this little clot* or stone before me, is to this vast and wide field that here I see: This gave me good encouragement for the space of two or three hours; in which time also me thought I saw by faith the Son of God as suffering for my sins. But because it tarried not, I therefore sunk in my spirit under exceeding guilt again.

[145. But chiefly by the aforementioned Scripture, concerning *Esaus* selling of his Birth-right, for that Scripture would lie all day long, all the week long; yea, all the year long in my mind, and hold me down, so that I could by no means lift up my self, for when I would strive to turn me to this Scripture, or that for relief, still that Sentence would be sounding in me; *For ye know how that afterwards, when he would have inherited the blessing, he found no place of repentance, though he sought it carefully with tears.*]

115. [146.] Sometimes also I should have a touch from that in *Luk.* 22. 31. *I have prayed for thee, that thy Faith fail not*; but it would not abide upon me: neither could I indeed, when I consider'd my state, find ground to conceive in the least, that there should be the root of that Grace within me, having sinned as I had done. Now was I tore and rent in heavy case, for many days together.

116. [147.] Then began I with sad and careful heart, to consider of the nature and largeness of my sin, and to search in the word of God, if I could in any place espy a word of Promise, or any encouraging Sentence by which I might take relief. Wherefore I began to consider that third of *Mark*, *All manner of sins and blasphemies shall be forgiven unto the sons of men, wherewith soever they shall blaspheme*: Which place me thought, at a blush, did contain a large and glorious Promise for the pardon of high offences; but considering the place more fully, I thought it was rather to be understood, as relating more chiefly to those who had, while in a natural estate, committed such things as there are mentioned, but not to me, who had not onely received light and mercie but that had both after and also contrary to that, so slighted Christ as I had done.

117. [148.] I feared therefore that this wicked sin of mine might be that sin unpardonable,* of which he there thus speaketh, *But he*

*that shall blaspheme against the Holy Ghost, hath never forgiveness, but
is in danger of eternal damnation* [Mar. 3]: And I did the rather give
credit to this, because of that sentence in the *Hebrews, For you know
how that afterwards, when he would have inherited the blessing, he was
rejected; for he found no place of repentance, though he sought it carefully with tears.*

[149. And *now* was I both a burden and a terror, to my self, nor
did I ever so know, as *now*, what it was to be weary of my life, and
yet afraid to die. O how gladly *now* would I have been any body
but my self, any thing but a man, and in any condition but mine
own. For there was nothing did pass more frequently over my
mind, then that it was impossible for me to be forgiven my transgression, and to be saved from Wrath to come.]

118. [150.] And now began I to labour to call again time that was
past, wishing a thousand times twice told, that the day was yet to
come, when I should be tempted to such a sin; concluding with great
indignation, both against my heart and all assaults, how I would
rather have been torn in pieces, than found a consenter thereto: but
alas! these thoughts and wishings, and resolvings, were now too late
to help me; the thought had passed my heart, God hath let me go,
and I am fallen: *O*, thought I, *that it was with me as in months past, as
in the days when God preserved me!* Job 29. 2.

119. [151.] Then again, being loth and unwilling to perish, I began
to compare my sin with others, to see if I could find that any of those
that are saved had done as I had done. So I considered *David*'s
Adultery and Murder,* and found them most hainous crimes, and
those too committed after light and grace received: but yet by considering, I perceived that his transgressions were onely such as were
against the Law of *Moses*, from which the Lord Christ could with
the consent of his Word deliver him: but mine was against the *Gospel*,
yea, against the Mediator thereof.

120. [152.] Now again should I be as if racked upon the Wheel;
when I considered, that, besides the guilt that possessed me, I should
be *so* void of grace, *so* bewitched: What, thought I, must it be no sin
but this? must it needs be the *great transgression*? Psal. 19. 13. Must
that wicked one touch my Soul, 1 *Joh.* 5. 18. O what stings did I find
in all these Sentences!

[153. What? thought I, is there but one sin that is unpardonable! but one sin that layeth the Soul without the reach of Gods

mercy, and must I be guilty of that! Is there but one sin amongst so many millions of sins, for which there is no forgiveness, and must I commit this? Oh! unhappy sin! oh unhappy Man! These things would so break and confound my Spirit, that I could not tell what to do, I thought at times they would have broke my wits, and still to aggravate my misery, that would run in my mind, *you know how that afterwards, when he would have inherited the blessing, he was rejected.* Oh! none knows the terrors of these days but my self.]

121. [154.] After this, I came to consider of *Peters* sin which he committed in denying his Master;* and indeed this came nighest to mine, of any that I could find; for he had denied his Saviour as I, and that after Light and Mercy received; yea, and that too, after warning given him: I also considered that he did it both once and twice, and that after time to consider betwixt. But though I put all these circumstances together, that if possible I might find help, yet I considered again, that his was but *a denial of his Master*, but mine was *a selling of my Saviour*. Wherefore I thought with my self, that I came nearer to *Judas*, than either to *David* or *Peter*.

122. [155.] Here again, my torment would flame out, and afflict me; yea, it would grind me as it were to powder, to discern the preservation of God towards others, while I fell into the snare: For in my thus considering of other mens sins, and comparing of them with my own, I could evidently see how God preserved them notwithstanding their wickedness, and would not let them, as he had let me, to become a son of perdition.

123. [156.] But O how did my Soul at this time prize the preservation that God did set about his People! Ah how safely did I see them walk, whom God had hedged in! they were within his care, protection, and special providence:* though they were full as bad as I by nature, yet because he loved them, he would not suffer them to fall without the range of Mercy: but as for me, I was gone, I had done it; he would not preserve me, nor keep me, but suffered me, because I was a Reprobate, to fall as I had done. Now did those blessed places, that spake of *Gods keeping his People*, shine like the Sun before me, though not to comfort me, but to shew me the blessed state and heritage of those whom the Lord had blessed.

[157. Now I saw that as God had his hand in all providences and dispensations that overtook his Elect, so he had his hand in all the temptations that they had to sin against him, not to animate them unto wickedness, but to chuse their temptations and troubles for them, and also to leave them for a time to such sins only as might not destroy, but humble them; as might not put them beyond, but lay them in the way of the renewing of his mercie: but oh! what love, what care! what kindness and mercy did I now see mixing it self with the most severe and dreadful of all Gods ways to his People! He would let *David, Hezekiah, Solomon, Peter,* and others fall, but he would not let them fall into sin unpardonable, nor into Hell for sin. Oh! thought I, these be the men that God hath loved; these be the men, that God, though he chastizes them, keeps them in safety by him, and them whom he makes to abide under the shaddow of the Almighty.* But all these thoughts added sorrow, grief, and horror to me, as whatever I now thought on, it was killing to me. If I thought how God kept his own, that was killing to me; if I thought of how I was fallen my self, that was killing to me. As all things wrought together for the best, and to do good to them that were the called according to his purpose,* so I thought that all things wrought for my dammage, and for my eternal over-throw.]

124. [158.] Then again, I began to compare my sin with the sin of *Judas,* that if possible I might find that mine differed from that which in truth is unpardonable; and O thought I, if it should be but the breadth of an hair, what a happy condition is my Soul in! And, by considering, I found that *Judas* did his intentionally, but mine was against my strivings;* besides, his was committed with much deliberation, but mine in a fearful hurry, on a sudden. Thus I was tossed to and fro, like the Locusts,* and driven from trouble to sorrow; hearing always the sound of *Esau*'s fall in mine ears, and of the dreadful consequences thereof.

125. [159.] Yet this consideration about *Judas,* his sin, was for a while some little relief unto me: for I saw I had not, as to the circumstances, transgressed so foully as he: but this was quickly gone again, for I thought with my self there might be more ways then one to commit the unpardonable sin; and that too, there might be degrees of that, as well as of other transgressions: wherefore, for ought I yet could perceive, this iniquity of mine might be such as might never be passed by.

[160. I was often now ashamed that I should be like such an

ugly man as *Judas*: I thought also how loathsome I should be unto all the Saints at the Day of Judgment, insomuch that now I could scarce see a good Man, that I believed had a good Conscience, but I should feel my heart tremble at him, while I was in his presence. Oh! now I saw a glory in walking with God, and what a mercy it was to have a good Conscience before him.

161. I was much about this time tempted to content my self, by receiving some false Opinion, as that there should be no such thing as a Day of Judgment; that we should not rise again, and that sin was no such grievous thing. The Tempter suggesting thus, For if these things should indeed be true, yet to believe otherwise, would yield you ease for the present. If you must perish, never torment yourself so much beforhand, drive the thoughts of damning out of your mind, by possessing your mind with some such conclusions that *Atheists* and *Ranters* use to help themselves withal.

162. But Oh! when such thoughts have passed thorow my heart, how, as it were, within a step hath Death and Judgment been in my view. Methought the Judge stood at the door, I was as if 'twas come already: so that such things could have no entertainment; but methinks I see by this, that Satan will use any means to keep the Soul from Christ. He loveth not an awakened frame of spirit, security, blindness, darkness, and error, is the very Kingdom and Habitation of the Wicked one.

163. I found it hard work now to pray to God, because despair was swallowing me up. I thought I was as with a Tempest driven away from God, for always when I cried to God for mercy, this would come in, 'tis too late; I am lost, God hath let me fall, not to my correction, but condemnation: My sin is unpardonable, and I know concerning *Esau*, how that after he had sold his Birth-right, he would have received the Blessing, but was rejected.] [About this time I did light on that dreadful story of that miserable mortal *Francis Spira*;* A Book that was to my troubled Spirit, as Salt when rubbed into a fresh wound; every Sentence in that book, every groan of that man, with all the rest of his actions in his dolors, as his tears, his prayers, his gnashing of teeth, his wringing of hands, his twineing* and twisting, and languishing, and pineing away under that mighty hand of God that was upon him, was as Knives and Daggers in my Soul; especially that sentence of his was frightful to me, *Man knows the beginning of sin, but who*

*bounds the issues thereof?** Then would the former Sentence as the conclusion of all, fall like a hot thunder-bolt again upon my Conscience; *for you know how that afterwards when he would have inherited the blessing, he was rejected, for he found no place of Repentance, though he sought it carefully with tears.*]

126. [164.] Then was I struck into a very great trembling, insomuch that at sometimes I could for whole days together feel my very body as well as my minde to shake and totter under the sence of the dreadful Judgement of God, that should fall on those that have sinned that most fearful and unpardonable sin. I felt also such a clogging and heat at my stomach by reason of this my terrour, that I was, especially at some times, as if my breast-bone would have split in sunder. Then I thought of that concerning *Judas, Who by his falling headlong, burst asunder, and all his bowels gushed out,* Act. 1.

127. [165.] I feared also that this was the mark that the Lord did set on *Cain,** even continual fear and trembling under the heavy load of guilt that he had charged on him for the blood of his Brother *Abel.* Thus did I wind, and twine, and shrink under the burden that was upon me; which burden also did so oppress me, that I could neither stand nor go,* nor lie either at rest or quiet.

128. [166.]* Yet that saying would sometimes come to mind, *He hath received gifts for the rebellious,* Psal. 68. 18. *The rebellious?* thought I; Why surely they are such as once were under subjection to their Prince, even those who after they have sworn subjection to his Government, have taken up arms against him.

[and this thought I, is my very condition. I once loved him, feared him, served him, but now I am a rebel; I have sold him, I have said, *let him goe if he will,* but yet he has gifts for rebels, and then why not for me?]

129. [167.] This sometimes I thought on, and should labour to take hold thereof; that some, though small, refreshment might have been conceived by me: but in this also I missed of my desire, I was driven with force beyond it, like a man that is going to the place of execution, even by that place where he would fain creep in, and hide himself, but may not.

130. [168.] Again, After I had thus considered the sins of the Saints in particular, and found mine went beyond them; then I began to think thus with myself: Set case I should put all theirs together, and mine alone against them, might I not then finde some encour-

agement? for if mine, though bigger than any one, yet should but be equal to all, then there is hopes: for that Blood that hath vertue enough to wash away all theirs, hath also vertue enough to do away mine, though this one be full as big, if no bigger, then all theirs. Here again, I should consider the sin of *David*, of *Solomon*, of *Manasseh*,* of *Peter*, and the rest of the great offenders, and should also labour what I might, with fairness, to aggravate and heighten their sins by several circumstances: but, alas! 'twas all in vain.

[169. I should think with my self that *David* shed blood to cover his Adultery, and that by the Sword of the Children of *Ammon*, a work that could not be done but by continuance, deliberate contrivance, which was a great aggravation to his sin. But then this would turn upon me: Ah, but these were but sins against the Law, from which there was a Jesus sent to save them, but yours is against the Saviour, and who shall save you from that?

170. Then I thought on *Solomon* and how he sinned, in loving strange Women, in falling away to their Idols, in building them Temples, in doing this after light, in his old age, after great mercy received: but the same Conclusion that cut me off in the former consideration, cut me off as to this: namely, that all those were but sins against the Law, for which God had provided a remedy, but I had sold my Saviour, and there now remained no more Sacrifice for sin.

171. I would then add to these mens sins the sins of *Manasseh*, how that he built Altars for Idols in the house of the Lord, he also observed times, used inchantments, had to do with Wizzards, was a Witch, had his familiar spirits, burnt his Children in the fire in Sacrifice to Devils, and made the Streets of *Jerusalem* run down with the blood of Innocents—These thought I are great sins, sins of a bloudy colour, but yet* it would turn again upon me, they are none of them of the nature of yours, you have parted with Jesus! you have sold your Saviour!]

131. [172.] This one consideration would always kill my Heart, *My sin was point-blank against my Saviour*, and that too at that height, that I had in my heart said of him, *Let him go if he will*. O me thoughts, this sin was bigger than the sins of a Countrey, of a Kingdom, or of the whole World, no one pardonable, nor all of them together, was able to equal mine, mine out-went them every one.

132. [173.] Now I should feel my minde to flee from God, as from the face of a dreadful Judge; yet this was my torment, I could not escape his hand.* (*It is a fearful thing to fall into the hands of the living God*, Heb. 10.). But blessed be his grace, that Scripture in these flying fits would call, as running after me, *I have blotted out as a thick cloud thy transgressions, and as a cloud thy sins. Return unto me, for I have redeemed thee*, Isa. 44. 22.

[This, I say, would come in upon my mind when I was flying from the face of God; for I did flie from his face, that is, my mind and spirit fled before him, by reason of his highness, I could not endure; then would the text crie, *return unto me*. It would crie aloud, with a very great voice, return unto me, for I have redeemed thee;* indeed, this would make me make a little stop, and as it were look over my Shoulder behind me, to see, if I could discern that the God of grace did follow me with a pardon in his hand, but I could no sooner doe that, but all would be clouded and darkened again by that Sentence, for you know how that afterwards, when he would have inherited the blessing, he found no place of Repentance though he sought it carefully with tears;]

but I could not return, but fled, though at some times it cried, *Return*, as if it did hollow* after me: for I feared to close in therewith, lest it should not come from God, for that other was still sounding in my conscience, *For you know how that afterwards, when he would have inherited the Blessing, he was rejected*, &c.

[174. Once as I was walking to and fro in a good mans Shop, bemoaning to my self in my sad and doleful state, afflicting my self with self abhorrence for this wicked and ungodly thought; lamenting also this hard hap of mine, for that I should commit so great a sin, greatly fearing I should not be pardoned; praying also in my heart, That if this sin of mine did differ from that against the Holy Ghost, the Lord would shew it me: and being now ready to sink with fear, suddenly there was as if there had rushed in at the Window, the noise of Wind upon me, but very pleasant, and as if I had heard a Voice speaking, *Didst ever refuse to be justified by the Blood of Christ?* and withal, my whole life of profession past, was in a moment opened to me, wherein I was made to see, that designedly I had not; so my heart answered groaningly No. Then fell with power that Word of God upon me, *See that ye refuse not him that speaketh*, Heb. 12. 25.] [This made a strange seisure upon

my Spirit; it brought light with it and commanded a Silence in my
heart of all those tumultuous thoughts that before did use like
masterless hell-hounds to roar and bellow, and make a hideous
noise within me. It showed me also that Jesus Christ had yet a
Word of Grace and Mercie for me, That he had not, as I had
feared, quite forsaken and cast off my soul; yea, this was a kind of
a chide for my proneness to desperation; a kind of a threatning
of me if I did not, notwithstanding my sins and the hainousness
of them, venture my Salvation upon the Son of God. But as to
my determining about this strange dispensation,] [What this was,
I knew not; or from whence it came, I know not. I have not yet in
twenty years time, been able to make a Judgment of it. *I thought
then what here I should be loth to speak.* But verily that sudden
rushing Wind, was as if an Angel had come upon me; but both it
and the Salutation I will leave until the Day of Judgement, only
this I say, it commanded a great calm in my Soul, it perswaded
me there might be hope; it shewed me, as I thought, what the
sin unpardonable was, and that my Soul had yet the blessed priv-
iledge to flie to Jesus Christ for mercy. But I say, concerning
this dispensation, I know not what yet to say unto it, which was
also in truth the cause that at first I did not speak of it in the Book.
I do now also leave it to be thought on by men of sound Judgment.
I lay not the stress of my Salvation thereupon but upon the
Lord Jesus in the Promise; yet seeing I am here unfolding of my
secret things, I thought it might not be altogether inexpedient to
let this also shew it self, though I cannot now relate the matter as
there I did experience it. This lasted in the savour of it, for about
three or four dayes, and then I began to mistrust, and to despair
again.]

133. [175.] All this while my life hung in doubt before me, not
knowing which way I should tip; onely this I found my Soul desire,
even to cast it self at the foot of Grace by Prayer and Supplication.
But O 'twas hard for me to bear the face to pray to this Christ for
mercie, against whom I had thus most vilely sinned! yet I knew this
must be the way, for mercy was no where else.

['Twas hard work I say to offer to look him in the face, against
whom I had so vilely sinned; and indeed I have found it as difficult to come to God by prayer after back-sliding* from him, as to
do any other thing. O the Shame that did *now* attend me, specially

when I thought, I am *now* a going to pray to him for mercie that
I had so lightly esteemed but a while before. I was ashamed, yea
even confounded, because this villainie had been committed by
me; but I saw that there was but one way with me, I must go to
him and humble my self unto him, and beg that he of his wonderful mercie would shew pity to me and have mercy upon my
wretched sinful Soul.]

134. [176.] Which when the Tempter perceived, he strongly suggested to me, That I ought not to pray to God, for Prayer was not
for any in my case, neither could it do me good, because I had rejected
the Mediator, by whom all Prayers came with acceptance to God the
Father, and without whom no Prayer could come into his presence;
wherefore now to pray, is but to adde sin to sin: yea, now to pray,
seeing God hath cast you off, is the next* way to anger and offend
him more then ever you did before.

135. [177.] For God (said he) hath been weary of you for these
several years already, because you are none of his; your bauling in his
ears hath been no pleasant voice to him, and therefore he let you sin
this sin, that you might be quite cut off, and will you pray still? This
the Devil urged, and set forth by that in *Numbers*, which *Moses* said
to the children of *Israel*, *That because they would not go up to possess
the Land when God would have them, therefore for ever after he did bar
them out from thence, though they prayed they might with tears*, Num.
14. 36, 37, &c.

136. [178.] As 'tis said in another place, *Exod.* 21. 14: *The man that
sins presumptuously, shall be taken from Gods Altar, that he may die*:
Even as Joab was by King *Solomon*, when he thought to find shelter
there, 1 *King.* 2. 28, &c. These places did pinch me very sore; yet my
case being desperate, I thought with my self, I can but die; and if it
must be so, it shall once be said, That such a one died at the foot of
Christ in Prayer: this I did, but with great difficulty, God doth know;
for still that saying about *Esau* would be set at my heart, even like a
flaming sword, to keep the way of the tree of Life,* lest I should take
thereof, and live. O who knows how hard a thing I found it to come
to God in prayer!

137. [179.] I did also desire the Prayers of the People of God for
me, but I feared that God would give them no heart to do it; yea, I
trembled in my Soul to think that some or other of them shortly
would tell me, that God had said those words to them that he once

did say to the Prophet concerning the Children of Israel, *Pray not for this People, for I have rejected them*, Jer. 11. 14. So, *pray not for him, for I have rejected him*: Yea, I thought that he had whispered this to some of them already, onely they durst not tell me so, neither durst I ask them of it, for fear if it should be so, it would make me quite besides my self. *Man knows the beginning of sin* (said *Spira*) *but who bounds the issues thereof?*

[180. About this time I took an opportunity, to break my Mind to an Antient Christian; and told him all my case. I told him also, that I was afraid that I had sinned the sin against the Holy Ghost; and he told me, *he thought so too.** Here therefore I had but cold comfort but talking a little more with him, I found him, though a good man, a stranger to much Combate with the Devil. Wherefore I went to God again as well as I could, for Mercie still.]

138. [181.] Now also did the Tempter begin to mock me in my misery, saying, That seeing I had thus parted with the Lord Jesus, and provoked him to displeasure who should have stood between my Soul and the flame of devouring fire, the way was now but one, and that was, to pray that God the Father would be the Mediator betwixt his Son and me, that we might be reconciled again, and that I might have that blessed benefit in him that his blessed Saints enjoyed.

139. [182.] Then did that Scripture seize upon my Soul, *He is of one mind, and who can turn him?** Oh I saw 'twas as easie to perswade him to make a new world, a new Covenant, or new Bible besides that we have already, as to pray for such a thing: this was to perswade him that what he had done already was meer folly, and to perswade with him to alter, yea, to disanul the whole way of salvation; and then would that saying rent my Soul asunder, *Neither is there salvation in any other, for there is none other Name under heaven, given amongst men, whereby we must be saved*, Act. 4. 12.*

140. [183.] Now the most free, and full, and gracious words of the Gospel were the greatest torment to me; yea, nothing so afflicted me as the thoughts of Jesus Christ: for the remembrance of a Saviour, because I had cast him off, brought both the villany of my sin, and my loss by it, to mind.

[Nothing did twinge my Conscience like this: Every time that I thought of the Lord Jesus, of his Grace, Love, goodness, kindness, gentleness, meekness, death, blood, promises and blessed

exhortations, comforts and consolations, it went to my Soul like a
Sword; for still, unto these my considerations of the Lord Jesus
these thoughts would make place for themselves in my heart; Ay,
This is the Jesus, the loving Saviour, the Son of God, whom you
have parted with, whom you have slighted, despised, and abused.
This is the *only* Saviour, the *only* Redeemer, the *only* one that could
so love sinners as to wash them from their sins in his own most
precious Blood: but you have no part nor lot in this Jesus, you have
put him from you, you have said in your heart, *Let him go if he
will.* Now therefore you are severed from him; you have severed
your self from him; behold then his goodness, but your self to be
no partaker of it. Oh! thought I, what have I lost! what have I
parted with! what have I disinherited my poor Soul of!]

O 'tis sad to be destroyed by the grace and mercy of God; to have
the Lamb, the Saviour, turn Lyon and Destroyer, *Rev.* 6. I also trembled at the sight of the Saints of God, especially at those that greatly
loved him, and that made it their business to walk continually with
him in this world: for they did both in their words, their carriages,
and all their expressions of tenderness and fear to sin against their
precious Saviour, condemn, lay guilt upon, and also add continual
affliction and shame unto my Soul.

141. [184.] Now also the Tempter began afresh to mock my Soul,
saying, That Christ indeed did pity my case, and was sorry for my
loss: but forasmuch as I had sinned, and transgressed as I had done,
he could by no means help me, nor save me from what I feared; for
my sin was not of the nature of theirs, for whom he bled and died,
neither was it counted with those that were laid to his charge when
he hanged on the tree;* therefore unless he should come down from
Heaven, and die anew for this sin, though indeed he did greatly pity
me, yet I could have no benefit of him.

[These things may seem ridiculous to others, even as ridiculous as
they were in themselves, but to me they were most tormenting
cogitations; every of them augmented my misery, that Jesus Christ
should have so much love as to pity me, when yet he could not
help me; nor did I think that the reason why he could not help
me, was because his Merits were weak, or his Grace and Salvation
spent on others already, but because his faithfulness to his threatning, would not let him extend his mercie to me. Besides I thought,
as I have already hinted, that my sin was not within the bounds of

that pardon, that was wrapped up in a promise, and if not, then I
knew assuredly, that it was more easie for heaven and earth to pass
away then for me to have eternal life; so that the ground of all
these fears of mine did arise from a stedfast belief that I had of
the stability of the holy word of God, and also, from my being
misinformed of the nature of my sin.]

142. [185.] But O how this would add to my affliction, to conceit
that I should be guilty of such a sin, for which he did not die! These
thoughts would so confound me, and imprison me, and tie me up
from Faith, that I knew not what to do: but Oh thought I, that he
would come down again, O that the work of Mans Redemption was
yet to be done by Christ; how would I pray him, and intreat him to
count and reckon this sin amongst the rest for which he died? But
that would strike me down: *Christ being raised from the dead, dieth no
more: Death hath no more Dominion over him*, Rom. 6. 9.

 [186. Thus by the strange and unusual assaults of the tempter,
was my Soul like a broken Vessel,* driven, as with the Winds,
and tossed sometimes head-long into despair, sometimes upon
the Covenant of works, and sometimes to wish that the New
Covenant, and the conditions thereof, might so far forth as I
thought my self concerned, be turned another way, and changed.
But in all these, I was but as those that josle against the Rocks,
more broken, scattered and rent. Oh, the unthought of imaginations, frights, fears, and terrors that are effected by a thorow application of guilt, and yielding to desparation! This is the man that
hath his dwelling among the Tombs with the dead; that is always
crying out, and cutting himself with stones, *Mark* 5. 2–5.* But, I
say, all in vain, desparation will not comfort him, the old Covenant
will not save him. Nay, Heaven and Earth shall pass away before
one jot or tittle of the Word and Law of Grace shall fail or be
removed:* this I saw, this I felt and under this I groaned. Yet this
advantage I got thereby, namely, a further confirmation of the certainty of the way of Salvation, and that the Scriptures were the
Word of God. Oh! I cannot now express what then I saw and felt
of the steadiness of Jesus Christ, the Rock of Man's Salvation,
what was done, could not be undone, added to nor altered; indeed,
sin might drive the Soul beyond Christ, even the sin which is
unpardonable; but woe to him that was so driven,* for the word
would shut him out.]

143. [187.] Thus was I always sinking, whatever I did think or do. So one day I walked to a Neighbouring Town, and sate down upon a Settle* in the Street, and fell into a very deep pause about the most fearful state my sin had brought me to; and after long musing, I lifted up my head, but methought I saw as if the Sun that shineth in the heavens did grudge to give me light, and as if the very stones in the street, and tiles upon the houses, did bend themselves against me.* O how happy now was every creature over I was! for they stood fast, and kept their station, but I was gone and lost.

144. [188.] Then breaking out in the bitterness of my Soul, I said with a grievous sigh, *How can God comfort such a wretch as I?* I had no sooner said it, but this returned upon me, as an eccho doth answer a voice, *This sin is not unto death.* At which I was as if I had been raised out of a grave, and cryed out again, *Lord, how couldst thou find out such a word as this?* For I was filled with admiration at the fitness, and also at the unexpectedness of the sentence.

[The fitness of the Word, the rightness of the timeing of it: the power, and sweetness, and light, and glory that came with it also, was marvelous to me to find. I was now, for the time, out of doubt, as to that about which I somuch was in doubt before, my fears before *were* that my sin was not pardonable, and so that I had no right to pray, to repent, &c. or that if I did, it would be of no advantage, or profit to me, but now thought I, if *this sin* is not unto death, then it is pardonable, therefore from this I have encouragement to come to God by Christ for mercie, to consider the promise of forgiveness, as that which stands with open arms to receive me as well as others; this therefore was a great easment to my mind, to wit, that my sin was pardonable, that it was not the sin unto death. (1 *Jo.* 5. 16, 17.) None but those that know what my trouble (by their own experience) was, can tell what relief came to my soul by this consideration; it was a release to me, from my former bonds, and a shelter from the former storm, I seemed now to stand upon the same ground with other sinners and to have as good right to the word and prayer as any of they.]

145. [189.] Now I was in hopes that my sin was not unpardonable, but that there might be hopes for me to obtain forgiveness. But O how Satan now did lay about him, for to bring me down again! But he could by no means do it, neither this day, nor the most part of the next: for this good sentence stood like a Mill-post* at my back. Yet

towards the evening of the next day, I felt this word begin to leave me, and to withdraw its supportation from me, and so I returned to my old fears again, but with a great deal of grudging and peevishness, for I feared the sorrow of it.

146. [190.] But the next day at evening, being under many fears, I went to seek the Lord; and as I prayed, I cryed to him in these words: *O Lord, I beseech thee shew me that thou hast loved me with an everlasting love*, Jer. 31. 3. I had no sooner said it, but with sweetness it returned upon me, *I have loved thee with an everlasting love*. Now I went to bed at quiet, also when I awaked the next morning, it was fresh upon my Soul.

147. [191.] But yet the Tempter left me not, for it could not be so little as an hundred times that he that day did labour to break my peace. O the combats and conflicts that I did then meet with! as I strove to hold by this word, that of *Esau* would flie in my face, like to Lightning: I should be sometimes up and down twenty times in an hour. Yet God did bear me up,* and keep my heart upon this word, from which I had also for several days together very much sweetness and comfortable hopes of pardon. For thus it was made out to me, *I loved thee whilst thou wast committing this sin, I loved thee before, I love thee still, and I will love thee for ever.*

148. [192.] Yet I saw my sin most barbarous, and a filthy crime, and could not but conclude, and that with great shame and astonishment, that I had horribly abused the holy *Son of God*: wherefore I felt my soul greatly to love and pity him, and my bowels to yearn towards him: for I saw he was still my friend, and did reward me good for evil: yea, the love and affection that then did burn within to my Lord and Saviour Jesus Christ, did work at this time such strong and hot desire of revengement upon my self for the abuse I had done unto him, that, to speak as then I thought, had I had a thousand gallons of blood within my veins, I could freely have spilt it all at the command and feet of this my Lord and Saviour.

149. [193.] And as I was thus in musing, and in my studies how to love the Lord and to express my love to him, that saying came in upon me, *If thou, Lord, shouldst mark iniquity, O Lord, who should stand? but there is forgiveness with thee, that thou mayst be feared*, Psal. 130. 3, 4. These were good words to me, especially the latter part thereof, to wit, that there is forgiveness with the Lord, that he might be feared; that is, as then I understood it, that he might be

loved, and had in reverence: for it was thus made out to me, *That the great God did set so high an esteem upon the love of his poor Creatures, that rather then he would go without their love, he would pardon their transgressions.*

150. [194.] And now was that word fulfilled on me, and I was also refreshed by it, *Then shall they be ashamed and confounded, and never open their mouth any more because of their shame, when I am pacified towards thee for all that thou hast done, saith the Lord God*, Ezek. 16. 36. Thus was my Soul at this time (and as I then did think for ever) set at liberty from being again afflicted with my former guilt and amazement.

151. [195.] But before many weeks were over, I began to dispond again, fearing lest notwithstanding all that I had injoyed, that yet I might be deceived and destroyed at the last: for this consideration came strong into my mind, That whatever comfort and peace I thought I might have from the word of the Promise of Life; yet unless there could be found in my refreshment a concurrance and agreement in the Scriptures, let me think what I will thereof, and hold it never so fast, I should finde no such thing at the end: *For the Scriptures cannot be broken*, John 10. 35.

152. [196.] Now began my heart again to ake, and fear I might meet with disappointment at the last. Wherefore I began with all seriousness to examine my former comfort, and to consider whether one that had sinned as I have done, might with confidence trust upon the faithfulness of God laid down in those words by which I had been comforted, and on which I had leaned my self; but now was brought those sayings to my minde, *For it is impossible for those who were once enlightned and have tasted the heavenly gift, and were made partakers of the holy Ghost, and have tasted the good word of God, and the Powers of the World to come; if they shall fall away, to renew them again unto repentance*, Heb. 6. *For if we sin wilfully after we have received the knowledge of the truth, there remains no more sacrifice for sin, but a certain fearful looking for of Judgement and fiery Indignation, which shall devour the adversaries*, Heb. 10. *Even as Esau, who for one morsel of meat sold his Birthright; for ye know how that afterwards, when he would have inherited the Blessing, he was rejected, for he found no place of repentance, though he sought it carefully with tears*, Heb. 12.

153. [197.] Now was the word of the Gospel forced from my Soul, so that no Promise or Encouragement was to be found in the Bible

for me: and now would that saying work upon my spirit to afflict me, *Rejoyce not, O Israel, for joy, as other People*, Hos. 9. 1. For I saw indeed there was cause of rejoycing for those that held to Jesus; but as for me, I had cut my self off by my transgressions, and left my self neither foot hold, nor hand-hold amongst all the stayes and props in the precious Word of Life.

154. [198.] And truly I did now feel my self to sink into a gulf, as an house whose foundation is destroyed. I did liken my self in this condition unto the case of some Child that was fallen into a Mill-pit,* who though it could make some shift to scrable and spraul in the water, yet because it could find neither hold for hand nor foot, therefore at last it must die in that condition. So soon as this fresh assault had fastened on my Soul, that Scripture came into my heart, *This is for many days*, Dan. 10. 14. and indeed I found it was so: for I could not be delivered nor brought to peace again until well-nigh two years and an half were compleatly finished. Wherefore these words, though in themselves they tended to discouragement, yet to me, who feared this condition would be eternal, they were at some times as an help and refreshment to me.

155. [199.] For, thought I, *many days* are not for ever; *many days* will have an end; therefore seeing I was to be afflicted not a few, but *many days*, yet I was glad it was but *for many days*. Thus, I say, I could recal my self sometimes, and give my self a help: for as soon as ever the words came in, at first I knew my trouble would be long, yet this would be but sometimes, for I could not always think on this, nor ever be helped though I did.

156. [200.] Now while these Scriptures lay before me, and laid sin at my door, that saying in the 18 of *Luke*,* with others, did encourage me to prayer: then the Tempter again laid at me very sore, suggesting, That neither the mercy of God, nor yet the blood of Christ, did at all concern me, nor could they help me, for my sin: yet thought I, I will pray, but said the Tempter, Your sin is unpardonable. Yet said I, I will pray.* So I went to prayer to God; and while I was at prayer, I uttered words to this effect: *Lord, Satan tells me, That neither thy mercy nor Christs blood is sufficient to save my soul: Lord, shall I honour thee most by believing thou wilt and canst, or* by believing thou neither wilt nor canst? Lord, I would fain honour thee by believing thou wilt and canst.*

157. [201.] And as I was thus before the Lord, that Scripture

fastned on my heart, *O man, great is thy Faith*, [Matt. 15. 28.]
even as if one had clapt me on the back, as I lay on my knees before
God; yet I was not able to believe this, till almost six months after,
for I could not think that I had Faith, or that there should be a word
for me to act Faith on; therefore I should still be as sticking in the
jaws of desparation, and went mourning up and down, crying, *Is his
mercy clean gone? is his mercy clean gone for ever?* And I thought sometimes, even while I was groaning in these expressions, they did
seem to make a question whether it was or no; yet I greatly feared it
was.

[202. There was nothing that I longed for more, then to be put
out of doubt as to this thing, and as I was vehemently desiring to
know if there was hope, these words came rowling into my mind,
*will the Lord cast off forever and will he be favourable no more? Is his
mercie clean gone for ever? doth his promise fail for evermore? Hath
God forgotten to be gracious! hath he in anger shut up his tender
mercies*, Psal. 77. 7, 8, 9. and all the while they run in my minde,
methought I had this still as the answer, 'Tis a question whether
he hath or no; It may be he hath not:] [yea, the interrogatory
seemed to me to carry in it a sure affirmation that indeed he
had not, nor would so cast off, but would be favourable, that his
promise doth not fail, and that he had not forgotten to be gracious,
nor would in anger shut up tender mercie;] [something also there
was upon my heart at the same time which I cannot now call to
minde, which with this Text did sweeten my heart, and make me
conclude that his mercie might not be quite gone, not clean gone
for ever.]

158. [203.] At another time I remember I was again much under
the Question, Whether the blood of Christ was sufficient to save my
Soul? In which doubt I continued from morning till about seven or
eight at night; and at last, when I was, as it were, quite worn out with
fear lest it should not lay hold on me, those words did sound suddenly within me, *He is able*: but me thought this word *able*, was spoke
so loud unto me, it shewed such a great word, and gave such a justle
to my fear and doubt, (I mean for the time it tarried with me, which
was about a day) as I never had from that, all my life either before or
after that, *Heb*. 7. 25.

159. [204.] But one morning when I was again at prayer and trembling under the fear of this, that no word of God could help me, that

piece of a sentence darted in upon me, *My Grace is sufficient*.* At this me thought I felt some stay, as if there might be hopes: But O how good a thing is it for God to send his Word! for about a fort-night before, I was looking on this very place, and then I thought it could not come near my Soul with comfort, and threw down my Book in a pet; but now it was as if it had arms of grace so wide, that it could not onely inclose me, but many more besides.

160. [205.] By these words I was sustained, yet not without exceed-ing conflicts, for the space of seven or eight weeks: for my peace would be in and out sometimes twenty times a day: Comfort now, and Trouble presently; Peace now, and before I could go a furlong, as full of Fear and Guilt as ever heart could hold; and this was not onely now and then, but my whole seven weeks experience: for this about the sufficiency of grace, and that of *Esau*'s parting with his Birth-right, would be like a pair of scales within my mind, some-times one end would be uppermost, and sometimes again the other, according to which would be my peace or trouble.

161. [206.] Therefore I still did pray to God, that he would come in with this Scripture more fully on my heart, to wit, that he would help me to apply the whole sentence; for as yet it only helped me thus far, *My grace is sufficient*; and tho it came no farther, it answered my former question, to wit, that there was hope; yet, because *for thee*, was left out, I was not contented, but prayed to God for that also: Wherefore, one day as I was in a Meeting of Gods People, full of sadness and terrour, for my fears again were strong upon me, and as I was now thinking, my Soul was never the better, but my case most sad and fearful, these words did with great power suddainly break in upon me, *My grace is sufficient for thee, my grace is sufficient for thee, my grace is sufficient for thee*;* three times together; and, O me-thought that every word was a mighty word unto me; as *my* and *grace*, and *sufficient*, and *for thee*; they were then, and sometimes are still, far bigger than others be.

162. [207.] At which time, my Understanding was so enlightned, that I was as though I had seen the Lord Jesus look down from Heaven through the Tiles upon me, and direct these words unto me; this sent me mourning home, it broke my heart, and filled me full of joy, and laid me as low as the dust, only it staid not long with me, I mean in this glory and refreshing comfort, yet it continued with me for several weeks, and did encourage me to hope. But so soon as that

powerfull operation of it was taken off my heart, that other about *Esau* returned upon me as before, so my soul did hang as in a pair of Scales again, sometimes up, and sometimes down, now in peace, and anon again in terror.

163. [208.] Thus I went on for many weeks, sometimes comforted, and sometimes tormented, and, especially at some times my torment would be very sore, for all those Scriptures fore-nam'd in the *Hebrews* would be set before me, as the only Sentences that would keep me out of Heaven. Then again I should begin to repent, that ever that thought went thorow me; I should also think thus with my self, why, How many Scriptures are there against me? there is but three or four, and cannot God miss them, and save me for all them? Sometimes again I should think, O if it were not for these three or four words, now how might I be comforted! and I could hardly forbear at some times, but to wish them out of the Book.

164. [209.] Then methought I should see as if both *Peter*, and *Paul*, and *John*, and all the Writers did look with scorn upon me, and hold me in derision; and as if they said unto me, All our words are truth, one of as much force as another; it is not we that have cut you off, but you have cast away your self; there is none of our sentences that you must take hold upon but these, and such as these; *It is impossible; there remains no more sacrifice for sin*, Heb. 6. *And it had been better for them not to have known the will of God, than after they have known it, to turn from the holy commandment delivered unto them*, Heb. 10. *For the Scriptures cannot be broken*, 2 Pet. 2. 21.

[210. These, as the Elders of the City of Refuge, I saw were to be the Judges both of my Case and me, while I stood with the avenger of blood at my heels, trembling at their Gate for deliverance; also with a thousand fears and mistrusts, I doubted* that they would shut me out for ever, *Josh*. 20. 3, 4.]

165. [211.] Thus was I confounded, not knowing what to do nor how to be satisfied in this question, whether the Scriptures could agree in the salvation of my Soul? I quaked at the Apostles; I knew their words were true, and that they must stand for ever.

166. [212.] And I remember one day, as I was in divers frames of Spirit, and considering that these frames were still according to the nature of the several Scriptures that came in upon my mind; if this of Grace, then I was quiet; but if that of *Esau*, then tormented. Lord, thought I, if both these Scriptures would meet in my heart at once,

I wonder which of them would get the better of me. So me thought I had a longing mind that they might come both together upon me; yea, I desired of God they might.

167. [213.] Well, about two or three dayes after, so they did indeed; they boulted both upon me at a time, and did work and struggle strangly in me for a while; at last, that about *Esaus* birthright began to wax weak, and withdraw, and vanish; and this about the sufficiency of Grace prevailed, with peace and joy. And as I was in a muse about this thing, that Scripture came home upon me, *Mercy rejoyceth against Judgment* [Jas. 2. 13].

168. [214.] This was a wonderment to me, yet truly I am apt to think it was of God, for the Word of the Law and Wrath, must give place to the Word of Life and Grace; because, though the Word of Condemnation be glorious, yet the Word of Life and Salvation, doth far exceed in glory, 2 *Cor.* 3. 8, 9, 10, 11. *Mar.* 9. 5, 6, 7. *John.* 6. 37. Also, that *Moses* and *Elias* must both vanish, and leave Christ and his Saints alone.

169. [215.] This Scripture also did now most sweetly visit my soul; *And him that cometh to me I will in no wise cast out.** O the comfort that I have had from this word, *in no wise!* as who should say, by no means, for no thing, what-ever he hath done. But Satan would greatly labour to pull this promise from me, telling of me, that Christ did not mean me, and such as I, but sinners of a lower rank, that had not done as I had done. But I should answer him again, Satan, here is in this word no such exception; but *him that comes*, *him*, any *him*, *him that cometh to me*, *I will in no wise cast out*. And this I well remember still, that of all the slights that Satan used to take this Scripture from me, yet he never did so much as put this Question, But do you come aright? And I have thought the reason was, because he thought I knew full well, what coming was for I saw that to come aright was to come as I was, a vile and ungodly sinner, and to cast my self at the feet of Mercy, condemning my self for sin: If ever Satan and I did strive for any word, it was for this in *John*; he pull'd, and I pull'd, but God be praised, I got some sweetness from it.

170. [216.] But, notwithstanding all these helps and blessed words of grace, yet that of *Esaus* selling of his birth-right, would still at times distress my Conscience; for though I had been most sweetly comforted, and that but just before, yet when that came into mind, 'twould make me fear again. I could not be quite rid thereof, 'twould

every day be with me: wherefore now I went another way to work, even to consider the nature of this blasphemous thought; I mean if I should take the words at the largest, and give them their own natural force and scope, even every word therein: So when I had thus considered, I found that if they were fairly taken, they would amount to this, That I had freely left the Lord Jesus Christ to his choice, whether he would be my Saviour or no, for the wicked words were these, *Let him go if he will*. Then that Scripture gave me hope, *I will never leave thee nor forsake thee*, Heb. 13. 5. O Lord, said I, but I have left thee; then it answered again, *but I will not leave thee*. For this I thank God also.

171. [217.] Yet I was grievous afraid he should, and found it exceeding hard to trust him, seeing I had so offended him: I could have been exceeding glad that this thought had never befallen, for then I thought I could with more ease and freedom abundance* have leaned upon his grace: I see it was with me as it was with *Josephs* Brethren, the guilt of their own wickedness did often fill them with fears, that their Brother would at last despise them, *Gen.* 50. 15, 16, 17, 18.

172. [218.] But above all the Scriptures that yet I did meet with, that in the twentieth of *Joshua*, was the greatest comfort to me, which speaks of the slayer that was to fly for refuge. *And if the avenger of blood pursue the slayer*, then, saith Moses, *they that are the Elders of the City of Refuge, shall not deliver him into his hand; because he smote his Neighbour unwittingly, and hated him not afore-time.* O blessed be God for this word! I was convinced that I was the slayer, and that the avenger of blood pursued me, that I felt with great terrour; only now it remained that I enquire, whether I have right to enter the City of Refuge. So I found, That he must not, *who lay in wait to shed blood*, but he who *unwittingly*, or that did *unawares shed blood*, even he who did not *hate his Neighbour before*. Wherefore,

173. [219.] I thought verily I was the man that must enter, for because I had smitten my Neighbour *unwittingly, and hated him not afore-time*. I hated him not afore-time, no I prayed unto him, was tender of sinning against him; yea, and against this wicked Temptation, I had strove for a twelve-moneth before; yea, and also when it did pass thorow my heart, it did it in spite of my teeth: Wherefore I thought I had right to enter this City, and the Elders,

which are the Apostles, were not to deliver me up. This therefore was great comfort to me, and did give me much ground of hope.

174. [220.] Yet being very critical, for my smart had made me that I knew not what ground was sure enough to bear me, I had one question that my Soul did much desire to be resolved about; and that was, *Whether it be possible for any Soul that hath indeed sinned the unpardonable sin, yet after that to receive, though but the least true spiritual comfort from God thorow Christ?* the which, after I had much considered, I found the answer was, No, they could not: and that for these reasons:

175. [221.] First, Because those that have sinned that sin, they are debarred a share in the Blood of Christ, and being shut out of that, they must needs be void of the least ground of hope, and so of spiritual comfort; *for to such there remains no more sacrifice for sin*, Heb. 10. 26, 27. Secondly, Because they are denied a share in the promise of Life: they shall never be forgiven, neither in this world, nor in that which is to come, *Mat.* 12. 32. Thirdly, The Son of God excludes them also from a share in his blessed intercession, being for ever ashamed to own them both before his holy Father, and the blessed Angels in heaven, *Mark* 8.

176. [222.] When I had with much deliberation considered of this matter, and could not but conclude that the Lord had comforted me, and that too after this my wicked sin: then methought I durst venture to come nigh unto those most fearful and terrible Scriptures, with which all this while I had been so greatly affrighted, and on which indeed before I durst scarce cast mine eye, (yea, had much ado an hundred times to forbear wishing of them out of the Bible, for I thought they would destroy me) but now, I say, I began to take some measure of incouragement, to come close to them, to read them, and consider them, and to weigh their scope and tendence.

177. [223.] The which when I began to do, I found their visage changed; for they looked not so grimly on me as before I thought they did: And first, I came to the sixth of the *Hebrews*, yet trembling for fear it should strike me; which, when I had considered, I found that the falling there intended was a falling *quite away*; that is, as I conceived, a falling from, and an absolute denial of, the Gospel of Remission of sins by Christ: for from them the Apostle begins his argument, *ver.* 1, 2, 3. Secondly, I found that this falling away must

be openly, even in the view of the World, even so as to *put Christ to an open shame*. Thirdly, I found that those he there intendeth were for ever shut up of God both in blindness, hardness, and impenitency: *It is impossible they should be renewed again unto repentance*. By all these particulars, I found, to Gods everlasting praise, my sin was not the sin in this place intended.

[First, I confessed I was fallen, but not fallen away, that is from the profession of Faith in Jesus unto eternal Life.

Secondly, I confessed that I had put Jesus Christ to *shame* by my sin, but not to open *shame*. I did not deny him before men, nor condemn him as a fruitless one before the World.

Thirdly, nor did I find that God had shut me up, or denied me to come (though I found it hard work indeed to come) to him by sorrow and repentance; blessed be God for unsearchable Grace.]

178. [224.] Then I considered that in the tenth of the *Hebrews*; and found that the *wilful Sin* there mentioned, is not every wilful sin, but that which doth throw off Christ, and then his Commandments too. Secondly, That must also be done openly, before two or three witnesses, to answer that of the Law, *ver.* 28. Thirdly, This sin cannot be committed but with great despite done to the Spirit of Grace; despising both the disswasions from that sin, and the perswasions to the contrary: But the Lord knows, though this my sin was devilish, yet it did not amount to these.

179. [225.] And as touching that in the twelfth of the *Hebrews*, about *Esau's* selling his Birth-right, though this was that which kill'd me, and stood like a Spear against me; yet now I did consider, First, That his was not a hasty thought against the continual labour of his mind; but a thought consented to, and put in practice likewise, and that too after some deliberation, *Gen.* 25. Secondly, it was a publick and open action, even before his Brother, if not before many more; this made his sin of a far more hainous nature then otherwise it would have been. Thirdly, He continued to slight his Birth-right: *He did eat and drink, and went his way*; thus Esau *DESPISED his Birth-right*: Yea, twenty year after he was found to despise it still. *And Esau said, I have enough, my Brother, keep that thou hast to thyself*, Gen. 33. 9.

180. [226.] Now as touching this, That *Esau sought a place of repentance*; thus I thought: First, This was not for the *Birth-right*, but for

the *Blessing*; this is clear from the Apostle, and is distinguished by *Esau* himself, *He hath taken away my Birth-right* (that is, formerly); *and now he hath taken away my Blessing also*, Gen. 27. 36. Secondly, Now this being thus considered, I came again to the Apostle, to see what might be the mind of God in a New-Testament stile and sence* concerning *Esau's* sin; and so far as I could conceive, this was the mind of God, That the *Birth-right* signified *Regeneration*, and the *Blessing* the *Eternal Inheritance*; for so the Apostle seems to hint, *Lest there be any profane person, as Esau, who for one morsel of meat sold his Birth-right*: as if he should say, Lest there be any person amongst you that shall cast off all those blessed beginnings of God that at present are upon him, in order to a new Birth, lest they become as *Esau*, even be rejected afterwards, when they would inherit the Blessing.

181. [227.] For many there are, who in the day of Grace and Mercy despise those things which are indeed the Birth-right to Heaven, who yet when the deciding-day appears, will cry as loud as *Esau, Lord, Lord, open to us*; but then, as *Isaac* would not repent, no more will God the Father, but will say, *I have blessed these, yea, and they shall be blessed*; but as for you, *Depart, you are workers of iniquity.* Gen. 27. 32. Luk. 13. 25, 26, 27.

182. [228.] When I had thus considered these Scriptures, and found that thus to understand them was not against but according to other Scriptures, this still added further to my encouragement and comfort, and also gave a great blow to that objection, to wit, *That the Scriptures could not agree in the salvation of my Soul.* And now remained only the hinder part of the Tempest, for the thunder was gone beyond me, onely some drops did still remain, that now and then would fall upon me: but because my former frights and anguish were very sore and deep, therefore it did oft befall me still as it befalleth those that have been scared with fire, I thought every voice was fire, fire; every little touch would hurt my tender Conscience.

183. [229.] But one day, as I was passing in the field, and that too with some dashes on my Conscience, fearing lest yet all was not right, suddenly this sentence fell upon my Soul, *Thy righteousness is in Heaven*; and methought withall, I saw with the eyes of my Soul Jesus Christ at Gods right hand, there, I say, as my Righteousness; so that wherever I was, or whatever I was a doing, God could not say of me,

He wants my Righteousness, for that was just before him. I also saw moreover, that it was not my good frame of Heart that made my Righteousness better, nor yet my bad frame that made my Righteousness worse: for my Righteousness was Jesus Christ himself,* *the same yesterday, to day, and for ever*, Heb. 13. 8.

184. [230.] Now did my chains fall off my Legs indeed, I was loosed from my affliction and irons, my temptations also fled away: so that from that time those dreadful Scriptures of God left off to trouble me; now went I also home rejoycing, for the grace and love of God: So when I came home, I looked to see if I could find that Sentence, *Thy Righteousness is in Heaven*, but could not find such a Saying, wherefore my Heart began to sink again, onely that was brought to my remembrance, *He is made unto us of God, Wisdom, Righteousness, Sanctification, and Redemption*; by this word I saw the other Sentence true.

185. [231.] For by this Scripture, I saw that the Man Christ Jesus, as he is distinct from us, as touching his bodily presence, so he is our Righteousness and Sanctification before God: here therefore I lived, for some time, very sweetly at peace with God thorow Christ; O methought Christ! Christ! there was nothing but Christ that was before my eyes: I was not now onely for looking upon this and the other benefit of Christ apart, as of his Blood, Burial, or Resurrection, but considered him as whole Christ; as he in whom all these, and all his other Vertues, Relations, Offices, and Operations met together, and that on the right hand of God in Heaven.

186. [232.] 'Twas glorious to me to see his exaltation, and the worth and prevalencie of all his benefits, and that because of this; Now I could look from my self to him, and should reckon that all those Graces of God that now were green in me, were yet but like those crack'd-Groats and Four-pence-half-pennies* that rich men carry in their Purses, when their Gold is in their Trunks at home: O I saw my Gold was in my Trunk at home! In Christ my Lord and Saviour! Now Christ was all; all my Wisdom, all my Righteousness, all my Sanctification, and all my Redemption.

187. [233.] Further, The Lord did also lead me into the mystery of Union with this Son of God, that I was joyned to him, that I was flesh of his flesh, and bone of his bone; and now was that a sweet word to me, in *Ephes*. 5. 30.* By this also was my faith in him, as my Righteousness, the more confirmed to me; for if he and I were one,

then his Righteousness was mine, his Merits mine, his Victory also mine. Now could I see my self in Heaven and Earth at once; in Heaven by my Christ, by my Head, by my Righteousness and Life, though on Earth by my Body or Person.

188. [234.] Now I saw Christ Jesus was looked on of God, and should also be looked upon by us as that common or publick person, in whom all the whole Body of his Elect are always to be considered and reckoned, that we fulfilled the Law by him, died by him,* rose from the dead by him, got the Victory over sin, death, the devil, and hell, by him: when he died we died, and so of his Resurrection: *Thy dead men shall live, together with my dead body shall they arise*, saith he, *Isa.* 26. and again, *After two dayes he will revive us, and the third day we shall live in his sight*, Hos. 6. 2. which is now fulfilled by the sitting down of the Son of Man on the right hand of the Majesty in the Heavens; according to that to the *Ephesians*, *He hath raised us up together, and made us sit together in heavenly places in Christ Jesus*, Ephes. 2. 6.

189. [235.] Ah these blessed considerations and Scriptures, with many other of a like nature, were in those days made to spangle in mine eyes, *Praise ye the Lord God in his Sanctuary, praise him in the firmament of his power, praise him for his mighty acts, praise him according to his excellent greatness*, Psal. 150. 1, 2.

190. [236.] Having thus in few words given you a taste of the sorrow and affliction that my Soul went under by the guilt and terror that this my wicked thought did lay me under; and having given you also a touch of my deliverance therefrom, and of the sweet and blessed comfort that I met with afterwards, (which comfort dwelt about a twelve-month with my heart, to my unspeakable admiration) I will now (God willing) before I proceed any further, give you in a word or two, what, as I conceive, was the cause of this Temptation; and also after that, what advantage at the last it became unto my Soul.

191. [237.] For the causes, I conceived they were principally two, of which two also I was deeply convinced all the time this trouble lay upon me. The first was, For that I did not, when I was delivered from the Temptation that went before,* still pray to God to keep me from Temptations that were to come: for though, as I can say in truth, my Soul was much in prayer before this tryal seized me, yet then I prayed onely, or at the most principally, for the removal of

present troubles, and for fresh discoveries of love in Christ: which I saw afterwards was not enough to do; I also should have prayed that the great God would keep me from the evil that was to come.

192. [238.] Of this I was made deeply sensible by the Prayer of holy *David*, who when he was under present mercy, yet prayed that God would hold him back from sin and temptation to come: *For then*, saith he, *shall I be upright, and I shall be innocent from the* GREAT *transgression*, Psal. 19. 13. By this very word was I gauled* and condemned, quite thorow this long temptation.

193. [239.] That also was another word that did much condemn me for my folly, in the neglect of this duty, *Heb.* 4. 16. *Let us therefore come boldly unto the Throne of grace, that we may obtain mercy, and find grace to help in time of need*: this I had not done, and therefore was suffered thus to sin and fall, according to what is written, *Pray, that ye enter not into temptation*: and truly this very thing is to this day of such weight and awe upon me, that I dare not, when I come before the Lord, go off my knees until I intreat him for help and mercy against the temptations that are to come: and I do beseech thee, Reader, that thou learn to beware of my negligence, by the affliction that for this thing I did for days, and months, and years, with sorrow undergoe.

194. [240.] Another cause of this temptation was, That I had tempted God; and on this manner did I do it: Upon a time my Wife was great with Child,* and before her full time was come, her pangs, as of a woman in travel,* were fierce and strong upon her, even as if she would immediately have fallen in labour, and been delivered of an untimely birth: now at this very time it was, that I had been so strongly tempted to question the being of God; wherefore, as my Wife lay crying by me, I said, but with all secresie imaginable, even thinking in my heart, *Lord, if thou wilt now remove this sad affliction from my Wife, and cause that she be troubled no more therewith this night* (and now were her pangs just upon her) *then I shall know that thou canst discern the most secret thought of the heart.*

195. [241.] I had no sooner said it in my heart, but her pangs were taken from her, and she was cast into a deep sleep, and so she continued till morning; at this I greatly marvelled, not knowing what to think; but after I had been awake a good while, and heard her cry no more, I fell to sleeping also: So when I waked in the morning, it came upon me again, even what I had said in my heart the last night, and

how the Lord had shewed me that he knew my secret thoughts, which was a great astonishment unto me for several weeks after.

196. [242.] Well, about a year and an half afterwards, that wicked sinful thought, of which I have spoken before, went thorow my wicked heart, even this thought, *Let Christ go if he will*; so when I was fallen under guilt for this, the remembrance of my other thought, and of the effect thereof, would also come upon me with this retort, which carried also rebuke along with it, *Now you may see that God doth know the most secret thoughts of the heart, now you may see that God doth know the most secret thoughts of the heart!*

197. [243.] And with this, that of the passages that was betwixt the Lord, and his servant *Gideon*, fell upon my spirit; how because that *Gideon* tempted God with his Fleece, both wet and dry,* when he should have believed and ventured upon his Word, therefore the Lord did afterwards so try him, as to send him against an innumerable company of Enemies, and that too, as to outward appearance, without any strength or help, *Judg. Chap.* 6, 7. Thus he served me, and that justly, for I should have believed his Word, and not have put an *if* upon the all-seeingness of God.

198. [244.] And now to shew you something of the advantages that I also gained by this Temptation: And first, By this I was made continually to possess in my Soul a very wonderful sence both of the being and glory of God, and of his beloved Son; in the temptation before, my Soul was perplexed

> [with unbelief, blasphemy, hardness of heart, questions about the being of God, Christ, the Truth of the Word and certainty of the World to come: I say, then I was greatly assaulted, and tormented]

with Atheism, but now the case was otherwise, now was God and Christ continually before my face, though not in a way of comfort, but in a way of exceeding dread and terrour. The glory of the Holiness of God did at this time break me to pieces, and the Bowels and Compassion of Christ did break me as on the Wheel; for I could not consider him but as a lost and rejected Christ, the remembrance of which was as the continual breaking of my bones.

199. [245.] The Scriptures now also were wonderful things unto me; I saw that the truth and verity of them were the Keys of the Kingdom of Heaven; those the Scriptures favour, they must inherit bliss; but those they oppose and condemn, must perish for evermore:

O this word, *For the Scriptures cannot be broken*,* would rend the caul of my heart,* and so would that other, *Whose sins ye remit, they are remitted, but whose sins ye retain, they are retained*:* Now I saw the Apostles to be the Elders of the City of Refuge, *Josh.* 20. 4. those they were to receive in, were received to Life, but those that they shut out, were to be slain by the avenger of blood.

200. [246.] O! one sentence of the Scripture did more afflict and terrifie my mind, I mean those sentences that stood against me, (as sometimes I thought they every one did) more, I say, than an Army of forty thousand men that might have come against me. Wo be to him against whom the Scriptures bend themselves.

201. [247.] By this Temptation I was made see more into the nature of the Promise, then ever I was before: for I lying, now trembling under the mighty hand of God, continually torn and rent by the thunderings of his Justice; this made me, with careful heart and watchful eye, with great seriousness to turn over every leaf, and with much diligence mixt with trembling, to consider every sentence, together with its natural force and latitude.

202. [248.] By this Temptation also, I was greatly beaten off my former foolish practice, of putting by the Word of Promise when it came into my mind: for now, though I could not suck that sweetness and comfort from the Promise, as I had done at other times, yet, like to a man asinking, I should catch at all I saw: formerly I thought I might not meddle with the Promise, unless I felt its comfort; but now 'twas no time thus to do, the Avenger of blood too hardly did pursue me.

203. [249.] Now therefore I was glad to catch at that word, which yet I feared I had no ground or right to own; and even to leap into the Bosom of that Promise, that yet I feared did shut its heart against me. Now also I should labour to take the word as God had laid it down, without restraining the natural force of one syllable thereof: O what did I now see in that blessed sixth of *John, And him that comes to me, I will in no wise cast out!* [John. 6. 37] now I began to consider with my self, that God had a bigger mouth to speak with, than I had heart to conceive with; I thought also with my self, that he spake not his words in haste, or in an unadvised heat, but with infinite wisdom and judgement, and in very truth and faithfulness, 2 *Sam.* 7. 28.*

204. [250.] I should in these dayes, often in my greatest agonies,

even flounce* towards the Promise (as the horses do towards sound ground, that yet stick in the mire) concluding (though as one almost bereft of his wits through fear) on this I will rest and stay, and leave the fulfilling of it to the God of heaven that made it. O! many a pull* hath my heart had with Satan, for that blessed sixth of *John*: I did not now, as at other times, look principally for comfort (though O how welcome would it have been unto me!) but now a Word, a Word to lean a weary Soul upon, that I might not sink for ever!*

205. [251.] Yea, often when I have been making to the Promise, I have seen as if the Lord would refuse my Soul for ever; I was often as if I had run upon the pikes,* and as if the Lord had thrust at me, to keep me from him, as with a flaming sword. Then I should think of *Esther*, who went to petition the King contrary to the Law, *Esth.* 4. 16. I thought also of *Benhadad*'s servants, who went with ropes upon their heads to their Enemies for mercy, 1 *Kin.* 20. 31, &c. the woman of *Canaan* also, that would not be daunted, though called dog by Christ, *Mat.* 15. 22, &c. and the man that went to borrow bread at midnight, *Luk.* 11. 5, 6, 7, 8, &c. were great encouragements unto me.

206. [252.] I never saw those heights and depths in grace, and love, and mercy, as I saw after this temptation: great sins do draw out great grace;* and where guilt is most terrible and fierce, there the mercy of God in Christ, when shewed to the Soul, appears most high and mighty. When *Job* had passed thorow his captivity, *he had twice as much as he had before*, Job 42. 10. Blessed be God for Jesus Christ our Lord. Many other things I might here make observation of, but I would be brief, and therefore shall at this time omit them; and do pray God that my harms may make others fear to offend, lest they also be made to bear the iron yoak as I.*

[I had two or three times, at or about my deliverance from this temptation, such strange apprehensions of the Grace of God, that I could hardly bear up under it; it was so out of measure amazing, when I thought it could reach me, that I do think, if that sense of it had abode long upon me, it would have made me uncapable for business.]

207. [253.] Now I shall go forward to give you a relation of other of the Lords dealings with me, of his dealings with me at sundry other seasons, and of the temptations I then did meet withall. I shall begin with what I met when I first did joyn in fellowship with the

People of God in *Bedford*.* After I had propounded to the Church, that my desire was to walk in the Order and Ordinances of Christ with them, and was also admitted by them; while I thought of that blessed Ordinance of Christ, which was his last Supper with his Disciples before his death, that Scripture *Do this in remembrance of me*, Luk. 22. 19. was made a very precious word unto me; for by it the Lord did come down upon my conscience with the discovery of his death for my sins, and as I then felt, did as if he plunged me in the vertue of the same. But behold, I had not been long a partaker at that Ordinance, but such fierce and sad temptations did attend me at all times therein, both to blaspheme the Ordinance, and to wish some deadly thing to those that then did eat thereof;* that lest I should at any time be guilty of consenting to these wicked and fearful thoughts, I was forced to bend my self all the while to pray to God to keep me from such blasphemies; and also to cry to God to bless the Bread and Cup to them, as it went from mouth to mouth: The reason of this temptation I have thought since was, because I did not with that reverence at first approach to partake thereof.

208. [254.] Thus I continued for three quarters of a year, and could never have rest nor ease; but at last the Lord came in upon my Soul with that same Scripture by which my Soul was visited before; and after that, I have been usually very well and comfortable in the partaking of that blessed Ordinance, and have I trust therein discerned the *Lords Body** as broken for my sins, and that his precious Blood had been shed for my transgressions.

209. [255.] Upon a time I was somewhat inclining to a Consumption,* wherefore, about the Spring, I was suddenly and violently seized with much weakness in my outward man; insomuch that I thought I could not live. Now began I afresh to give myself up to a serious examination after my state and condition for the future, and of my Evidences for that blessed world to come. For it hath, I bless the name of God, been my usual course, as alwayes, so especially in the day of affliction, to endeavour to keep my interest in Life to come,* clear before mine eye.

210. [256.] But I had no sooner began to recall to mind my former experience of the goodness of God to my Soul, but there came flocking into my mind an innumerable company of my sins and transgressions, amongst which these were at this time most to my affliction, namely, my deadness, dulness, and coldness in holy Duties;

my wandrings of heart, my wearisomness in all good things, my want of love to God, his wayes and people, with this at the end of all, *Are these the fruits of Christianity? are these the tokens of a blessed man?**

211. [257.] At the apprehension of these things, my sickness was doubled upon me, for now was I sick in my inward man, my Soul was clog'd with guilt, now also was all my former experience of Gods goodness to me quite taken out of my mind, and hid as if it had never been, nor seen: Now was my Soul greatly pinched between these two considerations. *Live I must not, Die I dare not*: now I sunk and fell in my Spirit, and was giving up all for lost; but as I was walking up and down in the house, as a man in a most woful state, that word of God took hold of my heart, *Ye are justified freely by his grace, through the redemption that is in Christ Jesus*, Rom. 3. 24.

212. [258.] Now was I as one awakened out of some troublesome sleep and dream, and listening to this heavenly sentence, I was as if I heard it thus expounded to me; Sinner, thou thinkest that because of thy sins and infirmities, I cannot save thy Soul; but behold my Son is by me, and upon him I look, and not on thee, and will deal with thee according as I am pleased with him: at this I was greatly lightened in my mind, and made to understand that God could justifie a sinner at any time; it was but looking upon Christ, and imputing of his benefits to us, and the work was forthwith done.

213. [259.] And as I was thus in a muse, that Scripture also came with great power upon my Spirit, *Not by works of righteousness that we have done, but according to his mercy he saved us*, &c. 2 Tim. 1. 9. Tit. 3. 5. Now was I got on high; I saw my self within the arms of Grace and Mercy; and though I was before afraid to think of a dying hour, yet now I cried, Let me die; now death was lovely and beautiful in my sight, for I saw we shall never live indeed till we be gone to the other World: O methought this life is but a slumber in comparison of that above: at this time also I saw more in those words, *Heirs of God* Rom. 8. 17. then ever I shall be able to express while I live in this world: *Heirs of God!* God himself is the portion of the Saints: this I saw and wondered at, but cannot tell you what I saw.

[260. Again, as I was at another time very ill and weak, and all that time also the Tempter did beset me strongly, (for I find he is much for assaulting the Soul, when it begins to approach towards the Grave, then is his Opportunity) labouring to hide from me my former experience of Gods goodness: Also setting before me the terrours of Death and the Judgment of God; insomuch, that at this time, through my fear of miscarrying for ever, (should I now die) I was as one dead before Death came, and did as if I had felt my self already descending into the Pit; methought, I said, there was no way but to Hell I must: but behold, just as I was in the midst of those fears, these words of the Angels carrying *Lazarus* into *Abrahams* bosom,* darted in upon me, as who should say, *So it shall be with thee when thou dost leave this World.* This did sweetly revive my spirit, and help me to hope in God; which when I had with comfort mused on awhile, that word fell with great weight upon my mind, O *Death, where is thy sting? O Grave, where is thy victory?* 1 Cor. 15. 55. At this I became both well in body and mind at once, for both my sickness did presently vanish, and I walked comfortably in my Work for God again.]

214. [261.] At another time, though just before I was pretty well and savoury in my spirit, yet suddenly there fell upon me a great cloud of darkness, which did so hide from me the things of God and Christ, that I was as if I had never seen or known them in my life;* I was also so over-run in my Soul, with a senceless heartless frame of spirit, that I could not feel my Soul to move or stir after grace and life by Christ; I was as if my loyns were broken, or as if my hands and feet had been tied or bound with chains. At this time also I felt some weakness to seiz my outward man, which made still the other affliction the more heavy and uncomfortable.

215. [262.] After I had been in this condition some three or four days, as I was sitting by the fire, I suddenly felt this word to sound in my heart, *I must go to Jesus*; at this my former darkness and atheism fled away, and the blessed things of heaven were set within my view; while I was on this sudden thus overtaken with surprize, Wife, said I, is there ever a such Scripture, *I must go to Jesus?* she said she could not tell; therefore I sat musing still to see if I could remember such a place; I had not sat above two or three minutes, but that came bolting in upon me, *And to an innumerable company of Angels*; and withal *Hebrews* the twelfth about the mount *Zion* was set before mine eyes. [*Heb.* 12. 22, 23, 24.]*

216. [263.] Then with joy I told my Wife, O now I know, I know! but that night was a good night to me, I never had but few better; I longed for the company of some of Gods people, that I might have imparted unto them what God had shewed me:* Christ was a precious Christ to my Soul that night; I could scarce lie in my Bed for joy, and peace, and triumph, thorow Christ; this great glory did not continue upon me until morning, yet that twelfth of the Author to the *Hebrews*, Heb. 12. 21, 22, 23. was a blessed Scripture to me for many days together after this.

217. [264.] The words are these, *You are come to mount Zion, to the City of the living God, to the heavenly Jerusalem, and to an innumerable company of Angels, to the general assembly and Church of the firstborn which are written in heaven, to God the Judge of all, and to the spirits of just men made perfect, and to Jesus the Mediator of the New Testament, and to the blood of sprinkling, that speaketh better things than that of Abel*: Thorow this blessed Sentence the Lord led me over and over, first to this word, and then to that, and shewed me wonderful glory in every one of them. These words also have oft since this time been great refreshment to my Spirit. Blessed be God for having mercy on me.

A brief Account of the Authors Call to the Work of the Ministery.

218. [265.] And now I am speaking my Experience, I will in this place thrust in a word or two concerning my preaching the Word, and of Gods dealing with me in that particular also: For after I had been about five or six years awakened, and helped* to see both the want and worth of Jesus Christ our Lord, and inabled to venture my Soul upon him: some of the most able among the Saints with us, I say the most able for Judgement, and holiness of Life, as they conceived, did perceive that God had counted me worthy to understand something of his Will in his holy and blessed Word, and had given me utterance in some measure to express, what I saw, to others for edification; they desired me, and that with much earnestness, that I would be willing at sometime to take in hand in one of the Meetings to speak a word of Exhortation unto them.*

219. [266.] The which, though at the first it did much dash and abash my spirit, yet being still by them desired and intreated, I consented to their request, and did twice at two several Assemblies (but in private) though with much weakness and infirmity, discover my Gift amongst them; at which they not onely seemed to be, but did solemnly protest as in the sight of the great God, they were both affected and comforted, and gave thanks to the Father of Mercies for the grace bestowed on me.

220. [267.] After this, sometimes when some of them did go into the Countrey to teach, they would also that I should go with them; where, though as yet I did not, nor durst not make use of my Gift in an open way, yet more privately still, as I came amongst the good People in those places, I did sometimes speak a word of Admonition unto them also; the which they, as the other, received with rejoycing at the mercy of God to me-ward, professing their Souls were edified thereby.

221. [268.] Wherefore, to be brief, at last, being still desired by the Church, after some solemn prayer to the Lord, with fasting, I was more particularly called forth,* and appointed to a more ordinary and publick preaching the Word, not onely to and amongst them that believed, but also to offer the Gospel to those that had not yet received the faith thereof: about which time I did evidently find in my mind a secret pricking forward thereto: (tho I bless God not for desire of vain-glory, for at that time I was most sorely afflicted with the firy darts of the devil, concerning my eternal state).*

222. [269.] But yet I could not be content unless I was found in the exercise of my Gift, unto which also I was greatly animated, not onely by the continual desires of the Godly, but also by that saying of *Paul* to the *Corinthians*, *I beseech you, Brethren (ye know the houshold of Stephanas, that it is the first fruits of Achaia, and that they have addicted themselves to the ministery of the Saints) that you submit your selves unto such, and to every one that helpeth with us and laboureth*, 1 Cor. 16. 15, 16.

223. [270.] By this Text I was made to see that the holy Ghost never intended that men who have Gifts and Abilities should bury them in the earth,* but rather did command and stir up such to the exercise of their gift, and also did commend those, that were apt and ready so to do, *they have addicted themselves to the ministery of the Saints*: this Scripture in these days did continually run in my mind, to incourage me, and strengthen me in this my work for God: I have also been incouraged from several other Scriptures and examples of the Godly, both specified in the Word and other ancient Histories.

Act 8. 4. & 18. 24, 25, &c. 1 *Pet.* 4. 10; *Rom.* 12. 6. Fox *Acts and Mon.**

224. [271.] Wherefore, though of my self, of all the Saints the most unworthy, yet I, but with great fear and trembling at the sight of my own weakness, did set upon the work, and did according to my Gift, and the proportion of my Faith, preach that blessed Gospel that God had shewed me in the holy Word of truth: which when the Countrey understood, they came in to hear the Word by hundreds, and that from all parts, though upon sundry and divers accounts.

225. [272.] And I thank God, he gave unto me some measure of bowels* and pity for their Souls, which also did put me forward to labour with great diligence and earnestness, to find out such a Word as might, if God would bless, lay hold of and awaken the Conscience; in which also the good Lord had respect to the desire of his Servant: for I had not preached long, before some began to be touched by the Word, and to be greatly afflicted in their minds at the apprehension of the greatness of their sin, and of their need of Jesus Christ.

226. [273.] But I at first could not believe that God should speak by me to the heart of any man, still counting my self unworthy; yet those who thus were touched, would love me, and have a peculiar respect for me; and though I did put it from me that they should be awakened by me, still they would confess it and affirm it before the Saints of God, they would also bless God for me (unworthy Wretch that I am!) and count me Gods Instrument that shewed to them the Way of Salvation.

227. [274.] Wherefore seeing them in both their words and deeds to be so constant, & also in their hearts so earnestly pressing after the knowledge of Jesus Christ, rejoycing that ever God did send me where they were: then I began to conclude it might be so, that God had owned in his Work such a foolish one as I;* and then came that Word of God to my heart with much sweet refreshment, *The blessing of them that were ready to perish is come upon me; yea, I caused the widows heart to sing for joy*, Job. 29. 13.

228. [275.] At this therefore I rejoyced; yea, the tears of those whom God did awaken by my preaching, would be both solace and encouragement to me; for I thought on those Sayings, *Who is he that maketh me glad, but the same that is made sorry by me?* 2 Cor. 2. 2. and again, *Though I be not an Apostle to others, yet doubtless I am unto you,*

for the seal of my Apostleship are ye in the Lord, 1 Cor. 9. 2. These things therefore were as another argument unto me that God had called me to and stood by me in this Work.

229. [276.] In my preaching of the Word, I took special notice of this one thing, namely, That the Lord did lead me to begin where his Word begins with Sinners, that is, to condemn all flesh, and to open and alledge that the curse of God by the Law doth belong to and lay hold on all men as they come into the World, because of sin. Now this part of my work I fulfilled with great sence;* for the terrours of the Law, and guilt for my transgressions, lay heavy on my Conscience. I preached what I felt, what I smartingly did feel,* even that under which my poor Soul did groan and tremble to astonishment.

230. [277.] Indeed I have been as one sent to them from the dead; I went my self in chains to preach to them in chains, and carried that fire in my own conscience that I perswaded them to beware of. I can truly say, and that without dissembling, that when I have been to preach, I have gone full of guilt and terrour even to the Pulpit-Door, and there it hath been taken off, and I have been at liberty in my mind until I have done my work, and then immediately, even before I could get down the Pulpit-Stairs, have been as bad as I was before. Yet God carried me on, but surely with a strong hand: for neither guilt nor hell could take me off my Work.

231. [278.] Thus I went for the space of two years, crying out against mens sins, and their fearful state because of them.* After which, the Lord came in upon my own Soul with some staid peace and comfort thorow Christ; for he did give me many sweet discoveries of his blessed Grace thorow him: wherefore now I altered in my preaching (for still I preached what I saw & felt); now therefore I did much labour to hold forth Jesus Christ in all his Offices, Relations, and Benefits unto the World, and did strive also to discover, to condemn and remove those false supports and props on which the World doth both lean, and by them fall and perish. On these things also I staid as long as on the other.

232. [279.] After this, God led me into something of the mystery of union with Christ: wherefore that I discovered and shewed to them also. And when I had travelled thorow these three chief points of the Word of God, about the space of five years or more; I was caught in my present practice, and cast into Prison, where I have

lain as long,* to confirm the Truth by way of Suffering, as I was before in testifying of it according to the Scriptures, in a way of Preaching.

233. [280.] When I have been in preaching, I thank God my heart hath often, all the time of this and the other exercise, with great earnestness cried to God that he would make the Word effectual to the salvation of the Soul; still being grieved lest the Enemy should take the Word away from the Conscience, and so it should become unfruitful: Wherefore I should labour so to speak the Word, as that thereby (if it were possible) the sin and person guilty might be particularized by it.

234. [281.] Also when I have done the Exercise, it hath gone to my heart to think the Word should now fall as rain on stony places; still wishing from my heart, O that they who have heard me speak this day, did but see as I do what sin, death, hell and the curse of God, is; and also what the grace, and love, and mercy of God is, thorow Christ, to men in such a case as they are, who are yet estranged from him; and indeed I did often say in my heart before the Lord, *That if to be hanged up presently before their eyes, would be a means to awaken them, and confirm them in the truth, I gladly should be contented.*

235. [282.] For I have been in my preaching, especially when I have been engaged in the Doctrine of Life by Christ, without Works,* as if an Angel of God had stood by at my back to encourage me: O it hath been with such power and heavenly evidence upon my own Soul, while I have been labouring to unfold it, to demonstrate it, and to fasten it upon the Conscience of others, that I could not be contented with saying, I believe and am sure; methought I was more then sure, if it be lawful so to express my self, that those things which then I asserted, were true.

236. [283.] When I went first to preach the Word abroad, the Doctors and Priests of the Countrey did open wide against me;* but I was perswaded of this, not to render rayling for rayling, but to see how many of their carnal Professors* I could convince of their miserable state by the Law, and of the want and worth of Christ: for thought I, *This shall answer for me in time to come, when they shall be for my hire before their face*, Gen. 30. 33.*

237. [284.] I never cared to meddle with things that were controverted, and in dispute amongst the Saints, especially things of the lowest nature; yet it pleased me much to contend with great

earnestness for the Word of Faith, and the remission of sins by the Death and Sufferings of Jesus: but I say, as to other things, I should let them alone, because I saw they engendered strife,* and because I saw that they neither in doing, nor in leaving undone, did commend us to God to be his: besides, I saw my Work before me did run in another channel, even to carry an awakening-Word;* to that therefore did I stick and adhere.

238. [285.] I never endeavoured to, nor durst make use of other men's lines, *Rom.* 15. 18. (though I condemn not all that do) for I verily thought, and found by experience, that what was taught me by the Word and Spirit of Christ, could be spoken, maintained and stood to, by soundest and best established Conscience: and though I will not now speak all that I know in this matter; yet my experience hath more interest in that text of Scripture, *Gal.* 1. 11, 12.* than many amongst men are aware.

239. [286.] If any of those who were awakened by my Ministry, did after that fall back (as sometimes too many did) I can truly say their loss hath been more to me, then if one of my own Children, begotten of my body, had been going to its grave; I think verily I may speak it without an offence to the Lord, nothing hath gone so near me as that, unless it was the fear of the loss of the salvation of my own Soul: I have counted as if I had goodly buildings and lordships in those places my Children were born: my heart hath been so wrapt up in the glory of this excellent work, that I counted my self more blessed and honored of God by this, than if he had made me the Emperour of the Christian World, or the Lord of all the glory of Earth without it: O that word, *He that converteth a sinner from the error of his way, doth save a soul from death!* [Jam. 5. 20.]

[*The fruit of the Righteous, is a Tree of Life; and he that winneth Souls, is wise,* Prov. 11. 30. *They that be wise, shall shine as the brightness of the Firmament; and they that turn many to Righteousness, as the Stars for ever and ever,* Dan. 12. 3. *For what is our hope, or joy, or crown of rejoycing? are not even ye in the presence of our Lord Jesus Christ at his coming? For, ye are our glory and joy,* 1 Thes. 2. 19, 20. These, with many others of a like nature, have been great refreshment to me.]

240. [287.] I have observed, that where I have had a work to do for God, I have had first as it were the going of God upon my Spirit to desire I might preach there: I have also observed, that such and such

Souls in particular have been strongly set upon my heart, and I stirred up to wish for their Salvation; and that these very Souls have after this been given in as the fruits of my Ministry. I have also observed, that a word cast in by the by, hath done more execution in a Sermon then all that was spoken besides: sometimes also when I have thought I did no good, then I did most of all; and at other times when I thought I should catch them, I have fished for nothing.

[288. I have also observed this that where there hath been a work to do upon Sinners, there the Devil hath begun to roar in the hearts, and by the mouths of his Servants. Yea often-times when the wicked World hath raged most, there hath been souls awakened by the Word: I could instance particulars, but I forbear.]

241. [289.] My great desire in my fulfilling my Ministry, was, to get into the darkest places in the *Countrey*, even amongst those people that were furthest off of profession; yet not because I could not endure the light (for I feared not to shew my Gospel to any) but because I found my spirit did lean most after awakening and converting-Work, and the Word that I carried did lead it self most that way; *Yea, so have I strived to preach the Gospel, not where Christ was named, lest I should build upon another mans foundation*, Rom. 15. 20.

242. [290.] In my preaching, I have really been in pain, and have as it were travelled* to bring forth Children to God, neither could I be satisfied unless some fruits did appear in my work: if I were fruitless it matter'd not who commended me; but if I were fruitful, I cared not who did condemn. I have thought of that, *He that winneth souls is wise*, Pro. 11. 30. and again, *Lo Children are an heritage of the Lord, and the fruit of the Womb is his Reward: as arrows in the hand of a mighty man, so are Children of the youth; happy is the man that hath filled his quiver with them, they shall not be ashamed, but they shall speak with the Enemies in the gate*, Psal. 127. 3, 4, 5.

[291. It pleased me nothing to see people drink in Opinions, if they seemed ignorant of Jesus Christ, and the worth of their own salvation, sound conviction for sin, especially for unbelief, and an heart set on fire to be saved by Christ, with strong breathings after a truly sanctified Soul: that was it that delighted me; those were the souls I counted blessed.]

243. [292.] But in this work, as in all other, I had my temptations attending me, and that of divers kinds: as sometimes I should be

assaulted with great discouragement, therein fearing that I should not be able to speak sence unto the people; at which times I should have such a strange faintness and strengthlessness seiz upon my body that my legs have scarce been able to carry me to the place of Exercise.

244. [293.] Sometimes again, when I have been preaching, I have bin violently assaulted with thoughts of blasphemy, and strongly tempted to speak them with my mouth before the Congregation. I have also at some times, even when I have begun to speak the Word with much clearness, evidence, and liberty of speech, yet been before the ending of that Opportunity so blinded, and so estranged from the things I have been speaking, and have also bin so straitned in my speech, as to utterance before the people, that I have been as if I had not known or remembred what I have been about; or as if my head had been in a bag all the time of the *exercise*.

245. [294.] Again, When at sometimes I have been about to preach upon some smart and scorching portion of the *Word*, I have found the tempter suggest, What! will you preach this? this condemns your self; of this your own Soul is guilty; wherefore preach not of it at all, or if you do, yet so mince it as to make way for your own escape, lest instead of awakening others, you lay that guilt upon your own soul, as you will never get from under.

[295. But I thank the Lord I have been kept from consenting to these so horrid suggestions, and have rather, as *Sampson*, bowed my self with all my might to condemn sin and transgression where ever I found it, yea though therein also I did bring guilt upon my own Conscience; *Let me die*, thought I, *with the Philistines*, Judg. 16. 29, 30, rather than deal corruptly with the blessed Word of God, *Thou that teachest another, teachest thou not thyself?* it is far better that thou do judge thy self, even by preaching plainly unto others, then that thou, to save thy self, imprison the Truth in unrighteousness: Blessed be God for his help also in this.]

246. [296.] I have also, while found in this blessed work of Christ, been often tempted to pride and liftings up of heart; and though I dare not say, I not been infected with this, yet truly the Lord of his precious mercy hath so carried it towards me, that for the most part I have had but small joy to give way to such a thing: for it hath been my every-days portion to be let into the evil of my own heart, and still made to see such a multitude of corruptions and infirmities

therein, that it hath caused hanging down of the head under all my Gifts and Attainments: I have felt this thorn in the flesh (2 *Cor.* 12. 8, 9.) the very mercy of God to me.

247. [297.] I have had also together with this, some notable place or other of the Word presented before me, which word hath contained in it some sharp and piercing sentence concerning the perishing of the Soul, notwithstanding gifts and parts; as for instance, that hath been of great use unto me, *Though I speak with the tongue of men and angels, and have not charity, I am become as sounding-brass, and a tinkling cymbal*, 1 Cor. 13. 1, 2.

248. [298.] A tinkling Cymbal is an instrument of Musick with which a skilful player can make such melodious and heart-inflaming Musick, that all who hear him play, can scarcely hold from dancing; and yet, behold, the Cymbal hath not life, neither comes the musick from it, but because of the art of him that playes therewith: so then the instrument at last may come to nought and perish, though in times past such musick hath been made upon it.

249. [299.] Just thus I saw it was and will be with them who have Gifts, but want saving-Grace;* they are in the hand of Christ, as the Cymbal in the hand of *David*; and as *David* could with the Cymbal make that mirth in the service of God, as to elevate the hearts of the Worshippers; so Christ can use these gifted men, as with them to affect the Souls of his People in his Church, yet when he hath done all hang them by, as lifeless, though sounding *Cymbals*.

250. [300.] This consideration therefore, together with some others, were for the most part as a maul* on the head of pride and desire of vain-glory: What, thought I, shall I be proud because I am a sounding Brass? is it so much to be a Fiddle? hath not the least Creature that hath life, more of God in it than these? besides, I knew 'twas Love should never die, but these must cease and vanish: So I concluded a little Grace, a little Love, a little of the true Fear of God, is better then all these Gifts: Yea, and I am fully convinced of it, that it is possible for a Soul that can scarce give a man an answer, but with great confusion as to method, I say it is possible for them to have a thousand times more Grace, and so to be more in the love and favour of the Lord, then some who by vertue of the Gift of Knowledge, can deliver themselves like Angels.

[301. Thus therefore I came to perceive, that though gifts in themselves were good, to the thing for which they are designed, to wit, the Edification of others, yet empty and without power to save the soul of him that hath them, if they be alone: Neither are they any signe of a mans state to be happy] [, being only a dispensation of God to some, of whose improvement, or non improvement they must when a little life more is over, give an account to him that is ready to judge the quick, and the dead.]

[302. This shewed me too, that gifts being alone, were dangerous, not in themselves, but because of those evils that attend them to wit, pride, desire of vain glory, self-conceit, &c., all of which were easily blown up at the applause, and commendation of every unadvised Christian, to the endangering of a poor Creature to fall into the condemnation of the Devil.

303. I saw therefore that he that hath Gifts had need be let in to a sight of the nature of them that they come short of making of him to be in a truly saved condition, least he rest in them, and so fall short of the grace of God.

304. He hath also cause to walk humbly with God, and be little in his own eyes, and to remember with all, that his Gifts are not his own, but the Churches, and that by them he is made a servant to the Church, and he must also give at last an account of his Stewardship unto the Lord Jesus, and to give a good account, will be a blessed thing!

305. Let all men therefore prize a little with the fear of the Lord, (gifts indeed are desirable) but yet great grace and small gifts are better then great gifts and no grace. It doth not say, the Lord gives gifts and glory, but the Lord gives grace and glory! and blessed is such an one! to whom the Lord gives grace] [, true grace, for that is a certain forerunner of glory.

306. But when Satan perceived that his thus tempting and assaulting of me would not answer his design; to wit, to overthrow my ministry, and make it ineffectual as to the ends thereof: then he tryed an other way, which was to stir up the mindes of the ignorant, and malicious, to load me with slanders and reproaches; now therefore I may say, That what the Devil could devise, and his instruments invent, was whirled up and down the Countrey against me, thinking as I said, that by that means they should make my ministry to be abandoned.

307. It began therefore to be rumored up and down among

the People that I was a Witch,* a Jesuit, a High-way-man, and the like.

308. To all which, I shall only say, God knows that I am innocent. But as for mine accusers, let them provide themselves to meet me before the tribunal of the Son of God, there to answer for these things (with all the rest of their Iniquities) unless God shall give them Repentance for them, for the which I pray with all my heart.

309. But that which was reported with the boldest confidence, was, that I had my *Misses*, my *Whores*, my *Bastards*, yea *two wives at once*,* and the like. Now these slanders (with the other) I glory in, because but slanders, foolish, or knavish lies, and falshoods cast upon me by the devil and his Seed; and should I not be dealt with thus wickedly by the World, I should want one sign of a Saint and Child of God. Blessed are you (said the Lord Jesus) when men shall revile you and persecute you, and shall say all manner of evil of you falsly for my sake; rejoyce and be exceeding glad for great is your reward in Heaven: for so persecuted they the Prophets which were before you, Mat. 5. 11.*

310. These things therefore upon mine own account trouble me not, no, though they were twenty times more then they are. I have a good Conscience, and whereas they speak evil of me, as an evil doer, they shall be ashamed that falsly accuse my good conversation in Christ.

311. So then, what shall I say to those that have thus bespattered me? shall I threaten them? shall I chide them? shall I flatter them? shall I entreat them to hold their tongues? no, not I: were it not for that these things make them ripe for damnation that are the authors and abettors, I would say unto them: *report it!* because 'twill increase my glory.

312. Therefore I bind these lies and slanders to me as an ornament, it belongs to my Christian Profession to be villified, slandered, reproached, and reviled: and since all this is nothing else, as my God and my Conscience doe bear me witness: I rejoyce in reproaches for Christs sake.

313. I also calling all these fools, or knaves that have thus made it anything of their business to affirm any of the things aforenamed of me, namely that I have been naught* with other Women, or the like, when they have used to the utmost of their endeavours, and

made the fullest enquiry that they can to prove against me truly, that there is any woman in Heaven, or Earth, or Hell, that can say, that I have at any time, in any place, by day or night, so much as attempted to be naught with them, and speak I thus, to beg mine enemies into a good esteem of me? no, not I. I will in this beg beliefe of no man: believe, or disbelieve me in this, all is a case to me.

314. My Foes have mist their mark in this their shooting at me. I am not the man, I wish that they themselves be guiltless, if all the Fornicators and Adulterers in England were hang'd by the Neck till they be dead,* *John Bunyan*, the object of their Envie, would be still alive and well. I know not whether there be such a thing as a woman breathing under the Copes of the whole Heaven but by their apparel, their Children, or by common Fame, except my Wife.

315. And in this I admire the Wisdom of God that he made me shie of women from my first Convertion until now. Those know, and can also bear me witness, with whom I have been most intimately concerned, that it is a rare thing to see me carry it pleasant towards a Woman;* the common Salutation of women I abhor, 'tis odious to me in whomsoever I see it. Their Company alone I cannot away with. I seldom so much as touch a womans hand, for I think these things are not so becoming me, When I have seen good men Salute those women that they have visited, or that have visited them, I have at times made my objection against it, and when they have answered that it was but a peice of Civilitie, I have told them it is not a comely sight; some indeed have urged the holy kiss,* but then I have asked why they made baulks,* why they did salute the most hansom, and let the ill favoured go, thus how laudable so ever such things have been in the eyes of others, they have been unseemly in my sight.

316. And now for a wind up in this matter, I calling not only men, but Angels to prove me guilty of having carnally to do with any woman save my wife, nor am I afraid to do it a second time, knowing that it cannot offend the Lord in such a case, to call God for a Record upon my Soul that in these things I am innocent. Not that I have been thus kept, because of any goodness in me more then in any other, but God has been merciful to me and has kept me, to whom I pray that he will keep me still, not only from this

but from every evil way and work, and preserve me to his Heavenly Kingdom. Amen.

317. Now as Satan laboured by reproaches and slanders to make me vile among my Countrymen, that, if possible, my preaching might be made of none effect, so there was added here to a long and tedious Imprisonment that thereby I might be frighted from my Service for Christ, and the world terrified, and made afraid to hear me preach, of which I shall in the next place give you a brief account.]

A brief Account of the Authors Imprisonment

251. [318.] Having made profession of the glorious Gospel of Christ a long time, and preached the same about five year; I was apprehended at a Meeting of good People in the Countrey,* (amongst whom, had they let me alone, I should have preached that day, but they took me away from amongst them) and had me before a Justice,* who, after I had offered security for my appearing at the next Sessions yet committed me, because my Sureties would not consent to be bound that I should preach no more to the people.

252. [319.] At the Sessions after, I was indicted for an Upholder and Maintainer of unlawful Assemblies and Conventicles, and for not conforming to the National Worship of the Church of England;* and after some conference there with the Justices, was sentenced to perpetual banishment because I refused to Conform.* So being again delivered up to the Goalers hands, I was had home to Prison again, and there have lain now above five year and a quarter,* waiting to see what God would suffer these men to do with me.

253. [320.] In which condition I have continued with much content thorow Grace, but have met with many turnings and goings upon my heart both from the Lord, Satan, and my own corruptions; by all which (glory be to Jesus Christ) I have also received, among many things, much conviction, instruction, and understanding, of which at large I shall not here discourse; onely give you, in a hint or two, a word that may stir up the Godly to bless God, and to pray for me; and also to take encouragement, should the case be their own, *Not to fear what man can do unto them.**

254. [321.] I never had in all my life so great an inlet into the Word of God as now: them Scriptures that I saw nothing in before, are made in this place and state to shine upon me. Jesus Christ also

was never more real and apparent then now; here I have seen him, and felt him indeed: O that word, *We have not preached unto you cunningly devised fables*, 2 Pet. 1. 16. and that, *God raised Christ from the dead, and gave him glory, that your faith and hope might be in God*, 1 Pet. 1. 21. were blessed words unto me in this my imprisoned condition.

255. [322.] These three or four Scriptures also have been great refreshment, in this condition, to me: *Joh.* 14. 1, 2, 3, 4. *Joh.* 16. 33. *Col.* 3. 3, 4. *Heb.* 12. 22, 23, 24. So that sometimes, when I have been in the savour of them, I have been able to laugh at destruction, *and to fear neither the Horse nor his Rider*.* I have had sweet sights of the forgiveness of my sins in this place, and of my being with Jesus in another world: *O the mount Zion, the heavenly Jerusalem, the innumerable company of Angels, and God the Judge of all, and the Spirits of just men made perfect, and Jesus*,* have been sweet unto me in this place: I have seen that here, that I am perswaded I shall never, while in this world, be able to express; I have seen a truth in that scripture, *Whom having not seen, ye love; in whom, though now ye see him not, yet believing, ye rejoyce with joy unspeakable, and full of glory*, 1 Pet. 1. 8.

256. [323.] I never knew what it was for God to stand by me at all turns, and at every offer of Satan, *&c.* as I have found him since I came in hither; for look how [when] fears have presented themselves, so have supports and encouragements; yea, when I have started even as it were at nothing else but my shadow, yet God, as being very tender of me, hath not suffered me to be molested, but would with one Scripture and another strengthen me against all: insomuch that I have often said, *Were it lawful, I could pray for greater trouble, for the greater comforts sake*, Eccles. 7. 14. 2 Cor. 1. 5.

257. [324.] Before I came to Prison, I saw what was a coming,* and had especially two Considerations warm upon my heart; the first was, How to be able to endure, should my imprisonment be long and tedious; the second was, How to be able to encounter death, should that be here my portion. For the first of these, that Scripture *Col.* 1. 11, was great information to me, namely, to pray to God *to be strengthened with all might, according to his glorious power, unto all patience and long-suffering with joyfulness*: I could seldom go to prayer before I was imprisoned, but for not so little as a year together, this Sentence, or sweet Petition, would as it were thrust it self into my

mind, and perswade me that if ever I would go thorow long-suffering, I must have all patience, especially if I would endure it joyfully.

258. [325.] As to the second Consideration, that Saying, 2 *Cor.* 1. 9. was of great use unto me, *But we had the sentence of death in our selves, that we might not trust in our selves, but in God that raiseth the dead*: by this Scripture I was made to see that if ever I would suffer rightly, I must first pass a sentence of death upon every thing that can properly be called a thing of this life, even to reckon my Self, my Wife, my Children, my health, my enjoyments and all, as dead to me, & my self as dead to them.*

259. [326.] The second was, to live upon God that is invisible; as *Paul* said in another place, The way not to faint, is *to look not at the things that are seen, but at the things that are not seen; for the things that are seen are temporal; but the things that are not seen, they are eternal*, 2 Cor. 4. 18. And thus I reasoned with my self; If I provide only for a prison, then the whip comes at unawares, and so does also the pillory; again, if I provide onely for these, then I am not fit for banishment; further, if I conclude that banishment is the worst, then if death come, I am surprized; so that I see the best way to go thorow sufferings, is to trust in God thorow Christ, as touching the world to come; and as touching this world, to *count the grave my house, to make my bed in darkness, to say to Corruption, Thou art my Father, and to the Worm, Thou art my Mother and Sister*;* that is, to familiarize these things to me.

260. [327.] But notwithstanding these helps, I found my self a man, and compassed with infirmities; the parting with my Wife and poor Children hath oft been to me in this place, as the pulling the flesh from my bones; and that not onely because I am somewhat too fond of these great mercies, but also because I should have often brought to my mind the many hardships, miseries and wants that my poor family was like to meet with, should I be taken from them, especially my poor blind Child,* who lay nearer my heart than all I had besides; O the thoughts of the hardship I thought this might go under, would break my heart to pieces.

261. [328.] Poor Child! thought I, what sorrow art thou like to have for thy portion in this world? Thou must be beaten, must beg, suffer hunger, cold, nakedness, and a thousand calamities, though I cannot now endure the wind should blow upon thee: but yet recalling my

self, thought I, I must venture you all with God, though it goeth to
the quick to leave you: O I saw in this condition I was as a man who
was pulling down his house upon the head of his Wife and Children;
yet thought I, I must do it, I must do it: and now I thought of those
*two milch Kine that were to carry the Ark of God into another Country,
and to leave their Calves behind them*, 1 Sam. 6. 10, 11, 12.

262. [329.] But that which helped me in this temptation was divers
considerations, of which three in special here I will name; the first
was the consideration of those two Scriptures, *Leave thy fatherless
children, I will preserve them alive, and let thy widows trust in me*: and
again, *The Lord said, Verily it shall go well with thy remnant, verily I
will cause the enemy to entreat thee well in the time of evil, &c.* [Jer.
49. 11. Chap. 15. 11.]

263. [330.] I had also this consideration, that if I should now
venture all for God, I engaged God to take care of my concernments;
but if I forsook him and his ways, for fear of any trouble that should
come to me or mine, then I should not only falsifie my profession,
but should count also that my concernments were not so sure if left
at Gods feet, while I stood to and for his Name, as they would be if
they were under my own tuition, though with the denial of the way
of God. This was a smarting consideration, and was as spurs unto
my flesh: that Scripture also greatly helped it to fasten the more upon
me, where Christ prays against *Judas*, that God would disappoint
him in all his selfish thoughts, which moved him to sell his Master.
Pray read it soberly, *Psal*. 109. 6, 7, 8, &c.*

264. [331.] I had also another consideration, and that was, The
dread of the torments of Hell, which I was sure they must partake
of, that for fear of the Cross do shrink from their profession of
Christ, his Word and Laws, before the sons of men: and of the glory
that he had prepared for those that in faith, and love, and patience
stood to his ways before them. These things, I say, have helped me,
when the thoughts of the misery that both my self and mine might,
for the sake of my profession, be exposed to, hath lain pinching on
my mind.

265. [332.] When I have indeed conceited that I might be banished
for my Profession, then I have thought of that Scripture, *They were
stoned, they were sawn asunder, were tempted, were slain with the sword,
they wandered about in sheep-skins and goat-skins, being destitute,
afflicted, tormented, of whom the world was not worthy*, [Heb. 11. 37,

38,] for all they thought they were too bad to dwell and abide amongst them. I have also thought of that saying, *The Holy Ghost witnesseth in every city, that bonds and afflictions abide me*;* I have verily thought that my Soul and it have sometimes reasoned about the sore and sad estate of a banished and exiled condition, how they are exposed to hunger, to cold, to perils, to nakedness, to enemies, and a thousand calamities; and at last it may be to die in a ditch like a poor forlorn and desolate sheep. But I thank God hitherto I have not been moved by these most delicate reasonings, but have rather by them more approved my heart to God.

266. [333.] I will tell you a pretty business: I was once above all the rest in a very sad and low condition for many weeks, at which time also I being but a young Prisoner, and not acquainted with the Laws, had this lay much upon my spirit, That my imprisonment might end at the Gallows for ought that I could tell;* now therefore Satan laid hard at me to beat me out of heart, by suggesting thus unto me: But how if when you come indeed to die, you should be in this condition; that is, as not to savour the things of God, not to have any evidence upon your soul for a better state hereafter (for indeed at that time all the things of God were hid from my soul).

267. [334.] Wherefore when I at first began to think of this, it was a great trouble to me: for I thought with my self, that in the condition I now was in, I was not fit to die, neither indeed did think I could if I should be called to it: besides, I thought with my self, if I should make a scrabling shift to clamber up the Ladder, yet I should either with quaking or other symptoms of faintings, give occasion to the enemy to reproach the way of God and his People, for their timerousness: this therefore lay with great trouble upon me, for methought I was ashamed to die with a pale face, and tottering knees, for such a Cause as this.

268. [335.] Wherefore I prayed to God that he would comfort me, and give me strength to do and suffer what he should call me to; yet no comfort appear'd, but all continued hid: I was also at this time so possessed with the thought of death, that oft I was as if I was on the Ladder, with the Rope about my neck; onely this was some encouragement to me, I thought I might have now an opportunity to speak my last words to a multitude which I thought would come to see me die; and, thought I, if it must be so, if God will but convert one Soul

by my very last words, I shall not count my life thrown away, nor lost.

269. [336.] But yet all the things of God were kept out of my sight, and still the tempter followed me with, *But whither must you go when you die? what will become of you? where will you be found in another world? what evidence have you for heaven and glory, and an inheritance among them that are sanctified?* Thus was I tossed for manie weeks, and knew not what to do; at last this consideration fell with weight upon me, That it was for the Word and Way of God that I was in this condition, wherefore I was ingaged not to flinch a hairs bredth from it.

270. [337.] I thought also, that God might chuse whether he would give me comfort now, or at the hour of death; but I might not therefore chuse whether I would hold my profession or no: I was bound, but he was free: yea, twas my dutie to stand to his Word, whether he would ever look upon me or no, or save me at the last: Wherefore, thought I, the point being thus, I am for going on, and venturing my eternal state with Christ, whether I have comfort here or no; if God doth not come in, thought I, I will leap off the Ladder even blindfold into Eternitie, sink or swim, come heaven, come hell;* Lord Jesus, if thou wilt catch me, do; I will venture for thy Name.

271. [338.] I was no sooner fixed upon this resolution, but that Word dropt upon me, *Doth Job serve God for nought?* as if the accuser had said, Lord, *Job* is no upright man, he serves thee for by-respects, hast thou not made a hedge about him, &c. But put forth now thy hand, and touch all that he hath, and he will curse thee to thy face:* How now? thought I, is this the sign of an upright Soul, to desire to serve God when all is taken from him? is he a godlie man that will serve God for nothing rather then give out? blessed be God, then I hope I have an upright heart, for I am resolved (God give me strength) never to denie my profession, though I have nothing at all for my pains; and as I was thus considering, that Scripture was set before me, Psa. 44. 12. &c.*

272. [339.] Now was my heart full of comfort, for I hoped it was sincere; I would not have been without this trial for much, I am comforted everie time I think of it, and I hope shall bless God for ever for the teaching I have had by it. Many more of the Dealings of God

towards me I might relate, but these out of the spoils won in Battel have I dedicated to maintain the House of God, 1 Chron. 26. 27.

The CONCLUSION

1. Of all the Temptations that ever I met with in my life, to question the being of God and truth of the Gospel, is the worst, and worst to be born; when this temptation comes, it takes away my girdle from me, and removeth the foundation from under me: O I have often thought of that word, *Have your loyns girt about with truth*; [Eph. 6: 14.] and of that, *When the foundations are destroyed what can the Righteous do?**

[2.] [Sometimes, when after sin committed, I have looked for sore chastizement from the hand of God, the very next that I have had from him hath been the discovery of his Grace. Sometimes, when I have been comforted, I have called my self a fool for my so sinking under trouble. And then again when I have been cast down, I thought I was not wise to give such way to comfort. With such strength and weight have both these been upon me.*]

2. [3.] I have wondered much at this one thing, that though God doth visit my Soul with never so blessed a discoverie of himself, yet I have found again, that such hours have attended me afterwards, that I have been in my spirit so filled with darkness, that I could not so much as once conceive what that God and that comfort was with which I have been refreshed.

3. [4.] I have sometimes seen more in a line of the Bible then I could well tell how to stand under, & yet at another time the whole Bible hath been to me as drie as a stick, or rather my heart hath been so dead and drie unto it, that I could not conceive the least dram of refreshment, though I have lookt it over.

4. [5.] Of all tears, they are the best that are made by the Blood of Christ; and of all joy, that is the sweetest that is mixt with mourning over Christ: O tis a goodly thing to be on our knees with Christ in our arms, before God: I hope I know something of these things.

5. [6.] I find to this day seven abominations in my heart: 1. Inclinings to unbelief, 2. Suddenlie to forget the love and mercie that Christ manifesteth, 3. A leaning to the Works of the Law, 4. Wandrings and coldness in prayer, 5. To forget to watch for that I

pray for, 6. apt to murmur because I have no more, and yet readie to abuse what I have, 7. I can do none of those things which God commands me, but my corruptions will thrust in themselves; When I would do good, evil is present with me.*

6. [7.] These things I continuallie see and feel, and am afflicted and oppressed with; yet the Wisdom of God doth order them for my good: 1. They make me abhor myself; 2. They keep me from trusting my heart: 3. They convince me of the insufficiencie of all inherent righteousness; 4. They shew me the necessity of fleeing to Jesus; 5. They press me to pray unto God; 6. They shew me the need I have to watch and be sober; 7. And provoke me to look to God thorow Christ to help me, and carry me thorow this world. *Amen.*

FINIS

A RELATION OF THE IMPRISONMENT OF MR. JOHN BUNYAN

A
RELATION
OF THE
IMPRISONMENT
OF
Mr. JOHN BUNYAN,
Minister of the Gospel at BEDFORD,
In November, 1660

His Examination before the Justices, his Conference with the Clerk of the Peace, what passed between the Judges and his Wife, when she presented a Petition for his Deliverance, &c.

Written by himself, and never before published.

Blessed are ye which are persecuted for righteousness sake, for theirs is the kingdom of Heaven.

Blessed are ye when men shall revile you and persecute you, and shall say all manner of evil against you falsly for my name's sake.

Rejoice and be exceeding glad, for great is your reward in Heaven, for so persecuted they the Prophets which were before you. MAT. V. 10, 11, 12.

LONDON:
Printed for JAMES BUCKLAND, at the Buck,
in Paternoster-Row.

MDCCLXV.

The Relation of my Imprisonment in the month of November, 1660, when, by the good hand of my God, I had for five or six years together, without any great interruption, freely preached the blessed Gospel of our Lord Jesus Christ; and had also, through his blessed Grace, some encouragement by his blessing thereupon: The Devil, that old enemy of mans salvation, took his opportunity to inflame the hearts of his vassall against me, insomuch that at the last, I was laid out for by the warrant of a

*justice, and was taken and committed to prison. The relation thereof is as
followeth:*

Upon the 12th of this instant November, 1660, I was desired by some
of the friends in the country to come to teach at *Samsell* by
Harlington, in *Bedfordshire*. To whom I made a promise, if the Lord
permitted, to be with them on the time aforesaid. The justice hearing
thereof, (whose name is Mr. *Francis Wingate*) forthwith issued out
his warrant to take me, and bring me before him, and in the mean
time to keep a very strong watch about the house where the meeting
should be kept, as if we that was to meet together in that place
did intend to do some fearful business, to the destruction of the
country;* when alas, the constable, when he came in, found us only
with our Bibles in our hands, ready to speak and hear the word of
God; for we was just about to begin our exercise. Nay, we had begun
in prayer for the blessing of God upon our opportunity, intending to
have preached the Word of the Lord unto them there present: But
the constable coming in prevented us. So that I was taken and forced
to depart the room. But had I been minded to have played the
coward, I could have escaped, and kept out of his hands. For when
I was come to my friend's house, there was whispering that that day
I should be taken, for there was a warrant out to take me; which when
my friend heard, he being somewhat timorous, questioned whether
we had best have our meeting or not: And whether it might not be
better for me to depart, lest they should take me and have me before
the Justice, and after that send me to prison, (for he knew better than
I what spirit they were of, living by them) to whom I said, no: By no
means, I will not stir, neither will I have the meeting dismissed for
this. Come, be of good chear, let us not be daunted, our cause is good,
we need not be ashamed of it, to preach Gods word, it is so good a
work, that we shall be well rewarded, if we suffer for that; or to this
purpose—(But as for my friend, I think he was more afraid of me,*
than of himself.) After this I walked into the close,* where I somewhat seriously considering the matter, this came into my mind: That
I had shewed myself hearty and couragious in my preaching, and
had, blessed be Grace, made it my business to encourage others;
therefore thought I, if I should now run, and make an escape, it will
be of a very ill savour in the country. For what will my weak and
newly converted brethren think of it? But that I was not so strong in

deed, as I was in word. Also I feared that if I should run now there was a warrant out for me, I might by so doing make them afraid to stand, when great words only should be spoken to them. Besides I thought, that seeing God of his mercy should chuse me to go upon the forlorn hope* in this country;* that is, to be the first, that should be opposed, for the Gospel; if I should fly, it might be a discouragement to the whole body that might follow after. And further, I thought the world thereby would take occasion at my cowardliness, to have blasphemed the Gospel, and to have had some ground to suspect worse of me and my profession, than I deserved. These things, with others, considered by me, I came in again to the house, with a full resolution to keep the meeting, and not to go away, though I could have been gone about an hour before the officer apprehended me; but I would not; for I was resolved to see the utmost of what they could say or do unto me: For blessed be the Lord, I knew of no evil that I had said or done. And so, as aforesaid, I begun the meeting: But being prevented by the constable's coming in with his warrant to take me, I could not proceed: But before I went away, I spake some few words of counsel and encouragement to the people, declaring to them, that they see we was prevented of our opportunity to speak and hear the word of God, and was like to suffer for the same: desiring them that they should not be discouraged: For it was a mercy to suffer upon so good account: For we might have been apprehended as thieves or murderers, or for other wickedness; but blessed be God it was not so, but we suffer as christians for well doing: And we had better be the persecuted, than the persecutors, &c. But the constable and the justice's man waiting on us, would not be at quiet till they had me away, and that we departed the house: But because the justice was not at home that day, there was a friend of mine engaged for me to bring me to the constable on the morrow morning. Otherwise the constable must have charged a watch with me, or have secured me some other ways, my crime was so great. So on the next morning we went to the constable, and so to the justice.* He asked the constable what we did, where we was met together, and what we had with us. I trow, he meant whether we had armour or not;* but when the constable told him that there was only met a few of us together to preach and hear the word, and no sign of any thing else, he could not well tell what to say: Yet because he had sent for me, he did adventure to put out a few proposals to me, which was to this effect. Namely, What

I did there? and why I did not content myself with following my calling: For it was against the law, that such as I should be admitted to do as I did.

John Bunyan. To which I answered, that the intent of my coming thither, and to other places, was to instruct, and counsel people to forsake their sins, and close in with Christ, lest they did miserably perish; and that I could do both these without confusion, (to wit) follow my calling, and preach the word also.*

At which words, he* was in a chafe, as it appeared; for he said that he would break the neck of our meetings.

Bun. I said, it may be so. Then he wished me to get me sureties to be bound for me, or else he would send me to the jail.

My sureties being ready, I call'd them in, and when the bond for my appearance was made, he told them, that they was bound to keep me from preaching; and that if I did preach, their bonds would be forfeited. To which I answered, that then I should break them; for I should not leave speaking the word of God: Even to counsel, comfort, exhort, and teach the people among whom I came; and I thought this to be a work that had no hurt in it: But was rather worthy of commendation, than blame.

Wing. Whereat he told me, that if they would not be so bound, my mittimus* must be made, and I sent to the jail, there to lie to the quarter-sessions.

Now while my mittimus was a making, the justice was withdrawn; and in comes an old enemy to the truth, Dr. *Lindale*,* who, when he was come in, fell to taunting at me with many reviling terms.

Bun. To whom I answered, that I did not come thither to talk with him, but with the justice. Whereat he supposing that I had nothing to say for myself, triumphed as if he had got the victory. Charging and condemning me for medling with that for which I could shew no warrant.* And asked me if I had taken the oaths?* and if I had not, 'twas pity but that I should be sent to prison, &c.

I told him, that if I was minded, I could answer to any sober question that he should put to me. He then urged me again, how I could prove it lawful for me to preach, with a great deal of confidence of the victory.

But at last, because he should see that I could answer him if I listed, I cited to him that in Peter, which saith, *As every man hath received the gift, even so let him minister the same, &c.**

Lind. I,* saith he, to whom is that spoken?

Bun. To whom, said I, why to every man that hath received a gift from God. Mark, saith the Apostle, *As every man that hath received a gift from God, &c.* And again, *You may all prophesy one by one.** Whereat the man was a little stopt, and went a softlier pace: But not being willing to lose the day, he began again, and said:

Lind. Indeed I do remember that I have read of one Alexander a Coppersmith,* who did much oppose, and disturb the Apostles. (Aiming 'tis like at me, because I was a Tinker.)

Bun. To which I answered, that I also had read of very many priests and pharisees, that had their hands in the blood of our Lord Jesus Christ.

Lind. I, saith he, and you are one of those scribes and pharisees, for you, with a pretence, make long prayers to devour widows houses.*

Bun. I answered, that if he had got no more by preaching and praying than I had done, he would not be so rich as now he was. But that Scripture coming into my mind, *Answer not a fool according to his folly,** I was as sparing of my speech as I could, without preju-dice to truth. Now by this time my mittimus was made, and I com-mitted to the constable to be sent to the jail in Bedford, &c. But as I was going, two of my brethren met with me by the way, and desired the constable to stay, supposing that they should prevail with the justice, through the favour of a pretended friend, to let me go at liberty. So we did stay, while they went to the justice, and after much discourse with him, it came to this; that if I would come to him again, and say some certain words to him, I should be released. Which when they told me, I said if the words was such that might be said with a good conscience, I should, or else I should not. So through their importunity I went back again, but not believing that I should be delivered: For I feared their spirit was too full of opposition to the truth, to let me go, unless I should in something or other, dishonour my God, and wound my conscience. Wherefore as I went, I lift up my heart to God, for light, and strength, to be kept, that I might not do any thing that might either dishonour him, or wrong my own soul, or be a grief or discouragement to any that was inclining after the Lord Jesus Christ.

Well, when I came to the justice again, there was Mr. *Foster** of Bedford, who coming out of another room, and seeing of me by the light of the candle (for it was dark night when I went thither) he said unto me, who is there, *John Bunyan?** with such seeming affection, as if he would have leaped in my neck and kissed me, which made me somewhat wonder, that such a man as he, with whom I had so little acquaintance, and besides, that had ever been a close opposer of the ways of God, should carry himself so full of love to me: But afterwards, when I saw what he did, it caused me to remember those sayings, *Their tongues are smoother than oil, but their words are drawn swords.* And again, *Beware of men, &c.** When I* had answered him, that blessed be God I was well, he said, What is the occasion of your being here? or to that purpose. To whom I answered, that I was at a meeting of people a little way off, intending to speak a word of exhortation to them; the justice hearing thereof (said I) was pleased to send his warrant, to fetch me before him, &c.

Fost. So (said he) I understand: But well, if you will promise to call the people no more together, you shall have your liberty to go home: for my brother* is very loath to send you to prison, if you will be but ruled.

Bun. Sir (said I) pray what do you mean by calling the people together? my business is not any thing among them when they are come together, but to exhort them to look after the salvation of their souls, that they may be saved, &c.

Fost. Saith he, we must not enter into explication, or dispute now; but if you will say you will call the people no more together, you may have your liberty; if not, you must be sent away to prison.

Bun. Sir, said I, I shall not force or compel any man to hear me, but yet if I come into any place where there is a people met together, I should, according to the best of my skill and wisdom, exhort and counsel them to seek out after the Lord Jesus Christ, for the salvation of their souls.

Fost. He said, that was none of my work; I must follow my calling, and if I would but leave off preaching, and follow my calling, I should have the justice's favour, and be acquitted presently.

Bun. To whom I said, that I could follow my calling and that too, namely, preaching the word: And I did look upon it as my duty to do them both, as I had an opportunity.

Fost. He said, to have any such meetings was against the law; and therefore he would have me leave off, and say, I would call the people no more together.

Bun. To whom I said, that I durst not make any further promise: For my conscience would not suffer me to do it. And again, I did look upon it as my duty to do as much good as I could, not only in my trade, but also in communicating to all people wheresoever I came, the best knowledge I had in the word.

Fost. He told me, that I was the nearest the Papists of any, and that he would convince me of immediately.

Bun. I asked him wherein?

Fost. He said, in that we understood the Scriptures literally.

Bun. I told him, that those that was to be understood literally we understood them so; but for those that was to be understood otherwise, we endeavoured so to understand them.

Fost. He said, which of the Scriptures do you understand literally?

Bun. I said, this, *He that believes shall be saved.** This was to be understood, just as it is spoken; that whosoever believeth in Christ, shall, according to the plain and simple words of the text, be saved.

Fost. He said, that I was ignorant, and did not understand Scriptures; for how (said he) can you understand them, when you know not the original Greek? &c.

Bun. To whom I said, that if that was his opinion, that none could understand the Scriptures, but those that had the original Greek, &c. then but a very few of the poorest sort should be saved, (this is harsh) yet the Scripture saith, *That God hides his things from the wise and prudent*, (that is from the learned of the world) *and reveals them to babes and sucklings.**

Fost. He said there was none that heard me, but a company of foolish people.

Bun. I told him that there was the wise as well as the foolish do hear me; and again, those that are most commonly counted foolish by the world, are the wisest before God. Also that God had rejected the wise, and mighty and noble, and chosen the foolish, and the base.*

Fost. He told me, that I made people neglect their calling; that God had commanded people to work six days, and serve him on the seventh.

Bun. I told him, that it was the duty of people, (both rich and poor) to look out for their souls on them days, as well as for their bodies: And that God would have his people exhort one another daily, while it is called to day.*

Fost. He said again, that there was none but a company of poor simple ignorant people that come to hear me.

Bun. I told him, that the foolish and the ignorant had most need of teaching and information; and therefore it would be profitable for me to go on in that work.

Fost. Well, said he, to conclude, but will you promise that you will not call the people together any more? and then you may be released, and go home.

Bun. I told him, that I durst say no more than I had said. For I durst not leave off that work which God had called me to.

So he withdrew from me, and then came several of the justices servants to me, and told me, that I stood so much upon a nicity. Their* master, they said, was willing to let me go; and if I would but say I would call the people no more together, I might have my liberty, &c.

Bun. I told them, there was more ways than one, in which a man might be said to call the people together. As for instance, if a man get upon the market-place, and there read a book, or the like, though he do not say to the people, Sirs, come hither and hear; yet if they come to him because he reads, he, by his very reading, may be said to call them together; because they would not have been there to hear, if he had not been there to read. And seeing this might be termed a calling the people together, I durst not say, I would not call them together; for then, by the same argument, my preaching might be said to call them together.

Wing. and Fost. Then came the Justice and Mr. Foster to me again (we had a little more discourse about preaching, but because the method of it is out of my mind, I pass it) and when they saw that I was at a point,* and would not be moved nor perswaded,

Mr. Foster* told the justice, that then he must send me away to prison. And that he would do well also, if he would present all them that was the cause of my coming among them to meetings. Thus we parted.

And verily as I was going forth of the doors, I had much ado to forbear saying to them, that I carried the peace of God along with me: But I held my peace, and blessed be the Lord, went away to prison with God's comfort in my poor soul.

After I had lain in the jail five or six days, the brethren sought means again to get me out by bondsmen, (for so run my mittimus, that I should lie there till I could find sureties). They went to a justice at Elstow, one Mr. Crumpton,* to desire him to take bond for my appearing at the quarter-sessions. At the first he told them he would, but afterwards he made a demur at the business, and desired first to see my mittimus, which run to this purpose; That I went about to several conventicles in this county, to the great disparagement of the government of the church of England, &c. When he had seen it, he said that there might be something more against me, than was expressed in my mittimus: And that he was but a young man, therefore he durst not do it. This my jailor told me. Whereat I was not at all daunted, but rather glad, and saw evidently that the Lord had heard me, for before I went down to the justice, I begged of God, that if I might do more good by being at liberty than in prison, that then I might be set at liberty: But if not, his will be done; for I was not altogether without hopes, but that my imprisonment might be an awakening to the Saints in the country, therefore I could not tell well which to chuse. Only I in that manner did commit the thing to God. And verily at my return, I did meet my God sweetly in the prison again, comforting of me and satisfying of me that it was his will and mind that I should be there.

When I came back again to prison, as I was musing at the slender answer of the Justice, this word dropt in upon my heart with some life, *For he knew that for envy they had delivered him.**

Thus have I in short, declared the manner, and occasion of my being in prison; where I lie waiting the good will of God, to do with me, as he pleaseth; knowing that not one hair of my head can fall to the ground without the will of my Father* which is in Heaven. Let the rage and malice of men be never so great, they can do no more, nor go no farther than God permits them: But when they have done their worst, we know all things shall work together for good to them that love God.*

Farewell.

Here is the Sum of my Examination, before Justice Keelin, Justice Chester, Justice Blundale, Justice Beecher, and Justice Snagg, &c.*

After I had lain in prison above seven weeks, the quarter-sessions was to be kept in Bedford, for the county thereof; unto which I was to be brought; and when my jailor had set me before those Justices, there was a bill of indictment preferred against me. The extent thereof was as followeth: That John Bunyan of the town of Bedford, labourer, being a person of such and such conditions, he hath (since such a time) devilishly and perniciously abstained from coming to church to hear divine service, and is a common upholder of several unlawful meetings and conventicles, to the great disturbance and distraction of the good subjects of this kingdom, contrary to the laws of our sovereign lord the king, &c.

The Clerk. When this was read, the clerk of the sessions said unto me; What say you to this?

Bun. I said, that as to the first part of it, I was a common frequenter of the church of God. And was also, by grace, a member with them people, over whom Christ is the Head.

Keelin. But saith Justice *Keelin* (who was the judge in that court) Do you come to church (you know what I mean) to the parish church, to hear divine service?

Bun. I answered, no, I did not.

Keel. He asked me, why?

Bun. I said, because I did not find it commanded in the word of God.

Keel. He said, we were commanded to pray.

Bun. I said, but not by the Common Prayer-book.*

Keel. He said, how then?

Bun. I said with the spirit. As the Apostle saith, *I will pray with the spirit and with understanding*. 1 Cor. xiv. 15.

Keel. He said, we might pray with the spirit, and with understanding, and with the Common Prayer-book also.

Bun. I said that those prayers in the Common Prayerbook, was such as was made by other men, and not by the motions of the Holy Ghost, within our Hearts; and as I said the Apostle saith, he will pray with the spirit and with understanding; not with the spirit and the Common Prayerbook.

Another Justice. What do you count prayer? Do you think it is to say a few words over before, or among a people?

Bun. I said, no, not so; for men might have many elegant, or excellent words, and yet not pray at all: But when a man prayeth, he doth through a sense of those things which he wants (which sense is begotten by the spirit) pour out his heart before God through Christ; though his words be not so many, and so excellent as others are.

Justices. They said, that was true.

Bun. I said, this might be done without the Common Prayer-book.

Another. One of them said, (I think it was Justice *Blundale*, or Justice *Snagg*) How should we know, that you do not write out your prayers first, and then read them afterwards to the people? This he spake in a laughing way.

Bun. I said, it is not our use, to take a pen and paper and write a few words thereon, and then go and read it over to a company of people.

But how should we know it, said he?

Bun. Sir, it is none of our custom, said I.

Keel. But said Justice Keelin, it is lawful to use Common Prayer, and such like forms: For Christ taught his disciples to pray, as John also taught his disciples. And further, said he, cannot one man teach another to pray? Faith comes by hearing:* And one man may convince another of sin, and therefore prayers made by men, and, read over, are good to teach, and help men to pray. While he was speaking these words, God brought that word into my mind, in the eighth of the Romans, at the 26th verse: I say God brought it, for I thought not on it before: but as he was speaking, it came so fresh into my mind, and was set so evidently before me, as if the Scripture had said, Take me, take me; so when he had done speaking,

Bun. I said, Sir, the Scripture saith, that *it is the spirit as helpeth our infirmities*; for we know not what we should pray for as we ought: But the spirit itself maketh intercession for us, with sighs and groanings which cannot be uttered. Mark, said I, it doth not say the Common Prayer-book teacheth us how to pray, but the spirit. And it is the spirit that helpeth our infirmities, saith the Apostle; he doth not say it is the Common Prayer-book.

And as to the Lord's Prayer, although it be an easy thing to say; *Our Father, &c.* with the mouth; yet there is very few that can, in the spirit, say the two first words of that Prayer; that is, that can call God their Father, as knowing what it is to be born again, and as having experience, that they are begotten of the spirit of God: Which if they do not, all is but babbling, &c.

Keel. Justice *Keelin* said, that that was a truth.

Bun. And I say further, as to your saying that one man may convince another of sin, and that faith comes by hearing, and that one man may tell another how he should pray, &c. I say men may tell each other of their sins, but it is the spirit that must convince them.*

And though it be said that *faith comes by hearing*: Yet it is the spirit that worketh faith in the heart through hearing, or else* *they are not profited by hearing*.

And that though one Man may tell another how he should pray: Yet, as I said before, he cannot pray, nor make his condition known to God, except the spirit help. It is not the Common Prayer-book that can do this. It is the* *spirit that sheweth us our sins*, and the* *spirit that sheweth us a Saviour*: And the spirit that stireth up in our hearts desires to come to God, for such things as we stand in need of, even sighing out our souls unto him for them with *groans which cannot be uttered*. With other words to the same purpose. At this they were set.*

Keel. But says Justice *Keelin*, what have you against the Common Prayer-book?

Bun. I said, Sir, if you will hear me, I shall lay down my reasons against it.

Keel. He said I should have liberty; but first, said he, let me give you one caution; take heed of speaking irreverently of the Common Prayer-book: For if you do so, you will bring great damage upon yourself.

Bun. So I proceeded, and said, my first reason was; because it was not commanded in the word of God, and therefore I could not do it.

Another. One of them said, where do you find it commanded in the Scripture, that you should go to *Elstow*, or *Bedford*, and yet it is lawful to go to either of them, is it not?

Bun. I said, to go to *Elstow* or *Bedford*, was a civil thing, and not material, though not commanded, and yet God's word allowed me to go about my calling, and therefore if it lay there, then to go thither, &c. But to pray, was a great part of the divine worship of God, and therefore it ought to be done according to the rule of God's word.

Another. One of them said, he will do harm; let him speak no further.

Just. Keel. Justice *Keelin* said, No, no, never fear him, we are better established than so; he can do no harm, we know the Common Prayer-book hath been ever since the Apostles time, and is lawful to be used in the church.

Bun. I said, shew me the place in the epistles, where the Common

Prayer-book is written, or one text of Scripture, that commands me to read it, and I will use it. But yet, notwithstanding, said I, they that have a mind to use it, they have their liberty; that is,* I would not keep them from it, but for our parts, we can pray to God without it. Blessed be his name.

With that one of them said, who is your God? Beelzebub? Moreover, they often said, that I was possessed with the spirit of delusion and of the Devil.* All which sayings, I passed over, the Lord forgive them! And further, I said, blessed be the Lord for it, we are encouraged to meet together, and to pray, and exhort one another; for we have had the comfortable presence of God among us, for ever blessed be his holy name.

Keel. Justice *Keeling* called this pedlers French,* saying that I must leave off my canting. The Lord open his eyes!

Bun. I said, that we ought to exhort one another daily, while it is called to-day,* &c.

Keel. Justice *Keeling* said, that I ought not to preach. And asked me where I had my authority?* with many other such like words.

Bun. I said, that I would prove that it was lawful for me, and such as I am, to preach the word of God.

Keel. He said unto me, by what Scripture?

I said, by that in the first epistle of *Peter*, the ivth chap., the 11th ver. and *Acts* the xviiith, with other Scriptures, which he would not suffer me to mention. But said, hold; not so many, which is the first?

Bun. I said, this. *As every man hath received the gift, even so let him minister the same unto another, as good stewards of the manifold grace of God: If any man speak, let him speak as the oracles of God, &c.*

Keel. He said, let me a little open that Scripture to you. *As every man hath received the gift*; that is, said he, as every man hath received a trade, so let him follow it. If any man have received a gift of tinkering, as thou hast done, let him follow his tinkering. And so other men their trades. And the divine his calling, &c.

Bun. Nay, Sir, said I, but it is most clear, that the Apostle speaks here of preaching the word; if you do but compare both the verses together, the next verse explains this gift what it is; saying, *If any man speak, let him speak as the oracles of God*: So that it is plain, that the Holy Ghost doth not so much in this place exhort to civil callings, as to the exercising of those gifts that we have received from God. I would have gone on, but he would not give me leave.

Keel. He said, we might do it in our families but not otherways.

Bun. I said, if it was lawful to do good to some, it was lawful to do good to more. If it was a good duty to exhort our families, it is good to exhort others: But if they held it a sin to meet together to seek the face of God, and exhort one another to follow Christ, I should sin still; For so we should do.

Keel. He said he was not so well versed in Scripture as to dispute, or words to that purpose. And said, moreover, that they could not wait upon me any longer; but said to me, then you confess the indictment, do you not? Now, and not till now, I saw I was indicted.

Bun. I said, this I confess, we have had many meetings together, both to pray to God, and to exhort one another, and that we had the sweet comforting presence of the Lord among us for our encouragement, blessed be his name therefore. I confessed myself guilty no otherwise.

Keel. Then said he, hear your judgment. You must be had back again to prison, and there lie for three months following; at three months end, if you do not submit to go to church to hear divine service, and leave your preaching, you must be banished the realm: And if, after such a day as shall be appointed you to be gone, you shall be found in this realm, &c. or be found to come over again without special licence from the King, &c. you must stretch by the neck for it, I tell you plainly; and so he bid my jailor have me away.

Bun. I told him, as to this matter, I was at a point* with him: For if I was out of prison to day, I would preach the Gospel again tomorrow, by the help of God.

Another. To which one made me some answer: But my jailor pulling me away to be gone, I could not tell what he said.* Thus I departed from them; and I can truly say, I bless the Lord *Jesus Christ* for it, that my heart was sweetly refreshed in the time of my examination, and also afterwards, at my returning to the prison: So that I found *Christ's* words more than bare trifles, where he saith, he *will give a mouth and wisdom, even such as all the adversaries shall not resist, or gainsay.** And that his peace no man can take from us.

Thus have I given you the substance of my examination. The Lord make these profitable to all that shall read or hear them.

Farewell.

The Substance of some Discourse had between the Clerk of the Peace and myself; when he came to admonish me, according to the tenor of that Law by which I was in Prison.

When I had lain in prison other twelve weeks, and now not knowing what they intended to do with me, upon the third of *April*, comes Mr. *Cobb** unto me, (as he told me) being sent by the Justices to admonish me, and demand of me submittance to the church of *England*, &c. The extent of our discourse was as followeth.

Cobb. When he was come into the house he sent for me out of my chamber; who, when I was come unto him, he said, Neighbour *Bunyan*, how do you do?

Bun. I thank you Sir, said I, very well, blessed be the Lord.

Cobb. Saith he, I come to tell you, that it is desired, you would submit yourself to the laws of the land, or else at the next sessions it will go worse with you, even to be sent away out of the nation, or else worse than that.*

Bun. I said, that I did desire to demean myself in the world, both as becometh a man and a christian.

Cobb. But, saith he, you must submit to the laws of the land, and leave off those meetings which you was wont to have: For the statute law is directly against it; and I am sent to you by the Justices to tell you that they do intend to prosecute the law against you, if you submit not.

Bun. I said, Sir, I conceive that that law by which I am in prison at this time, doth not reach or condemn, either me, or the meetings which I do frequent: That law was made against those, that being designed to do evil in their meetings, make the exercise of religion their pretence to cover their wickedness. It doth not forbid the private meetings of those that plainly and simply make it their only end to worship the Lord, and to exhort one another to edification. My end in meeting with others is simply to do as much good as I can, by exhortation and counsel, according to that small measure of light which God hath given me, and not to disturb the peace of the nation.

Cobb. Every one will say the same, said he; you see the late insurrection at *London*,* under what glorious pretences they went, and yet indeed they intended no less than the ruin of the kingdom and commonwealth.

Bun. That practice of theirs, I abhor, said I; yet it doth not follow, that because they did so, therefore all others will do so. I look upon it as my duty to behave myself under the King's government, both as becomes a man and a christian; and if an occasion was offered me, I should willingly manifest my loyalty to my Prince, both by word and deed.*

Cobb. Well, said he, I do not profess myself to be a man that can dispute; but this I say truly, neighbour *Bunyan*, I would have you consider this matter seriously, and submit yourself; you may have your liberty to exhort your neighbour in private discourse, so be you do not call together an assembly of people; and truly you may do much good to the church of Christ, if you would go this way; and this you may do, and the law not abridge you of it. It is your private meetings that the law is against.

Bun. Sir, said I, if I may do good to one by my discourse, why may I not do good to two? And if to two, why not to four, and so to eight, &c.

Cobb. I, saith he, and to a hundred, I warrant you.

Bun. Yes, Sir, said I, I think I should not be forbid to do as much good as I can.

Cobb. But, saith he, you may but pretend to do good, and indeed, notwithstanding, do harm, by seducing the people; you are therefore denied your meeting so many together, lest you should do harm.

Bun. And yet, said I, you say the law tolerates me to discourse with my neighbour; surely there is no law tolerates me to seduce any one; therefore if I may by the law discourse with one, surely it is to do him good; and if I by discoursing may do good to one, surely, by the same law, I may do good to many.

Cobb. The law, saith he, doth expresly forbid your private meetings, therefore they are not to be tolerated.

Bun. I told him, that I would not entertain so much uncharitableness of that parliament in the 35th of *Elizabeth*, or of the Queen herself, as to think they did by that law intend the oppressing of any of God's ordinances, or the interrupting any in the way of God; but men may, in the wresting of it, turn it against the way of God, but take the law in itself, and it only fighteth against those that drive at mischief in their hearts and meetings, making religion only their cloak, colour, or pretence; for so are the words of the statute. *If any meetings, under colour or pretence of religion, &c.*

Cobb. Very good; therefore the King seeing that pretences are usual in, and among people, as to make religion their pretence only; therefore he, and the law before him, doth forbid such private meetings, and tolerates only public; you may meet in public.

Bun. Sir, said I, let me answer you in a similitude; set the case that, at such a wood corner, there did usually come forth thieves to do mischief, must there therefore a law be made, that every one that cometh out there shall be killed? May not there come out true men as well as thieves, out from thence? Just thus is it in this case; I do think there may be many, that may design the destruction of the commonwealth: But it doth not follow therefore that all private meetings are unlawful; those that transgress, let them be punished: And if at any time I myself, should do any act in my conversation as doth not become a man and christian, let me bear the punishment. And as for your saying I may meet in public, if I may be suffered, I would gladly do it: Let me have but meetings enough in public, and I shall care the less to have them in private. I do not meet in private because I am afraid to have meetings in public. I bless the Lord that my heart is at that point, that if any man can lay any thing to my charge, either in doctrine or practice, in this particular, that can be proved error or heresy, I am willing to disown it, even in the very market-place. But if it be truth, then to stand to it to the last drop of my blood. And Sir, said I, you ought to commend me for so doing. To err, and to be a heretic, are two things; I am no heretic, because I will not stand refractorily to defend any one thing that is contrary to the word; prove any thing which I hold to be an error, and I will recant it.

Cobb. But goodman *Bunyan*, said he, methinks you need not stand so strictly upon this one thing, as to have meetings of such public assemblies. Cannot you submit, and, notwithstanding do as much good as you can, in a neighbourly way, without having such meetings?

Bun. Truly Sir, said I, I do not desire to commend myself, but to think meanly of myself; yet when I do most despise myself, taking notice of that small measure of light which God hath given me, also that the people of the Lord (by their own saying) are edified thereby: Besides, when I see that the Lord, through grace, hath in some measure blessed my labour, I dare not but exercise that gift which God hath given me, for the good of the people. And I said further, that I would willingly speak in public if I might.

Cobb. He said, that I might come to the public assemblies and hear. What though you do not preach? you may hear: Do not think yourself so well enlightened, and that you have received a gift so far above others, but that you may hear other men preach. Or to that purpose.

Bun. I told him, I was as willing to be taught as to give instruction, and I looked upon it as my duty to do both; for, said I, a man that is a teacher, he himself may learn also from another that teacheth; as the Apostle saith: *We may all prophecy one by one, that all may learn.** That is, every man that hath received a gift from God, he may dispense it, that others may be comforted; and when he hath done, he may hear, and learn, and be comforted himself of others.

Cobb. But, said he, what if you should forbear awhile; and sit still, till you see further, how things will go?

Bun. Sir, said I, *Wickliffe* saith,* that he which leaveth off preaching and hearing of the word of God for fear of excommunication of men, he is already excommunicated of God, and shall in the day of judgment be counted a traitor to Christ.

Cobb. I, saith he, they that do not hear shall be so counted indeed; do you therefore hear.

Bun. But Sir, said I, he saith, he that shall leave off either preaching or hearing, &c. That is, if he hath received a gift for edification, it is his sin, if he doth not lay it out in a way of exhortation and counsel, according to the proportion of his gift; as well as to spend his time altogether in hearing others preach.

Cobb. But, said he, how shall we know that you have received a gift?

Bun. Said I, let any man hear and search, and prove the doctrine by the Bible.

Cobb. But will you be willing, said he, that two indifferent persons shall determine the case, and will you stand by their judgment.

Bun. I said, are they infallible?

Cobb. He said, no.

Bun. Then, said I, it is possible my judgment may be as good as theirs: But yet I will pass by either, and in this matter be judged by the Scriptures; I am sure that is infallible, and cannot err.

Cobb. But, said he, who shall be judge between you, for you take the Scriptures one way, and they another.

Bun. I said, the Scripture should, and that by comparing one Scripture with another; for that will open itself, if it be rightly compared. As for instance, if under the different apprehensions of the word *Mediator*, you would know the truth of it, the Scriptures open it, and tell us, that he that is a mediator, must take up the business between two, and a mediator is not a mediator of one, *but God is one, and there is one mediator between God and man, even the man Christ Jesus.** So likewise the Scripture calleth Christ a *compleat*, or perfect, or able *high-priest.** That is opened in that he is called man, and also God. His blood also is discovered to be effectually efficacious by the same things. So the Scripture, as touching the matter of meeting together, &c. doth likewise sufficiently open itself and discover its meaning.

Cobb. But are you willing, said he, to stand to the judgment of the Church?

Bun. Yes Sir, said I, to the approbation of the church of God: the church's judgment is best expressed in Scripture. We had much other discourse, which I cannot well remember, about the laws of the nation, submission to governments; to which I did tell him, that I did look upon myself as bound in conscience to walk according to all righteous laws, and that whether there was a King or no; and if I did any thing that was contrary, I did hold it my duty to bear patiently the penalty of the law, that was provided against such offenders; with many more words to the like effect. And said, moreover, that to cut off all occasions of suspicion from any, as touching the harmlessness of my doctrine in private, I would willingly take the pains to give any one the notes of all my sermons: For I do sincerely desire to live quietly in my country, and to submit to the present authority.

Cobb. Well, neighbour *Bunyan*, said he, but indeed I would wish you seriously to consider of these things, between this and the quarter-sessions, and to submit yourself. You may do much good if you continue still in the land: But alas, what benefit will it be to your friends, or what good can you do to them, if you should be sent away beyond the seas into *Spain*, or *Constantinople*, or some other remote part of the world? Pray be ruled.

Jaylor. Indeed, Sir, I hope he will be ruled.

Bun. I shall desire, said I, in all godliness and honesty to behave myself in the nation whilst I am in it. And if I must be so dealt withall, as you say, I hope God will help me to bear what they shall lay upon me. I know no evil that I have done in this matter, to be so used. I speak as in the presence of God.

Cobb. You know, saith he, that the Scripture saith, *the powers that are, are ordained of God.**

Bun. I said, yes, and that I was to submit to the King as supreme, also to the governors, as to them that are sent by him.

Cobb. Well then, said he, the King then commands you, that you should not have any private meetings; because it is against his law, and he is ordained of God, therefore you should not have any.

Bun. I told him, that *Paul* did own the powers that were in his day, as to be of God; and yet he was often in prison under them for all that. And also, though *Jesus Christ* told *Pilate*, that he had no power against him, but of God, yet he died under the same *Pilate*; and yet, said I, I hope you will not say, that either *Paul*, or Christ, was such as did deny magistracy, and so sinned against God in slighting the ordinance. Sir, said I, the law hath provided two ways of obeying: The one to do that which I in my conscience do believe that I am bound to do, actively; and where I cannot obey actively, there I am willing to lie down, and to suffer what they shall do unto me. At this he sate still and said no more; which when he had done I did thank him for his civil and meek discoursing with me; and so we parted.

O! that we might meet in Heaven!

Farewell. *J. B.*

Here followeth a Discourse between my Wife and the Judges, with others, touching my Deliverance at the Assizes following: the which I took from her own Mouth.

After that I had received this sentence of banishing, or hanging from them, and after the former admonition, touching the determination of Justices, if I did not recant; just when the time drew nigh, in which I should have abjured, or have done worse (as Mr. *Cobb* told me) came the time in which the King was to be crowned.* Now at the coronation of Kings, there is usually a releasement of divers prisoners, by virtue of his coronation; in which privilege also I should have had my share; but that they took me for a convicted person, and therefore, unless I sued out a pardon, (as they called it) I could have no benefit thereby, notwithstanding, yet forasmuch as the coronation proclamation did give liberty from the day the King was crowned, to that day twelvemonth to sue them out: Therefore, though they would not let me out of prison, as they let out thousands, yet they could not meddle with me, as touching the execution of their sentence; because of the liberty offered for the suing out of pardons. Whereupon I continued in prison till the next assizes, which are called *Midsummer* assizes, being then kept in *August*, 1661.

Now at that assizes, because I would not leave any possible means unattempted that might be lawful; I did, by my wife, present a petition to the Judges three times, that I might be heard, and that they would impartially take my case into consideration.

The first time my wife went, she presented it to Judge *Hales*,* who very mildly received it at her hand, telling her that he would do her and me the best good he could; but he feared, he said, he could do none. The next day again, least they should, through the multitude of business, forget me, we did throw another petition into the coach to Judge *Twisdon*;* who, when he had seen it, snapt her up, and angrily told her that I was a convicted person, and could not be released, unless I would promise to preach no more, &c.

Well, after this, she yet again presented another to Judge *Hales* as he sate on the bench, who, as it seemed, was willing to give her audience. Only Justice *Chester* being present, stept up and said, that I was convicted in the court, and that I was a hot spirited fellow (or words to that purpose) whereat he waved it, and did not meddle therewith. But yet, my wife being encouraged by the High Sheriff,* did venture once more into their presence (as the poor widow did to the unjust Judge*) to try what she could do with them for my liberty, before they went forth of the town. The place where she went to them, was to the *Swan Chamber*,* where the two Judges, and many Justices and Gentry of the country, was in company together. She then coming into the chamber with a bashed face, and a trembling heart, began her errand to them in this manner.

Woman. My Lord, (directing herself to Judge *Hales*) I make bold to come once again to your Lordship to know what may be done with my husband.

Judge Hales. To whom he said, Woman, I told thee before I could do thee no good; because they have taken that for a conviction which thy husband spoke at the sessions: And unless there be something done to undo that, I can do thee no good.

Woman. My Lord, said she, he is kept unlawfully in prison, they clap'd him up before there were any proclamation against the meetings;* the indictment also is false: Besides, they never asked him whether he was guilty or no; neither did he confess the indictment.

One of the Justices. Then one of the Justices that stood by, whom she knew not, said, My Lord, he was lawfully convicted.

Wom. It is false, said she; for when they said to him, do you confess the indictment? He said only this, that he had been at several meetings, both where there was preaching the word, and prayer, and that they had God's presence among them.

Judge Twisdon. Whereat Judge Twisdon answered very angrily, saying, what, you think we can do what we list; your husband is a breaker of the peace, and is convicted by the law, &c. Whereupon Judge *Hales* called for the Statute Book.

Wom. But said she, my Lord, he was not lawfully convicted.

Chester. Then Justice *Chester* said, my Lord, he was lawfully convicted.

Wom. It is false, said she; it was but a word of discourse that they took for a conviction (as you heard before.)

Chest. But it is recorded, woman, it is recorded, said Justice *Chester.* As if it must be of necessity true because it was recorded. With which words he often endeavoured to stop her mouth, having no other argument to convince her, but it is recorded, it is recorded.

Wom. My Lord, said she, I was a-while since at *London,* to see if I could get my husband's liberty, and there I spoke with my Lord *Barkwood,** one of the house of Lords, to whom I delivered a petition, who took it of me and presented it to some of the rest of the house of Lords, for my husband's releasement; who, when they had seen it, they said, that they could not release him, but had committed his releasement to the Judges, at the next assises. This he told me; and now I come to you to see if any thing may be done in this business, and you give neither releasement nor relief. To which they gave her no answer, but made as if they heard her not.

Chest. Only Justice *Chester* was often up with this, He is convicted, and it is recorded.

Wom. If it be, it is false, said she.

Chest. My Lord, said Justice *Chester*, he is a pestilent fellow, there is not such a fellow in the country again.

Twis. What, will your husband leave preaching? If he will do, then send for him.

Wom. My Lord, said she, he dares not leave preaching, as long as he can speak.

Twis. See here, what should we talk any more about such a fellow? Must he do what he lists? He is a breaker of the peace.

Wom. She told him again, that he desired to live peaceably, and to follow his calling, that his family might be maintained; and moreover said, my Lord, I have four small children, that cannot help themselves, of which one is blind, and have nothing to live upon, but the charity of good people.

Hales. Hast thou four children? said Judge *Hales*; thou art but a young woman to have four children.

Wom. My Lord, said she, I am but mother-in-law* to them, having not been married to him yet full two years. Indeed I was with child when my husband was first apprehended: But being young and unaccustomed to such things, said she, I being smayed at the news, fell into labour, and so continued for eight days, and then was delivered, but my child died.

Hales. Whereat, he looking very soberly on the matter, said, Alas poor woman!

Twis. But Judge *Twisden* told her, that she made poverty her cloak; and said, moreover, that he understood, I was maintained better by running up and down a preaching, than by following my calling.

Hales. What is his calling? said Judge *Hales*.

Answer. Then some of the company that stood by, said, A Tinker, my Lord.

Wom. Yes, said she, and because he is a Tinker, and a poor man; therefore he is despised, and cannot have justice.*

Hales. Then Judge *Hales* answered, very mildly, saying, I tell thee, woman, seeing it is so, that they have taken what thy husband spake, for a conviction; thou must either apply thyself to the King, or sue out his pardon, or get a writ of error.*

Chest. But when Justice *Chester* heard him give her this counsel; and especially (as she supposed) because he spoke of a writ of error, he chaffed, and seemed to be very much offended; saying, my Lord, he will preach and do what he lists.

Wom. He preacheth nothing but the word of God, said she.

Twis. He preach the word of God! said *Twisdon* (and withal, she thought he would have struck her) he runneth up and down, and doth harm.

Wom. No, my Lord, said she, it's not so, God hath owned him, and done much good by him.

Twis. God! said he, his doctrine is the doctrine of the Devil.

Wom. My Lord, said she, when the righteous judge shall appear, it will be known, that his doctrine is not the doctrine of the Devil.

Twis. *My* Lord, said he, to Judge *Hales*, do not mind her, but send her away.

Hales. Then said Judge *Hales*, I am sorry, woman, that I can do thee no good; thou must do one of those three things aforesaid, namely; either to apply thyself to the King, or sue out his pardon or get a writ of error; but a writ of error will be cheapest.

Wom. At which *Chester* again seemed to be in a chaffe, and put off his hat, and as she thought, scratched his head for anger: But when I saw, said she, that there was no prevailing to have my husband sent for, though I often desired them that they would send for him, that he might speak for himself, telling them, that he could give them better satisfaction than I could, in what they demanded of him; with several other things, which now I forget; only this I remember, that though I was somewhat timerous at my first entrance into the chamber, yet before I went out, I could not but break forth into tears, not so much because they were so hard-hearted against me, and my husband, but to think what a sad account such poor creatures will have to give at the coming of the Lord, when they shall there answer for all things whatsoever they have done in the body, whether it be good, or whether it be bad.*

So, when I departed from them, the book of Statute was brought, but what they said of it, I know nothing at all, neither did I hear any more from them.

Some Carriages of the Adversaries of God's Truth with me at the next Assises, which was on the nineteenth of the first Month, 1662.

I shall pass by what befel between these two assizes, how I had, by my Jailor, some liberty granted me,* more than at the first, and how

I followed my wonted course of preaching, taking all occasions that
was put into my hand to visit the people of God, exhorting them to
be stedfast in the faith of Jesus Christ,* and to take heed that they
touched not the Common Prayer, &c. but to mind the word of God,
which giveth direction to Christians in every point, being able to
make the man of God perfect in all things through faith in Jesus
Christ, and thoroughly to furnish him up to all good works. Also how
I having, I say, somewhat more liberty, did go to see Christians at
London, which my enemies hearing of, was so angry, that they had
almost cast my Jailor out of his place, threatning to indite him, and
to do what they could against him. They charged me also, that I went
thither to plot and raise division, and make insurrection,* which,
God knows, was a slander; whereupon my liberty was more straight-
ened than it was before; so that I must not look out of the door. Well,
when the next sessions came, which was about the 10th of the 11th
month, I did expect to have been very roundly dealt withal; but they
passed me by, and would not call me, so that I rested till the assises,
which was the 19th of the first month following; and when they
came, because I had a desire to come before the judge, I desired my
Jailor to put my name into the Kalender* among the felons, and made
friends to the Judge and High Sheriff, who promised that I should
be called; so that I thought what I had done might have been effectual for the obtaining of my desire: But all was in vain; for when the
assises came, though my name was in the kalender, and also though
both the Judge and Sheriff had promised that I should appear before
them, yet the Justices and the Clerk of the peace, did so work it about,
that I, notwithstanding, was defered, and might not appear: And
though I say, I do not know of all their carriages towards me, yet this
I know, that the Clerk of the peace did discover himself to be one of
my greatest opposers: For, first he came to my Jailor, and told him
that I must not go down before the Judge, and therefore must not be
put into the kalender; to whom my Jailor said, that my name was in
already. He bid him put me out again; my Jailor told him that he
could not: For he had given the Judge a kalender with my name in
it, and also the Sheriff another. At which he was very much displeased, and desired to see that kalender that was yet in my Jailor's
hand, who, when he had gave it him, he looked on it, and said it was
a false kalender; he also took the kalender and blotted out my accusation, as my Jailor had writ it. (Which accusation I cannot tell what
it was, because it was so blotted out) and he himself put in words to

this purpose: That *John Bunyan* was committed in prison; being law-fully convicted for upholding of unlawful meetings and conventicles, &c. But yet for all this, fearing that what he had done, unless he added thereto, it would not do, he first run to the Clerk of the assises; then to the Justices, and afterwards, because he would not leave any means unattempted to hinder me, he comes again to my Jailor, and tells him, that if I did go down before the Judge, and was released, he would make him pay my fees, which he said was due to him; and further, told him, that he would complain of him at the next quarter sessions for making of false kalenders, though my Jailor himself, as I after-wards learned, had put in my accusation worse than in itself it was by far. And thus was I hindred and prevented at that time also from appearing before the Judge: And left in prison. Farewell.

JOHN BUNYAN

CONFESSIONS

Richard Norwood

Jesus Christ came into the world to save sinners of whom I am chief*
Rich Norwood

I was born of christian parents and under them educated till about
15 years of age: In whom there was a severe Disposition and cariage
towards me suitable to that mass of sin and folly which was bound
up in my heart.* Whereby it was moderated in some good measure.
Until ten years of age I lived with them at Stephnage, being taught
to read, (and I think) entered in writing, and my accidence;* afterwards I lived with them at Barkamsted till twelve years of age, where
was a Grammar school, a free-school, where I went through the Latin
Grammar and other books appertayning, and entered into the Greek;
at what time my parents went from thence to Shitlanger and from
thence to Stony-stratford.

Whilst I was at Stephnage, going to school with my sister about
a mile from home (the very day that I left of my long coats to wear
breeches) I was in danger to have bene drowned,* by swinging on a
stake by a ditch of water, which brake and I fell into the ditch, my
head forwards but by Gods providence I was drawn out by one that
came with a cart (as I remember) to a pit near adjoining. During this
time that I lived at Stephnage and Barkamsted the Lord was pleased,
by means of my parents, School-dame, School-masters and sermons
to plant in my heart some seeds of religion and the fear of God,
which though no fruits of regeneration yet through the blessing of
God they were special preservatives to keep me for many years after
from diverse enormous sins whereof I was in danger, and wherein in
likelyhood I should have perished. These and many other pledges of
thy grace and mercy thou wast pleased O Lord and father to vouchsafe me in my childhood and tender years; making the remembrance
of those times sweet and savory unto the present. But for the excessive vanity and wickednes of my heart and mind even then, and the
fruits thereof which began to put forth apace, it was just I should be
deprived of those blessings and favours, and left more to the vanity
of myne own heart as I was. Whence for many years next ensuing
I so greivously stayned my life, and lived so dissolutely, that I even

abhor the remembrance of those times. Surely God made me sensible of the misery ensuing when I came from Barkamsted, for my School-master there being as I conceived something sharper to me then to my fellows when I knew I must shortly go from him I thought I would then be even with him, for I purposed then to carry my self very chearfully without any sign of greif at departure, that so he might see I did not love him. But as the day drew nearer qualms of greif and dismay began to seaze on my heart, and much more when that woful day was come, and that my master called me aside giving me good admonitions, and I to take my leave of him and my fellows; then my heart was ready to break, and myne eyes to gush out aboundantly with tears. And not without cause, for from that time forwards I went no more to school to any purpose, not meeting with an able schoolmaster, and my father much decaying in his estate, but passed my time in a more fruitless and dissolute manner. At Stratford when I was near 15 years of age being drawn in by other yong men of the town, I acted a womans part in a stage play;* I was so much affected with that practice, that had not the Lord prevented it, I should have chosen it before any other course of life. About 14 years of age I was taken with a dangerous sickness at the end of harvest. But it pleased the Lord to spare me, and to restore me to health. Also to preserve me from the plague being about that time very rife in the town and at the next house.*

[*Norwood digresses here to speak of his dame school at Stevenage before the age of 10.*]

And my Dame (as it seems) was a very religious woman, and had a daughter also very pyous in her talk and conversation, so far as I was able then to judge of godlines and religion. I thought them to be both in the special love of God, and near unto him, her daughter was sickly, I think in a consumption, and dyed shortly after. They would often use pyous persuasions both to learning and other things, which took good impression in me, and praise me for learning so well, and teaching my sisters, and tell me that God would love me, and that he did love me, and others told me so also. I thought it no small matter to be beloved of God, but I doubted much whether that were so; or how they could know that it was so, besides I knew my self to be worse then they took me to be.* But yet I thought that they were near to God and might know much more of his mind then I did. These thoughts and affections* (so far as I can judge) were serious but usually mixed with self conceipt and vanity of mind, and I had even then much inward pride [as may appear in this instance and many others. There came a gentlewoman a stranger one day to visit my Dame, and we (the scholars) being at play, and she sitting at the door I merely of pride ran before her with all my might that she might see how fast I could run, thinking she would praise me for it, and just as I came against her, fell and brake my face sorely, that I think I could nor rise again till my Dame came and took me up, and paid me well for it.] And so it pleased the Lord to meet with that sin of pride and self conceiptednes usually from my childhood with sharp and greivous stripes, insomuch as in my natural estate* I usually observed it, and feared it, which was a great means to restrayne that corruption . . .

There was also a good minister [at Berkhamstead], one Mr Newman, who preached twice every Lords day, and besides did catechise* us children apart in the chancel before his afternoon sermon. There also through Gods mercy I profited well in religion and the fear of God; there I heard the word with reverence, and often with much attention and good affection, and good purpose and res-olutions, at least for the present till play put them out of my mind again. So that sometimes I seemed to my self to be indeed almost converted.

But surely they were only fleeting perswasions, and I did not well understand from what to convert, nor to what, nor could distinctly discern what pyety was but only in a general and very confused and uncertain manner.* Neither was it doubtless at best any more then moral,* being without any spark of the right knowledge and appre-hension of Christ, that I can remember. Yet surely very profitable for me, and a means through the grace of God to preserve me for many years after from falling into such gross sins as else I should have fallen into.

I was also in those times frequent in private prayer, and sometimes made vows to God, which I was careful to observe. But these prayers proceeded of a very wavering heart without any true faith that I can discern, but rather as it were of opinion, thinking: it may be God doth hear mens prayers and will grant me what I now crave. And my prayers were usually for childish things as often on the Lords day at night or Monday morning I prayed to escape beating that week, or, when I was sent on an errand two or three miles into the country, that I might not lose my way, or such other occasions; for the most part they were moved by some danger feared. I remember not that I sought to the Lord in my greatest greif when I was taken from school . . .

It was a great mercy of God to me that my father came to live at Barkamsted, although it was great losses which he sustayned that had brought him thither; for having been brought up from his youth as a gentleman, when afterwards he was married he took a farm at Stephnage called Cannix (being I think the manor house; I remember I was present at a court kept there) and whether through his unskilfulnes in that course of life or otherwise I know not but he had very great losses in sheep and otherwise;* Whereupon he gave it over and came to Barkamsted where he lived two years upon his means in a very fair house at great charge, but had little or nothing coming in, which moved him also to leave that.

There was at Barkamsted a gentlemans son, about my years, my scholefellow and usual companion, his name, Adolphus Speed, of a moderate soft and sweet disposition. I had oftentimes secretly in my heart much emulation or jealousie touching him above all others, for though sometimes I thought I was before him in piety and in the favor of God (and this sometimes in hearing the word together I thought somethings were applyable to me in the best sense, which were not to him) yet at other times again I thought though I was before him in learning, yet God had endued him with sundry gifts and virtues which I had not, and that he was much in the favor of God, but that I was not, or not so much, and this jealousy possest me for the most part yet I loved him very well. I did also much reverence and affect my master there, though I scarce knew it then, fear more prevailing. And though I then thought him to be more sharp and severe towards me then to others, yet doubtless he did affect me very tenderly, as was manifest by his frequent commendations of me in such companies where he had occasion to come, shewing the verses and latins* I had made and otherwise. I had an aptnes and readines in versifying above the rest of my school-fellows for which they called me Ovid and sometimes in scorn or derision Naso,* the first I was proud of, the other I could not endure.

Also when my father, mother, and their family departed from

Barkamsted, my master stayed me there I think a month after, and had dealt with my Lady Paget, the patroness of the school, to maintain me at school, and so it was thought I should have continued there, but it fell out otherwise, the Lord in his wisdom seeing it fit that I should drink deep of a most bitter cup, the remembrance whereof is even an abhorring unto me to this day, chiefly for that I lost my time in sinful and dissolute courses. I have heard that Mr Speed, being (I think) then steward to my Lady Paget, prevailed with her that his son Adolphus might have that maintenance which was before moved and intended for me. And he surely was fitter for such a happy condition, being of a tender, gentile, and sweet disposition (so far as I could then judge) but I of a more rough and violent, and of an aspiring mind, ayming at the highest things *Per fas aut nefas,** and possest with much inward pride and vanity of mind, and yet on the contrary (as a just punishment of the former) as often subject to a very dejected and dispairing mind without any very notable cause for either.

When that dismal day came that I must depart, I had sundry thoughts, as to hide my self in some corner near the school, etc., but I thought al would be in vayne, I should then be sent away with disgrace. So I departed with a most sorrowful heart, sprinkling the way with tears, and not without cause in respect of those many evils which were to ensue. From thenceforth I went no more to school to any purpose, nor came not where there was any powerful ministry neither had the society of any forward in religion ... At fifteen years of age I came to London where I was bound apprentice to a fishmonger who also dealt in sea-cows,* a stern man, where before two years were expired, his house being visited with the plague, I was sick also and was like to dy. But the Lord in his mercy spared me then also and restored me to health. His house being often frequented by mariners I heard them sometimes discourse of their sea-affairs and of the art of navigation, wherewith I was so much affected that I was most earnestly bent both to understand the art which seemed to me to reach [as it] were to heaven, and to see the World ...

Thus having forsaken the calling wherein my parents had placed me* and betaken my self to another course of life [at sea] without and against their liking and without any due calling or encouragement from God or men, I met with many troubles. In this three years,

especially whilst I was at London by the fishmonger, the corruption
of my heart showed it self abundantly. [Norwood here deletes con-
fessional references to his lust (his behaviour towards two maids and
'wantonness with my master's daughter') and 'appareling'.] In vanity
of mind and self conceiptednes. Which notwithstanding the Lord
was pleased somewhat to moderate, by sending usually some sharp
chastisement or affliction upon me when that sin did much prevail,
insomuch as I took notice of it and did expect and fear it, which did
something repress that vice. Also as a fruit and fomentor of the
former I had a great delight in reading vayne and corrupt books
as *Palmerin de Oliva*, *The Seaven Champions*,* and others like. Also
assoon as I was recovered of the plague, and before I was quite recovered, I fell to reading of Virgils Eneade with much affection, but had
no love nor delight nor faith in the word of God, never spent any
time (that I remember) in those three years and much less in many
years after in reading of that. I think, that acting a part in a play, the
reading of play-books and other such books as aforementioned, and
the vayne conceipts which they begat in me was the principal thing
that alienated my heart from the Word of God which afterwards grew
to that height that scarce any book seemed more contemptible to me
then the Word of God . . .

[*Norwood goes to the Netherlands where he fights for the Dutch United
Provinces against the Spanish until peace is concluded in 1609. Enfeebled
by sickness, he then wanders aimlessly to Brussels; and from there makes
for England.*]

Now again I was alone, and travailing towards England, and
approaching somewhere near the place where I was to take shipping.
When I began again to enter into a serious consideration with my
self (as I had sometimes done before) what I should do when I came
into England. To further me in my desired course to sea, I thought
my freinds would be as opposite as formerly they had bene. To be
bound apprentice again to any land trade was an abhorring to me to
think upon, yea even to a seafaring man except I might be sure to go
some long voyages, as the East or West Indies or the like, and otherwise then as an apprentice I thought none would take me especially
being without freinds, cloathes, etc. I began to think that seeing I
could not have opportunity as I desired to travail by sea, it would not
be amiss to spend some time in travail by land, and to go see Rome.
But then I considered I must have the Popes Nuntios Letters (as I

had bene informed) and for the obtayning of that I must have a letter from one of the English priests or Jesuits in Lovayne, which they graunted not till after confession, and receiving their sacrament, and so dissembling at least to be a papist. This dissembling I conceived to be very offensive to God. I further considered the greatnes of the journey, and in what a poor condition I was to pass it. I thought upon my parentage, Education, and friends in England, and into what a poor condition I was now come to be releeved from place to place by the Bores or husbandmen and others, and how I was like to continue in this condition if I went to Rome.

Notwithstanding being destitute of meet furtherance in England in my desired course I enclyned to that, namely to see Rome but to dissemble so grossly as I must greived me exceedingly, and being much perplexed in mind with objections on both sides, and in consideration of my forlorn condition and no longer able to contayn my self I went aside out of the way into the standing corn (being harvest time) and there wept aboundantly till I think I was something distracted. But it growing towards evening, and I to resolve either upon the one or the other, I at last resolved to go to Rome, childishly hoping that time would wear out, and alter my condition and give me better opportunity for accomplishing my desired ends. And thus did I now as it were bid adieu to parentage, Education, freinds, country, Religion, etc., though I thought and purposed it should be but for a little time, and then to return to all again. But miserable and foolish man, I understood not the many dangers of soul and body whereinto I cast my self and how every step I went, as it was farther from my native country, so it led me and alienated my heart farther from God, from Religion and from a desire to return. My heart after this grew more hardened,* scarce any affliction or misery would move a tear for many years after till about the time of my conversion. Now Satan was leading away in triumph his poor vanquished vassal, never likely to have bene recovered again out of his hands, had not the Lord, who hath the hearts of all men in his hands, by his almighty power and gracious providence brought me back again. But as I say being resolved for Rome I arose and began to travail back again and whether it was through horrour of conscience (which notwithstanding I remember not that I was very much sensible of) or whether I was somewhat distracted or weak headed through perplexity and greif, I know not, but I could not endure that men should see me. I was so vexed at them for looking upon me, that in my heart I was ready to fall on some of them to do them a mischeife, and yet (or at least I conceived so) they gazed more upon me then, then ever they had wont to do before. Whereupon so soon as I gate out of sight I went and hid my self till night, and so travailed by night, and hid my self for the most part by day, and went through by ways for several nights. I think also it was because I thought they would be apt to stay me, seeing me to travail back again . . .

Coming to Lovayne to the English priests, there being a Colledge of them (as I remember) I was very curteously intertained by them (as it seems their custom is in such cases) and there was one of them assigned to instruct me in their religion; Who used divers arguments, and showed me sundry books for that purpose; all which prevailed little or nothing with me, save only that I did dissemble, and would seem to be perswaded for the end afore mentioned. Thus after some weeks spent there I very desperately dissembled seeming to be convinced, and to embrace that religion, confessed to a priest, and received their sacrament, and then had a letter commendatory from one of the chief of them to the Popes Nuntios at Bruxells for procuring his letter for my journey to Rome, which he readily upon the sight of that letter granted; and so about michelmas (I think it was) I went towards Rome . . .

Notwithstanding though I seemed now to have more peace of conscience then before [being half persuaded by a travelling companion of the claims of Roman Catholicism] yet about the same time, or presently after, before I parted company with that man, the Lord strook me with a greivous judgement, the marks and symptoms whereof I am like to bear to my grave, and even the thing it self in some measure . . .

[*Norwood, with his companion Thomas, makes a hazardous journey over the Alps.*]

About the same time or presently after my entring into Italy, I began first to be troubled with that nightly disease which we call the mare, which afterwards encreased upon me very greivously, that I was scarce any night free from it, and seldom it left me without nocturnal polutions;* besides, whilst it was upon me I had horrible dreams and visions; oft-times I verily thought that I descended into Hell and there felt the pains of the damned, with many hideous things.

Usually in my dreams me thought I saw my father always greivously angry with me. This disease brought me very weak, and surely without the special power of God sustaining me I see not how life should have bene continued. Besides having often a light burning in the room as is usual in those places, though I was not able to stir when the disease was upon me, yet I could usually remember where I was and who was in the room with me, and if they talked could understand what they said and could open my eyelids a little and see the light in the room; and sometimes I seemed to see a thing on my breast or belly like a hare or cat etc; whereupon I have sometimes taken a naked knife in my hand when I went to sleep, thinking there-with to strike at it and it was Gods mercy that I had not by this means slain my self, but after I had observed the danger whereinto the wily feind was like to draw me, I left of that. When I departed out of Italy to go for England, this desease began to abate and afterwards more when I came into England. About 26 years of age when it pleased the Lord of his free grace and mercy to deliver me from the bonds of my corruptions into the glorious liberty of his saints and children, I was altogether freed from those nocturnal polutions, yet have bene troubled with that disease unto this day, but seldom and remissly, I give God thanks, as 3 or four times in a year. It was a just judgment of God for my wilful blindnes and apostacy contrary to myne own conscience, and contrary to that light and those principles which by education were planted in me.

Many other dangers I passed more then I knew or can remember. . . . Yet so was my heart hardned, that these and many other calamities could not move it to relent or take any pity or compassion on my self only I think once or twice for a short time my heart did relent a little, and I had some thoughts and purposes to return into England and to settle my self I cared not in how mean a calling* so I might have the favor of God and turn away his displeasure, which I conceived lay heavily upon me but these purposes were not con-stant but soon vanished again . . .

[*Norwood reaches Rome, considers joining a pilgrimage to the Holy Land (first visiting Mt Etna and the Sybil's caves in Sicily, which he had read about in Virgil), is surprised by the kindness of some English merchants, and is persuaded by them to return with them to England.*]

And so being come home I went to no Protestant church, nor freinds of that side, but went down to Cornebury Park near Oxford to a kinsman, my mothers brother there, where I lived some three or four months as one of his keepers, in all which time, my father nor my other freinds heard not of me. But then an opportunity being offered which I could scarce avoyd (my uncle as I think going to London and being to see my father) I wrote a letter to my father, dwelling then at London being much decayed in estate; and though I was much estranged, as in religion, so likewise in myne affection towards them, yet I seemed in my writing to put on a childlike affection and somewhat to bewail my time mispent, and the courses I had taken contrary to the liking of them my parents and other my freinds though I had no purpose then of reformation. The letter through the good providence of God came very opportunely to my father who at that time lay dangerously sick, not like to recover; but upon the receipt of my letter was much revived and comforted, and by the return as I think of my uncle wrote me an answer, wherein he expressed much tender and fatherlike affection towards me and withal did lovingly invite and earnestly perswade me to come up to London, to resolve upon some good course of life, wherein I might as he said serve God, and live comfortably another day, and whatsoever course it were, whether to go to sea or to live on shoare, though his estate was now much decayed, I should be sure of his best fartherance . . .

When I received and had read the letter, I layd it by, without any great regard, yet was something affected with it; but I thought, I am not the man my father takes me to be. I seemed in my letter, to have some child-like affection, and desire of reformation, but have no such purpose, and besides to all former greivances have added this that I am not as my father thinks of me, a protestant. Yet after some consideration, I read it again and again and was more and more affected.* I considered though I had written many things in a fained stile of good affection, yet he had written truly and unfainedly as he was affected indeed, and why should I to all other his greivances add this, namely to dash those good hopes that he conceived of me. Amongst other things he wrote *I doubt not but God hath reserved thee to some special good end if good use be made of his admirable providence*. I could not then, nor many years after entertayn this saying, as any ways suteable or belonging to me, but thought: this is the nature of parents to hope well of their children, how bad so ever, especially because I have now bene long absent; but by that time he knows me a little better he wilbe of another mind.

But though I thought thus of this saying then, yet I loved to read it often, and always after to have it often in my thoughts, and sometimes thought (though with no stedfastnes) Who knows what God may do? and for the present I thought Let me not make things worse then they are; yea rather let me conceal the worse a while. What though I be not such as my father takes me to be, yet let him enjoy the comforts of his hopes, at least wise till it must needs appear to the contrary. Hereupon, though altogether unresolved what course to settle in, yet I resolved to go up to London to see him; and so did forthwith . . .

At my first coming up to London I was a while at my Uncle Carpenters in Barnsby-street, till I might otherwise be settled. She my aunt being a religious woman, observing that I went not to church, and suspecting that I was infected with popery, questioned with me of myne opinion that way, which I did not hide but readily declare, and would maintain till better reasons could be brought to the contrary. Hereupon she got Mr Elton then minister there to come to her house, to deal with me about it. He began with me something sharply to this purpose, namely pressing upon me my disobedience to my parents, forsaking the calling wherein they had placed me, and betaking my self to another contrary to their liking,* and hereupon God had laid several afflictions upon me. I was destitute of a calling and prospered not, and besides God had left me to err so fouly in religion. His words though true did touch me very nearly, yet withal I apprehended my self to be contemned of him because I was poor, and as it were in a forlorn condition,* and so I answered with some stomack* and passion, that touching the calling which I left, it was not likely I should have done much good in it seeing it could not be managed without a good stock, which my father now had bene noways able to furnish me with, and for the calling which I desired, it was an honest, necessary and commendable calling. Touching my afflictions they might befall the best men, even in a good way, instancing Job and others: and for any errour I had made in religion, all this did not prove any such thing; with other such speeches, which I uttered more sharply and stiffly then was meet to such a reverend Devine. Whereupon after a few other speeches he left me, not desiring (as I remember) any further conference with me, esteeming me (as I suppose) obstinate, though indeed I desired to have bene resolved of sundry doubts and to be setled in my religion either the one or the other, for which I should see best ground: and I on the contrary conceived my self to be despised of him because he was so sharp, and left me, never desiring to speak with me any more. Notwithstanding I was greived that our meeting took no better success, and began to bethink my self what course I should take to be resolved and setled in my religion. I thought being in that poor condition if I should make tryal of any other devine in England I should find no better success;* they would only use an imperious strain (as it seemed to me) and not so much abase themselves as to use that familiarity, nor spend that time and labour to resolve me that were necessary. Whereupon being then bound forth on a voyage into the straights, I thought when I came into Spayne or Italy I would seek resolution of the preists and Jesuits there remembering how courteously and familiarly I had bene formerly used by them in the like case at Lovaine. Yet to my best remembrance I much rather desired to be resolved in England, and so the Lord in mercy was pleased to vouchsafe. For my father dwelling then in Aldersgate-Street, there was there a worthy Divine one Mr Topsall* who preached without Aldersgate, to whom my father would have me go with him. When we came he was in his study, and my father went in and brake the matter to him, desiring him that he would confer with me; he answered yes if I would confer, and calling me in though I was in a poor habit, yet he caused me to sit down by him, began at first (as I remember) to confer about my travails in a loving and familiar manner, afterwards touched gently upon religion etc. and used me with marveilous courtesy and familiarity, then and at all other times afterwards sparing neither time nor diligence in resolving all my doubts, and for setling me firmly in the Protestant religion. What thanks and praise can I render unto thy majesty oh heavenly father for all that goodnes and mercy which thou wast pleased to dispense and confer upon me by the ministry of that thy servant. The Lord recompense it into his bosom an hundred fold if he be yet living, otherwise I doubt not but he rests from his labour, and that with the rest of his works follow him.

I was at this time near about the age of 20 years, and had now also sundry thoughts and motions inwardly of a full conversion to God,

and newnes of life. I thought it a blessed condition to live and especially to dy in the favour of God, and began to forecast for such a
condition, and hapely if I had continued on land to hear the word,
and to have bene conversant with such as were indeed regenerate this
work might then through the grace of God have been effected, but
going presently to sea amongst those which were strangers to these
misteries, I soon grew cold and careless; besides I yet understood not
what piety was, but had rather a monastical concept of it then true,
esteeming it to consist in a kind of austerity of life, renouncing all
the pleasures of the world (even those which are honest and allow-
able) and a retyring a mans self to solitarines and prayre etc. . . . And
further I often thought upon those words in the Epistle to the Hebr.
for if we sin willingly after we have received etc., and other the like;
and feared being then in the prime of my youth that I should not
persevere,* but that some corruptions of nature* would prevail
against me, and then thought it would be according to the words of
the Apostle: It had bene better not to have known the way of righteousnes then to turn from the holy commaundement etc.* These and
the like thoughts were always a Lyon in the way . . .

[*Bound as apprentice to a master's mate at Limehouse, Norwood makes
two hazardous merchant voyages—to Spain, Italy, and Turkish domin-
ions in Southern Greece. A heightened sense of danger, sea-sickness, and
frustration that his master gives him little opportunity to study navigation combine to convince him that he should seek his freedom: 'the calling
I never much affected, but only as it was a means whereby I might see
the World, and learn the art of navigation. Hereupon I thought to give
it over if I could agree with my master to let me go'. He has also taken
with enthusiasm to the study of mathematics, 'for it so fell out by the providence of God that in our first voyage there went one with us as passen-
ger who had diverse mathematical books . . . the Lord thus giving me a
good entrance and settling in that which should afterwards be my calling'.
He obtains his freedom (having made some money from a cousin's invest-
ment in his merchant voyages) but agrees to stay with his ship until it is
sold.*]

And now lying at home in the ship, having means allowed me, and
leisure enough for half a year together (for about so long it was as I
remember before she was sold) a man would have thought I should
have made a very good progress in my studies; but it fell out clean
contrary; for though I might seem now to be myne own man, being

gotten free from a good master (who I think respected me well and intended his daughter to me for wife as I have heard) yet I was under an evil master Satan who in this time finding me idle and unsetled employed me in his drudgery, tyrannizing over me; and I became more his vassal then ever before. Whereby I have further occasion to see and to acknowledge the good providence of God towards me, that from my youth I had never bene much at myne own hand, but had bene for the most part either under some strict government, or some other hard condition which by the blessing of God kept me from much evil, which otherwise I was apt to have run into, being enthralled unto sin and Satan.* For at this time (as I say) I did not prosecute any laudable exercise but went often to stage plays,* where-with I was as it were bewitched in affection and never satiated, which was a great means to withdraw and take off my mind from any thing that was serious true or good, and to set it upon frivolous, false and fayned things; yea so far was I affected with these lying vanities that I began to make a play, and had written a good part of it. It happened after some time that I fell out with the players at the fortune* (which was the house I frequented) about a seat which they would not admit me to have, whereupon out of anger, and as it were to do them a despite, I came there no more that I remember. It was Gods mercy to give me this rub, that I had not run my self over head and ears in these vanities . . .

But as I say, after some four or six months one Mr. Manering (shortly after Capt: Manering and since his return from his voyage Sir Henry Manering) bought the ship of Mr. Phinehas Pett* (since Capt. Pett) wherein I was. The purser Bartholmew Nichols commended me much to him for my skill in Navigation, whereupon he caused him that was to be master of the ship to examine me, and upon his commendations also, Capt. Manering entertayned me for one of the masters mates, and as Tutor to himself in the Art of Navigation . . .

[*In this capacity, Norwood was to join a voyage transporting Sir Robert Shirley, as ambassador, to Persia under the patronage of Prince Henry; but Henry's death in November 1612 prevented this.*]

I had and have great cause to be thankful to God for the measure of skill and knowledge which he had then vouchsafed me; it being through the blessing of God the principal means whereby it pleased the Lord to raise me from that poor condition whereinto I had cast my self in myne outward estate. Besides it was doubtless some occasion at least to stir up my mind to look after the greatest things. For partly by nature and partly by many accidents that had befallen me, I was much enclyned to a dejected and despairing mind. But the Lord having given me so good success in my studies I began to think that the good things which belonged unto others, belonged also to me and what was attainable by others—might also be attained by me, if I did diligently use the means.* Some glances I had also at some times towards heaven and heavenly things, the Lord inviting and calling me, but I found no affection to those things, but such a violent stream of affections carrying me another way to evil—that it seemed to be altogether in vayne to strive against them.

But to return being disapointed of our voyage into Persia, Capt. Manering in regards of his great charge obtayned of the King Letters of mart, and when he was at sea, betook himself to pyracy for many years. This I had some knowledge of whilst we were at Limmington.* Whereupon debating with my self I resolved upon good considerations to give over the voyage; for I thought I had no cause to betake my self to such a desperate course, the Lord had given me occasion to hope for better things; and howsoever at present I found my self carried away with a stream of corrupt affections into foul and enormous sins and so conceived my self to be going along in that highway that leadeth unto hell: Yet I thought, let me not make the way shorter then needs must; Let me not cast my self into any desperate course needlessly. Whilst I forbear—who knows what time may bring forth. The Lord can change the disposition of my heart, which is so furiously bent upon evil; or as I grow in years it may be it will abate, and I shalbe better able to set my affections upon heavenly things; or something may betide, so long as I remayne, and do not desperately hasten myne own destruction; nor provoke God by more sins then those to which I am already enthralled. Thus resolving I got my chest and such things out of the ship to the shoare, and a day or two before the ship was to depart from Limmington I absented my self also being willing to lose the time I had spent if I could get clear so. And indeed having never in my life received wages I thought childishly as if there were scarce any due to me as to other men . . .

[*Norwood is pursued by the ship's lieutenant and other officers and*

*returned to the ship; he then escapes again but is later apprehended and
assaulted by Captain Mannering with a truncheon for having put it about
that his business was piracy. Finally he frees himself by subterfuge and
returns to London.*]

Thus then at twelve years old I was taken from school, my father
removing from Barkamsted; at fifteen years old I came to London to
be apprentice where I continued about two years, and then at Orford
and in the Netherlands and in my journey to Rome spent about three
years, so I was then about twenty years. Then at Cornebury, and two
voyages into the Straights, about two years or more and this was
almost a year after. So that at this time when I left Limmington, and
came up to London I was about twenty three years of age. [*Margin:*
'Anno 1613']

Being come up I joyned in partnership with Mr John Goodwin, a
man famous in his time, who had then begun to teach the mathe-
maticks. He furnished me with cloaths and money suteable to our
Calling, and I was to teach him some things which he desired, and I
learned also many things off him and he continued my constant
freind to the time of his death. We taught together, and shared alike,
and this by the good providence of God fell out well for me, especially if I had made a wise use of it; for I being still of a boyish disposition unacquainted with the world, and altogether ignorant how
to settle my self into any good course of life, the Lord thus brought
me into a way, and joyned me with one that, though about my years
yet had some better experience. And London was then one of the
most happy and flourishing places of the World, especially for the
light of the Gospel and life of true religion then flourishing there*
(though that was a thing then slighted and contemned by me). So
that I might seem to be settled in a very happy condition and course
of life if I had known myne own happines: in a calling also that was
suteable to myne own heart. But the Lord saw that such a settled and
happy condition was not fit for me as then, and therefore I could not
see the happines of it nor settle my self effectually* to it. Indeed the
frame* of my heart was so furiously bent upon wickednes as lust and
uncleaness, vanity of mind, pride and self-conceiptednes, a desire
and purpose to try other wicked practises, etc., that if the Lord had
given me rest and prosperity, in all likelyhood I should speedily have
run upon myne own ruin. So that I continued this course of life I
think not above eight or nine months. For by the time Mr Goodwin

and I had bene together four or five months he marryed and I then taught by my self some 3 or 4 months more . . .

[*Owing to the skill Norwood had once exhibited at Lymington in retrieving a cannon from the sea, the Bermuda Company approaches him to go to Bermuda as a pearl diver. There turn out to be no pearls, but Norwood is invited to survey the islands. A plague of rats, introduced by a captured Spanish frigate, leads to desperate food shortage, so Norwood goes in search of berries on a small neighbouring island in his makeshift boat.*]

The next morning when I purposed to depart the wind was come to the northeast direcly against me and blew very hard—and so continued five days that I could not go, this five days seemed to me the most tedious and miserable time that ever I underwent in all my life; yea though I had had experience of sundry difficulties, dangers, and hard conditions before; yet till then I never seemed to understand what misery was; yet I had victuals sufficient, only I seemed as banished from human society and knew not how long it might last. Yet at other times I was apt to retire my self much from company, but at this time I thought it one of the greatest punishments in the world, yea, I thought it was one of the greatest punishments in hell, and the sense and apprehension of it made me to think of hell as of hell indeed, a condition most miserable. The want of victuals had caused me often before to think and determine of going from hence in a boat to some of the Cariby or Bahama Islands uninhabited where was store of victuals, but now I thought I would rather suffer any thing then be deprived of human society* . . .

[*Norwood returns safely. Although 'there were many in those times that died daily for want of victuals', he never again has 'any great want of victuals' owing to the 'special favour' of the Governor, Mr Moore. He concludes his survey. Mr Moore returns to England in 1615 to be replaced by Captain Tucker. Norwood speaks of political infighting, gives details of where he lived, describes his work apportioning land, and returns to England in 1617. He speaks of his 'corruptions'.*]

I often thought with much perplexity; There is no doubt an excellency and beauty in heavenly things, but I cannot see it, it is such a beauty as is not suteable to my nature or to myne ey or myne ey not suteable to that, I have no delight in it. They are happy no doubt that can delight in them for whether there be any beauty and excellency in those heavenly things or not yet they are delivered from hell and they enjoy that which they delight in, there is no other thing that a man delights in that can promise so much. But I thought many dissembled and that they could not indeed have such delight in heavenly things as they seemed to have and that there were very few that did sincerely affect them, and those that do are men of another nature, differing from the common disposition of men . . . And so far did my blindnes in heavenly things & the ignorance and infidelity of my heart transport me, as to have the like evil thoughts of God himself, not without much fretting and murmuring, as if he allowed of no joy nor pleasure, but of a kind of melancholy demeanour and austerity . . . I desired to shun the torments of hell but was not much affected with the joys of heaven. I wished there were some midle estate between both,* and sometimes I flattered my self with such conceipts that there might be, Whereof I was the more perswaded, when I considered how there had been sundry Philosophers and other eminent persons who by their virtues and endowments had deserved much of the world, and in their moral conversation seemed not to be inferiour to the better sort of Christians. To adjudge these all to hell seemed to be a harsh judgement. Yet that they should be in the same condition with beleeving christians I thought it not probable, their institution and dispositions being so much different. Therefore I thought there might be some midle condition happy, though inferiour to the condition of true christians . . .

Thus I was often perswaded that the estate of a true christian was the best and surest of all other conditions, but had no courage nor full resolution to press earnestly for it feeling my self destitute of the wedding garment of love. But even as a woman that is much in debt and continual danger, hearing some possibility of a husband that would soon pay all her debts, and free her from danger would diligently listen after him, but if withal she found not in her self a conjugal affection to his person, would forbear marriage much after that maner it was with me; I was willing to be freed from hell, but had no delight in the kingdom of heaven in Christ nor in the things of Christ the relish of my soul being corrupted could savour nothing but carryon and what was corrupt; and so I thought there was little likelyhood of constancy and perseverance if I should begin, and that were worse then not to begin at all . . .

[*Norwood keeps his 'ey upon that imaginary middle estate': 'And so though I attayned not the joys of heaven and felicity of the saints, yet if I might escape the pains of hell, it should suffice me to have such pleasure and contentments as human things afford and especially learning.' He pursues his mathematical studies, but is distracted by the question: 'what do I endeavour after? What singular good do I hope for by these my studies?' For two years he makes 'no progress in any study'.*]

But by how much the more I neclected all diligent and serious employment, so much the more exceedingly did Satan prevail through my corruptions to captivate me in the basest kind of bondage, so that I might seem to be more beslaved unto sin and Satan actually then any other living. This drove me quite out of hope, not only of heaven but of any such middle estate as I had imagined, if there had bene any such, and I conceived that dying in this estate there was indeed no other to be expected but hell. To this dispair I was always subject in some remiss degree as it seems from my youth for after 12 or 14 years of age, being then taken from school and for the most part without that good nurture and education which till then I had enjoyed, the corruption of my heart did much more manifest it self actually then before, whereupon I doubted much of salvation if I should dy in that estate. This was more manifest when being near 17 years of age I lay sick of the plague having two or three very dangerous fits one so violent that it seemed to me the powers of nature were not able to continue agaynst it. I was then thinking, now I shall surely dy, and what then shal become of me. Surely I can expect none other but hell, are not the evil spirits here present already to carry me away? and I looked up for fear it was so: And thus I was always (to my remembrance) convinced in my thoughts that I was in an evil estate for the present, but had some uncertain hopes of some change that might befall me for the time to come. And such a hope there seemed to be in me in some measure even at this time also, which I conceive did somewhat moderate the despair. But very weak and almost a hopeless hope it seemed to be now, the rather because I observed such an averseness in my disposition from the Word and ways of God. I conceived it would be far more tolerable for any the principal ring-leaders of heresies then for me, for they seemed to be something affected to the Holy Scriptures else how could they be so much conversant in them to know them so well as they did; whereas nothing seemed to me more tedious and irksome then hearing the

Word preached or reading the Scriptures; Yea, the Holy Scriptures seemed then to me the most unsavoury and contemptible of all other writings,* and especially the Gospel of St. John. So that I did not only know my self to be in a damnable estate for the present, but was almost hopeless of ever being in a better.

I remember that a little before the Lord was pleased to work a change in me, sojourning then with Mr. Blanke it hapned that I burnt my finger, and complayning somewhat of the payne he replyed in jest: What doth a little burning of the finger trouble you so much? How dost thou think to endure the burning of Hell; But I having often thought of that before, answered in good earnest: I know not how I shall endure it. I conceive it to be very intolerable, but there wilbe many there besides me, and I must endure it as others do. He observing that I answered in good earnest grew into a great passion, and said with indignation, I would scorn to have such a base and abject mind as once to entertain such a thought. I answered, I thought there were very few that should be saved, even of those that live within the Church. He answered if there were but one man in all the world to be saved he would certainly believe that he was that man, etc.

But not long after the Lord in mercy was pleased to give me better hopes. Who showeth mercy where he will show mercy, and will have compassion on whom he will have compassion,* as he was pleased to manifest in me, the cheif of all sinners; the maner to my best remembrance was in this wise.

I was now near 25 years of age, marveilously captivated unto sin and Satan in all the faculties of my soul and body, even my thoughts and affections so wholy taken up with the lusts of the flesh with pride and self conceiptednes and with vanity and lying imaginations that there was scarce room at any time for any good thought or consideration. So as when I think upon it makes me stand and wonder at the patience and long suffering of the Lord that he had not by some suddayne stroke from heaven destroyed me;* and such an apprehension I had at that time, but not very forcible, the Lord doubtless having respect to my weaknes, having a heart wretchedly prone to cast away all hope and to fall into utter despair. But as I say I was stricken with a certain admiration or wonder to see how I did run post-hast and was hurryed on to hell. To hell I conceived surely I must needs tend, and it could be to no other where, that way that

I was running, and I could not be far off but holding on that pace I must needs shortly come thither. I seemed as it were to be within the ken of it, even as a ship after a long voyage descovers the place whereunto she saileth,* I apprehended my race to be almost finished and to be as it were within the hearing of the screichings and yellings of tormented souls, not by any sensible noise but as it were an impression of the species of it, as audible as a sensible noise . . .

[*Norwood vows to God 'to forbear my sins, especially my master sin for one week' (this appears to be masturbation); he succeeds for the week but fails to sustain the effort. Haphazardly, he begins to read St Augustine's* Tractate upon John *and finds in himself, to his surprise, a warming towards Christ and 'the children of God'. He also reads William Perkins and the Bible. He is sceptical of the change others seem to observe in him: 'these are some such vayne hopes as my father conceived of me at my return from Rome, and others at other times.' Nevertheless he is arrested by the question: 'Whence is it that I am drawn and affected with the Word of God, which hereto fore I have hated and slyghted so much?' He counsels himself to 'use all good means': 'If I should neclect so great grace, Who knows whether I shall ever have the like opportunity again?'*]

About this time also began all those false conceipts of God wherewith my evil heart was forestalled, to vanish away by degrees. That beam of light of the knowledge of God in Christ which shined into my heart, began to dissolve all those foggy mists of darknes by little and little. I conceived and understood him to be he who giveth to all things not only their beings but also their welbeings, whose mercy is over all his works, who hath a care of all his creatures giving them food in due season, filling the hearts of all with food and gladnes; who giveth to every thing its grace and comelynes; and, whatsoever true contentment, lovelynes, comfort or joy there is in any thing in this world it is not from Satan (though he said to our Saviour, and whispers doubtless in the carnal and corrupt heart of man, the glory of these is delivered unto me and to whomsoever I will I give it) but from God, all worldly pleasures seemed before to me to be as stolen things which God did not allow of. I scarce thought that he created them. Satan secretly suggesting to the heart as if there were nothing from God and accompanying piety but austerity and sad things, and as if he or some kind of heathenish Gods were the giver of pleasure, happines and joyful things. But now I began to apprehend well that as God hath made us, so those affections and dispositions in us, and the objects of those affections, and their suteablenes whereby they become pleasing, and doth confer them upon us so far forth as may not tend to our prejudice but for our good; and doth not forbid us taking delight in that wherein there is indeed true delight but is the author and giver of it. Neither requires us to delight in that wherein there is no delight (as heavenly things seemed to me) but that they are indeed the most ravishing delights of all, if our natures were not so fouly corrupted that we cannot savour them as they are . . .

And surely my heart was deeply and dangerously poisoned and fore-stalled with a heathenish and harsh conceipt of God and of his ways, which I can very hardly shake off unto this day . . .

[*For 18 to 20 months Norwood continues to experience a 'freedom from that miserable captivity wherein I was', though his sense of progress is shaken by awareness of veering into spiritual pride and passionate enter-tainment of murderous thoughts towards a neighbour. He then relapses (the date recorded in the margin as October 1616) into his 'master sin' which brings back 'black thoughts'. Reflecting miserably, however, on how he can approach Christ when he has 'poluted myself' (a phrase he crosses out in favour of 'sinned'), he suddenly experiences 'a clear and heavenly apprehension of my Saviour Jesus Christ with comfort and joy unspeak-able'. He has 'an undoubted assurance of the remission of my sins and sure reconciliation with God in Christ'. His 'heavenly raptures' continue for nearly an hour, when, prompted by memory of Perkins's advice to improve such experiences, he takes his Bible and alights on the words in Col. 1: 12–13: 'Giving thanks unto the Father who hath made us meet to be partakers of the inheritance of the saints in light; who hath deliv-ered us from the power of darkness and hath translated us into the kingdom of his dear son'. Thus, 'the Lord was pleased to seal unto my soul a sweet and comfortable assurance that he had most certainly dealt so with me, and to fill my heart with joy unspeakable and glorious: in comparison whereof I could not but acknowledge all earthly pleasures to be altogether base and muddy and of no account, and that one hour of these joys did far surpass all the joy and pleasure that I had had all my life long if it were all put together.' The joys last some hour and a half, and are followed by an evening in company when he feels 'as one that had found some inestimable treasure which none knew but my self'. For nearly seven months he uses the times before breakfast and after his long working day to read through 'the Old Testament about five times, and the new, ten, with wonderful solace and delight'. He labours against the 'disacquaintance that I observed to grow in my heart towards Christ'.]*

Amongst other means, I read often a treatise of Mr. Perkins entitled The Right Knowledge of Christ Crucified,* but could not sensibly find my heart so disposed towards him as that treatise describes it should: Neither could I draw my heart to that nearnes and affection towards Christ that I desired, but still there seemed to be much strangenes though I sought it often by prayre and framed a prayre out of that treatise for that purpose. Nor even unto this day though it be now 24 years past, and I have through his grace continued asking, seeking, and knocking in some measure, yet I have not attayned that knowledge and acquaintance nor cannot in my soul and spirit come so near unto Christ as might in any good measure content my heart. Yet he hath graciously supported me unto this present, and as often as I have bene at a loss through distrust, doubtfulnes and a dejected mind (my frequent maladies) he hath directed, quickened and comforted me. Yet seems to keep at a distance though I trust he will at last frame my heart to be such as he may take pleasure to dwell there, and to manifest himself more clearly . . .

[Norwood departs from Summer Islands for England, with pious intentions to 'use all diligence and striving with myself', yet remains 'unsetled, I confess' after four months. Not wishing to share the opprobrium of the godly, yet having little regard for 'carnal people', he spends much of his time alone. He is assailed by 'blasphemous thoughts' and 'false opynions and heresies', among which he found most damaging 'errors . . . of an Arminian tincture'.* He assents 'in some sort to that temptation of doubting of my salvation, or at least to hide from my self for a time the certainty of it'. He is 'assailed at certain times, and as it were by fits with dispair,* which by degrees encreased, and grew worse and worse'.]

Besides there was joyned with it (though no visible appearance) yet a very sensible annoyance of Satan; sometimes waking sometimes sleeping which in short time also grew to be almost continual. It is hard to express the maner of it but sometimes he seemed to lean on my back or arm or shoulder, sometimes hanging on my cloak or gown.* Sometimes it seemed in my feeling as if he had stricken me in sundry places, sometimes as it were handling my heart and working withal a wonderful hardnes therein accompanyed with many strange passions affections lusts and blasphemies. Also in bed sometimes pressing sometimes creeping to and fro, sometimes ready to take away my breath, sometimes lifting up the bed, sometimes the pillow, sometimes pulling the cloathes or striking on the bed and on the pillow; sometimes as it were flashing in my head and all my body, sometimes working a strange and stirring fear and amazednes, whether I would or not though I was very firmly resolved against them, and often an expectation of some apparition. Also sometimes as I was walking in the streets my senses grew benummed and dizy, and every thing seemed as death or as it were covered with the shadow of death. It seems also he had some power in transforming or deforming my countenance which I was sensible of, and at those times my countenance seemed very strange and deformed to my father and others that knew me well.

What more? My wonted apprehensions of the joyful presence of Gods holy spirit were turned into an apprehension of the presence of Satan, in soul and body, stirring up horrible blasphemies in my mind, and sundry annoyances in my body . . . But blessed be the Lord who returned my captivity, and delivered my soul from the snare of the hunter, opening myne eyes to see the deadly danger that was before me and into which I had so far run already. Me thought as I looked back I saw my self far entered within the gates of hell, and now if the percullis should be let fall I should be kept in and could no more return, and I feared upon my offer to return the percullis would be presently let fall, such a kind of apprehension I had in my imagination: And indeed I found my self so weak, and so habituated and prone to dispair, and Satan to have gotten such power over me by custom, that I much feared that as soon as he should perceive me about to return, and to lay hold upon the promises (which I had long neglected) he would assail me with all his power and be ready to overwhelm me with utter dispair. Therefore though I desired and endeavoured with all speed to recover my self yet I thought to do it secretly and as it were to steal away, that if it were possible Satan might not perceive it at first till I had gotten some strength, conceiving that he knew not our thoughts. And therefore I laboured in my heart to apply those promises I could think upon and to recover my wonted comfort and assurance. And the Lord did not deny me nor hide his face from me. And so before from time to time the Lord had dealt very graciously with me: for when sometimes through horrible thoughts, lusts and blasphemies I was tempted to doubt whether I were a man indeed endued with a reasonable soul, or whether I were not rather a divel incarnate in the likeness of man and a very enemy to God, and therefore did seem to wish that I had never bene or that I might fly somewhere from God, Even in these temptations seeking the Lord he did usually shew me his wonted gracious countenance. Whereby I was in some good measure restored from time to time; And so at this time as I say he did not hide his face from me, but I seemed to have some joy and comfort, even upon the first purpose and thought of returning.

But notwithstanding my secrecy it seems that Satan perceived my drift* (whether by turning to some places of Scripture or otherwise I know not) and thereupon did assault me more furiously then ever before. And I think it was the night following, or not long after, being asleep, I was troubled with the disease called the mare (wherein a man seems to be neither quite awake nor quite asleep) and in that fit I was most suddainly and vehemently assaulted with a number of blasphemous and horrible thoughts and temptations or perswasions, As that God was not just and faithful in his word that he was hard and unmerciful, etc. and that he had now certainly given me over to Satan and that I was now become a companion of the divel and his angels, and that I did hate God and rage against him as the damned spirits do, and surely my heart seemed to be in a maner so disposed for a moment, but then it pleased the Lord to bring it to my remembrance* and knowledge that all this was but a temptation, and that things were not so indeed as they seemed to be, but was only a delusion of Satan, and provocation to blasphemy.

Hereupon though in myne own apprehension I seemed to be wholly both body and soul in the hands of Satan and no ways able to move or help my self yet the Lord enabled me to desire earnestly to renounce and detest Satan . . . At last overcoming the disease and being quite awake, my feeling smelling and relishing being annoyed as it were with some loathsome thing, there being a kind of noise and the bed rising up in sundry places, and in several places the cloathes being pressed down heavy, with being removed or I removing from that the place became very chill; so was my whole body after I awaked, also the ayre seemed to strike here and there, sometimes upon me, sometimes upon the bed. Hereupon fearing there was some

sin which I had not yet found out for which God had sent these
judgements and threatnings, I arose, put on my cloathes and lighted
a candle, and though it was my usual practise, yet then I began again
to examine my self according to the commandments. Many dismal
thoughts suspicions and doleful doubts arising and presenting themselves, also turbulent passions and murmurings took hold of me,* but
no certainty could I discern of any thing that was not before known
nor scarce of that; hereupon the Lord was graciously pleased by
his holy Spirit to check me inwardly for foolishnes and slownes or
softnes in suffering my self to be holden in the snares and delusions
of Satan and for too much timorousnes in all my carriage towards
God and man. Upon this the bands of Satan became presently as flax
that is burnt with fire,* and I was stirred up from being holden in
his snares, and incouraged not to beleeve delusions, nor to suspect
and doubt in that maner without some greater evidence, and to order
my passions and affections by a certain and well grounded judgment
and well known causes. My faith was quickned, and I had good confidence in God and he seemed to be the very same gracious, loving
and merciful as he was wont to be, and I felt my self enabled to pray
and went to prayre. All heaviness, troublesome doubts, terrours, suspicions and turbulent passions were gone, and I had much peace and
quiet. And then I saw clearly that I was too much afraid of Satan,
too distrustful of the constant mercy of God, too soft and yeilding
in suffering my self to be holden of temptations, and listning too
much to them; too curious in outward circumstances and things;
Whereas the Lord required roundnes, sincerity and truth, and to do
things boldly not wavering about this or that circumstance or esteeming of God as if he lay at a catch* for my failings . . .

[*Norwood seeks pastoral help from two ministers, Mr Elton and Mr
Meacock.*]

It was about two hours after I was up when I set forth to go to Mr.
Meacock, at which time I began again to be much troubled with
inward terrours and threatnings, and all things seemed in their kinds
to be myne enemyes and surely going through the streets I escaped
the horses and carts but narrowly twice or thrice, which might also
be occasioned partly by the present weaknes and dizines of my head
and great perturbations, but it seemed then in my apprehension to
proceed from indignation, wrath and as it were a gnashing of the
teeth against me. I was exceedingly opprest and deprived in the

powers and faculties of my mind and soul, and all things seemed to my sight, hearing and other senses very deadly, and as the shadow of death. And withal an inward whispering of Satan, as if he should say: Seest thou not how I am Lord of the earth, and have domynion over all creatures? tis true indeed God created them at first and indued them with much more vigour grace and beauty then now they have; but now through sin all is divolved into my hands, and I am the God of this world; I strike with lameness, blindness, deafnes, foolishnes madnes and death, where and when I list. Seest thou not at this present the shadow of death upon all things? which also is to be seen upon them at all times in some measure, but now thou seest it more evidently. And as I can thus blast their grace and beauty, so I could as instantly confound and destroy them if I please; for by reason of sin God hath in a maner forsaken the world and cares not for it. And for thy self thou art as surely in my hands and power as ever was any man; Well may I give thee leave to wriggle a while this way or that way, better were it for thee to be quiet, thou shalt no whit avail, but rather increase my rage so much the more to sweep thee away suddainly, and torment thee so much the more greivously when thou art in hell; and indeed thy time is even at hand, thou needest not provoke me to make it shorter then it is; thou shalt see speedily what shal become of thee etc. . . .

It may seem strange that a man should be so suddainly changed from so much peace and comfort to such perturbations and terrours, and it seemed strange to me even at those times. And when I was comforted and in peace I resolved often I would not be so much moved or dismayed with any terrours; the Lord had aboundantly confirmed his grace and mercy towards me, and why should I give place to such temptations and fears? But still when they came they prevailed and I could not withstand them, my comforts being almost wholy withdrawn or rather retyred and hidden. And Satan had power to overwhelm all as it were with a thick dark cloud* and to captivate me in all the powers and faculties of mind and body;* And so it was with me at this time . . .

[*Mr Meacock in particular is 'loving and compassionate'; yet, Norwood feels, both ministers were 'very willing to be rid of my company, though they were loath to tell me so'.*]

The fearful blasphemies and annoyances of Satan, I did but lightly touch upon, concealing my greatest greivances and fears, supposing that if I should lay open all, I should be rejected of christians as a reprobate, a man forsaken of God and given over unto Satan;* Which (being at the pits brink already) would be a means to throw me into utter despair, and would further deprive me of that communion, and such other helps as I might enjoy, especially if the Lord should leave me to a real possession of Satan which I often feared, and seemed sometimes evidently to feel. Besides if it were so indeed, that the Lord had or should utterly cast me off,* yet I conceived it would be no whit to the glory of God for me to publish or declare it; he had manifested the greatnes of his power in my conversion, when I was running headlong into destruction, if he had not stayed me, he had magnifyed his grace and favor towards me in comfortable communion of his holy spirit aboundantly, etc. and if he should now forsake me or (according to my blackest thoughts) if he had thus lifted me up to make my fall the more terrible,* there was surely some secret cause for it more then I knew of, therefore I thought it best to put my mouth in the dust* and to be silent in many things even unto death . . .

[*Mr Elton advises restraint in religious exercises 'to give my self more liberty and contentment for the recovery of my health and strength.'*]

But towards the evening, adressing my self homewards, I began again to have some qualms of heavines and fear, because of the night approaching, and being in the winter near five of the clock, as I went through Canning Street, there was a stranger preaching at the church by London Stone, I went in and heard him; The drift of his sermon (or of that part which I heard) was to shew that God doth sometimes inflict strange and fearful judgements upon men for sin, and yet not withdraw his love and mercy from them, citing and pressing with much emphasys that place, My son despise not thou the Chastening of the Lord, neither faint when thou art rebuked of him, for whom the Lord loveth he chastneth, and scourgeth every son whom he receiveth, etc.* Which things he handled so, that I thought there was some other there present that was troubled in like sort as I was, who had acquainted him with his estate to whom he did especially apply himself.* As I was going home, and thinking on the sermon, and in special on the place aforementioned I was comforted and encouraged and exceedingly strengthned against all fear and terrour, insomuch that I could in some sort bid defyance to the powers of darknes, and resolve with my self that if I were sure to find my chamber full of divels I would not be afraid of them having in my heart a lively and powerful assurance of the love and mercy of God in Christ. Yet by and by after I came into the chamber, I began to have such feelings as I was wont to have at other times, sometimes as if one had handled myne arm; sometimes as if they had leaned on my back, and being at praire I was much more troubled, having a feeling as if I were sometimes peirced through the back, sometimes the reynes, sometimes the side, and feeling as it were the motion of the ayre round about me . . .

[*Norwood takes one of the servants of the house to bed with him, and this helps him to sleep. In the morning, and for about a month following, he is encouraged by 'heavenly and savoury meditations'. Believing his chamber to be haunted, he takes to sleeping with a friend in Walbrook, and experiences trouble only on the occasions when he returns. Following Mr. Elton's advice, he is treated by a physician (negligently, with leeches). He also takes Mr Clitheroe, the master of the house, as his sleeping companion. Clitheroe 'shreeked out often with fear and perturbation' and, questioned by Norwood in the morning, avers that he is generally so afflicted when he has spent the day virtuously. After heavy drinking he is untroubled. Convinced that the house is haunted, Norwood moves to a chamber with a Christian family where, in spite of suspecting the woman of the house of witchcraft, he 'continued above four years till I married.'*]

This temptation hath doubtless had a strong influence in me in the whole course of my life since that time, being now 24 years past. But whether be more the benefit or the prejudice that hath come unto me by it, hath bene always doubtful. But surely upon due consideration I may say, and that from experience, that even these things have wrought together for the best, and that it is good for me that I have bene afflicted.* And that I have borne the yoake in my youth, and as the prophet saith psa: 94.12, Blessed is the man whom thou chastisest, O Lord: and teachest him in thy law; That thou maist give him rest from the days of evil, whilst the pit is digged for the wicked. And surely the Lord was pleased by this chastisement to teach me many things, as also to give me much rest. I have seemed indeed ever since to be more feeble both in body and mind then before, more cold and slow and timorous in and to holy excercises and the spiritual combat, prone to doubting distrusfulnes and qualms of despair,* and in general to have lost much of that youthful heat and vigour in the ways of God which before I enjoyed; which youthful heat and vigour is in no sort to be despised, being a sweet furtherance and advantage in holy excercises carrying a man sweetly forwards as a prosperous gale, who else must row against wind and tide, not that it can do this of it self, but being sanctifyed and quickned by the spirit of God; and so it is a singular blessing and happines where the Lord hath humbled the heart and made it meet to enjoy such a blessing with sobriety and moderation.

But it may be yea it is most likely* that these losses have bene gain to me, and have prevented far greater losses and dangers that might have befallen me some other ways, I might have bene left to some scandalous and shameful fall for the mortifying of spiritual pride, and I may justly conceive, that such a thing would have befallen me at one time or other, considering my desperate and precipitate dis-position to sin in temptation. But the Lord was pleased rather to use this medicine. I remember as a further fruit of this pride that at my first coming into England from Sommer Islands, having some busines with my cousin Rudd, I came acquainted with his wife also, a sweet and gracious woman without doubt. She was then far spent in a consumption, whereof she dyed not long after, and had other heavy afflictions. But at that time she seemed very desirous of my further and more familiar acquaintance, and as if she had bene privy to my spiritual disease she would in conference often interlace such speeches as might remove any prejudicate opynion or offence in me, because of that outward forlorn condition that she seemed to be in at the time, expressing often her faith and sure confidence in God, notwithstanding her afflictions. But I being altogether unexperienced in the ways of God was (like a wretch) so far from judging merci-fully of the poor, that I rather thought her to be a hipocrite or at least to have procured those judgements by some greivous sin.* And if I had no other fruit of my temptation but this, namely to have a tender heart and to judge mercifully of the poor afflicted, and a more pre-cious estimation of the least of Gods saints and children it were a large compensation. *Why then art thou cast down my soul, and why art thou still disquieted within me? Wait on God, for I will yet give him thanks, who is my present help and my God.** Besides I could not before that find in my heart that filial fear and awful regard of God which is usually in his children ...

And thus this temptation, the thought whereof hath bene always

some abhorring to me and dampning of spirit, seems upon due consideration to have bene most expedient and profitable and a further
pledge of Gods free grace and mercy to me in Christ.

O Lord discover thy ways unto me more and more; Give me a
sanctifyed use of all thy dealings towards me, and as thou hast bene
unto me from my childhood a gracious God and merciful father in
Jesus Christ, and art not like man that thou shouldest repent: oh let
it not repent thee of all that grace and goodnes, but continue the
same unto me, now that the evening of my life and age approacheth.
Make me mindful of that great deliverance out of Egypt, from those
cruel taskmasters who would soon have made me wholy unfit for
earth, much more unfit for heaven, spoiling me daily of whatsoever
good thou hadst given me, and hurrying me forwards unto everlasting destruction; Make me mindful of all thy gracious deliverances.
Oh Lord whatsoever I am, whatsoever I have is thine, thyne by a
manifold right. Enlarge my heart to offer up my self my soul and
body; a living sacrifice holy and acceptable unto thee, fit me unto the
trials and temptations whereunto thou hast reserved me, strengthen`
me to stand in the evil day, thou hast engaged thy faithfulnes. Leave
me not to be tempted above what I am able, but give a comfortable
issue with the temptation that I may be able to bear it; give what thou
requirest, and require what thou wilt; make me to be such as thou
maist take pleasure and delight in. Conform me unto Jesus Christ,
my head, reveal thy self unto me daily more and more in him, that
I may account all things but loss, for the excellent knowledge sake of
Jesus Christ, my Lord, and judge them to be dung that I may win
Christ and be found in him not having myne own righteousnes but
that which is through the faith of Christ even the righteousnes which
is of God through faith; That I may know him, and the virtue of his
resurrection, and the fellowship of his afflictions, and be made con-
formable unto his death if by any means I might attayn unto the resurrection of the dead. That I may comprehend with all thy saints
what is the length and breadth and height and depth, and know the
love of Christ which passeth knowledge.

Unto thee who art able to do exceeding aboundantly above all
which we ask or think, according to thy power which worketh in us,
be praise in thy church by Christ Jesus   Amen 1640

A SHORT HISTORY OF
THE LIFE OF JOHN CROOK

History of the life of John Crook, *A Quaker, Containing Some of his Spiritual Travels* and Breathings after God,* in his Young and Tender Years: Also an Account of various Temptations wherewith he was Exercised, and the Means by which he came to the Knowledge of the Truth. The Manuscript hereof, Written by his own Hand, was found since his other Works were Published in Print.* London, Printed and Sold by F. Sowle, in White-Hart-Court in Gracious Street, 1706.

I remember . . . when I was tempted or troubled in my Mind, I would get into some Corner or secret Place, and pray unto God;* and when I had committed Sin and Evil, I was still troubled afterward, and then I would pray to God for his Strength against them: And when I was alone, I was sure to hear of all my Doings, they would come so fresh in my remembrance, and be so set before me, that I could not get them out of my sight, but endeavoured to get into some private Place to pray and weep; and then would promise and covenant in secret with God, that if he would forgive these, and help me for the time to come, I would never do the like again: But for all this, Evils prevailed against me, and I could not keep my Promises with God. So that Trouble came upon my Spirit, and I often mourned and went heavily, not taking that delight in Play and Pastime which I saw other Children took; which made me often conclude in my Mind, that they were in a better Condition than I, and that surely God was angry with me,* which made him so correct me, that I could have no Peace, whenas I saw other Children merry and chearful, and not at all as I was. Yet sometimes I had Ease, and was chearful, but it seldom held long, without some intermixture of Trouble. I had also many Openings* in my Mind, which did sometimes much amaze me; about Heaven and Hell, and wicked Men and good Men; and also I saw many of the Priests Prophane in those Parts, giving up themselves to divers kinds of Wickedness.

About Ten or Eleven Years of Age I went to *London*, and there went to several Schools, until I was about Seventeen Years of Age; in all which time, I was not without much Trouble and Exercises in my Mind; notwithstanding I lived in a wicked Family, and amongst those that scoffed at all strictness in Religion; yet I would get into some by-Corner, and pray and weep bitterly, from the sense of my own Sins, and would often reprove my School-Fellows and Companions for their Wickedness; I often walking alone by my self in some secret Place, when they would be at Play and Pastime. Thus I passed away my youthful Days, in Reading and Praying oft times when Trouble was upon me, which I was seldom free from whole Weeks, more or less, either in the Night or Day-time; but all this time I did not mind* hearing of Sermons, being little acquainted with any that frequented such Exercises, until I went to be an Apprentice, about the 17th Year of my Age.*

About this time I was placed in a Parish in *London*, where was a Minister, who was in those Days called a Puritan,* where I came acquainted with those young People that frequented Sermons and Lectures,* so often as we had any Liberty from our Occasions, being Apprentices; yet Trouble grew upon me more and more, as I grew in knowledge and understanding of the things of God; and still I applied my self to reading the Bible, and other good Books, and prayed often, insomuch, as those in the Family where I was an Apprentice, took much notice of it, and would stand in secret Places to hear me, tho' I then knew it not.

But I remember when I was most fervent in my Devotion, something in me would be still pulling me back (as it were) as if I would not wholly yet leave those Evils I knew my self guilty of, but would gladly have them pardoned and forgiven, and yet would I continue in them: Such a thing I found within my self, gainsaying my earnest Cries and Petitions, as if I would have had Peace with God, and yet also have continued still in those things I prayed against; which at last made me conclude, I was but an Hypocrite,* and did not belong to the Election of Grace, but was to become some eminent Spectacle of God's Displeasure,* and that which gainsayed my earnest Cries was the Devil; and therefore concluded I was possessed with the Devil;* and would often, as I had occasion, be enquiring of Professors how it was with them,* and how they understood the Condition of those to be, that were possessed with unclean Spirits in Christ's time;* but all that I could get from any, could not remove this out of my Mind, but that I was possessed with the Devil; for I thought I often felt in my self something sensible, and manifestly opposing those good Motions and Desires that were in me, as if two had been striving in me for Victory:* And when I was so tired out with Resistings and Fightings in my self, I could get no Relief or sensible Ease, but by going to Prayer, either secretly within my self, or down upon my Knees in some secret Place; and oft times when I was at Prayer, I was so possessed with fear, that I looked behind me, lest the Devil stood there ready to take me so soon as I rose up; and then I was troubled for giving way so far, as to look behind me; yet I durst not leave praying for all this,* And that which troubled me often times, was, that those which heard me pray, admired my Gift in Prayer, and believed me to be a Child of God, when I concluded nothing less of my self, than that I should deceive them,* and cause God's Name to be blasphemed by my miscarriage at last, which I concluded must needs be at one time or other; for I thought it impossible for me to continue in that Condition long, but I should be made an Example to all Hypocrites.*

Thus I continued Professing, and Praying, and Hearing, and Reading, and yet I could not perceive any Amendment in my self; but the same youthful Vanities drew away my Mind when Opportunities offered, as before; which was never much to outward gross Prophaneness, but only to idle Talk, and vain Company, in misspending my time, and minding Pride too much in my Apparel, and such things, for all which I was condemned; as also for wearing long Hair, and spending my Money in vain, which I thought might have been better imployed, if I had bought some good Books, or been charitable to the Poor: All that I did was condemned, and my self for doing of it also; yet I durst not leave off my Duties, for then I thought the Devil would prevail over me, to make me destroy my self; for I was afraid to see a Knife if I was alone, or to have any in the Room at Night where I lay.* And thus I continued, running to Lectures when I had any time allowed me by my Master from my Occasions, which I endeavoured to get, by doubling my Diligence in the Day time, and also from my Sleep in the Night time, that so I might the more easily gain Opportunities of my Master; all which I imployed in private Meetings and Lectures, going after any eminent Man I heard of, which by this time I had obtained the Knowledge of, by my much Acquaintance with constant Hearers of Sermons, and Frequenters of private Fasts and Meetings.

I have often been in Congregations, hearing Sermons, when I have had much ado to forbear crying out in the midst of the Assembly

(I am damned, I am damned) but did not, though I went often away full of Horrour and Misery in my Mind. The Ministers then commonly preaching by Marks and Signs, how a Man might know himself to be a Child of God, if [h]e were so; and how it would be with him if he were not so;* which made me sometime to conclude, I had saving Grace, and by and by to conclude, I was but an Hypocrite: And thus I was tossed up and down, from Hope to Despair;* and from a sign of Grace to me one while, and then presently to a sign of an Hypocrite and Reprobate* again; so that I could not tell what to do with my self, or whether it were best to go to Church, or stay at Home; for I could get no Rest, or lasting Peace, by all my hearing and running up and down: And yet I had no freedom in my self, to go to any of those Ministers in private, to acquaint them with my Condition; partly, because I thought they could not help me; and partly out of fear, lest they should discourage me, and tell me I was an Hypocrite,* and then Satan should prevail to force me to destroy my self; for I was afraid of any thing that might confirm my own Thoughts of my miserable State, which I believed to be bad enough, but was exceeding afraid to have my Thoughts seconded by the Sentence and Judgment of any other:* So that I remember not that ever I went to any Minister to acquaint them with my Condition, but bore it secretly in my own Bosom, few knowing how it was with me. Then I resolved one First Day* afternoon (called then the Lord's Day), being full of Trouble, when I was an Apprentice to go that time which way I should be moved or enclined in my Spirit, whether it was up Street, or down Street, East or West, North or South, without any predetermination or forecast, or so much as fore-thinking, either of any Man or Place to go to, or hear that Day, but only (as the Staff should fall, as it were, or) as I should be led;* accordingly I did come down Stairs, and went, as I was led by something within me, which I believed in and followed, until it brought me into a Parish-Church (so called)* where I went in and sate down, and within a small season of time, a young Man went up into the Pulpit, and preached out of this Text, *Isa.* 50 10. *He that walketh in Darkness, and hath no Light, let him trust in the Name of the Lord, and stay upon his God.* Upon which Text he had preached before, and was at that time to pick out, or discover, who that Man was that feared the Lord, and yet walked in Darkness; the which he performed, as if he had known my Condition and aimed at, and spake to me in particular;* which did much relieve me, and at that time much comfort me, being so providentially brought thither, where I never was before, neither heard of any such Man (that I remember) I went away much gladded, and continued so for some time; but Trouble came upon me again afterwards, through some Negligence and Coldness, which gendered to Distrust and Unbelief; so that the old Enemy, the Tempter, got in again, and tore me worse than before in my Mind; so that I questioned all that ever I had at any time given me to refresh me, as being but a Delusion, and no Truth in it; for I was a Cast-away, and all these things were but to leave me without Excuse.* Then I began to be full of Horrour, so that my Sleep was much taken from me, and Anguish and intolerable Tribulation dwelt in my Flesh; so that when I heard any of the meanest poor People cry any thing about *London* Streets, I even wished and desired that I were in their Condition; for I thought every Man or Woman to be in a better Condition than my self;* nay, I thought my self the only miserable Man in all the World; had I been made the most contemptible Creature in the whole Creation,* I had been happy in comparison of my most intolerable unexpressible Misery; all which was heightened by *Francis Spira*'s Book,* which came to my hand, but I could not read it over, I thought it so to resemble my present Condition; for when I had read but a little, I cast it from me,* and durst not look on it any more.

In this extream Misery I continued, keeping it to my self, mourning in secret, until one Morning, as I was solitarily sitting, lamenting my present State; on a suddain, there sprang in me a Voice,* saying, Fear not, O thou tossed, as with a Tempest, and not comforted, I will help thee; and although I have hid my Face from thee for a moment, yet with everlasting loving Kindness will I visit thee, and thou shalt be mine; fear not, for I am pacified towards thee, and will never leave thee nor forsake thee, saith I the Lord, the mighty God.

Whereupon all was hush'd and quieted within me, so that I wondered what was become of the many Vexations, tormenting Fears and Thoughts that just before attended me; here was such a Calm and Stilness in my Mind for a pretty time; so that it was brought to my Mind, that there was Silence in Heaven for half an Hour; and I was filled with Peace and Joy, like one overcome; and there shone such an Inward Light within me,* that for the space of Seven or Eight

Days time, I walked as one taken from the Earth; I was so taken up in my Mind, as if I walked above the World, not taking notice (as it seemed to me) of any Persons or Things as I walked up and down *London* Streets, I was so gathered up in the marvellous Light of the Lord, and filled with a joyful Dominion over all things in this World. In which time, I saw plainly, and to my great Comfort and Satisfaction, that whatever the Lord would communicate and make known of himself, and the Mysteries of his Kingdom, he would do it in a way of Purity and Holiness; for I saw then such a Brightness in Holiness, and such a Beauty in an upright and pure righteous Conversation, and close circumspect walking with God in an Holy Life, although I had before obeyed to the uttermost that I could, yet I could not get Peace thereby, nor find and feel that Acceptance and Justification before God, as I did at this time when it sprang freely in me, that, as it were, all Religion lay in it truly so, and all Profession besides, or without it, were as nothing in comparison of this Communion. For I remember, while I abode and walked in that Light and Glory which shone so clearly in my Mind and Spirit within me, there was not a wrong Thought appearing or stirring in me, but it vanished presently, finding no Entertainment; my whole Mind and Soul was so taken up with, and swallowed up of, that glorious Light and satisfactory Presence of the Lord thus manifested in me.

After this, I perceived an Abatement of the Glory, and I began to read and perform Duties as I had done before (which for about Eight Days time, I could not perform so formally as I did use to do before (I was so filled with Joy and Peace) but with much more Livingness and Zeal, Faith and Confidence than before, which caused many of my Acquaintance to admire my Gift in Prayer,* and upon all occasions to put me upon that Duty. I begining about this time much to follow those Ministers that came out of *Holland*,* and some others that were more for the way of Separation from the Parish Assemblies, disliking in my Mind those mixed Communions; much thirsting after, and longing for a pure Communion with such as were most Spiritual, and walked in the closest Fellowship with God in Holiness, and Watchfulness one over another, for Good and Encrease in a Holy Life, which much I longed for, since I had seen the Beauty of it.

I did also walk with a Company of young Men, who met together so often as our Occasions would permit, and prayed and conferred together about the things of God; and I remember, when several would be speaking out of the Scriptures, by way of Exposition, &c. I had little to say from thence, not having much acquaintance with them, being brought up, mostly in my young Days, under such Tutors, and in such Families, as did not much regard the Scriptures, accounting them Puritans and Sectaries that addicted themselves that way: But I would be speaking forth my own Experiences, delighting in, and loving those most who could speak most from Experience, my Heart being most warmed and enlivened in those experimental Discourses and Conferences; so that those who were most spiritual, delighted to be with me, and I with them; they would tell me, that I spake from Experience; for I thought I could speak to most Conditions and Things by Experience, as if I had had a Volume of all Subjects within me, while most gathered their Discourses from the Scriptures without them.*

In Two or Three Years time after this, I began to gather Scriptures into my Mind and Memory, what from hearing of others, and my own Studies, which occasioned me to dwell more without, and less within; so that by degrees, the Knowledge in my natural Understanding and Judgment began to out-grow and over-top the sense of my inward Experiences; at last, having little besides the remembrance (now a great way off) of those things which once were lively and fresh, growing and sprouting up in me, as if it had always been Spring Time in my Heart and Mind: But afterwards my inward Parts were like a Winter, all retired out of sight, as into an hidden Root;* and many Questionings about the way of Worship, and Ordinances of the New Testament began to arise in my Mind, judging my self, that now the Lord had done so much for me, I could not but be chargeable with Unthankfulness before the Lord for his Mercies, if I did not now seek out the purest way of Worship, that I might enjoy all his Ordinances in the Purity of them: Wherefore, after I had gone amongst several sorts of Professors, of divers Judgments, trying with whom my Spirit could most sit down and close with; at last, I met with some particular Persons, with whom I joined in Communion, in the way of Independancy;* and at times, we had many Refreshings together, while we were kept watchful and tender, with our Minds inwardly retired, and our Words few and savoury; which frame of Spirit* we were preserved in, by communicating our Experiences each to other;* as, how our Hearts had been kept towards the Lord all the Week; with an Account of most Days Passages between God and our own Souls, from the Beginning of the Week unto the End; which continued some Years, until it grew formal;* and then we began to consider our Church-State, whether we were in the right Order of the Gospel, according to the Primitive Patterns,* and in the Consultation of the proper Administrator of Baptism, and the right Subject thereof, we began to be divided and shattered in our Minds and Judgments about it;* from whence arose many Questionings about divers things not at all questioned before, which gendered unto much uncertainty and insta-bility. Afterwards, we began not only to be remiss in our Meetings, but also confused in our Preachings and Services, when we were Assembled; so that at last we did not meet at all, but grew by degrees into Estrangedness one from another, and into Carelesness, consult-ing Principles of Liberty, and Ease to the Flesh, and from thence, to encourage and justifie our present Remisness and Coldness in Religious Performances. But I was not so given up, or devoted to Remisness and Ease, as that that I was wholly without Checks and Reproofs for my so doing; and oftentimes the inward Distress and Trouble of my Spirit roused me up again to Religious Duties, as Praying, Reading, etc. I found also by Experience, that when I was over-born in my Judgment and natural Understanding, by Principles and Tenents, which were offer'd to me in my shattered State, to draw my Mind unto Carelesness about all Religion, and to a slighting of my former Strictness (as well as others now) and as for Sin and Evil, those Principles would have forced me into a Belief, that my former Apprehensions of the Wickedness and Danger thereof, was more from a suddain Fright, together with a Traditional Belief of the thing, than from any grounded Certainty from Reason, or deliberate Consideration thereof in true Judgment. But against all this, and much more of like Nature, which I was exercised with Day and Night, and often tempted to embrace, both by inward Suggestions, and outward Allurements, from those that sometimes had been as Religious as my self, and no less acquainted with inward Experiences of like kind with my own: Yet from a Sense and deep Impression, which yet remained upon my Spirit, both of great Troubles (in being delivered from them all) and sweet Consolation I had tasted; I say, the sensible Remembrance of the former Days (did stick upon me so, as to keep me from those Principles of Ranterism and Atheism, which were rife and much stirring in those Times,* and through Faith in what I had tasted, I was supported under many a bitter Combate, and deep Wave and Billow) made me say and conclude in my Heart and Mind, That the Righteous was more excellent than his Neighbour; and that there was a far better State and Condition to be known and enjoyed in this World, by walking with God in Holiness and Purity, than by all licentious and voluptuous Living, or covetous gathering of Riches together, to get a Name in the Earth. And this I knew from what Sweetness I my self had once enjoyed therein. The Result of all which, together with an inward Cry, that was still continued underneath all Reasonings and Observations I could make, and lay deeper lodged in my inward Parts, than all overly floating Apprehensions and Wanderings to get and obtain Relief and Satisfaction. I say, this continued Cry and Sound in my Ears inwardly, called for Watchfulness over my Ways, and Obedience unto what was made manifest to be the Will of God in my Conscience, as being more available to afford me Rest and Peace, than either all my Notions, Observations, Beliefs or Sacrifices (outward) whatsoever;* the meaning whereof, to know them distinctly, was as unknown to me, as the struglings of the Twins in *Rebekah*'s Womb;* until it pleased the Lord to send one of his Servants (called a Quaker) to join himself unto my Condition, in his Ministring, as *Philip* did unto the Chariot of the Eunuch* (who before understood not what he read) but afterwards, by Philip's expounding the Scripture to him, believed what before he was ignorant of: So it was with me, through that Servant and Instrument of the most high God, opening my Eyes, and speaking plainly, and not in Parables, nor in dark Sayings; whereby I came to see what it was that had so long cried in me, upon every Occasion, of serious inward retiring in my own Spirit: So that I could say of Christ, A greater than Solomon was here, and one that divided aright between the Living and the Dead, and manifested plainly to whom the Living Child belonged,* and what was the true Woman, or Church, in God (the Father of our Lord Jesus Christ) and what was the Harlot,* or false Church and Synogogue of Satan, whatever she could say to justifie her self, as the true Mother-Church.

And indeed this kind of Preaching by the fore-mentioned Quaker (so called) appeared unto me, at the first hearing thereof, like as if the old Apostles were again risen from the Dead, and began to preach again in the same Power, Life and Authority, in which they ministred when they gave forth, and first writ and published the Gospel and New Testament of Jesus Christ.

I could truly say with *Jonathan*,* after I had heard and tasted of the Honey and sweet Ministration of the blessed Gospel, that my Eyes were opened, and Strength renewed from the same Power again, by which it was preached at first, as free from the Dreggs and Lees of Man's Wit and Inventions, by which they had darkened Counsel by Words without Knowledge: I say the Truth and Lye not; after I had heard and tasted of that Honey of *Canaan*, that flowed freely, without the forced Inventions of Man's Brain, my Eyes were opened, and my Strength was renewed, and Victory I obtained (through that Grace of the Gospel) over those Lusts and corrupt Desires which rose against those little Stirrings and Movings after the living God, which I had felt working at times in my Heart, even from my Youth, until the time of my being born again of the incorruptible Seed, and received the Earnest of the Inheritance and Seal of the Covenant, &c.

When the glad Tidings of the Gospel came thus to be sounded in my Ears, and reaching my Heart and Conscience, they did not make void my former Experiences of the Love and Mercy of God to my poor Soul, nor in the least beget my Mind into a Contempt of his sweet Refreshings in my wearied Pilgrimage,* all along as Streams of that Brook which *Israel* drank of by the way in their Travels; but on the contrary, brought all my former Revivings that he gave me in my sore Bondage fresh to my Remembrance, and set in order before me my manifold Rebellions against his Wooings, as also my ill Requitings of him for his tender-Dealings, often Visits and long-Suffering towards me; all which challenged a Subjection from me, as most due unto this tender dealing God and Father towards me, and made me cry out, What was God so near me in a Place I was not aware of! that I found my Heart to be broken and overcome with his Love and Mercy to me ...

Here followeth a Relation of the working of Truth *in my Heart since I was called a* Quaker, *'till near the time of my Departure.*

I was convinced of the Truth towards the end of the Year, 1654. (as I remember) through the Servant of the Lord, before mentioned, called *William Dewsbury*,* not knowing of what Judgment he was when I went to him, (for if I had known he had been a *Quaker*, I think I should not have heard him, being afraid of strange Opinions, lest I should be deceived, but) being providentially cast where he was declaring, I heard him; and his Words, like Spears, pierced and wounded my very Heart; yet so, as they seemed unto me, as Balm also, healing and comforting, as well as searching and piercing; And I remember the very Words that took the deepest Impression upon me at that present, speaking of several States and Conditions of Men and Women: Such Words passed from him, as implied the miserable Life of such, who notwithstanding their Religious Duties or Performances, had not Peace and Quietness in their Spirits; who through the want of an Understanding, where to know and find a stay to their Minds, to exercise them at all times, and in all places, were like Children tossed to and fro,* and frighted with every Bug-bear and cunning Craftiness of Men, to promote their own Opinions and Ways; which I knew was my own Condition at that time, as well as the State of many more poor shattered People at that Day compassing our selves about with the Sparks of our own kindling, which did but procure us Sorrow, when we came to lie down and be still, and commune with our own Hearts, having nothing inwardly to feed and stay upon, but either formal Duties, which perished with the using, or disputatable Opinions about Christ, and Doctrinal Things, in the natural Understanding and Memory; but wanted a spiritual Understanding of that which might then have been known of God within;* which afterward I came to know and behold, as the Appearance of the tryed Corner-stone laid in *Zion*, most elect and precious unto them that believed in him; whereby I understood certainly, that it is not an Opinion, but Christ Jesus the Power and Arm of God, who is the Saviour, and that felt in the Heart, and kept dwelling there by Faith; which differs as much from all Notions in the Head and Brain, as the Living Substance differeth from the Picture or Image of it. . . .

THE LOST SHEEP FOUND

Lawrence Clarkson

The Lost sheep Found: or The Prodigal returned to his Fathers house, after many a sad and weary Journey through many Religious Countreys,*

Where now, notwithstanding all his former Transgressions, and breach of his Fathers Commands, he is received in an eternal Favor, and all the righteous and wicked Sons that he hath left behinde, reserved for eternal misery;*

As all along every Church or Dispensation may read in his Travels, their Portion after this Life.*

Written by Laur. Claxton, the onely true converted Messenger of Christ Jesus, Creator of Heaven and Earth.

London:
Printed for the Author. 1660.

Having published several Writings in confirmation of this spiritual last Commission that ever shall appear in this unbelieving World, a Well-wisher to this Commission, yea a man of no mean parts nor Parentage in this Reasons kingdom,* much importuned me to publish to this perishing world, the various leadings forth of my spirit through each Dispensation, from the year 1630, to this year 1660, and that for no other end, than that Reason, or the Devils mouth might be stopped, with the hypocrisie of his heart laid naked, and the tongues of Faith with praises opened, to consider what variety of By-paths, and multiplicity of seeming realities, yet absolute notions, the souls of the Elect may wander or travel through, seeking rest, and yet find none till the day unexpected, that Soul as a brand be plucked out of the fire* of his own righteousness, or professed wickedness, unto the true belief of a real Commission which quencheth all the fiery darts of sin, that Dispensations have left cankering in his soul, [minde this] as have but patience, and thou shalt hear the more I labored for perfect cure and peace in my soul, the further I was from it, insomuch that I was resolvd to seek forth no more, supposing my self in as perfect health and liberty in my spirit, as any then professing an unknown God whatsoever.

As do but seriously minde this ensuing Epistle, and thou mayest in me read thy own hypocrisie and dissimulation in point of Worship all along;* as in that year 1630, being of the Age of fifteen yeares, and living with my Parents in the town of Preston in Amounderness, where I was born, and educated in the Form and Worship of the Church of England, then established in the Title of the Episcopal, or Bishops Government; then, and in that year, my heart began to enquire after the purest Ministery held forth under that Form, not being altogether void of some small discerning, who preached Christ more truly and powerfully, as I thought, than another, and unto them was I onely resolved to follow their Doctrine above any other, and to that end my brethren being more gifted in the knowledge of the Scriptures than my self, and very zealous in what they knew, that they did prevail with Mr. Hudson our Town-Lecturer,* to admit of such Ministers as we judged were true laborious Ministers of Christ, who when they came, would thunder against Superstition, and sharply reprove Sin, and prophaning the Lords-day; which to hear, tears would run down my cheeks for joy: so having a pitiful superstitious fellow the Minister of our Town, I spared no pains to travel to Standish and other places, where we could hear of a Godly Minister,* as several times I have gone ten miles, more or less, fasting all the day, when my Parents never knew of it, and though I have been weary and hungry, yet I came home rejoycing. Then the Ministers had an Order, that none should receive the Sacrament, but such as would take it at the rayled Altar kneeling,* which I could not do, and therefore went to such Ministers in the Countrey that gave it sitting: Now a while after Mr. Starby the Minister of our Town, taking notice of leaving our Parish, informed our father the dangers of his children going into Heresie, and the trouble that would ensue upon our father and his children, besides the disgrace of all good Church-men, which did much incense our father, but all to no purpose, for I thought it conscience to obey God before man;* however I being under my fathers tuition, he cast a strict eye over me, and would force me to read over the prayers in the book of *Common-prayer* and *Practice of Piety*,* which I have done, till they have fallen asleep and my self, this was our devotion in those days; but increasing in knowledge, I judged to pray another mans form, was vaine babling, and not acceptable to God: and then the next thing I scrupled, was asking my parents blessing,* that often times in the winter mornings, after I have been out of my bed, I have stood freezing above, and durst not come down till my father was gone abroad, and the reason I was satisfied, the blessing or prayers of a wicked man God would not hear, and so should offend God to ask him blessing; for either of these two ways I must, down on my knees, and say, Father pray to God to bless me, or give me your blessing for Gods sake, either of which I durst not use with my lips, but was in me refrained; and I improved my knowledge in the Doctrine of these men I judged was the true Ministers of God, so that with teares many times I have privately sought the Lord as I thought, whether those things that the puritanical Priests preached, was my own,* and the more I was troubled, that I could not pray without a Book as my brethren did, fain would I have been judged a Professor with them, but wanted parts,* yet often times have had motions to tender my self to prayer amongst them, but durst not, and to that end I might be admitted to pray with them, I have prayed alone to try how I could pray, but could not utter my self as I knew they did: so I remember their was a day of Humiliation* to be set apart by the Puritans so called,* to seek God by prayer and expounding of Scriptures, against which day I took my pen, and writ a pretty form of words, so got them by heart, and when the day came I was called to improve my gifts, at which I was glad, yet in a trembling condition lest I should be foyled; however, to prayer I went, with a devotion as though I had known the true God, but alas, when I was in the midst of that Prayer, I lost my form of words, and so was all in a sweat as though I had been sick, and so came off like a hypocrite as I was, which so seized on my soul, that I thought for my hypocrisie damnation would be my portion;* however it humbled me, that I was glad to become one of the meanest of the number, still full of fears that when I died, I should go to hell; in which time I writ all the hypocrisie of my heart in a Letter to send to Mr. Hudson our Lecturer, to know his judgement whether such a soul as there related might be saved?* in the interim comes a motion within me, saying, A fool, why dost thou send to man that knows not what will become of his own soul? burn it, and wait upon me; which Letter I did burn, and not many weeks after I had a gift of Prayer that was not inferior to my brethren, for which I was glad for the goodness of God to my soul; and as I increased in knowledge, so was my zeal, that I have many times privately prayed with rough hard Sinders under my bare knees, that so

God might hear me; and when I could not end my Prayers with tears running down my cheeks, I was afraid some sin shut the attention of God from me: and thus did I do for a few years, in which time the Bishops began to totter and shake,* yea, for their cruelty and superstition, was totally routed.

Now if then you had asked me what I thought God was, the Devil was, what the Angels nature was, what Heaven and Hell was, and what would become of my soul after death?

My answer had plainly bin this: That my God was a grave, ancient, holy, old man, as I supposed sat in Heaven in a chair of gold, but as for his nature I knew no more than a childe: and as for the Devil, I really believed was some deformed person out of man, and that he could where, when, and how, in what shape appear he pleased; and therefore the devil was a great Scar-croe, in so much that every black thing I saw in the night, I thought was the devil:* But as for the Angels, I knew nothing at all; and for Heaven I thought was a glorious place with variety of rooms suitable for Himself, and his Son Christ, and the Holy Ghost: and Hell, where it was I knew not, but judged it a local place, all dark, fire and brimstone, which the devils did torment the wicked in, and that for ever; but for the soul at the hour of death, I believed was either by an Angel or a Devil fetcht immediately to Heaven or Hell. This was the height of my knowledge under the Bishops Government, and I am perswaded was the height of all Episcopal Ministers then living; so that surely if they shall be established for a National Ministry, they will not impose such ceremonies as then they did, but are grown wiser about God and Devil; for they will finde the major part of England is grown wiser, so cannot stoop to an inferior Light; therefore if ye now begin to stand, take heed lest ye fall.*

Secondly, After this I travelled into the Church of the Presbyterians, where still I made Brick of straw and clay, nay there I found my soul the more oppressed, and further ensnared in the land of Egypt, burning Brick all the day;* but I knowing no further light, I was willing to bear their yoke, and sometimes found it pleasant; for herein consisted the difference of the Presbyterian and Episcopal, onely in a few superstitious Rites and Ceremonies, as also their Doctrine was more lively than the Episcopal, for they would thunder the Pulpit with an unknown God, which then I thought was true, and sharply reprove sin, though since I saw we were the greatest sinners; but however their Doctrine I liked, it being the highest I then heard of: So war being begun betwixt the Episcopal and the Presbyterian,* I came for London, where I found them more precise* than in our Popish Countrey of Lancashire;* for with us the Lords-day was highly profaned by the toleration of May-poles, Dancing and Rioting, which the Presbyterians hated, and in their Doctrine cryed out against, which thing my soul also hated, though yet I was not clear but the Steeple was the house of God,* from that saying of David, Psalm 84.10 saying, For a day in thy Courts is better than a thousand: I had rather be a Door-keeper in the house of my God than to dwell in the tents of wickedness; so that I finding out the ablest Teachers in London, as then I judged was Mr. Calamy, Case, Brooks* and such like, unto whom I daily referred, if possible, to get assurance of Salvation,* not neglecting to receive the Ordinance of Breaking of Bread from them, judging in so doing, I shewed forth the Lords death till he came. Now the persecution of the Bishops fell so heavy upon the Presbyterian Ministers, that some fled for New England; and Hooker had left several Books in print, which so tormented my soul, that I thought it unpossible to be saved;* however, I labored what in me lay, to finde those signs and marks in my own soul, and to that end neglected all things that might hinder it; and thus for a certain time I remained a hearer of them till such time that Wars began to be hot, and they pressed the people to send out their husbands and servants to help the Lord against the Mighty,* by which many a poor soul knowing no better, was murthered, and murthered others, taking the Bible in their Pockets, and the Covenant in their Hats,* by me was esteemed the work and command of the Lord, not at all minding the command of the Second Commission* to the contrary, as in 2 Cor. 10.4. saying, We do not war after the flesh, for the weapons of our warfare are not carnal, but mighty through God to the pulling down of strong holds, &c. This was not by me understood, but as they did in the old time in Moses his Commission, so I thought we might do then; in which time the Presbyterians began to be great people, and in high esteem, and at that time there was a great slaughter of the Protestants in Ireland,* that London was thronged with their Ministers and people, and several Collections was gathered for them; but this I observed, that as the Presbyterians got power, so their pride and cruelty increased against such as was contrary to them, so that

Thirdly I left them, and travelled to the Church of the Independents; for this I observed as wars increased, so variety of Judgements increased: and coming to them, of which was Mr. Goodwin,* and some others, I discerned their Doctrine clearer, and of a more moderate spirit: Now the greatest difference betwixt them, was about baptizing of infants, pleading by Scripture, that none but the infants or children of Believers ought to be baptized; and that none of them must receive the Sacrament, as then it was called, but such as was Church-members, judging all that was not congregated into fellowship, were not of God, but the world: So that about these things I was searching the truth thereof, and labored in the letter of the Scripture to satisfie my judgement; in the interim hearing of one Doctor Crisp,* to him I went, and he held forth against all the aforesaid Churches, That let his people be in society or no, though walked all alone, yet if he believed that Christ Jesus died for him, God beheld no iniquity in him: and to that end I seriously perused his Bookes, and found it proved by Scripture, as it is written Numbers 23.21. He hath not beheld iniquity in Jacob, neither hath he seen perverseness in Israel. This was confirmed by other Scriptures, that I conceived whose sins Christ died for, their sin was to be required no more; for thus thinking when the debt was paid, the Creditor would not look upon him as indebted to him, yet this I ever thought Christ never died for all,* though the Scripture was fluent to that purpose, yet I found Scriptures to the contrary,* and was ever as touching that satisfied, that as Christ prayed for none but such as was given him out of the world, I pray for them, I pray not for the world, so that I thought he did not die for them he would not pray for, which thought now I know is true, and have by pen, and can by tongue make good the same: But I must return to the time then under Doctor Crisp's Doctrine, in which I did endeavor to become one of those that God saw no sin, and in some measure I began to be comforted therewith, but how, or which way to continue in the same I could not tell; having as yet but little understanding in the Scripture I was silent, onely still enquiring after the highest pitch of Light then held forth in London, in which time Mr. Randel* appeared, with Mr. Simpson,* with such a Doctrine as Doctor Crisp, onely higher and clearer, which then was called Antinomians, or against the Law, so that I left all Church-fellowship, and burning of Brick in Egypt, and travelled with them up and down the borders, part Egypt, and part Wilderness.

Fourthly, take notice in this Sect I continued a certain time, for Church it was none, in that it was but part form, and part none; in which progress I had a great sort of professors acquainted with me, so began to be some body amongst them, and having a notable gift in Prayer, we often assembled in private, improving my gifts, judging then the best things of this world was onely prepared for the Saints, of which then I judged my self one, not knowing any other but that God was a Spirit, and did motion in and out into his Saints, and that this was Gods Kingdom, and we his people; and therefore I judged God did fight for us against our enemies, that so we might enjoy him in liberty: At which time Paul Hobson* brake forth with such expressions of the in-comes and out-goes of God, that my soul much desired such a gift of preaching, which after a while Hobson and I being acquainted, he had a Captains place under Colonel Fleetwood for Yarmouth, so that thither with him I went, and there tarried a soldier with them, at which time I had a small gift of Preaching, and so by degrees increased into a method, that I attempted the Pulpit at Mr. Wardels Parish in Suffolk, and so acquainted my gifts more and more in publick, that having got acquaintance at Norwich, I left the company at Yarmouth; so after a few dayes I was admitted into a Pulpit two or three times: so coming a man from Pulom side in Norfolk and hearing of me, was greatly affected with my Doctrine, but especially my Prayer, and was very urgent with me to go to their Parish of Russel, which within two weeks after I assented to be there such a day, which was against the Fast-day; for at that time the Parliament had established a Monethly Fast, which was the last wednesday of the moneth: at the set time I came to the place appointed, where this man had given notice to the best affected people in those parts, what a rare man was to preach that day, which thing I was ambitious of, as also to get some silver: Well, to the matter I went, and as was my Doctrine, so was their understanding, though I say't, as young as I was, yet was not I inferior to any Priest in those days: So in conclusion of my days work there came several in the Church-yard to me, and gave me thanks for my paines, yea, hoped the Lord would settle me among them, which news I was glad to hear; so for the next Lords-Day by Goodman Mays and Burton was

I invited to preach at Pulom, which was a great Parish; so upon liking I went, and was well approved of by all the Godly, so there for a time was I settled for twenty shillings a week, and very gallantly was provided for, so that I thought I was in Heaven upon earth, judging the Priests had a brave time in this world, to have a house built for them, and means provided for them, to tell the people stories of other mens works.* Now after I had continued half a year, more or less, the Ministers began to envy me for my Doctrine, it being free Grace, so contrary to theirs, and that the more, their people came from their own Parish to hear me, so that they called me Sheep-stealer for robbing them of their flock, and to that end came to catch and trap me at several Lectures where I was called, that at last they prevailed with the Heads of the Parish to turn me out, so I slighting them as they could me, we parted, and then having many friends, I was importuned to come and live with them, so above all I chose Robert Marchants house my Lodging place, because his Daughter I loved; and for a certain time preached up and down several Churches, both of Suffolk and Norfolk, and many times in private, that I had great company. Now in the interim there was one John Tyler a Colchester man frequented those parts where then I inhabited who was a Teacher of the Baptists, and had a few scattered up and down the Countrey, which several times we had meetings and converse about a lawful Minister: now I knowing no other but that those sayings, Go ye teach all Nations, baptizing them, and lo I am with you to the end of the world;* that continuance to the end of the world, was the Load-stone that brought me to believe that the Baptism of the Apostles was as much in force now, as in their days, and that Command did as really belong to me as to them; so being convinced, for London I went to be further satisfied, so that after a little discourse with Patience, I was by him baptized in the water that runneth about the Tower, after which I stayed at London about a week.

Fifthly, then for Suffolk again I travelled through the Church of the Baptists, and was of Robert Marchants family received with joy, for I had the love of all the family; and though he had four Daughters marriageable, yet there was one I loved above any in that Countrey, though I was beloved of other friends daughters far beyond her in estate, yet for her knowledge and moderation in spirit, I loved her;* so there up and down a certain time I continued preaching the

Gospel, and very zealous I was for obedience to the Commands of Christ Jesus; which Doctrine of mine converted many of my former friends and others, to be baptized, and so into a Church-fellowship was gathered to officiate the order of the Apostles, so that really I thought if ever I was in a true happy condition, then I was, knowing no other but as aforesaid, that this Command of Christ did as really belong to me as to them; and we having the very same rule, as Elders and Deacons, with Dipping,* and Breaking of bread in the same manner as they, I was satisfied we onely were the Church of Christ in this world.

Thus having a great company, and baptizing of many into that Faith, there was no small stir among the priests what to do with me, which afterwards they got a Warrant from the Parliament,* to apprehend Mr. Knowles* and my self, ...

[*Early in 1645, Clarkson is arrested at Eye and taken, accompanied by his wife, to Bury St Edmunds to be interrogated by the Suffolk County Committee concerning his practice of dipping. Confronted with the rumour that he dipped six sisters naked one night, and 'which of them you liked best, you lay with her in the water', Clarkson replies: 'Surely your experience teacheth you the contrary, that nature hath small desire to copulation in water, at which they laughed; But, said I, you have more cause to weep for the unclean thoughts of your heart.' The chairman also asks the couple about their marriage: 'Where were you married? At* Waybread *in my fathers house. Who married you? My husband, with the consent of my parents, and the Church. At that there was great laughter, and said, your husband marry you to himself, that is against the law; I being vexed at their folly, answered, Marriage is no other, but a free consent in love each to the other before God, and who was sufficient to publish the Contract as my self? . . .'* Clarkson preaches the necessity of 'the true baptism' from the window of the private chamber in which he is imprisoned.*]

After I had lain there a long time, Mr. Sedgewick* and Mr. Erbery* came to visit me, with whom I had great discourse, and after they were gone, I had a great contest in my minde, as touching the succession of Baptism, which I could not see but in the death of the Apostles, there was never since no true Administrator;* for I could not read there was ever any that had power by imposition of hands, to give the Holy Ghost, and work miracles as they did; so that in the death of them I concluded Baptism to either young or old, was ceased. Now observe, I could discern this, but could not by the same rule see that preaching and prayer was to cease:* for this now I know, as in the death of the Apostles, and them commissionated by them, the Commission ceased, as unto all their Form and Worship: So finding I was but still in Egypt burning Brick, I was minded to travel into the Wilderness; so seeing the vanity of the Baptists, I renounced them and had my freedom. Then

Sixthly, I took my journey into the society of those people called Seekers, who worshipped God onely by prayer and preaching, therefore to Ely I went, to look for Sedgwick and Erbery but found them not, onely their people were assembled: with whom I had discourse, but found little satisfaction; so after that for London I went to finde Seekers there, which when I came, there was divers fallen from the Baptists as I had done, to coming to Horn in Fleet lane, and Fleten in Seacoal-lane, they informed me that several had left the Church of Patience, in seeing the vanity of Kiffin* and others, how highly they took it upon them, and yet could not prove their Call successively; so glad was I there was a people to have society withal; then was I moved to put forth a book which was the first that ever I writ, bearing this Title, *The pilgrimage of Saints, by church cast out, in Christ found, seeking truth*,* this being a sutable peece of work in those days, that it wounded the Churches; which book Randel owned, and sold many for me. Now as I was going over London-bridge, I met with Thomas Gun* a teacher of the Baptists, who was a man of a very humble, moderate spirit, who asked me if I own'd *the Pilgrimage of Saints*? I told him yea: then said he, you have writ against the church of Christ, and have discovered your self an enemy to Christ. Then I said, it is better be a hypocrite to man then to God, for I finde as much dissimulation, covetousness, back-biting and envy, yea as filthy wickedness among some of them, as any people I know: and notwithstanding your heaven-like carriage, if all your faults were written in your forehead, for ought I know, you are a hypocrite as well as I; which afterwards it was found out he had lain with his Landlady many times; and that he might satisfie his Lust, upon flighty errands, he sent her husband into the country, that so he might lodge with his wife all night; which being found out, so smote his conscience, that he privately took a Pistol and shot himself to death in Georges-fields. As all along in this my travel I was subject to that sin, and yet as saint-like, as though sin were a burden to me, so that the fall of this

Gun did so seize on my soul, that I concluded there was none could live without sin in this world; for notwithstanding I had great knowledge in the things of God, yet I found my heart was not right to what I pretended, but full of lust and vain-glory of this world, finding no truth in sincerity that I had gone through, but meerly the vain pride and conceit of Reasons imagination, finding my heart with the rest, seeking nothing but the praise of men in the heighth of my prayer and preaching, yet in my doctrine through all these opinions, pleading the contrary, yea abasing my self, and exalting a Christ that then I knew not. Now after this I return'd to my wife in Suffolk, and wholly bent my mind to travel up & down the country, preaching for monies, which then I intended for London, so coming to Colchester where I had John Aplewhit, Purkis, and some other friends, I preached in publick; so going for London, a mile from Colchester, I set my Cane upright upon the ground, and which way it fell, that way would I go; so falling towards Kent, I was at a stand what I should do there, having no acquaintance, and but little money, yet whatever hardship I had withal, I was resolved for Gravesend, so with much a do I got that night to a town called Bilrekey, it being in the height of Summer, and in that town then having no friends, and I think but six pence, I lodged in the Church porch all night, so when day appeared, I took my journey for Gravesend, and in the way I spent a groat of my six pence, and the other two pence carried me over the water; so being in the town, I enquired for some strange opinionated people in the town,* not in the least owning of them, but seemingly to ensnare them, which they directed me to one Rugg a Victualler, so coming in, though having no monies, yet I called for a pot of Ale, so after a few words uttered by me, the man was greatly taken with my sayings, in so much that he brought me some bread and cheese, with which I was refreshed, and bid me take no care, for I should want for nothing, you being the man that writ The Pilgrimage of the Saints, I have had a great desire to see you, with some soldiers and others, so for the present he left me, and informed Cornet Lokier and the rest, that I was in town, who forthwith came to me, and kindly received me, and made way for me to preach in the Blockhouse; so affecting my doctrine, they quatered me in the Officers lodging, and two days after they carried me to Dartford, where there I preached; so against the next Lords-day came for Gravesend; and there preached in the Market-place, which was such a wonder to the town and countrey, that some for love, and others for envy, came to hear, that the Priest of the town had almost none to hear him, that if the Magistrate durst, he would have apprehended me; for I boldly told them God dwelled not in the Temple made with hands, neither was any place more holy then another, proving by Scripture, that where two or three were gathered in his name, God was in the midst of them, and that every Believer was the Temple of God . . .

[*Clarkson continues his itinerant preaching, meeting 'a maid' in Canterbury 'of pretty knowledge, who with my Doctrine was affected, and I affected to lye with her, so that night prevailed, and satisfied my lust'. He deceives the woman by pledging to return and marry her, revisits his wife, settles some domestic affairs, and finds new employment.*]

. . . the Town of Sanderidge took me for their Minister, and setled me in the Vicaridge, where Sir John Garret, Colonel Cox, and Justice Robotom came constantly to hear me, and gave me several Gifts, so that in heaven I was again; for I had a high pitch of free Grace, and mightily flown in the sweet Discoveries of God, and yet not at all knowing what God was, onely an infinite Spirit, which when he pleased did glance into his people the sweet breathings of his Spirit; and therefore preached, it was not sufficient to be a professor, but a possessor of Christ, the possession of which would cause a profession of him, with many such high flown notions, which at that time I knew no better, nay, and in truth I speak it, there was few of the Clergy able to reach me in Doctrine or Prayer; yet notwithstanding, not being an University man, I was very often turned out of employment, that truly I speak it, I think there was not any poor soul so tossed in judgement, and for a poor livelihood, as then I was. Now in this my prosperity I continued not a year, but the Patron being a superstitious Cavelier, got an Order from the Assembly of Divines* to call me in question for my Doctrine, and so put in a drunken fellow in my room: and thus was I displaced from my heaven upon earth . . .

[*Clarkson is appointed by Captain Cambridge as teacher to their company. He quarters in a private house in Smithfield, and learns 'of a people called* My one flesh '* to which Giles Calvert can direct him.*]

so coming to Calvert,* and making enquiry after such a people, he was a fraid I came to betray them, but exchanging a few words in the height of my language, he was much affected, and satisfied I was a friend of theirs,* so he writ me a Note to Mr. Brush, and the effect thereof was, the bearer hereof is a man of the greatest light I ever yet heard speak, and for ought I know instead of receiving of him you may receive an Angel,* so to Mr. Brush I went, and presented this Note, which he perused, so bid me come in, and told me if I had come a little sooner, I might have seen Mr. Copp,* who then had lately appeared in a most dreadful manner; so their being Mary Lake, we had some discourse, but nothing to what was in me, however they told me, if next sunday I would come to Mr. Melis in Trinity-lane, there would that day some friends meet. Now observe at this time my judgment was this, that there was no man could be free'd from sin, till he had acted that so called sin, as no sin,* this a certain time had been burning within me, yet durst not reveal it to any, in that I thought none was able to receive it, and a great desire I had to make trial, whether I should be troubled or satisfied therein: so that

Seventhly, I took my progress into the Wilderness, and according to the day appointed, I found Mr. Brush, Mr. Rawlinson, Mr. Goldsmith, with Mary Lake, and some four more: now Mary Lake was the chief speaker, which in her discourse was some thing agreeable, but not so high as was in me experienced, and what I then knew with boldness declared, in so much that Mary Lake being blind, asked who that was that spake? Brush said the man that Giles Calvert sent to us, so with many more words I affirmed that there was no sin, but as man esteemed it sin, and therefore none can be free from sin, till in purity it be acted as no sin, for I judged that pure to me, which to a dark understanding was impure, for to the pure all things, yea all acts were pure;* thus making the Scripture a writing of wax, I pleaded the words of Paul, That I know, and am perswaded by the Lord Jesus, that there was nothing unclean, but as man esteemed it, unfolding that was intended all acts, as well as meats and drinks,* and therefore till you can lie with all women as one woman, and not judge it sin, you can do nothing but sin: now in Scripture I found a perfection spoken of,* so that I understood no man could attain perfection but this way, at which Mr. Rawlinson was much taken, and Sarah Kullin being then present, did invite me to make trial of what I had expressed, so as I take it, after we parted she invited me to Mr. Wats in Rood-lane, where was one or two more like her self, and as

I take it,* lay with me that night: now against next sunday it was noised abroad what a rare man of knowledge was to speak at Mr. Brushes; at which day there was a great company of men and women, both young and old; and so from day to day increased, that now I had choice of what before I aspired after, insomuch that it came to our Officers ears; but having got my pay I left them, and lodged in Rood-lane, where I had Clients many, that I was not able to answer all desires, yet none knew our actions but our selves; however I was careful with whom I had to do. This lustful principle encreased so much, that the Lord Mayor with his Officers came at midnight to take me, but knowing thereof, he was prevented. Now Copp was by himself with a company ranting and swearing, which I was seldom addicted to, onely proving by Scripture the truth of what I acted; and indeed Solomons Writings was the original of my filthy lust, supposing I might take the same liberty as he did, not then understanding his Writings was no Scripture, that I was moved to write to the world what my Principle was, so brought to publick view a Book called *The Single Eye*,* so that men and women came from many parts to see my face, and hear my knowledge in these things, being restless till they were made free, as then we called it. Now I being as they said, Captain of the Rant,* I had most of the principle women came to my lodging for knowledge, which then was called The Head-quarters. Now in the height of this ranting, I was made still careful for moneys for my Wife, onely my body was given to other women: so our Company encreasing, I wanted for nothing that heart could desire, but at last it became a trade so common, that all the froth and scum broke forth into the height of this wickedness,* yea began to be a publick reproach, that I broke up my Quarters, and went into the countrey to my Wife, where I had by the way disciples plenty which then Major Rainsborough,* and Doctor Barker was minded for Mr. Walis of Elford, so there I met them, where was no small pleasure and delight in praising of a God that was an infinite nothing,* what great and glorious things the Lord had done, in bringing us out of bondage, to the perfect liberty of the sons of God,* and yet then the very notion of my heart was to all manner of theft, cheat, wrong, or injury that privately could be acted, though in tongue I professed the contrary, not confiding I brake the Law in all points (murther excepted:) and the ground of this my judgement was, God had made all things good, so nothing evil but as man judged it; for I apprehended there was no such thing as theft, cheat, or a lie, but as man made it so: for if the creature had brought this world into no propriety, as Mine and Thine, there had been no such title as theft, cheat, or a lie; for the prevention hereof Everard and Gerrard Winstanley* did dig up the Commons, that so all might have to live of themselves, then there had been no need of defrauding, but unity one with another, not then knowing this was the devils kingdom, and Reason* lord thereof, and that Reason was naturally enclined to love it self above any other, and to gather to it self what riches and honor it could, that so it might bear sway over its fellow creature; for I made it appear to Gerrard Winstanley there was a self-love and vain-glory nursed in his heart, that if possible, by digging to have gained people to him, by which his name might become great among the poor Commonality of the Nation, as afterwards in him appeared a most shameful retreat from *Georges-hill*, with a spirit of pretended universality, to become a real Tithe-gatherer of propriety;* so what by these things in others, and the experience of my heart, I saw all that men spake or acted, was a lye, and therefore my thought was, I had as good cheat for something among them,* and that so I might live in prosperity with them, and not come under the lash of the Law;* for here was the thought of my heart from that saying of Solomon, Eccles. 3.19. For that which befalleth the sons of men, befalleth beasts, even one thing befalleth them; as the one dieth, so dieth the other, yea, they have all one breath, so that a man hath no preheminence above a beast; for all is vanity, all go into one place, all are of the dust, and all turn to dust again. So that the 18th and 19th verses of Ecclesiastes was the rule and direction of my spirit, to eat and to drink, and to delight my soul in the labor of my minde all the days of my life, which I thought God gave me as my portion, yea to rejoyce in it as the gift of God, as said that wise Head-piece Solomon; for this then, and ever after, till I came to hear of a Commission, was the thought of my heart, that in the grave there was no more remembrance of either joy or sorrow after. For this I conceived, as I knew not what I was before I came in being, so for ever after I should know nothing after this my being was dissolved; but even as a stream from the Ocean was distinct in it self while it was a stream, but when returned to the Ocean, was therein swallowed and become one with the Ocean; so the spirit of man while in the body, was distinct from God, but when death came it returned to God, and so became one with God, yea God it self; yet notwithstanding this, I had sometimes a relenting light in my soul, fearing this should not be so,* as indeed it was contrary; but however, then a cup of Wine would wash away this doubt.

But now to return to my progress, I came for *London* again, to visit my old society; which then *Mary Midleton** of *Chelsford*, and Mrs. *Star* was deeply in love with me, so having parted with Mrs. *Midleton*, Mrs. *Star* and I went up and down the countries as man and wife, spending our time in feasting and drinking, so that Tavernes I called the house of God; and the Drawers, Messengers; and Sack, Divinity; reading in *Solomons* writings it must be so, in that it made glad the heart of God; which before, and at that time, we had several meetings of great company, and that some, no mean ones neither, where then, and at that time, they improved their liberty, where Doctor *Pagets* maid stripped her self naked, and skipped among them, but being in a Cooks shop, there was no hunger, so that I kept my self to Mrs. *Star*, pleading the lawfulness of our doings as aforesaid, concluding with *Solomon* all was vanity . . .

[*Once again Clarkson is arrested, this time to be brought before a Committee of Parliament. He is interrogated concerning his sexual practices and those of this 'disciples', the authorship of* A Single Eye *(which Clarkson does not name), and his association with Coppe. Clarkson denies that he has disciples, disavows the book, and says of Coppe: 'Yea I know him, and that is all, for I have not seen him above two or three times.' He receives sentence, fourteen weeks later, of banishment after one month in New Bridewell prison. But the sentence of banishment is not carried out. After reacquainting himself with his wife, he resumes his progress in Cambridgeshire 'where still I continued my Ranting principle, with a high hand'.*]

Now in the interim I attempted the art of Astrology, and Physick, which in a short time I gained, and therewith travelled up and down Cambridgeshire and Essex as Linton and Saffron-walden, and other countrey towns, improving my skill to the utmost, that I had clients many, yet could not be therewith contended, but aspired to the art of Magick, so finding some of Doctor *Wards* and *Woolerds* Manuscripts.* I improved my genius to fetch Goods back that were stoln, yea to raise spirits, and fetch treasure out of the earth, with many such diabolical actions, as a woman of Sudbury in Suffolk assisted me, pretending she could do by her witch-craft whatever she pleased; now something was done, but nothing to what I pretended, however monies I gained, and was up and down looked upon as a dangerous man, that the ignorant and religious people was afraid to come near me, yet this I may say, and speak the truth, that I have cured many desperate Diseases, and one time brought from Glenford to a village town wide of Lanham to Doctor Clark, two women and one man that had bewitched his daughter, who came in a frosty cold night, tormented in what then Clark was a doing, and so after that his daughter was in perfect health, with many such like things, that it puffed up my spirit, and made many fools believe in me, for at that time I looked upon all was good, and God the author of all, and therefore have several times attempted to raise the devil, that so I might see what he was, but all in vain, so that I judged all was a lie, and that there was no devil at all, nor indeed no God but onely nature, for when I have perused the Scriptures I have found so much contradiction as then I conceived, that I had no faith in it at all, no more then a history, though I would talk of it, and speak from it for my own advantage, but if I had really then related my thoughts, I neither believed that Adam was the first Creature, but that there was a Creation before him, which world I thought was eternal, judging that land of Nod where Cain took his wife, was inhabited a long time before Cain, not considering that Moses was the first Writer of Scripture, and that we were to look no further than what there was written; but I really believed no Moses, Prophets, Christ, or Apostles, nor no resurrection at all: for I understood that which was life in man, went into that infinite Bulk and Bigness, so called God, as a drop into the Ocean, and the body rotted in the grave, and for ever so to remain.*

In the interim came forth a people called Quakers, with whom I had some discourse, from whence I discerned that they were no further than burning brick in Egypt, though in a more purer way than their fathers before them; also their God, their devil, and their resurrection and mine, was all one, onely they had a righteousness of the Law which I had not; which righteousness I then judged was to be destroyed, as well as my unrighteousness, and so kept on my trade of Preaching, not minding any thing after death, but as aforesaid, as also that great cheat of Astrology and Physick I practised, which not long after I was beneficed in Mersland, at Torington and

St. Johns, and from thence went to Snetsham in Norfolk, where I was by all the Town received, and had most of their hands for the Presentation, then for London I went, and going to visit Chetwood my former acquaintance, she, with the wife of Middleton, related to me the two Witnesses; so having some conference with Reeve* the prophet, and reading his Writings, I was in a trembling condition; the nature thereof you may read in the Introduction of that Book [_Look about you, for the devil that you fear is in you_*] considering how sadly I had these many years spent my time, and that in none of these seven Churches could I finde the true God, or right devil; for indeed that is not in the least desired, onely to prate of him, and pray to him we knew not, though it is written, It is life eternal to know the true God, yet that none of them mindes, but from education believeth him to be an eternal, infinite Spirit, here, there, and every where; which after I was fully perswaded, that there was to be three Commissions upon this earth,* to bear record to the three Titles above, and that this was the last of those three: upon the belief of this I came to the knowledge of the two Seeds,* by which I knew the nature and form of the true God, and the right devil, which in all my travels through the seven Churches I could never finde, in that now I see it was onely from the revelation of this Commission to make it known.

Now being at my Journeys end, as in point of notional worship, I came to see the vast difference of Faith from Reason, which before I conclude, you shall hear, and how that from Faiths royal Prerogative all its seed in Adam was saved, and all Reason in the fallen Angel was damned, from whence I came to know my election and pardon of all my former transgressions;* after which my revelation growing, moved me to publish to the world, what my Father was, where he liveth, and the glory of his house, as is confirmed by my writings now in publick; So that now I can say, of all my formal righteousness, and professed wickedness, I am stripped naked, and in room thereof clothed with innocency of life, perfect assurance, and seed of discerning with the Spirit of revelation. I shall proceed to answer some Objections that may be raised, as unto what I have already asserted ...

THE NARRATIVE OF
THE PERSECUTION
OF AGNES BEAUMONT

[*The following note is prefaced to the original manuscript:*]
Written by one Agnes (Beaumont) of Edworth, Beds. intimately
acquainted with John Bunyan, and to whose meetings she went contrary to her father's wishes, he objecting to his daughter attending
such. She mentions his name in several parts of the MS.

The Lord hath been pleased, since I was Awakened,* to Exercise me
with many and great tryals; but, blessed be his gratious name, he hath
caused all to work together for good* to my poor soul, and hath often
given me cause to say it was good for me that I have been afflicted.*
And oh, how great hath the kindness of god been to me in afflicting
dispensations! In tryals and temptations he never left me without
his teaching and comforting presence, and I have often Observed
that, the more trouble and sorrow I have had, Either from within, or
without, the more of gods presence I have had;* when I have been
helped to keep Close to him by prayre and supplication. And oh, how
sweet is his presence when a poor soul is surrounded on every side
with trouble! And for my part I have found trouble and sorrow, as
David saith,* None knoweth but god the sore tryals and temptations
that I have warded through in my day, some Outward, but more
Inward. O the fiery darts from hell with which my soul hath been
battred!* But, on the other hand, none knows but god the sweet
Communion and consolation that it hath pleased a gratious god
to give me in many of these hours of trouble. Oh, the great
Consolations* and inlargements of heart, with fervent desires after
Jesus Christ* and his grace, which hath often made me thank god for
trouble when I have found it drive me neerer to himself, to the throne
of his grace. The Lord hath made troublesome times to me; Praying
times, humbling, and mourning, and heart searching times. But one
thing I have great Cause to Admire Gods great goodness to me in,
That before a tryal hath come upon me I have had great consolations
from god; Insomuch that I have Expected some thing to come upon
me, and that I had some trouble to meet with, which hath often fallen
out According to my thoughts: some times one scripture after
Another would run in my mind several days together.* That would

signifie something I had to meet with, and that I must prepare for a tryal, which would drive me into corners, to cry to the Lord to be with me. And oh, how hath the Lord as it were taken me up into the mount,* that my soul hath been so raisd and comforted as if it had been out of the body for a time. Many times in a day would the Lord lead me into his banqueting house, and his banner over me was love.* Now when I found these things in a more then Ordinary manner, then I did begin to thinck I had something to meet with; but so long as I was kept awake in my soul and in a humble empty praying frame,* he never sent me away from the throne of grace without his presence, which hath been so sweet to me that, when I have gone away from the throne of grace, I have thought long to be their again. Oh, it Canot be Exprest with a tounge what sweetness their is in one promise of god when he is pleased to Apply it to the soul by his spirit. It turns sorrow into Joy, fears into faith; it turns weeping and mourning into rejoycing, which, blessed be god, I have experienced these things and many more In that great fiery tryal* Concerning my fathers death which now I am About to tell you of.

About a quarter of a year before god was pleased to take away my father, I had great and frequent injoyments of god, and he was pleased to pour out a spirit of grace and supplication upon me in a wonderful maner, day and night, I may say. And, the Lord knowest it, their was scarce a Corner in the house, or Barns, or Cowhousen, or Stable, or Closes, under the hegges, or in the wood, but I was made to pour out my soul to god.* And some times before I have risen from my knees, I have been as if I had been in heaven, and as if my very heart would have Brake in peeces with Joy and Consolation, which hath Caused floods of teers to fall from mine Eyes with admiration of the love of Christ to such a great Sinner as I was.

I have wept and cryed as if I should have brake my heart strings in sunder, only with Consolation. And when some have seen me weep, they thought sorrow had filled my heart. Indeed, often times I have been sincking in a sea of sorrow; but not in that Quarter of the year before my father dyed. But some would say to me, *Agnes, why do you greive and go Crying about thus, are you minded to kill yor self with sorrow*, when indeed my teers have been for Joy and not for greef; they was sweetned with the love of Christ.

And before god brought that tryal upon me, I had many Scriptures that would run in my mind to signifie I had something to meet with, and then it may be my heart would begin to sinck; But presently I should have one promise to bear me up.* I did thinck I had some hard thing to meet with, because that Scripture would often dart into my mind, *Call upon me in a time of trouble and I will deliver thee, and thou shalt glorifie me*. Where ever I was this would run in my mind, *Call upon me in the time of trouble*.* Thought I this must poynt at some thing to come, for now I have more Comfort then trouble. And that other Scripture would run in my mind, *When thou goest through the fier I will be with thee, and through the Waters, they shall not over flow thee*.* And many such Scriptures that I see had bitter and sweet in them. And I often said to Sister Prudon, *I have some heavy thing coming upon me, but I know not what it will be.*

And the many Dreams that I had, which I beleeve some of them was of God.* I should often dream I was like to lose my life, and could hardly Escape with it. Sometimes I have thought that men have run after me to take it away; & sometimes that I was tryed for my life before a Judge & Jewry, and me thought I did Escape with it, and that was all.

One Dream I tould Sister Prudon, which she tould me of after my father was ded. Me thoughts in my fathers yard grew an old Aple tree, and it was full of fruit. And one night, about the midle of the night, their came a very suddaine storm of wind, and blew this tree up by the roots, and I was sorely troubled to see this tree so suddenly blew down.

I run to it, as it lay upon the ground, to lift it up, to have it grow in its place again. I thought I see it turnd up by the roots, and my thoughts I stood lifting at it as long as I had any strength, as it lay upon the ground, first at one Arm, then at another, but could not stir it out of its place to have it grow in its place again; at last left it, and run to my Brothers* to Call help to set this tree in its place again. & I thought when my Brother and his men did Come, they could not make this tree grow in its place again; and, oh, how troubled was I for this tree, and so greived that the wind should blow that tree down and let others stand. And many such things that I see afterwards did signifie some thing.

And a while after their was to be a Church meeting at Gamgey.* And About a week before, I was very much in prayre with god for two things, for which I set many hours Apart day and night.

And One was that god would please to make way for my going,

and make my father willing, who would sometimes be Against my going. And in those days it was like death to me to be kept from such a meeting. And I found at last by Experience that the only way to prevail with my father to let me go to a meeting was to pray hard to god before hand to make him willing. And before that I had often found success according as my crys had been to god in that matter; when I have prayed hard I have found my father Willing, when I have feared other wise; and when I have not, I have found it more defficult.

And the other thing that I was begging of the Lord for was that he would please to give me his presence their at his Table,* which many times before had been a sweet sealing ordinance* to my soul; And that I might have such a sight of my dying, bleeding Saviour that might melt my heart, and inlarge it with love to him.

In those days I was Always laying up many a prayre in heaven Against I came to the Lords Table, Where I often found a very plentiful return. I could say a great deal more what I have met with, and how I have been in that Ordinance, But I shall for bear.

Well, It did please the Lord to grant me those two things; One in a large manner indeed when I came to the Lords table. And the day before the meeting I asked my father to let me go to it, and he seemd as if he was not very willing; but pleading with him, I tould him I would do what I had to do in the morning before I went, and come home Again at night. At last he was willing. So on friday morning, which was the day the meeting was to be, I made me ready to go. My father Asked me who caried me. I said I thought Mr Wilson, who was to Call at my Brothers that morning as he went, and I would pray him to Cary me; for my Brother spake with him the Tuesday before, who tould him he had thought to Call at his house on friday morning to go with him to Gamgy. So my father said nothing to these things.

So when I was ready, I went to my Brothers, Expectin to meet with Mr Wilson to ride behind him. And their I waited some time; And no body came. At last my heart began to ake, and I fell a Crying for fear I should not go, for my Brother tould me he could not let me have a horse to go for they was all at work, and he was to Cary my sister behind him to the Meeting, so that he could no ways help me thither. And it was the deep of Winter, I could not go on foot.

Now I was Afraid all my prayers would be lost upon that Account.

Thought I, *I prayed to god to make my father Willing to let me go, and that I might have the presence of god in that meeting, But now my way is hedged up with thorns.** And their I weighted, and lookt, many a long look, with a broken heart.

Said my Brother to me, *Mr Wilson said he would come this way and Cary you.* But he did not come. *Oh,* thought I, *that god would please to put it into the heart of some body to come this way and Cary me, and make some way or other for my going.* Well, still I waighted, with my heart full of fears least I should not go.

At last un Expected came mr Bunyan, and Cald at my Brothers as he went to the meeting; but the sight of him Caused sorrow, and Joy, in me; I was glad to see him but I was afraid he would not Cary me to the meeting behind him; and how to Ask him I did not know, for fear he should deny me. So I got my Brother to ask him.

So my Brother said to him, *I must desire yow to Cary my Sister today behind you.*

And he Answered my Brother very roughly, and said, *No not I. I will not Cary her.** These was Cutting words to me indeed, which made me weep bitterly.

My Brother said to him Again, *If yow do not Cary her, yow will break her heart.*

And he replyed with the same words Again, that he would not cary me, that he would not Cary me. And he said to me, *If I should cary yow, yor father would be greivous Angry with me.* Said I, *If you please to carry me, I will venture that.* So with a great many intreatyes, at last my Brother did prevail with him, and I did git up be hind him. But oh how glad was I that I was going.

But I had been but Just on horseback, as I heard after wards, But my father Came to my brothers, to some of the men that was at work, and askt them who his daughter rode behind. They Answered such an one, with that my father fell into a pastion, and ran down to the Close End, thincking to have met me in the fields, where he intended to have pulled me off of the horse back, he was so Angry, because some had incenst him Against mr Bunyan; But we was gone by first.

But to speak the truth I had not gone fer behind him, but my heart was pufft up with pride, and I began to have high thoughts of my self, and proud to thinck I should ride behind such a man as he was; and I was pleasd that any body did look after me as I rode A long.

And sometimes he would be speaking to me A bout the things of god as we went Along. And indeed I thought my self a happy body that day; first that it did please god to make way for my going to the meeting; & then that I should have the honour to ride behind him. But, as yow will understand, my pride had a fall.

So Coming to the towns End, their met with us a priest one Mr Lane who, as I remember, lived then at Bedford, but was use to preach at Edworth; and he knew us both, and spoke to us, and lookt of us, as we rode Along the way as if he would have staird his Eyes Out; and afterward did scandalise us after a base maner, and did raise a very wicked report of us, which was altogether false, blessed be god.*

So we Came to Gamgy; and after a while the meeting began, and god made it a blessed meeting to my soul indeed. Oh, it was a feast of fat things* to me! My soul was filled with Consolation, and I sat under his Shadow, with great delight, and his fruit was pleasant to my tast* when I was at the Lords table.

I found such a return of prayre that I was scarse able to bear up under it. Oh, I had such a sight of Jesus Christ that brake my heart to peeces. Oh, how I longed that day to be with Jesus Christ; how fain would I have dyed in the place, that I might have gone the next way* to him, my blesced saviour. A sence of my sins, and of his dying love, made me love him, and long to be with him; and truly it was infinite Condesention in him, and I have often thought of his grace and goodness to me, that Jesus Christ should so gratiously visit my poor soul that day. He knew what tryals and temptations I had to meet with that night, and in a few days. Oh, I have seen what bowels of pity and Compation he had towards me, that he should give me such new manifestations of his love that very day.

Well, when the meeting was done, I began to thinck how I should get home, for Mr Bunyan was not to go by Edworth though he came that way. And it was almost night and very Durty, and I had promised my father to come home at night. And my thoughts began to work, and my heart to be full of fears least I should not get home that night. As I was troubled to get thither, so I was to get home, but in the time of the meetin, blessed be god, it was kept out. So I went first to One, and then to Another, to ask who went that way that could Cary me some part of the way home; but their was no body could supply my wants, but a maid that lived at hincksworth, half a mile off my fathers, and, the ways being so durty and deep, I was afraid to venture behind her. But I did, and she set me down at sister Prudons gate.

So I came home ploshing through the durt, over shoes having no pattings* on. I made what hast I could, hoping I should be at home before my father was a bed; but when I came neer the house, I see no light in it. So I went to the door, and found it Lockt, with the key in it. Then my heart began to Ake with fear; for if I have not been at home, if my father hath hapned to go to bed before I came home, he would Cary the key to bed with him, and give me it out at Window. But now I perceived what I was Like to trust to; but how ever, I went to his Chamber window, and Called to him.

He asked who was their. *It is I, father*, said I, *pray will you let me in; I am come home wet and dirty*.

Said he, *Where you have been all day, go at Night*; and many such like things, for he was very Angry with me, for riding behind mr Bunyan, and said I should never come within his doors Again, Except I would promise him to leave going after that man; for some Enemyes in the town had set my father Against him with telling of him of some false reports that was raisd of him;* and they affirmed them to my father for truth, and, poor man, he beleeved them because such persons affirmed it!*

So then I stood at his Chamber Window pleading and Intreating of him to let me in, beggin and Crying. But all in vain; instead of letting me in, he bid me begone from the Window, or Else he would rise and set me out of the yard. So then I stood a while at the window silent, and that Consideration Came into my mind, *How if I should Come at last when the door is shut and Jesus Christ should say to me, 'Depart from me I know yow not'*.* And it was secretly put into my mind to spend the night in prayre, Seing my father would not let me come in. *Oh*, thought I, *so I will, I will go into the barn and spend this night in prayre to god, that Jesus Christ will not shut me out at last*. But these thoughts presently darted in upon my mind: *No, go to your Brothers; their yow may have a good supper, and a warm bed, and the night is long and could*.

No, said I, *I will go, and cry to heaven for mercy for my soul, and for some new discoveryes of the love of Christ*. But these and Many frightful thoughts came into my mind, as this, how did I know but I might be knockt o th head in the barn before morning; or if not so, I might Catch my death by the Cold.

At last my mind began to comply with these fears. Thought I, *it may be so indeed, it being a lone house, & none neer it;—And it is a very cold night, I shall never be able to abide in the barn till morning*. But at last one Scripture after another came into my mind to incourage me in that work, as that word, *Pray to thy father that seeth in secret, and thy father that seeth thee in secret—shall reward thee openly*;* And that Scripture, *Call upon me, and I will Ansure thee, and shew the great and mighty things, and thow knowest not*;* and many a good word beside that I have forgot. I thought I had need go pray to my heavenly father indeed.

So into the barn I went, and it was a very dark night; and when I came in to the barn, I found I was Again asaulted, by Sathan, but having received some strength from god and his word, As I remember I spake out with these and such like words; *Sathan, my father hath thee in a Chain;* thou Canst not hurt me*. So I went to the throne of grace, to spread my Complaints before the Lord.* And indeed it was a blessed night to me; a Night to be remembered to my lifes End;* and I hope I shall remember it with Comfort to Eternity. It was surely a night of prayre, and a night of praise, and thanks giving. The Lord was pleased to keep scaires out of my heart all the night after. Oh the spirit of faith and prayre that god gave me that night. Surely the Lord was with me after a wonderful maner. Oh, the heart ravishing visits that he gave me. It frose vehemently that night, but I felt no Cold; the dirt was frosen upon shoues in the morning. My heart was wonderfully drawn out in prayre, and, as I was in prayre, that Scripture came with mighty power upon my heart, *Beloved, thinck it not strange Concerning the fiery tryals that are to try yow*.* Oh, this word (Beloved) made Such Melody in my heart,* that I canot tell yow; and yet the other part of the words had dread in it—*thinck it not strange, conserning the fiery tryals that are to try yow*.

I see that was a great tryal, my fathers shutting me out of doors. I thought what could be worse to me then that, & still when I was in prayre, the same scripture would run throw and throw my heart; but that first word *Beloved* I thought sounded lowder in my heart then all the rest. It run very much in my mind all night; I see it had bitter and sweet in it; but to be the Beloved of god, I thought that was my mercy, what ever I had to meet with. I did then direct my Crys to god to stand by me and strengthen me, what ever I had to meet with. And many a blessed promise I had before the Morning light. One time in the night I was a little Cast down, & greife began to sease upon me. Notwithstanding god had been so good to me, I was greived to thinck I should lose my fathers love, for going to Seek after Jesus Christ.* So I went to the throne of grace Again to Shew unto him my trouble, and I was bewailing the loss of my fathers love, and saing, *Lord, what will become of me if I should fail of thy love too*? that good word darted upon my mind, *The father him self loveth yow.** Oh blessed be god, said I, *then that is enough; do with me what seems good in thy sight.**

So the morning Came on, and when it was light, I peeked through the Cracks of the barn door to see when my father opened the door. So at last I see him unlock the door, and when he came out in to the yard, he lockt the door after him, and put the key in his pocket. Thought I, this looks very bad upon me, for I knew by that he was still resolved I should not go in, though [he] did not know I was so neer as I was. But that good word—(*Beloved*) *thinck it not strange Concerning the fiery tryals that are to try yow* still sounded in my heart.

So my father comes with his fork in his hand to serve the Cows, in to the barn where I was. And when he opened the door, he was at a stand to see me their with my riding Cloths on, as I came home. I suppose he thought I had been gone to my Brothers.

So said I to him *Goodmorrow, father. I have had a Could nights lodging hear; but god hath been good to me, Else I should have had a worse*. He said it was no matter. So I prayed him to let me go in; *I hope father*, said I, *yow are not Angry with me still*. So I followed him About the yard as he went to serve the Cows; but he would not hear me. The more I intreated him, the more Angry he was with me, and said I should never Come within his doors Again, unless I would promise him Never to go to a meeting Again as long as he lived.*

Father, said I, *my soul is of more worth then so, and if yow Could stand in my steed before god to give an Account for me at the great day, then I would obay yow in this as well as other things.** But all that I could say to him prevailed nothing with him.

At last some of my brothers men Came into the yard for

something their master sent them for, and they went home, and tould their Master that their Master had shut me out of doors; *for she*, said they, *hath her riding Cloths on still.*

My Brother hearing that was troubled, and came in haste to my fathers, and he did what he Could to perswade him to be reconsiled to me, and to let me in; but he was more pastionate with my Brother then with me, and would not hear him. So my Brother came to me and said, *Come Child, go home with me; thou wilt Catch thy death with the Cold.* So I bid him go home, for I see my father was more provoked with what he said then he was with me, though my brother spake very mildly to him; And I had a mind to stay a little longer, to see what I could do with my father.

So I followed him A bout the yard still, and some times got hold of his Arms and Cryed, and hung About him, saying, *Pray, father, let me go in;* which I afterwards wondered how I durst, he being a hasty man, that many times when he hath been Angry I have been glad to git me out of his presence, though when his Anger was over he was as good a natured man as lived.*

So I see I could not prevail with him to be reconsiled with me; I went and set me down at the door; and he walked about the yard, and would not come neer the House so long as I was their; and he had the key in his pocket, for their I sat at the door some time. At last I began to be faint with cold, for it was a very sharp morning, and it greived me to be the occation of my fathers staing in the cold so long, for I see he would not go in so long as I was their.

So I went to my Brothers and they gave me something to refresh me. So when I was warm and had refreshed my self, I did desire to be retired and to be alone. So I went up into one of my sisters Chambers to pour out my soul to god; for the more I met with, the more I cryed to the lord. The Lord was still pleased to pour out a spirit of grace and supplication upon me, and did not Leave me nor forsake me.*

So about the midle of the day, which was saterday, I said to my sister, *Will yow go with me to my fathers, to see what he will say to me now?* And she said yes, she would go with me. So we went, and when we came to the door, we found the door lockt, and my father in the house; for he would not go out, but he would lock the door, and put the key in his pocket. Neither would he go into the house but he would lock the door after him.

So we went to the window, and my sister said, *father, where are yow?* And he came to the window, and spake to us. Said my Sister, *father, I hope now yor Anger is over, and that yow will let my Sister come in.* So I prayed him to be reconsiled to me, and fell a Crying very much, for indeed at that time my heart was full of greif and sorrow to see my father so Angry with me still, and to heer what he said, which now I shall not mention; only this one thing He said, he would never give me a penny as long as he lived; Nor when he dyed,* but he would give it to them he never saw before.

Now to tell you the truth, these was very hard sayings to me, and at the hearing of it my heart began to sinck. Thought I to my self, *What will be come of me? To go to service and work for my living is a new thing to me; and so young as I am too. What shall I do?* thought I. And these thoughts Came suddenly into my mind, *Well, I have a good God to go to still*; and that word did Comfort me, *when my father and mother forsook me, then the Lord took me up*;* but my heart sanck quickly. So my sister stood pleading with him, but all in vain. Then I prayed my father, if he did not please to let me Come in, that he would give me my Bible and my pattings. But he would not, and said Again he was resolved I should never have one peny, nor penny worth, as long as he lived; Nor when he dyed.

As I said, I was very much Cast down at this. Now did my thoughts begin to work. Thought I, *what shall I do? I am Now in a miserable Case*, for I went home with my sister Again Crying bitterly, for indeed unbeleef and Carnal reasoning, was got in at a great rate, Notwithstanding god had been so wonderful good to me but the last night in the barn.

So away I went up stairs to Cry to the Lord that afternoon, who gave me hopes of an Eternal inheritance; and I was let to see I had a better portion then silver or gold.* Oh then I was willing to go to service, Or be stript of all for Christ. Now I was unconcernd, Again, at what my father had said. I was made to beleeve I should never want.

So at night I had a mind to go Again to my fathers; *but*, thought I, *I will go alone*; for I see he was more Angry with my brother that morning and with my sister at noon then he was with me. *And*, thought I, *now he hath been Alone one night, and hath no body to do anything for him, it may be he will let me Come in.*

And so I considered which way to go. Thought I, *I will go such a bye way that he shall not see me till I come to the door; And if I find it open, I will go in. He will thinck I will come no more to night, and so it may be the door may be opened. And if it is,* thought I, *I will go in, let my father do with me what he pleases when I am in. If he doth through me out, he does; I will venture.*

So in the Evening I went; and when I came at the door, it stood A Jar, with the key o th out side, and my father in the house. So I shoved it soughly* and was going in. But my father was a Coming through the Entry, to come out, who see me a Coming in; so he came hastily to the door and Clapt it to; and if I had not been very quick one of my legs had been between the door and the threshold. So he Clapt the door to with the key o th out side, for he had not time to take the key out, and then pinned the door within side, for he could not Lock it, the key being o th out side of the door. So I would not be so uncivil to lock my father in the house; but I took the key out of the door and put it in my pocket, and I thought to my self, *it may be my father will Come out presently to serve the Cows*; for I see they was not served up for all night. And thinck I, *when he is gone up in the yard, I will go in.* And thought I, *I will go stand behind the house, and when I hear him come out, I will go in; and when I am in, I will lye at his mercy.*

So their I stood lissening, and after a while I heard him Come out. But before he would go up in the yard to serve the Cows, he Comes and looks behind the house, and their he sees me stand. Now behind the house was a pond, Only a narrow path between the house and the pond, and their I stood close up to the wall. So my father Comes to me, and takes hould of my Arm.

Hussif, said he, *give me the key quickly, or I will through yow in the pond.*

So I very speedily pulled the key out of my pocket and gave it to him, and was very sad and silent; for I see it to be in vain to say any thing to him. So I went my way down into one of my fathers Closess to a wood side, sighing and groaning to god as I went Along. And as I was a going with my heart full of sorrow, that scripture came in upon my mind, *Call upon me and I will Answer thee, and shew thee great and mighty things that thou knowest not.**

So away I went to the Woodside (and it was very dark night) Where I powred out my soul with plenty of teers to thee Lord; and still this scripture would often dart in upon my mind,* *Call upon me and I* *will Answer thee, and shew thee great and mighty things that thou knowest not.* And sometimes I should be ready to say in my heart, *Lord what mighty things wilt thou shew me?* So their I remained sometime, Crying to the Lord very bitterly.

As any rational body must needs thinck, these was hard things for me to meet with. But that was a blessed word to me, *the Eyes of the lord are over the righteous, and his ears are open to their Cryes.** Oh, I did beleeve, his Ears was open in heaven to hear the Cryes of a poor disolate afflictd Creature, and that his heart did yearn towards me. That was a wonderful word to me, *in all their afflictions he was afflicted.** So staying so long, My brother and sister was much concernd for me, and sent some of thier men to my fathers on some Arrand, on purpose to see whither my father had let me come in. But they returned their master that Answer that their old mr was alone; I was not their.

So my brother and some of his family went About seeking for me but found me not. At last I came to my Brothers, (when I had spread my Complaints before the Lord). And now I began to resolve in my mind what to do, for this was the Case—That if I would promise my father never to go to a meeting Again, he would let me come in. So, thought I to my self, *that I will never do, If I beg my bread from door to door.* And I thought I was so strongly fixed in this resolution that nothing could move me; what ever I met with from my father, I should never yeild upon that Account. But poor weak Creature that I was, I was peeter like, as you will hear afterwards.*

Well, this was Saterday night. So when Sabboth day morning Came, I said to my Brother, *let us Go to my fathers as we go to the meeting.* But he said no, *It will but provoake him.* So we did not. And as my brother and I went to the meeting, he was talking to me as we went.

Sister, said he, *you are now brought upon the Stage to Act for Christ and his ways.* Said he, *I would not have yow Consent to my father upon his terms.*

No, Brother, said I, *if I beg my bread from door to door.* Thought I, *I do not want any of your Cautions, upon that Account.* So we went to the meeting; but as I sat in the meeting my mind was very much hurried, and afflicted, as no wonder Considering my Curcumstances. So when it was night, I said to my Brother as we went from the meeting, *let us go to my fathers.* So he consented to it.

And we went and found him in the yard a serving the Cows, but before we came into the yard, my Brother warned me Again that I did not Consent to promise my father to forsake the ways of god; but I thought I had no need of his Counsel upon that Account. So my Brother talked with him very mildly, and pleaded with him to be reconsiled to me. But he was so Angry with him that he would not hear him. So I whispered to my Brother, and bid him go hence. *No*, said he, *I will not go with out yow*. Said I, *Go, I will come presently*. But, as he afterwards said, he was afraid to leave me for fear I should yeild. But I thought I could as soon part from my life.

So my Brother and sister went on their way home. So their I remained in the yard, talking to my father who then had the key in his pocket. And I was pleading with him to let me go in; *father*, said I, *I will serve yow in any thing that lyes in me to do for yow as long as you live and I live; And father*, said I, *I desire time to go no whether but to hear gods word, if yow will but let me go a Sabbath days to the meeting; And I desire no more. Father*, said I, *yow Cant Answer for my sins, nor stand in my steed before god; I must look to the Salvation of my soul, or I am undone for ever.*

So he told me if I would promise him never to go to a meeting as long as he lived, I should go in, and he would do for me as for his other Children; but if not I should never have a farthing.

father, said I, *my Soul is of more worth then so; I dare not make such a promise*; And my poor Brothers heart Ackt that he did not see me follow him. So my father began to be very Angry and bid me begone, and not trouble him, for he was resolved what to do; *And therfore tell me; if yow will promise me Never to go to a meeting Again, I will give yow the key and yow shall go in.*

So-many times together held the key out to me, to see if I would promise him; And I as often refused to yeild to him.

So at last he began to be Impatiant; *hussif,** said he, *what do you say? If yow will promise me never to go to a meeting Again as long as I live, hear is the key; take it, and go in*; And held the key out to me.

Said he, *I will never offer it to yow more, and I am resolved yow shall never Come within my doors Again, while I live.* And I stood Crying by him in the yard. So he spake hastily to me, *What do yow say, hussif*, said he, *will yow promise me or no?*

Well father, said I, *I will promise yow that I will never go to a meeting;*

Again, as long as yow live, without your Consent; not thinking what doler and misery I brought upon my self in so Doing.* So when he heard me say so he gave me the key to go in. So I unlockt the door and went in; And so soon as I got within the door, that dreadful scripture Came upon my mind, *They that deny me before men, them will I deny before my father and the Angels that are in heaven;* And that word, *he that forsaketh not father and mother and all that he hath, is not worthy of me.* Oh, thought I, *what will become of me now? What have I done this night?* So I was a going to run out of the house Again; but, thought I, that wont help what I have done if I do. Oh, now all my Comforts and Injoyments was gone! In the room of which I had nothing but terrour, and gilt, and rendings of Contience. Now I see what all my resolutions was Come to. This was Sabbath day night, a Black night.

So my poor father Comes in and was very loving to me, and bid me git him some Supper; which I did. And when I had done so, he bid me Come and eat some. But oh bitter supper to me! So my poor brother was mightily troubled that I did not come to his house. He wondered that I stayed so long. He did fear and thinck what I had done; but to be satisfied he sent one of his men on some Arrand to see if I was in the house with my father. And he returned his master that Answer, that I was in the house with their Old master, and he was very Chearful with me; which when my Brother heard, was much troubled, for he knew that I had yeilded, Else my father would not have let me go in. But no tong Can Express what a doleful Condition I was in, Neither durst I hardly look up to god for mercy. *Oh now I must hear gods word no more*, thought I, oh, what a rech am I, that I should deny Christ and his ways; he that had so often visited my soul, and had been so gratious to me in all my troubles. But now I have turned my back upon him. *Oh black night, Oh, dismal night*, thought I, *in which I have denyed my dere saviour.* So I went to bed, when I had my father to bed; but it was a sad night to me.

So on the next morn, which was munday morning, Came, my Brother; And the first salutation that he gave me, *Oh, Sister*, said he, *what have you done? What do yow say to that scripture, he that denyes me before men, him will I deny before my father and the Angels that are in heaven?* Oh, thought I, *it is this that Cuts my heart*; but I said litle to him only wept bitterly.

So my father Coming in, he said no more, Only said, *goodmorrow,* *father*; And went Away. But I canot Express with words the doler I was in; I filled every Corner of the house and yard that day with bitter sighs and groans and teirs. I went Crying About as if my very heart would have burst in sunder with greif and horrour. But now and then one blessed promise or other would drop upon my mind; but I could take litle Comfort in them; As that word, *Simon, Sathan hath desired to have thee that he may sift thee as wheat, but I have prayed for thee*.* But oh, this lay uppermost, I must hear gods word no more. *Now*, thought I, *if my father Could give me thousands of gold what good would it do me?*

Thus I went groaning about till I was almost spent; and when my father was but gone out of the house, I made the house ring with dismal Cryes, but tould not my greif to my brother, for I thought he would not pity me. Neither did I ever tell him what I went through upon that Account. And when my father Came into the house, then I would go out into the barns or outhousen to vent my sorrowful groans and teirs to the lord.

So before night, as I stood sighing and Crying like a poor distracted body, leaning my head Against something in the house, saying, *Lord, what shall I do, what shall I do*, them words dropt upon my mind, *their shall be a way made for yow to Escape, that yow may be able to bear it*.* *Lord*, said I, *what way shall be made? wilt thou make my father willing to let me go to thine Ordinances?* But if it should be so, thought I, yet what a wrech was I to deny Christ. Oh Now hopes of the pardon of my sins was worth a world; for the forgiveness of my sins was that I Cryed much for, saying, *lord, pity and pardon, pity and pardon*.

So at Night as my father and I sat by the fire, he Asked me what was the matter with me; for he took notiss of me in what a sorrowful Condition I was in all day. So I burst out a Crying, *Oh, father*, said I, *I am so afflicted to thinck that I should promise yow never to go to a meeting Again without yor Consent; and the fears that I have lest yow should not be willing to let me go*; and I tould him what trouble I was in.

And he Wept like a Child.

Well, dont let that trouble yow, said he, *We shall not disagree.*

At this I was a litle Comforted. Said I, *Pray, father, forgive me where in I have been undutyful to you, or disobedient in Anything.* So he sat weeping, and tould me how troubled he was for me that night he shut me out, and Could not sleep. But he thought I had bene gone to my Brothers. But it was my riding behind John Bunyan, he said, that vext him; for that enemy in the town had often been in Censing of him Against Mr Bunyan, though sometime before my father had heard him preach gods word, & heard him with a broaken heart as he had done several others. For when I was first awakened, he was mightily Concernd, seeing me in such distress about my soul, and would say to some neighbours that Came some times to the house; said he, *I thinck my daughter will be distracted,** She scarse Eats, drincks, or sleeps; and I have lived these three score years and scarse ever thought of my Soul.* And afterwards would Cry to the Lord in Secret, as well as I, and would go to meetings for a great while together, and hath heard gods word with many teirs. But that evil minded man in the town would set him against the meetings. I have stood and heard him say to my father, *Have you lived to these years to be led away with them? These be they that lead silly women Captive into houses, and for a pretence make long prayers;** and so never leave till he had set him Against me and the meetings; and would I suppose Counsel him not to let me go. And laterly I met with a great deal from him upon that Account.

Well, this was munday night; but notwithstanding what my father had said to me, I was full of Sorrow, and gilt of Contience; and my worck was still to Cry to the Lord for pardon of sin and to humble my self before him for what I had done. And much time I spent that night in Crying to the Lord for mercy; now was I made to Cry for pardon of sin, and that god would keep me by his grace for time to Come, as if I never prayed before; and that he would keep me from denying of him and his ways. I see now what all my strong resolutions came to, and that I was but a poor weak Creature if god did not keep me by his grace.

And the next day Came, which was Tuesday, in which I still remained in a sorrowful frame, Weeping and Crying bitterly. But, as I remember, god brought me up out of this horrible pit before night, and set my feet upon a Rock,* and I was helped to beleeve the for-giveness of my sins; and many a good word I had Come in upon my heart, which I have forgot.

But now I began to look back with Comfort upon fryday night in the barn, and to thinck of that blessed word (Beloved) and I did beleeve that Jesus Christ was the same yesterday, and today, and for ever. But all day I spent in praying and Crying to god in Corners, unless it was to do my work about house, and git my father his dinner. And he did eat as good a dinner as ever I see him eat.

Well, Night Came on, which indeed was a very dismal night to me, and had not the lord stood by me, and strengthened me, I had certainly sanck down under gods hand that night. But he was faithful, who did not suffer me to be tempted and afflicted above what I was able. Towards night that Scripture would often run in my mind, *In six troubles I Will be with thee, and in seaven I will not leave thee.** And that was a mighty word to me, *The Eternal god is thy Refuge, and underneath are the everlasting Arms.**

So in the Evening, my father said, *It is a very Cold night; we will not sit up too long to night.* He, when the nights ware long, would sit up with me a Candles burning, as I have sat a spining or at other work. But then he said he would have his supper and go to bed because it was so Could.

So after supper, as he sat by the fyre, he took a pipe of Tobacco. And when he had done, he bid me take up the Coals and warm his bed; which I did. And as I was Covering of him, them words run through my mind, *the End is Come, The End is come, the time drayeth neer.* I could not tell what to make of these words, for they was very dark to me.* So when I had done, I went out of the Chamber into the Kitching.

Now the Chamber where my father and I lay had too beds, and it was a lower room, so that I could hear my father when he was a sleep as I sat by the fyre in the next room; for when he was a sleep, he used to snore so in his sleep that one might hear him all over the house. Now when I have heard him do so, I often took liberty to sit up the longer, wher god gave me a heart to improve my time. And that night he slept very sound as he used to do. And although he bid me make hast to bed, yet I did not, But went to the throne of grace, where I found my heart wounderfully drawn out in prayre for several things for which I had not found it in such a violent maner for some time before. And one thing that I was so Importunate with god for was that he would shew mercy to my dear father, and save his soul. This I could not tell when to have done pleading with god for. And that word still run thro my mind, *The End is Come, the End is Come, the time draweth near*; And that word, *The set time is Come.** But not one thought I had that it had respect to my fathers death. And anoth[er th]ing* I was Crying to the Lord for was that he would please to stand by me, and be with me, in whatsoever I had to meet with in this World; Not thincking what I had to meet with that night and week. But I was so helped to direct my Cryes to the Lord as if I had known what had been a Coming upon me, which I did not. And it was a very sweet season to my poor soul.

So after a great while I went to bed. And when I came into the Chamber, my father was still A sleep, which I was glad of; which I often used to be, when I had sat up a great while, for if he hath happened to hear me come to bed, he would often chide me for sitting up so late.

So I went to bed, I hope with a thanckful heart to god for what he had given me *that* night. And after I had been a bed a while, fell a sleep; but I suppose had not been a sleep long But heard a very doleful noyse. I thought it to be in the yard, not being quite awake. At last it wakened me more and more, and I perceived it was my father. So hereing of him make such a doleful noise I start up in my bed.

father, said I, *are you not well?* And he said, *no.* Said I, *How long have you not been well, pray?* Said he, *I was struck with a pain at my heart in my sleep; I shall dye presently.*

So I start out of my bed and slipt on my petty coats & shoes, and ran and light a Candle, and Came to his bed side. And he sat upright in his bed, Crying out to the Lord for mercy. Lord, said he, have mercy on me. I am a poor miserable sinner; Lord Jesus, wash me in thy pretious blood.

So I stood by him trembling to hear him in such distress of Soul for Christ, and to see him look so pale in the face. So I knelt down by his bed side and spent a litle time in prayre by him, so well as god helped me; and he seemed to Joyn with me so Earnestly. So when I had done—which was more then ever I did with him before—*father*, said I, *I must go Call some body, for I dare not stay with you Alone*; for I had no body with me, nor no house very neer.

Said he, *Yow shall not go out at this time of the night; dont be afraid of me.* And he still made the house ring with Cryes for mercy. So he said he would rise, and he put on his Cloths himself. And I ran and made a good fire Against he came out; and he all the while Cryed and prayed for mercy; And Cryed out of a pain at his heart. Thought I, may be it is Cold that is settled about his heart, for want of taking of hot things when he would not let me Come in, and had no body to do Any thing for him.

So I run and made him something hot, hoping he might be better. *Oh, I want mercy for my soul*, said he, *Oh Lord shew mercy to me; I am a great Sinner. Oh, Lord Jesus, if thow doest not show mercy to me now, I am undone for ever.*

father, said I, *their is mercy in Jesus Christ for sinners; Lord help yow to lay hould of it.*

Oh, said he, *I have been Against yow for seeking after Jesus Christ; the Lord forgive me, and lay not that sin to my Charge.**

So, when I had made him something hot, I prayed him to drinck some of it; and he dranck a litle of it, and straind to vomit, but did not. So I run to him to hold his head, as he sat by the fyre; and he Changed black in the face, as if he was a dying. And as I stood by him to hold his head, he leant Against me with all his Weight. Oh this was a very frightful thing to me indeed! Thought I, *if I leave him, he will drop in fier; And if I stand by him, he will dye in my Arms, And no body near me. Oh*, I Cryed out, *Lord help me, what shall I do?* Them words darted in upon my mind, *Fear not, I am with thee; be not dismaied, I am thy god, I will help thee, I will up hold thee.**

So after a litle it pleased god my father revived again, and Came to himself; And Cryed out Again for mercy, *Lord, have mercy upon me, I am a sinful man; Lord spare me one week more, one day more.* Oh, these was peirsing words to me! So sitting a while by the fier after he Came to himself, for I think he did swound Away for a time, he said, *give me the Candle to go in to the Chamber, for I shall have a stool.*

So he took the Candle & went into the Chamber; And I see him stagger as he went over the threshould. So I made a better fier Against he came out, and when I had done I went into the Chamber to him presently, and when I came within the door, I see him lye upon the grownd. And I run to him, screming and Crying, *father, father*; and I put my hands under his Arms, and lift at him to lift him up, and stood lifting at him, and Crying till my strength was gone, first at one Arm, then at Another. As some afterwards said, my dreaming of the Aple tree did signifie something of this. Their I stood, lifting, and Crying, till I was almost spent and Could perceive no life in him. Oh, now I was in a streight indeed. So I see I could not Lift him up, I left him and run through the house, Crying like a poor afflicted Creature that I was, and unloct the door to go Call my Brother.

Now it was the dead time of the night and no house neer. And as I ran to the door, these thoughts met me at the door, that their stood rouges ready at the door to knock me o th head, at which I was sadly frighted; but thinckin that my poor father lay dead in the house, I see I was now surrounded with trouble. So I opened the door, and rusht out much Affrighted. And it had snowed Aboundance that night; it lay very deep, and I had no stockings on so that the snow got into my shoues that I could not run a pace, and going to the stile, that was in my fathers yard, I stood Crying and Calling to my Brother. At last god helped me to Consider that it was Impossible to make them hear so fer off. Then I gat over the stile, and the snow water Caused my shoues that they would not stay on my feet for want of stockins; but I ran as fast as I could. And About the midle of the Close, as I was runing to my brothers, I was suddainly surprised with these thoughts, that there was rouges behind me, that would kill me. With that I hastily lookt behind me, and those word dropt upon my mind, *the Angels of the Lord Incampeth round About them that fear him.**

So Coming to my Brothers, I stood Crying out in a doleful manner, under his Chamber window, to the sad surprising and frighting of the whole family, they being in their midnight sleep. My poor brother was so afrighted that he did not know my voyce. He start out of his bed, and put his head out at window, and said, *Who are yow? what is the matter?*

Oh, Brother, said I, *my father is dead; Come away quickly.*

Oh, wife, said he, *this is my poor Sister. My father is dead.*

So he Called up his servants, but they was so frighted that they could scarse put on their Cloths. And when they came down out of doors, they did not know me at first. So my Brother and too or three of his men ran, and was their before me. And when my Brother Came into the Chamber my father was risen from the ground and layd upon the bed.

So my Brother spake to him, and stood Crying over him, but he Could speak but one word, or too, to him.

So when I came in, they would not let me go in to him, for they said he was Just a departing. Oh dismal night to me! Indeed, as I said, had not the lord been good to me, I had been frighted to death al most.

So presently one of my brothers men Came to me, and tould me he was departed. But in the midest of my trouble I had some hopes my father was gone to heaven Notwithstanding. So I sat Crying in a deismal manner, thincking what a great Change death had made up on my poor father of a suddain, who went well to bed and was in eternity by midnight. I said in my heart, *Lord, give me one seal more that I shall go to heaven* when death shall make this great Change upon me.* That scripture Came suddainly upon my mind, *The Ransomed of the lord shall return, and Come with singin to sion, and everlasting Joy shall be upon their heads; & they shall obtain Joy and gladness, & sorrow and sighing shall fly away.* Oh I longed to be gone to heaven, I had such a sence of the work the saints was now A bout in heaven. Thinck I, they are singing and I am sorrowing; but I see it to be a mercy that I had Any hopes through grace of going thither.

So my Brother, quickly after he Came, sent some of his men to Call in neighbours. So Among the rest Came mr fary* and his son, who so soon as they came in house, asked if my father was departed; and somebody tould him yeas. And he Answered it was no more then he lookt for. Now no body took notice of them words till afterwards. So some women Came in, who see me set without my stockings and scarse any thing on me, bewailed my sorrowful Case, and the terri- fying things I had met with that night.

Now this was Tuesday night my father dyed, and now I remem- ber that Scripture on friday night in the barn, *Beloved, thinck it not strange Concerning the fiery tryals that are to try yow.* Thought I, *I have had fiery tryals since fryday night indeed*; litle thincking I had as bad, or worse, to Come still, though god in his infinite goodness Caused it to work for good to my soul and made me say, it was good for me that I have been afflicted.*

Well, that day, which was Tuesday, their was a fair at baldocke; And this preist, mr Layne, that meet Mr Bunyan and I on horse back at Gamgey towns End, was at Baldocke that day, and tould it about the fair that he see me behind John Bunyan going to gamgey, and at the towns End, their we was naught* together. And, as I hard, it ran from one End of the fair to the other presently. So on Wedensday morning, the next day after the fair, when my poor father lay by the walls, Came somebody in and tould me what a report thir was of me at baldock fair. But that scripture bore me up, *Blessed are ye when men shall revile yow, and say all maner of evil of yow falsely, for my name sake.**

So the next day my brother and we Concluded for buryin my father on Thursday night; and he spake for wine and all things to Come in on Thursday. We also invighted all our freinds, and relations, and neighbours to Come in on Thursday; some we invighted several miles about. So when this was all done and Concluded of, Mr feery sends for my Brother to his house.

So on Wedensday night my Brother went. And when he Came, he had him in to his parlour to speak with him. So said he to my Brother, *I had a mind to speak with yow. Do yow thinck yor father dyed a natural death?*

My Brother was amased to hear him Ask such a question; But he Answered and said, *I know he did dye a natural death.*

But, said he to my Brother, *I beleeve he did not; and*, said he, *I have had my horse twise out of the stable to day, to fetch Mr Halfehead of Potten, the Doctor. But, I considered, yow are an officer in the town,* and so I will leave it to yow. Therefore, pray see yow do yor office.*

Said my brother, *How do yow thinck he came by his End, if he did not dye a natural death?*

Said he, *I beleeve yor Sister poysoned him.*

I hope, said my Brother, *we shall satisfie yow to the Contrary.*

So my poor brother Comes home with a heavy heart, for he did not know but I might lose my life, and he was very much troubled to thinck what I had yet to meet with. So he Calls my sister up stairs to speak with her, and told her; which Caused great distress in them both. And their was a good man in the Town at Sister prudons. So they sent for him, and my Brother told him of this thing. So they 3 went up into an upper room, and spread it before the lord. So my Brother Askt this man and my sister whither he had best Come to my fathers that night to tell me of it; And they said, *no, Let her have this night at quiet.* So he did not Come; but that night they spent much time in prayre.

So the next morning my Brother Comes early, and with a very sad Countenance Calls me up Stairs. *Sister*, said he, *I must speak with yow.* So I went up with him into the Chamber, and when he Came up, he fell a weeping.

Oh, Sister, said he, *pray god help yow; yow are like to meet with hard things.*

Hard things? said I, *what, worse then I have met with?*

Yes, worse then ever yow met with yet.

So he told me My neighbour feery Accused me with my fathers death, and said that I had poysoned him. At the first hearing of it, My heart sanck in me, and it was a very sad and suddain surprysal to me. But I quickly said to him, *Oh Brother, blessed be god for a Clear Contience.* But Although I knew my self Clear in the sight of god, yet any body must needs thinck these was hard things for one so young as I to meet with.

So my Brother said, *I must send to Potten for Mr Halfehead, who is a docter and Surgeon both.* And we was Also first to send to all those we had invited to my fathers funeral To desire them not to Come till they heard further from us. So all the town, and towns their A bouts, wondred what the matter was, knowing my father did not dye in debt.

So we sent for mr Halfehead, and tould him how things was; that such a one in the town, did thinck that I had poysoned my father. So he Examined me, how my father was before he went to bed; and what supper he eat. And I told him every thing that he asked me, and he seemed to be much Concerned for me. And when he had vewed the Corps, he went to mr feerys to talk with him, and tould him he wondred he should have such thoughts of me; their was no ground for it. But he said to Mr Halfehead, he did beleeve it was so.

So mr Halfehead sees no Arguments would Convince him, he Come back to my Brothers and I, and said we must have a Coroner and a Jewry. So I prayed him that he would please to open my father. *Sir*, said I, *as my Inocency is known to god, so I would have it known to men.*

No, said he, *their is no need to have him opened.*

So we desired him to Come the next day to meet the Coroner and the Jewry; and he said he would. So now I had a new work lay before me, and I did betake my self to prayre, to fly to god for help, and that he would please to appeer for me in this fiery tryal. I see my life lye at stake,* and the name of god lye their too; and many prayres & teers was powred out to god, and that sweet Cordial the Lord sent me to Comfort me; Oh it was a blessed promise indeed; and blessed be god he also made it good. *No weapon that is formed Against thee shall prosper; And every toung that shall rise up in Judgement Against thee, thou shall Condemn;** And that word would often Come into my mind, *as many as are incensed Against thee shall be Ashamed.**

So the next morning, which was friday Morning, my Brother sent for the Coroner and Jewry to Come that day. So mr feery, hearing my Brother had sent for them, He sent for my Brother to his house, and he went. So when he Came their, said he, *I hear yow have sent for the Coroner.*

Yes, said my brother.

Said he Again, *I would wish yow to meet the Coroner at biglesworth, and Agree it their, and not let him Come through; for it will be found petty Treason; She must be burned.**

Said my Brother, *We are not Afraid to let him Come throw.*

So my brother Came and told me what he said.

Brother, said I, *I will have him Come through, if it Cost me all that ever my father left me; for if we should not, then he and All the world might say I am guilty indeed.* Though, as I said, I see my life lye at stake; for I did not know how far god might suffer him and the divel to go. And this Also troubled me, that if I had suffered Another as Inocent as I must have suffred too; for mr feery said that I made a hand of* my father, And John Bunyan gave me Counsel to poyson him when he Caried me behind him to Gamgy; that then we did Consent to do it. Nay as I remember it was said that Mr Bunyan gave me stuff to do it with. But the Lord knew to the Contrary, that neither he nor I was gilty of that wickedness in thought, word, nor deed. But yet notwithstanding I knew my self Clear, yet I must tell yow, I see my self surrounded with straights and trouble; And Carnal reasoning gat in. Thought I, *Suppose god should suffer my enemyes to prevail, to take away my life; how shall I endure burning?* Oh, this made my heart Ake at a great rate; though, blessed be god, my heart did not Accuse me, in thought, word, nor deed. But the thoughts of burning would sometimes shake me all to peeces; and sometimes I should think of that scripture that would so often run in my mind before my father dyed, *When thou goest throw the fier, I will be with thee; and through the waters, they shall not over flow thee.* And then I should thinck thus, *Lord, thow knowest I am Inocent; therfore if it shall please thee to suffer them to take Away my life, yet Surely thow wilt be with me. Thou hast been with me in all my straights, and I hope thow* *will not leave me now in the greatest of all.* And Arguing thus from the Experience of gods goodness to me in times of tryal, at last I was made to beleeve that, if I did burn at a stake, the Lord would give me his presence. So I was made, in a solemn maner I hope, to resign my self up to god, to be at his disposing, for life or death. But still I was greatly Concernd for the name of god, that is like to suffer, let it go which way it will with me; for thinck I, *Though it may be some will not beleeve it, yet a great many will; Doubtless the Name of god will suffer. But,* thinck I, *I must leave it with god, who hath the hearts of all men in his hand.*

So that day the Coroner was to Come in the Afternoon, some of Gamgy freinds Came to me, and they spent several hours in prayer before the Crowner Came, that god would please to Appear gratiously for me, and for the glory of his one Name. So when they had done, I gat into a Corner by my self; for I had a great mind, to be with god Alone at the thrown of grace where I usually found releif, and Succur, and help. And that was very much upon my heart, to Cry to the Lord to give me his presence that day; So much of it that I might not have a dijected Countenance, nor be of a daunted spirit before them; for I see that to be brought before a Company of men, and to Come before them of being Accused of Murtherin my one father, that, although I knew my self clear in the sight of god, yet without A boundance of his presence, I should sinck before them.* Thought I, if they should see me degected and loock daunted, they would thinck I was gilty. I begged of the Lord that he would please to Cary me A bove the fears of men, and devils, and death it self; And that he would give me faith and Courage that I might look my Accuser in the face with boldness, and that I might lift up my head before him, with Conviction to themself.

And as I was earnestly Crying to the Lord, with many teirs, for his presence, that blessed word darted in upon my mind, *ye righteous shall hold on their way, and they that have clean hands, shall grow stronger and stronger.* Oh I brake out with these words, *Lord, thou knowest my hands and my heart is Clean in this matter.* I thought it was such a suitable word, I could scarse have had the like; And the lord made it good ere the sun went down, every litle of it. So I was helped to look my Accuser in the face with boldness.

So presently word was brought that the Coroner and the Jewry was Come to my brothers, and when they had set up their horses, and Come altogether, they Came to vew the Corpes. And I, with some Neighbours, was by the fyre; And as they passed through the house into the Chamber where my father was layd out, Some of the Jewrymen Came and took me by the hand, with teirs runing down their Cheecks, and said to me, *Pray god be thy Comfort, for thou art as Inocent as I am, I beleeve*. So Another would say to me, and truly I loockt upon this to be a mercy to me, to see them so Convinced of my Inocency.

So when the Coroner had loockt on my father, he comes out into the house, and stands and warms himself by the fier, and with a sted-fast look, Looks upon me.

Said he, Are yow the daughter of this man deceased?

Yes, Sir, said I.

And what are yow she that was in the house Alone with him when he dyed?

Yeas, Sir, I am She.

So he shook his head, which I thought his thoughts had been evil towards me and not good.

So when the Jewry had vewed the Corpes, they went back to my Brothers. And when they had dyned, they sat A bout the business. So my Brother sent for me, and I went. And as I was going, my heart went out mightily to god to stand by me; And such words as these passed through my heart, *Thow shall not return Again A shamed.** And before I came to my Brothers, my soul was made like the Chariots of Aminnadab,* and I was wounderfully bourn up, beyound what I did ask or thinck.

So when I came their, my brother sent for mr feery and he did not Come. So my Brother sent A gain, at last he Came. So then they sat A bout their business.

So the Coroner Cald for the witnesses, my Brothers men, that was with my father before he departed and gave them an oth; And Likewise mr feery was sworn, to speak the truth and nothing but the truth. So, as I remember, my Brothers men was Examined first. So they Answered to all the Coroner askt them, which was this, whether they was their before my father dyed. And they said yes. And how long he lived after they Came, and what words they heard him speak. So he had quickly done with them. Then he Called mr feery.

Come, said he, *you are the Occation of our Coming together, we would know what you have to say as to this Maids Murthering of her father, and what ground yow have to Accuse her.*

So he made such a strange preamble that no body knew what to make of it, of the defference that was between my father and I; And of my being shut out of doors; and my fathers dying too nights after I came in.

And their I stood in the parlour Among them, with my heart full of Comfort as ever it Could hold; and I was got Above the fears of men and devils.

So, said the Crowner, *This is nothing to the matter in hand; what have yow to A ccuse this Maid with?*

But he said but litle, or nothing to the purpose, So that the Coroner was very Angry at the Contrary Answers that he gave him to what he askt him; but I have forgot most of his pity full Answers. But at last the Coroner was very Angry, and bid him stand by, if their was all he Could say. So the Coroner Calls me, *Come, sweetheart*, said he, *tell us where yow was that night yor father shut yow out.*

Now the man that went to bedford for the Coroner had told him how all things was as they rid A long.

Sir, said I, *I was in the barn all night.*

And wast thow their Alone all night? Said he.

Yeas Sir, I had no body with me.

So he shook his head, And where did you go the next morning?

Sir, said I, *I layed in the yard with my father till about nine or ten A Clock to perswade him to let me go in; but he would not.*

And the Coroner seemed as if he was Concerned at the hearing of these things. So he askt me where I was that day.

Sir, I went to my brothers, said I.

And where was yow that night?

I told him that I lay at my brothers that night as my Brothers servants did witness.

So he askt me when my father let me Come in.

I told him it was sabboth day night.

And he askt me if he was well, and how long it was after I came in that he dyed.

Sir, said I, *it was sabboth day night that I went in, and he dyed the next Tuesday night.*

Was he well that day? said he.

Yes Sir, as well as ever I see him in my life, and Eat as good a dinner as ever I see him eat.

So he askt me what he eat at supper.

So I told him.

He askt me after what maner he was taken, and what time. *Sir,* said I, *the maner of his being taken was in his sleep, with a pain at his heart, he said; and as to the time, it was a litle before midnight. I, being in the same room, heard him groan; So I made hast to rise, and light a Candle, and went to him; & he sat upright in his bed, Crying out of a pain at his heart, and that he should dye presently; and I was sadly frighted, so that I could scarse git any Cloths on me. So he said he would rise; and I made a fire, and he sat by it, and I ran and got him something hot, and he dranck a litle of it, & straind to vomit and I run to him to hold his head; and he swounded away, and I Could not leave him to Call in any body; for if I had he would have dropt in the fire, for he lent Against me, with all his wait.*

Was their no body in the house with yow? said he.

No, Sir, said I, *no body with me but god.*

So he shook his head.

So when my father Came to himself, he said he should have a stool; and he went into the Chamber, and quickly after I followed him, and he lay all A long upon the ground. So I run scraming to him, and lift at him; but Could not lift him up, so left him, and ran in a very frightful Condition to my Brothers.

But the man that went for the Coroner had tould him how I frighted the family. So he said to me, *Sweetheart, I have no more to say to thee.*

So Next he spake to the Jewry, and when they had given up their verduit, and all was done, he. Turns himself to mr feery. Said the Coroner, *Yow that have defamed this maid after this manner, yow had need make it yor business now to repair her reputation A gain. Yow have taken Away her good name from her, and yow would have taken Away her life from her if yow Could. She met with Enough I thinck,* said he, *in being in the house alone that night he dyed. Yow needed not have added this to her affliction and sorrow. If yow should have given her five-hundred pounds, it would not make her amends.*

So the Coroner Comes to me, and takes me by the hand, *Come, Sweetheart,* said he, *do not be daunted, god will take Care of thy preferment, and provide a husband, notwithstanding the malice of this man;*

And bless god for this deliverance, and never fear but god will take Care of thee. But I Confess these are heard things for one so young as thow art to meet with.

So I had a mind to speak to the Coroner and Jewry before they departed; *Sir*, said I, *if yow are not all satisfied, I am freely willing that my father sould be opened. As my Inocency is known to god, so I would have it known to yow, for I am not afraid of my life.*

No, said he, *we are all well satisfied of thy Inocency; their is no need to have him opened. But*, said he, *bless god that the Malice of this man brake out before thy father was buryed.*

So the room, where we was, Was very full of people, and it seems great Observation was made of my Countenance, as I heard afterwards. Some gentlemen that was upon the Jewry said, they should never forget me, to see with what a Chearful Countenance I stood before them all. They said I did not look like one that was gilty. I know not how I Lookt, but I know my heart was full of peace And Comfort. All the Jewry was much concernd for me, though Carnal men, and it was observed they sat with wet Eyes Many of them while the Coroner was Examining of me. And indeed I had Cause to thanck god, that he did Convince them of my Inocency. And I hard that a twelvemonth after they would speak of me with teirs.

So then we sent to invite All our freinds to Come to my fathers funeral on Saterday night. So now I thought surely my troubles and tryals up on that Account was at an End. I thought mr feery had vented all his malice now; but he had not he was resolved to have Another pull with me.* Seeing he was prevented of my life, he did attempt to take Away what my father left me; for he sent for my brother in law, that had Maried my own Sister, from my fathers grave, and tould him how things was left as to my fathers Will, and that my father had given her but a shilling to Cut her off.* And he tould him he Could set him in a way to Come in for a part, which my brother* was glad to hear of.

Now my fathers Will was made three years before he dyed, and mr feery made it. And then he put my father on to give me more then my sister because of some design that he had then, but afterwards when I came to go to meetings he was turned Against me. And I did not know but that will that was made then had been Altered; But it was not. So the next thing I was to meet with I must spedely resign up a part of what my father had left me to my Brother in law, or else he would sue me. So this was a new trouble to me; I was threatned at a great rate. Mr feery said, *Hang her, dont let her go away with so much more then yor wife.* So to law they would have gone with me presently but I Agreed to give my Brother Threscore pounds for peace and quietness.

Well, one great mercy the lord was pleasd to Add to all the rest; he was pleasd to keep pregudise out of my heart to this man. And the lord did help me to Cry to him in secret, with many teirs, for mercy for his poor soul; And I longed After the salvation of it, and begged forgiveness of and for him for what he had done Against me.

Well, About a month after my father was buried, Another report was raised of me. It was hotly reported at Biglesworth that now I had Confest that I had poysoned my father, and that I was quite distracted. And their the people would get together to tell one Another this news.

But is it true? said some. *Yeas, it is true Enough,* said others. So I heard of it. *Well,* thought I, *if it please god to spare me, I will go the next market day to let them see I was not distracted.* I was troubled that the name of god did suffer. So when wedensday morning Came, I made me ready to go to biglesworth, and it was very sharp and Could; it was frost and snow, but I could not be contented without going. The Lord was wonderful good to my soul, That morning; that scripture run mightily through my mind as I was going to the market, *Blessed are ye, when men shall revile yow, and say all maner of evil of yow falsely for my name sake; rejoyce and be exceeding glad, for great is yor reward in heaven*; and that word, *As many as are incensed against thee shall be ashamed.* I was very comfortable in my soul, as I was going, and when I Came their.

So I went to my sister Everads to rest me; and when it was full market, I went to show my self among them. And when I came into the market, the poor people could not follow their business that they was A bout, but I thinck I may say almost all the Eyes of the market was fixt upon me. Hear I should see half a dozen stand together, whispering and poynting at me; And their I should see Another Company stand talking together. So I walkt through and through the market. Thought I, *If their was a thousand more of yow, I could lift up my head before yow all.* I was very chearful, for I was very well in my soul that day.*

So a great many came to me and said, *We see yow are not distracted.*
And I see some Cry, and some laugh. *Oh*, thought I, *mock on; their
is a day a Coming will clear all.* That was a wonderful scripture to me,
*he will bring forth thy righteousness as the light, and thy brightness shall
be as the noon day.**

Thus I have tould yow of the good and evil things that I met with
in that dispensation. I wish I was as well in my soul as I was then.

[*The following notes are added to the original manuscript:*]
her name Agnes.

Edworth where Agnes livd 3 3/4 miles from Biggleswade.

Revd John Bunyan, nam'd by ye writer as the Minister she heard,
was born at Elstow near Bedford 1628; had been a Soldier in the parliamentary Army; 1655 he was admitted a Member of ye Baptist
Meeting at Bedford & was soon after chosen their pastor & for
preaching the gospel was sent to Bedford Jail where he was kept
12½ yrs; he died in London 1688 agd 60.

N.B.—In the Jail he wrote his Pilgrims Progress.

[*In the other manuscript (Egerton 2128) these concluding paragraphs are
added:*]

After this Report there was another, raised in another place in the
Country, and that was, *Mr. Bunyan was a Widower, and he gave me
Councel to poyson my Father that so he might have me to be his Wife,
and this we agreed upon as we rid along to Gongey.* And truely this did
sometimes make me merry, as other things did make me sad, and not
long after it was said, *we were married*, but they were mistaken for he
had a good Wife before.

I could not but tell this News to several my self, and it did serve
to divert me sometimes.

Now I thought surely *Mr. Ferey* had done, but the next Sumer
after my ffather died, there happen'd to be a ffire in the Town, and
no Body could tell how this ffire came. But *Mr. Ferey* did secretly
affirm it, that I did set the House on ffire. But the Lord knows I knew
nothing of it till I heard the doleful cry of ffire in the Town.

FINIS

APPENDIX

RADICAL AND NONCONFORMIST GROUPS IN SEVENTEENTH-CENTURY ENGLAND

(This brief Appendix includes only those groups mentioned in this edition.)

ANABAPTISTS. Anabaptist ('re-baptizer') is the name given to various groups on the Continent who in the sixteenth century denied the validity of infant baptism on the grounds that baptism must be the voluntary undertaking of a believer. Many Anabaptists refused to take oaths or do military service and established communities based on communistic principles. In England during the sixteenth and seventeenth centuries, the term was very loosely applied and generally denoted a person whose religious views were considered to threaten the stability of the social order.

BAPTISTS. While generally characterized by the belief that adult baptism—the baptism of believers—should be the condition of reception into the church, Baptists in seventeenth-century England were a diverse group. The two main branches, the General and the Particular Baptists, shared the concern to institute the baptism of believers but differed fundamentally in the form of Protestantism they embraced. The General Baptists were Arminians; that is, they accepted the doctrine of the Dutch theologian Jacob Arminius (1560–1609), which stressed the efficacy of the human will in the attainment of salvation, revising the Calvinist belief in total human depravity and the predetermined fate of the soul. The Particular Baptists, by contrast, adhered to traditional Calvinist doctrine. John Bunyan belonged to the open-communion Baptist church, which was also Calvinist in theology but did not insist on the necessity of adult baptism. A fourth, smaller branch, the Seventh-Day or Sabbatarian Baptists, regarded Saturday as the true Sabbath.

DIGGERS. Founded in 1649 by Gerrard Winstanley, who equated the Fall of Man with the creation of private property rights and argued that true Christian principles dictated the common ownership of land. The Diggers called on the common people of England to cultivate crown property and common land, and in April 1649 began digging and manuring waste ground at St George's Hill in Surrey. Retaliation from local landowners followed, and the colony at St George's Hill, along with other similar experiments in communistic living, was soon suppressed. Although based on Genesis, Winstanley's political theory tends to secularize the Christian faith, identifying God with Reason.

FAMILISTS. The 'Family of Love' was founded in 1540 by Henry Niclaes (b. 1502 in Münster). His followers, called Familists, believed that it was only the Inner Light, the divine illumination within the believer, which could produce a full understanding of Scripture. They repudiated the ceremonies of the established church, adhered to principles of common ownership, and claimed that heaven and hell lay here on earth. Familism took root in England during the late sixteenth century, especially among the lower ranks of society. The sect survived through the seventeenth century, and the Inner Light emphasis of Niclaes led many Quakers to read his works.

FIFTH MONARCHISTS. Millenarianism—the belief in the imminence of the millennium, or Christ's Second Coming—was widespread in mid-seventeenth-century England. The Fifth Monarchists, whose disciples were largely Baptists and Congregationalists, tended to espouse a radical millenarianism which saw the overthrow of the old social and religious order as a necessary preparation for Christ's Second Coming. The 'Fifth Monarchy', prophesied in the Book of Daniel (2: 44), was their chosen term for the millennium. In 1661, under Thomas Venner, the Fifth Monarchists instigated an unsuccessful armed revolt against the restored monarchy.

INDEPENDENTS (or CONGREGATIONALISTS). Independents, who began to promote their views in 1641–2, disagreed with the concept of a single national church. They believed instead that individual churches, composed of members who made public testimony to their conversion and gave a solemn undertaking to join together in fellowship, should be autonomous, self-governing societies. Bunyan's church was Independent in organization and Baptist in doctrine.

LEVELLERS. This was the name given to a political and religious movement widely supported by the soldiers of the New Model Army during the Civil War. Leveller spokesmen included the radical puritans John Lilburne, Richard Overton, and William Walwyn. The Leveller programme had no place for monarchy, urged the abolition of the property requirement for the vote, and advocated total freedom of religious belief and practice. The Levellers agitated for a role in determining the shape of the post-Civil War settlement, but their democratic impulses proved too radical for a Parliament and army leadership dominated by the puritan gentry. Lilburne and other leaders were arrested, army mutinies were crushed, and the movement went into decline.

MUGGLETONIANS. Founded in 1652 by John Reeve and Lodowick Muggleton, who claimed to be the Two Last Witnesses of Revelation (11: 3–6), entrusted with God's final commission, Muggletonians held that God's granting of his final revelation to the 'two witnesses' rendered prayer and preaching redundant. They also rejected the doctrine of the Holy Trinity and condemned human reason as satanic in origin.

PRESBYTERIANS. Presbyterians opposed the government of the Church of England by bishops (episcopacy), on the grounds that it had no scriptural warrant, smacked of popery, and gave too much authority in spiritual matters to bishops who were appointed by the state. They advocated instead a Presbyterian system of church government, which empowered each congregation to elect its own minister(s) and lay elders. Presbyteries, consisting of ministers and elders from a particular area, would in turn send elected representatives to the General Assembly responsible for doctrine and discipline. In 1646, Parliament's attempt to establish Presbyterian church government was opposed by the Independents, who advocated the autonomy of individual congregations.

QUAKERS (Society of Friends). The Quakers began to flourish in the 1650s, under the leadership of George Fox and James Nayler. They believed in the Inner Light, or 'God within': that all people carry within themselves the potential for divine illumination. The Quaker stress on each individual's direct experience of the operation of God's spirit had several logical (and radical) consequences. The Bible, while still viewed as a valuable spiritual guide, was subordinated to the Inner Light. A formal ministry and a consecrated building in which to worship lost their relevance, while reliance on the promptings of the Spirit removed the need for religious rituals and sacraments. The Quakers' refusal to take oaths, their defiance of traditional social hierarchies, and their prioritizing of the Inner Light over any external authority led to conflict with the government. They were persecuted during the Commonwealth and more severely after the Restoration. The pacifist and quietist principles for which the Quakers are now known developed after 1660.

RANTERS. Although the existence of an organized Ranter movement has been the subject of debate among historians, the term 'Ranter' is generally applied to the writings of such sectaries as Abiezer Coppe, Lawrence Clarkson, Joseph Salmon, and Jacob Bauthumley. The published works of these men (which belong to the period 1649–51) differ markedly from each other, but tend to share a pantheistic identification of God with the natural world and an antinomian conviction that those who live by grace are above the moral law. Coppe and Clarkson in particular appear to have advocated a radical antinomianism, which held that the test of true spiritual liberty was the ability to commit 'sins' without feeling any remorse. The Ranters were widely accused of licentious behaviour, and the Blasphemy Act of 1650 was directed particularly against them and those with similar beliefs.

SEEKERS. Active from the early seventeenth century, the Seekers denied the legitimacy of all existing churches and believed that God would eventually appoint new apostles or prophets to establish a new church. They took a quietistic view of this process: the believer must wait passively for the revelation of God's will.

EXPLANATORY NOTES

Grace Abounding

3 *I being taken from you in presence*: Bunyan was, like his model the Apostle Paul, writing from prison, to which he had been consigned in November 1660. Internal dating suggests that the writing is quite close to the publication date of 1666.

edifying: a key word for puritans, emphasized here by the tautology ('building up'), which expressed the dissenting church's reliance, in the absence of a physical edifice, on the preached word (and the precedent of the early church) to hold it together.

I thank God upon every Remembrance of you: Phil. 1: 3. Bunyan clearly aligns himself with Paul by using his words.

while I stick between the Teeth of the Lions in the Wilderness: an implicitly optimistic allusion to Paul's typological use of Daniel: 'I was delivered out of the mouth of the lion' (2 Tim. 4: 17). As the conclusion to the Preface indicates ('The Milk and Honey is beyond this Wilderness'), the wilderness is this world. It is the terrain of 'dens' and 'lions' (see Ps. 10: 9; Amos 3: 4), the symbols of persecution of nonconformists under the Restoration's Clarendon Code (Corporation Act, 1661, Act of Uniformity, 1662, Conventicle Act, 1664, Five Mile Act, 1665).

For you are my glory and joy, 1 Thes. 2. 20: again Bunyan merges his identity with Paul's.

The Philistians understand me not: the allusion is to Judg. 14: 14. The Philistines could not solve Samson's riddle: 'Out of the eater came forth meat, And out of the strong came forth sweetness.' Puritans believed that the language of their spiritual experience was foreign to the worldly. They sometimes called it 'the Language of *Canaan*' (*PP* 74).

for he woundeth, and his hands make whole: Job 5: 18.

4 *Yea, it was for this reason I lay so long at Sinai*: Sinai was a metonym for the moral law of God (delivered to Moses on Mount Sinai as the Ten Commandments (Exod. 19: 20)), sometimes known as the first covenant or the covenant of the law, under which all humankind stood condemned. See *PP* 16–20.

and commanded also, that they did remember their forty years travel in the wilderness: memory, and consequently assurance, of elect experiences had awesome importance to puritans, as it was the basis on which they would be finally judged. The word 'remember' recurs twelve times in the Preface.

the hill Mizar: Ps. 42: 6.

5 *Remember also the Word . . . upon which the Lord hath caused you to hope*:
see Ps. 119: 49.

but out of them all the Lord delivered me: 2 Tim. 3: 11.

God did not play in convincing of me: the word 'convince' has a technical
sense: 'conviction of sin' was the first phase in the process of salvation,
although it was a phase that could be shared by the reprobate (see
Bunyan's *Mapp Shewing the Order and Causes of Salvation and Damnation*,
reprinted in Stachniewski, 196–7).

the Devil did not play in tempting of me: Bunyan deleted this clause from
edition 5, perhaps because his rhetoric inadvertently attributes sincerity
to the devil (the devil might well have been playing with him).

when I sunk as into a bottomless pit: the first of many anticipations of the
sinking in the Slough of Dispond (*PP* 13).

the pangs of hell caught hold upon me: the closest reference is Isa. 13: 8,
'pangs and sorrows shall take hold of them'.

wherefore I may not play in my relating of them: a higher style is equated
with adornment, which is a form of play, a negatively charged concept
for many puritans. Puritan preachers tended to favour a 'plain style'.

God be merciful to you . . . to go in to possess the Land: this return to typological identification of the separatist community with the Israelites
escaping Egyptian slavery to seek the promised land not only marks it as
a mental habit of puritan groups (including for example, Quakers (see
Crook, p. 168)); it also carries, with its concluding emphasis on
'possess[ing] the Land', a personal resonance for Bunyan, whose feeling
of spiritual dispossession seems to have been allied to his sense of his
family's social decline and loss of land. For a description of puritan typological practice, see Thomas M. Davis, 'The Exegetical Traditions of
Puritan Typology', *Early American Literature*, 5 (1970), 11–50.

6 *Grace Abounding to the chief of Sinners*: Bunyan's entire title is an allusion
to Paul's words to Timothy (1 Tim. 1: 14–15). The meaning of the last
phrase ('sinners; of whom I am chief') lay in subjective intensity rather
than comparison.

most despised of all the families in the Land: Bunyan's family had quite
recently declined from yeoman status to that of braziers or tinkers (there
are records of land being sold from 1548). It is the sense of being held in
social contempt by others ('despised'), rendered acute by recent decline,
that flavours this passage. The exaggeration (if there is any) is correlated
with the aggressive implication that high birth 'according to the flesh'
confers deceptive advantage: 'the flesh' being the worldly antagonist of
'spirit'.

it pleased God . . . to put me to School: fees and book purchase deterred
most parents of the poorer sort from sending their children to school.
Bunyan was well aware that the privileged classes saw him as uneducated:
'I never went to School to Aristotle or Plato, but was brought up at my

father's house, in a very mean condition, among a company of poor Country-men' ('Epistle to the Reader', *The Doctrine of the Law and Grace Unfolded* (1659), *MW* ii. 16).

natural: according to Calvinist theology, without the benefit of divine grace—selectively bestowed—depraved human nature inevitably succumbed to demonic promptings. (Compare Norwood's use of 'natural', p. 127)

7 *still*: ever.

bound down with the chains and bonds of eternal darkness: see 2 Pet. 2: 4.

These things, I say, when I was but a childe: edition 3 specifies 'about nine or ten years old'.

had not a miracle of precious grace prevented: Bunyan alludes to the doctrine of 'prevenient grace': God's grace came before human repentance, enabling it to take place.

shame before the face of the world: it is noteworthy that Bunyan's rhetoric subordinates the stroke of eternal justice to worldly disgrace, helping to justify the argument that the young Bunyan was reacting, in his spiritual distress, to a social predicament.

8 *O Lord, thou knowest my life, and my ways were not hid from thee*: the closest Bible verse is Ps. 69: 5: 'O God, thou knowest my foolishness; And my sins are not hid from thee.'

God . . . followed me still, not now with convictions, but Judgements: judgements were punitive external events or afflictions, while convictions were punitive pangs of conscience.

Bedford River: the Ouse.

but mercy yet preserved me alive: spiritual autobiographers usually record similar incidents ('special preservatives', Norwood calls them (p. 125)): since the unregenerate deserved death and punishment, any accident which might have been fatal was latched onto as betokening God's selective mercy, preserving the elect until the time of their reception of grace.

stounded: stunned.

This also I have taken notice of with thanksgiving; When I was a Souldier: Bunyan was mustered in the Parliamentary army not later than November 1644 (when he reached the legal age of 16), and posted to Colonel Richard Cokaynes's company, which was garrisoning Newport Pagnell under the command of Sir Samuel Luke. His regiment was demobilized on 21 July 1647. He probably saw little, if any, action.

9 *not having so much*: the word 'houshold-stuff' was added after 'not having so much' in edition 3: the need for scrupulous honesty overrides, in cooler retrospect, the earlier need to stress worldly lowliness.

The Plain Mans Path-way to Heaven, and The Practice of Piety: first published in 1601, Arthur Dent's *The Plaine Mans Path-way to Heaven* ran through twenty-five editions by 1640. It is a work of popular piety constructed as a conversation between an informed Christian, a scoffer, and an ignorant man, through whom evangelism is aimed at the reader. Bunyan took many hints from it when he wrote *The Pilgrim's Progress*. Lewis Bayly, author of the (also much published) popular devotional manual, *The Practice of Piety* (1612), was bishop of Bangor (1616–32). It is interesting to note that, while for Bunyan this book is associated with the first stirrings of puritan piety, for Laurence Clarkson it represented the dutiful conformist observance his father sought to impose on him when he was gadding to puritan preachers. The work is clearly Calvinist, but when Clarkson was an adolescent (around 1630), this theology did not of itself identify the puritan.

9 *a godly man*: the term 'godly', when applied to a person, is a fairly reliable way of identifying a 'puritan' in Bunyan's time. It tends to identify the user, as well as the referent.

how he would reprove and correct Vice: taking it on themselves to reprove their neighbours was both an identifying characteristic of many puritans and, naturally enough, a major reason for the hostility they tended to attract.

awaken: puritans used 'awaken' in a peculiar sense, not specifically distinguished in *OED* (but see example from 1746). Only loosely derived from certain biblical texts (such as 1 Cor. 15: 34), it refers to the beginning of the conversion experience: the awakening of a dormant spiritual faculty to the hideousness of sin and the need of divine grace. Compare Agnes Beaumont: 'since I was Awakened' (p. 193).

adored, and that with great devotion . . . belonging to the Church: Elstow Abbey (an eleventh-century foundation) was a grand and imposing church for a small village, and its clergy may have had pretensions to match. Christopher Hall, the vicar, had been beneficed under Archbishop Laud in 1639. 'Two-thirds of the Episcopal clergy' of Bedfordshire, says John Brown, 'remained undisturbed in their livings' (Brown, 70). To Bunyan's eyes, then, the ordained clergy of the national church would not have changed radically under the mainly presbyterian authority of the puritans' Westminster Assembly of Divines. The terms he uses heighten otherness with hostile colouring: 'high places' were destroyed as idolatrous in the Bible (2 Kgs. 23: 5–20); 'priest' disparages the clergy as scions of the Catholic priesthood; 'vestments' suggests liturgical garments, although a plain gown would probably have been worn. It was not unusual for separatists to stress how devout they had been within the established church, so that they could claim to transcend something of which they had taken the measure. See, for example, Jane Turner, *Choice Experiences* (1653), 11.

This conceit: conception.

10 *to treat of the Sabbath day . . . with labour, sports, or otherwise*: this sermon may have signalled the advent of a new puritan ethos to a village community in which games may previously have been viewed, in accordance

with the Royalist position, as a harmless pastime for the lower orders. They came to signify illiteracy, idleness, and probably reprobation, and were prohibited on Sundays by puritan legislation introduced in 1644. See Christopher Hill's excellent analysis of the politics of sabbatarianism and the reasons behind its emergence as a battle-ground between Royalists and puritans: 'The Uses of Sabbatarianism', ch. 5 in *Society and Puritanism in Pre-Revolutionary England* (1964; Harmondsworth, 1986).

believing that he made that Sermon on purpose to shew me my evil-doing: this piercing sense of being singled out, often by a sermon, is a common feature of the autobiographies (see Crook, pp. 162–3, and Norwood, p. 152).

cut: Sharrock prefers edition 3's 'did benum the sinews of my best delights' to 1's 'cut' on the reasonable grounds that the delights return (p. 135 n.). But the word 'benumming' occurs proximately (p. 11)—just the sort of thing a revising author, as distinct from a composing author, would be likely to overlook. Besides, one could argue that edition 1 conveys a greater immediacy of experience: it felt to the young Bunyan as though the sinews had been severed like a cut hamstring.

a game at Cat: cat, or tipcat, involved placing a six-inch oval-shaped piece of wood (the cat) on a spot on the ground (the hole), knocking it with a bat so that it jumped up, and then striking it in mid-air. That Bunyan was playing tipcat on the village green (adjacent to he church) on a Sunday suggests that the law of 1644 against Sunday sports was not rigorously enforced.

11 *and therefore I resolved in my mind, I would go on in sin*: this state of mind tended to be a product of the predestinarian theology and cultural restrictiveness of the church. Marlowe's *Doctor Faustus* is the most spectacular literary example: his desperate hedonism is premissed on the despair of salvation—'What will be, shall be' (*The Complete Plays*, ed. J. B. Steane (Harmondsworth, 1969), 1. i. 48)—expressed in his first speech. Opponents of Calvinism argued that its predestination tended to remove all moral restraint and thus promote social disorder.

returned to my sport again: edition 3 (followed by Sharrock) adds 'desperately' to 'returned'. This is gratuitous, since Bunyan goes on to talk of 'this kind of despair' which 'did so possess my Soul', and even falsifying in that it overlays a moralization on an experience which is at first more subtly conveyed (the despair is not consciously apprehended). This exemplifies the moralizing tendency of minor revisions of edition 1, which I prefer to omit.

frame of heart: this distinctively puritan use of 'frame' (present also in Norwood, p. 140) designated a spiritual state as it was experienced from the inside, colouring all perceptions. Bunyan finds it especially useful in *Grace Abounding* (e.g. pp. 11, 66, 74) (see also *PP* 15).

a secret conclusion . . . for they have loved sins, Jer. 2.25. & 18.12.: the quotation is loosely based on Jer. 2: 25; 'therefore after them will I go' is added in 3.

12 *swearing*: swearing was a criminal offence. New legislation, replacing James I's law of 1624, was enacted in 1650 to emphasize this: *An Act for the better Preventing and Suppressing of Prophane Swearing and Cursing*. *Parliamentary Proceedings* ii. 903–16.

Pauls Epistles: the Pauline epistles, especially Romans and Galatians, were the most fruitful source of puritan inspiration; responsiveness to their doctrine of grace was a litmus test of an awakened state. Interest in the 'historical part' signals Bunyan's subjection to the first covenant, based on God's contract with the Jewish people.

get help again: 3 adds: 'for then I thought I pleased God as well as any man in *England*.' The detachment of the revising author is again evident here. The moralistic thematizing (pride goes before a fall) probably distorts what he felt at the time.

13 *to something like a moral life*: 'moral' was a term which Puritans generally used negatively, since moral effort, implying a failure to see that God's grace alone enabled righteousness, was not only unavailing but self-deluding. Yet a phase of strenuous moral effort which led to a despairing and fearful recognition of sin and impotence (Christian's experience of Mount Sinai) was seen by many puritans as the necessary 'preparation' for the reception of grace (see Norman Pettit, *The Heart Prepared*: *Grace and Conversion in Puritan Spiritual Life* (New Haven, 1966), 15–18, 48–85).

Tom of Bedlam: Bethlehem Hospital in London (for the insane) gave its name to wandering beggars, some of whom had been discharged from the hospital and licensed to beg.

hanckered: Bunyan's experience is resonant of a widespread sense of loss as puritan strictures came into force (from 1644). His crises of conscience over recreational bell-ringing and dancing predate any encounter with the Bedford sectaries.

steeple house: sectaries such as Quakers and Baptists referred to churches as steeple-houses in order to desacralize them. 'Dost thou call the steeple-house the church?' challenged George Fox; "The church is the people, whom God hath purchased with his blood, and not the house' (*Journal of George Fox*, ed. John L. Nickalls, rev. edn (London, 1975), 261). The bell tower at Elstow Abbey, still solidly in evidence, had originally been built as a watch tower, and stands on its own a few feet from the church. One needs to know this in order to make architectural sense of Bunyan's thought-processes. He could continue, hankeringly, to watch the ringing from the thick-walled doorway.

14 *their miserable state by nature*: the word 'nature' conflates two senses: by birth they are miserable because unregenerate and deserving of damnation, but they are also poor.

abhor their own righteousness, as filthy, and insufficient to do them any good: Christian wears rags in *PP* (p. 8) in allusion to Isa. 64: 6: 'all our righteousnesses are as filthy rags'.

15 *I wanted the true tokens*: puritans were much occupied by the introspective search for 'marks' or 'signs' or 'tokens' of salvation. Many books, including for example Dent's *Plaine Mans Path-way*, listed and discussed these for their anxious readers.

16 *About this time, I met with some Ranters books*: Ranters published their books in 1649 and 1650, taking unprecedented advantage of the lapse of censorship of the press (since 1642). Scandalized by scare stories about the Ranters' blasphemous opinions and licentious behaviour (the true basis and extent of which remain a matter of dispute), and eager to demonstrate that Independency did not countenance immorality and disorder, Parliament introduced, on 9 August 1650, *An Act Against several Atheistical, Blasphemous and Execrable Opinions Derogatory to the Honor of God, and destructive to Human Society* (1650), *Parliamentary Proceedings* ii (1650), 979–84. Authors of allegedly Ranter works include: Jacob Bauthumley, Laurence Clarkson, Abiezer Coppe, and Joseph Salmon (see Smith).

pretend that he had gone through all Religions . . . till now: Clarkson's entire autobiography practises this kind of one-upmanship (he made his way through seven religions); he provides convincing evidence of the kind of jaunty superiority Bunyan seems to have encountered.

Professors: like 'the godly', this was a term favoured by puritans for their co-religionists. It left open the question whether those who 'professed' a Christian calling were genuinely elect, just as the term 'truly godly' drew attention to the possibility of hypocrisy. The invisible church of true saints was not commensurate with the visible claimants.

condemn me as legal and dark: Antinomians, those who believed that recipients of divine grace were above the moral law, pushed a Protestant tenet, that salvation is by faith alone, to an extreme, and used it against those with a qualified understanding of it which left them subject to guilt.

17 *especially the Epistles of the Apostle Paul*: see note to p. 12 above.

could not tell what to do: edition 3 (followed by Sharrock) adds: 'especially this word Faith put me to it, for I could not help it, but sometimes must question, whether I had any Faith or no'. The revising author anticipates something he is going to say anyway over the ensuing five paragraphs, exemplifying another unimproving tendency of the minor revisions.

Cast-away: a common puritan term for the reprobate, rejected by God.

I was loath to fall quite into despair: Bunyan seems here to make despair a necessary preparation for receiving grace. See Pettit, *The Heart Prepared*; and the critique of 'preparation theology' as Theodore Beza's distortion of Calvinism which fed into English Calvinism in R. T. Kendall, *Calvin and English Calvinism to 1649* (Oxford, 1979).

18 *plunge*: see *OED* sb. 5: overwhelmed in trouble; dilemma.

Be you the puddles: this incident could be seen as a temptation to blasphemy as God declares his power in Isaiah, saying 'to the deep, Be dry'

(44: 27). See Leopold Damrosch, Jr., *God's Plot and Man's Stories* (Chicago, 1985), 136; but see also note to p. 69.

18 *Vision represented to me*: Bunyan alters this phrase to 'a kind of Vision, presented to me'. But memory, one might argue, is diminishingly smoothed. Bunyan's description of his repeated striving to enter a narrow passage seems to be a more immediate experience than a vision (which implies his own detachment, as a spectator). Closer, in time at least, to the experience than this sober dilution is the uncertainty ('Dream or Vision') of the original version, suggestive of intense daydream.

19 *and so was comforted with the light and heat of their sun*: Jack Lindsay has suggested that this 'Dream or Vision' evokes birth trauma (Lindsay, 188–92). The specific detail which most struck Bunyan, in his first encounter with the poor Bedford women, was their talk of a 'New birth'. The terms of Bunyan's vision recall Christ's words, 'I am the door' (1 John 10: 9); and 'Enter ye in at the strait gate . . . strait is the gate, and narrow is the way, which leadeth unto life, and few there be that find it' (Matt. 7: 13–14).

O Lord, consider my distress: Bunyan quotes from the metrical version of Sternhold and Hopkins (*The Whole Book of Psalmes* (1609)).

how if the day of grace should now be past and gone?: Ostensibly, the idea of the day of grace implied, in contradiction to Calvinism, that human beings could resist God's call; but it related to the Calvinist dogma, apparent from William Perkins's 'Table' (prefixed to his *Works* (1603)), that some reprobates received 'A calling not effectuall'—a call from God to which they were destined not to respond adequately and which would never be repeated.

20 *unless the great God . . . had voluntarily chosen me to be a vessel of mercy*: see Rom. 9: 19–21 for Paul's analogy, much relied on by Calvinists, between a potter's right as creator to assign uses to his clay and God's to predetermine salvation and damnation for his human creations.

there lay all the question: it is striking how readily and widely the doctrine of the arbitrary decree was accepted in the Calvinist culture which hung over from the pre-Revolutionary period. Lodowick Muggleton affirms that both God's glory and the posture of praise of the elect depend on it: 'For if all Life were to be happy, or all Mankind sav'd, then where would God's Honour appear, But because the greatest part of Mankind are made Vessels of Wrath to bear eternal Torments therefore it is that God's Redeemed ones shall praise him' (*Acts of the Witnesses* (1699), 26).

went: walked.

21 *the promises*: the promises were the biblical texts, vital sources of succour for puritans, which gave assurances of mercy and salvation.

all that God would save in those parts: this gives some idea of Bunyan's statistical expectations. Arthur Dent's *Plaine Mans Path-way to Heaven*

(1601) reports estimates ranging from one in a hundred to one in a thousand (p. 290).

myself: Bunyan's compounding of 'myself' is both rare and significant. There are seven instances up to this paragraph but only four hereafter to the Conclusion. There are countless uses of 'my self'. The virtual disappearance of the conflation coincides with the growing introspection of the record: Bunyan's self becomes an object of scrutiny and concern; it develops into an important concept which, as we know, carries a complex and culturally important history.

23 *if I be not called, what then can doe me good?*: 3 adds: 'None but those who are effectually called, inherit the Kingdom of Heaven.' This addition slightly emboldens the theology behind the anxieties. Bunyan later warned people who doubted 'the truth of their Effectual Calling' that they would 'but plunge themselves into a deeper labyrinth of confusion' (*MW* xi. 88).

60. *[73.]*: paragraph number 73 is omitted in edn. 5, whose numeration is thus one out hereafter. I have followed Sharrock (who dates the omission from edition 6 rather than edition 5) in making the correction.

Oh I saw . . . they had a goodly heritage: Bunyan characteristically reaches for biblical metaphors which keep alive the idea of land-inheritance, and here, especially, the arbitrariness of inheritance.

24 *Mr. Gifford*: John Gifford, first pastor of the Bedford Independent congregation, had been a loose-living Royalist major who was condemned to death for his part in the Kentish rising of 1648. He escaped from prison, underwent conversion, and from 1650 played the leading role, as chosen pastor, in the gathered church Bunyan was to join. He stressed the need to avoid controversy over 'externalls', such as the proper form of baptism, held that communion was open to all who professed 'faith in Christ and holiness of life', and encouraged egalitarian behaviour amongst the saints. (See Tibbutt, 15–21).

clog: a metal or wooden weight used in taming hawks.

began to sink: this phrase, used also by Agnes Beaumont (p. 195), derives from Matt. 14: 30 where Peter is 'beginning to sink' as he walks, with failing faith, on the water to Jesus. It is paralleled when Christian 'began to sink' as he crosses the River of Death (*PP* 128).

25 *as to the act of sinning, I never was more tender then now*: edition 5 adds 'my hinder parts was inward': i.e. the shameful aspects of himself which had been kept from view were now brought into consciousness.

26 *a reprobate mind*: a reprobate mind—one of the phases of reprobate development on Bunyan's *Mapp Shewing the Order and Causes of Salvation and Damnation* (?1663)—was an irredeemable state of mind, with a governing attitude either of calloused resistance or despair. For discussion of Bunyan's belief in Calvinist predestination and its effects on him, see

Richard L. Greaves, *John Bunyan* (Abingdon, 1969), 51–8, and
Stachniewski, ch. 3.

26 *what a doe is here about such little things as these?*: the inward-
looking egotism induced by Calvinist theology is disturbingly apparent
here.

A wounded Spirit who can bear?: Prov. 18: 14.

unless guilt of conscience was taken off the right way: this was an anxiety
which could assail the Calvinist after a period of peace of mind.

27 *but they grew harder and blinder, and more wicked after their trouble*: each
experience represented a step towards fulfilment of either an elect or a
reprobate destiny. Sanctification was the gradual process of purification
following 'justification' which led to 'glorification' of the elect. But
reacted to differently, the same situation could contribute to a process
of blinding and hardening of the heart punitively inflicted by God (the
typological idea was based on texts in Exodus concerning Pharaoh).

a: colloquial contraction of 'have'.

rejoyced; had my condition been as any of theirs: compare John Donne: 'If
lecherous goats, if serpents envious | Cannot be damn'd; Alas; why
should I bee?' (*The Divine Poems*, ed. Helen Gardner (Oxford, 1978), 8).

dissertion: God's 'desertion' could either be a punitive temporary withdrawal, or a permanent 'forsaking his creature' (See William Perkins,
Works (1605), 496).

28 *look up*: a recurrent figure for seeking divine mercy. The scholars in
Marlowe's *Doctor Faustus* (unavailingly) encourage him to 'look up to
heaven, and remember mercy is infinite' (v. ii. 41); it signalled the capacity to believe in divine mercy.

and with that Rom. 8. 39: the text is a triumphant list of all that will be
unable 'to separate us from the love of God'.

29 *to my great confusion and astonishment*: Bunyan seems as unresponsible for
these compulsive blasphemies as for the visitations of divine grace. Some
of the blasphemies may have been suggested to his mind by the Ranter
books he had seen. To take an example at random: 'the devil and [God]
are one, . . . the devil is but a part of Gods backsides' (Anon., *Justification
of the Mad Crew*, repr. in Davis, *Fear, Myth and History: The Ranters and
the Historians* (Cambridge, 1986), 139).

30 *when God gave me leave to swallow my spittle*: cf. Job 7: 19. God gave him
some respite; Job had none.

31 *the sin against the Holy Ghost*: the unpardonable sin—blaspheming against
the Holy Ghost—is spoken of in Matt. 12: 31–2, Mark 3: 29, and Luke
12: 10. It was endlessly expounded by divines and ministers, and the
fear of having committed it is present in many autobiographical testi-
monies. Its vagueness made it a vortex of terror to those whose minds
had been drawn by the question of whether they were elect or reprobate.

Now I blessed the condition of the Dogge and Toad: see note to p. 27.

And now my heart was at times exceeding hard: the hardened heart was another worrying symptom for the puritan (compare Norwood, p. 131); William Perkins, in his famous Table, gave 'The hardening of the heart' as one of the phases of a reprobate's development. (See *GA* 26–7.)

I thought my condition was alone: Martin Luther described this radically alienated spiritual state in which the sufferer asks, 'Why does God pick on me alone?' (see Ernest Gordon Rupp, *The Righteousness of God: Luther Studies* (London, 1953), 107).

While this temptation lasted . . . I could attend upon none of the Ordinances of God: puritans often preferred this term to superstition-tainted 'sacraments' for Holy Communion (and baptism). 'Ordinances' had a broader application to divinely ordained duties, notably hearing sermons, Bible-reading, and prayer—of which Bunyan here proceeds to speak. See note to p. 72.

32 *I have thought I should see the Devil . . . pull my cloaths*: compare Norwood's record of tactile experiences of the devil (p. 147).

Besom; broom.

unexpressable groanings: See Rom. 8: 26 where 'groanings which cannot be uttered' bespeak the interceding activity of the Holy Spirit on behalf of the inarticulate worshipper.

for a spirt: a variant of 'for a spurt'—for a short space of time; also with the sense of a brief and unsustained effort.

33 *spoken and done evil things as we could*: Sharrock's edition reads 'though we have spoken and done as evil things as we could'. Edition 1 makes sense, however, meaning 'as we had the opportunity', which was commonly the Calvinist understanding of the operation of human depravity.

34 *this was a good day to me, I hope I shall not forget it*: in the act of writing down this memory Bunyan fulfils in miniature what his autobiography as a whole seeks to achieve.

false and unsound rests: a puritan term for spiritual consolations; sound rests were often 'places' in Scripture. The terms suggest the developed metaphor of the wayfaring Christian in *PP* (see Richard Baxter, *The Saints Everlasting Rest* (1650), *passim*. See also the excellent essay, James Turner, 'Bunyan's Sense of Place' in V. Newey (ed.), *The Pilgrim's Progress: Critical and Historical Views* (Liverpool, 1980)).

This was as seasonable to my Soul, as the former and latter rain in their season: see Jer. 5: 24; the allusion marks the typological contrast, in this case, between Bunyan and the refractory Israelites.

35 *that Jesus Christ is Lord, but by the holy Ghost*: 1 Cor. 12: 3.

36 *the errors of the Quakers*: Bunyan publicly disputed with Quakers, first, according to Quaker Edward Burrough's record, at Pavenham on 12 Apr.

1656; and his first published tract (*Some Gospel-truths Opened* (1656)) arose from such encounters. For a historical account of disputations in this period, see Ann Hughes, 'The Pulpit Guarded: Confrontations between Orthodox and Radicals in Revolutionary England' in Laurence.

36 *[124.]*: The didactic style and detail of this edition 5 addition depart from the tone of 1, and read as the interpolation of subsequent systematization of his objections when he became a disputant, or even later. The emphasis is on the authority of the Bible and the centrality and external reality of Christ, which Quaker preoccupation with the spirit within and the inner light seemed to compromise. See *Some Gospel-Truths Opened* (1656) and *A Vindication of . . . Some Gospel-Truths Opened* (1657) (*MW* i) for Bunyan's quarrel with Quakerism.

37 *talk with me*: omitted by Sharrock.

Now had I an evidence for Heaven, with many golden Seals thereon, all hanging in my sight: edition 3 alters this to 'Now had I an evidence, as I thought, of my salvation from Heaven'. Christian is given 'a Roll with a Seal upon it'. It represents 'the assurance of his life', or salvation (*PP* 31, 37). Assurance of salvation was, for most puritans, a condition of salvation. The true believer, said Calvin, 'with confidence glorieth that he is heyre of the kyngdome of heaven' (*The Institutes of Christian Religion*, trans. T. Norton (1561), 3. 2. 16). The idea of the seal is an instance of the linkage between the spiritual and the economic dimensions of life: a contractual objectivity was required (see David Zaret, *The Heavenly Contract: Ideology and Organization in Pre-Revolutionary Puritanism* (Chicago, 1985), 177).

38 *without going down themselves into the deep*: like Luther, Bunyan regards despair ambivalently: as well as posing, at the time, a dire threat, it powerfully authenticates spiritual experience. See Stachniewski, 18.

a book of Martin Luther, his comment on the Galathians: translated into English in 1575, this book might have been read by Bunyan in any of the nine editions published before 1640.

most fit for a wounded Conscience: there was a multitude of books, in the seventeenth century, on the 'wounded conscience'. See William Haller's ch. 1, 'Physicians of the Soul', in *The Rise of Puritanism* (New York, 1938).

cleave: Sharrock corrects this to 'cleaved', which may well be right. But it is also possible that Bunyan chose to inhabit this moment of the past with the vividness of a present tense.

I thought I should die in my nest: see Job 28: 18.

39 *those who were once effectually in Christ . . . could never lose him for ever*: the Calvinist doctrine of perseverance (see Norwood, p. 137) declared the impossibility of the elect falling away. But of course the key word, and possible catch here, is 'effectually'. He could have been the recipient of an *ineffectual calling*.

For the land shall not be sold for ever . . . Levit. 25. 23: see Hill, 68–74, and Stachniewski, 139–41.

by way of pushing or thrusting: edition 5 adds 'with my hands or elbows'.

40 *I must do it now, or I should displease God*: in edition 5 this is altered to direct speech ('*you must do it now, or you will displease God*'), clarifying the voice's source: narratized thus, the ambiguity of the original experience is dispelled.

though he sought it carefully with tears, Heb. 12. 16, 17: the aptness of the Esau text, which stays with Bunyan obsessively, may be reinforced by the idea of irrevocable forfeiture of land, which had relevance to both Esau and Bunyan. It is difficult otherwise to give any content to the notion of 'selling' Christ. See Lindsay, 64–95.

41 *lear*: skulk.

clot: clod.

that sin unpardonable: see note on p. 31.

42 *David's Adultery and Murder*: see 2 Sam. 11.

43 *I came to consider of Peters sin . . . in denying his Master*: see Matt. 26: 69–75; Mark 14: 66–72; Luke 22: 54–62; John 18: 25–7.

special providence: the particularized care, emphasized by Calvin, which God extended to his chosen (see, for example, *Institutes* 1. 16. 1; 1. 17. 6). Hamlet, apparently embracing such detailed providential control of his own life, says: 'There is special providence in the fall of a sparrow' (Arden edn. 5. 2. 215–16).

44 *abide under the shaddow of the Almighty*: Ps. 91: 1.

As . . . purpose: Rom. 8: 28. Bunyan adds the explicit Calvinist corollary which gave rise to a sense of double providence corresponding to double predestination: God's providence could be hostile and persecutory.

but mine was against my strivings: edition 3 (followed by Sharrock) inserts 'prayer and' before strivings. Mature reflection would have made Bunyan aware that, from a Calvinist point of view, his 'strivings' could not count for anything; prayer, however, was of God.

Thus I was tossed to and fro, like the Locusts: Ps. 109: 23.

45 *Francis Spira*: Francesco Spira was a Paduan lawyer who recanted his Protestant faith under inquisition and then fell into despair at his apostasy, which was made impregnable by predestinarian theology. He presented a fearful spectacle to numerous visitors in Venice in 1549: he argued so tenaciously, with detailed scriptural knowledge, for his own reprobation that a Catholic bishop who sought to counsel him, Pier Paulo Vergerio, was persuaded to espouse the reformed faith. Calvin himself wrote a stern preface to one of the published accounts based on eyewitness testimony (Anne Jacobson Schutte, *Pier Paulo Vergerio: The Making of an Italian Reformer* (Geneva, 1977), 244–6; Matteo Gribaldi, *A Notable and Marvelous Epistle*, trans. E. Aglionby (n.d.)). The story

exercised a powerful influence in puritan culture, Spira being added to biblical types of reprobation such as Cain and Judas. Bunyan would have read it in Nathaniel Bacon's frequently reissued translation, *A Relation of the Fearfull Estate of Francis Spira, in the Yeare, 1548* (1638). Like other puritan preachers Bunyan made cautionary use of Spira in his sermons (see *The Barren Fig-Tree; The Heavenly Foot-Man; The Greatness of the Soul: MW* v. 58; v. 151; ix. 167).

45 *twining*: Bunyan is credited by *OED* with the first use of 'twine' in this sense (now dialect only): v[1] 8 'To contort the body; to writhe, wriggle, squirm.' Bunyan strains to find language adequate to the intense introspective agonies he documents: the word, applied here to Spira, is transferred to himself at p. 46.

46 *Man knows the beginning of sin, but who bounds the issues thereof?*: the comment is Nathaniel Bacon's, not Spira's reported speech (see David Renaker, 'John Bunyan's Misattribution to Francesco Spira of a Remark by Nathaniel Bacon', *Notes and Queries*, 25 (1978), 25).

the mark that the Lord did set on Cain: Gen. 4: 15.

go: walk.

128. [166.]: In edition 1 paragraph number 127 is repeated here; and later on, paragraph number 161 is omitted. I have restored the correct sequence.

47 *the sin of David, of Solomon, of Manasseh*: see 2 Sam. 11, 1 Kgs. 11, and 2 Kgs. 21.

but yet: Sharrock is textually correct in adopting 'yea', but the intended, and logical, word is 'yet'—and the correction 'but yet' is made in edition 5.

48 *I could not escape his hand*: this was a common expression for the feeling of total circumvention by divine wrath.

for I have redeemed thee: absent from Sharrock's text, presumably through eyeslip, are the words 'It would crie aloud, with a very great voice, return unto me, for I have redeemed thee'. The whole passage is original to edition 5. The phrase 'with a very great voice' is surely an important one for anyone interested in the paranormal/psychological aspect of *Grace Abounding*.

hollow: call, often in hunting.

49 *back-sliding*: this was a puritan coinage: it was, says Beek, the typical puritan word for 'temporary relapse into sin' as against 'total falling away' (See Beek, 58).

50 *next*: nearest.

like a flaming sword, to keep the way of the tree of Life: in Gen. 3: 24 Adam and Eve's return to Eden and the Tree of Life is barred by a flaming sword.

51 *he told me, he thought so too*: Jane Turner reproached the Baptist community: 'But with grief of heart I must confess, that the greatest discouragement that I have met with have been from the Saints themselves' (*Choice Experiences* (1653), 6).

He is of one mind, and who can turn him?: Job 23: 13.

Act. 4. 12.: edition 3 adds to the paragraph: '*The dread of them was upon me, and I trembled at God's Samuels*, 1 Sam. 16. 4.'

52 *neither was it counted . . . when he hanged on the tree*: this conviction implies the influence of Theodore Beza's doctrine of limited atonement (departing from Calvin's understanding), according to which Christ died not for all mankind but only for the elect. But this was a hair-splitting distinction, since according to Calvin only the elect could benefit from Christ's death.

53 *broken Vessel*: Bunyan misunderstands the 'broken vessel' of Ps. 31: 12 as a boat rather than a pot.

This is the man that hath his dwelling among the Tombs . . . Mark 5. 2–5: Christian and Hopeful spectate surreally, from the Delectable Mountains, on other would-be pilgrims who have had their eyes put out by Giant Despair: 'And they perceived that the men were blind, because they stumbled sometimes upon the Tombs, and because they could not get out from among them' (*PP* 99).

Heaven and Earth shall pass away . . . shall fail or be removed: see Matt. 5: 18.

but woe to him that was so driven: the word 'driven' returns the reader to the driven vessel at the beginning of the paragraph, starkly conveying the passivity of committing the unpardonable sin.

54 *Settle*: wooden bench.

did bend themselves against me: paranoia of this kind was widely experienced. William Perkins presents it as part of the conversion process. See *Works*, 458.

Mill-post: the huge wooden post supporting a windmill.

55 *I should be sometimes up and down twenty times in an hour. Yet God did bear me up*: compare Donne: 'But our old subtle foe so tempteth me, | That not one houre I can my selfe sustaine; | Thy Grace may wing me to prevent his art . . .' (*Divine Poems*, 13).

57 *Mill-pit*: a mill-pond, holding water for driving a mill.

Luke: Luke 18: 1: 'Men ought always to pray, and not to faint.'

Yet said I, I will pray: edition 5 adds: ''Tis no boot, said he. Yet said I, I will pray'. Again, the devil's speaking part is slightly elaborated. Perhaps this suggests that the same narrative impulse produced him as an external entity in the first place.

57 *Lord, shall I honour thee most by believing thou wilt and canst, or*: edition 5 adds '*him,*'. This falsifies the thought process in dramatizing it. To ask, 'Shall I honour the devil?' is to prejudge the question too crudely. Moreover, the follow-up, '*I would fain honour thee by believing thou wilt and canst*', clearly implies that it was *God's* intentions about which he was doubtful. The change is a nervous sanitization. To the extent that he has persuaded himself that the counsel of despair is Satan's, things become quite simple. Again this makes clear the direction in which revision of experience moves in the process of narratization. It is a verbally tiny but nevertheless important instance of the ways in which the later editions are less reliable (if, that is, one wants to get as close as possible to what Bunyan claims to be giving us: '*the thing as it was*').

59 *My Grace is sufficient*: 2 Cor. 12: 9.

my grace is sufficient for thee: Hopeful's testimony records his rescue by this oft-quoted text (*PP* 116).

60 *I doubted*: omitted by Sharrock.

61 *And him that cometh to me I will in no wise cast out*: John 6: 37. This is another promise, much adduced by puritans, which came to Hopeful's aid (*PP* 117). It could be snagged, however, by frequent puritan discussion of what it meant to 'come aright'.

62 *freedom abundance*: Sharrock supplies an apparently missing 'and' between 'freedom' and 'abundance'; but may not Bunyan have intended the meaning 'abundance of freedom', using 'abundance' ambiguously, in part as an adjective?

65 *a New-Testament stile and sence*: the historical style of the Old Testament had spiritual applications. In this case the Apostle Paul has explicitly adapted the text to a New Testament context. As elsewhere, Bunyan seeks to understand the typological application to his own circumstances.

66 *for my Righteousness was Jesus Christ himself*: the doctrine whose meaning is suddenly revealed to Bunyan is that of 'imputed righteousness', whereby God sees only the righteousness of Jesus in place of the Christian's sin.

crack'd-Groats and Four-pence-half-pennies: groats, fourpenny pieces, were not issued after 1662. Cracked ones were a byword for worthlessness. The fourpence-halfpenny was an Irish sixpence.

Ephes. 5. 30: 'For we are members of his body, of his flesh, and of his bones.'

67 *died by him*: omitted by Sharrock.

the Temptation that went before: the temptation, that is, lasting 'about a year' (p. 31), to atheism and blasphemy (pp. 29–35).

68 *gauled*: galled; made sore by rubbing.

Upon a time my Wife was great with Child: Bunyan's first child, Mary, was baptized on 20 July 1650. The premature labour pains (when his wife was 'great with Child' but 'before her full time') probably occurred around May, dating the onset of temptation (see para. [242.]) around October 1651. That would mean the period of despair ran from October 1652 to the early months of 1655, if one takes the 'well-nigh two and a half years' of para. [198.], as it appears to do, to date from the moment of acquiescence. It seems likely enough that Bunyan was admitted to membership of the Bedford church (as he was in 1655) shortly after he came through this conflict.

travel: travail.

69 *Gideon tempted God with his Fleece, both wet and dry*: Gideon tested God by laying out a fleece to see whether God could make it wet with dew in the morning while the earth around it remained dry, and the other way round the following night (Judg. 6: 36–40). This story may have put into Bunyan's mind his earlier idea of making puddles in the horse tracks dry and the dry places puddles (p. 18).

70 *For the Scriptures cannot be broken*: John 10: 35.

would rend the caul of my heart: see Hos. 13: 8.

Whose sins ye remit, they are remitted, but whose sins ye retain, they are retained: John 20: 23.

2 Sam. 7. 28: 'Thy words be true, and thou hast promised this goodness unto thy servant.'

71 *flounce*: plunge, flounder.

many a pull: *OED* pull sb. 23: a turn or bout at pulling each other in wrestling.

that I might not sink for ever: Christian warns his neighbours that, if they stay in the City of Destruction, 'you will sink lower than the Grave' (*PP* 10). There are, it turns out, steps in the Slough of Despond, though it doesn't seem so at the time. Sinking and rising were very common tropes, linked to the topography of the afterlife.

pikes: infantry weapons with a long shaft and metal point.

great sins do draw out great grace: this hints at the spiritual kudos which accrued from having been the chief of sinners. See for example *MW* xi. 40: 'He that has most sin, if forgiven, is partaker of the greatest love, of the greatest forgiveness'.

lest they also be made to bear the iron yoak as I: see Deut. 28: 48; Jer. 28: 13, 14.

72 *when I first did joyn . . . with the People of God in Bedford*: Bunyan had attended meetings for some time (see, for example, p. 59). But he is now referring to the time when he was 'admitted' to church membership. This would have required a spoken testimony. His name appears in the *Church Book*'s list of members in 1655. The author of 'A Continuation of Mr. Bunyan's Life,' appended to the 7th edition of *Grace Abounding* (1692), also notes that Bunyan was baptized in 1655 (see Sharrock, appendix B, p. 171).

72 *wish some deadly thing to those that then did eat thereof*: the Lord's Supper could be a focus of anxiety because puritans stressed Paul's menacing words in 1 Cor. 11: 29: 'For he that eateth and drinketh unworthily, eateth and drinketh damnation to himself, not discerning the Lord's body.' It was a litmus test of spiritual identity, and Bunyan's irrepressible impulses of hostility towards both the elect and God would be understandable at such a moment if he still had doubts about himself. The following paragraph betrays, in its echo of Paul, the source of his agitation.

therein discerned the Lords Body: see 1 Cor. 11: 29.

Consumption: see *Law and Grace*, MW ii. 147-8.

my Evidences for that blessed world to come . . . my interest in Life to come: the evidence of heaven was supposed to inhere in the spiritual experiences of this life. This key term is derived from Heb. 11: 1: 'faith is . . . the evidence of things not seen'. There is also much in Jer. 32 about evidence of the purchase of land to which Jeremiah had the right of redemption. Bunyan tries to keep in view his 'interest' in the life to come. Arthur Dent had likened such evidence to that of tenure of land: 'Shall we hold the state of our immortall inheritance by hope, hope well, and have no writings, no evidences, no seale . . . to shew for it' (*Plaine Mans Path-way*, 264-5). Christian's evidence for and interest in heaven are expressed by the certificate he produces at the heavenly gate.

73 *my affliction, namely, my deadness, dulness, and coldness in holy Duties; . . . are these the tokens of a blessed man?*: the tediousness of religious duties often gave rise to such panicky self-questioning. Henry Scudder generalizes: 'Many yet complaine, They cannot Pray, Reade, Heare, Meditate, nor get any good by the best Companies . . . They are so dull, so forgetfull, so full of distractions, and so unfruitfull . . . that they feare they haue no grace at al in them' (*The Christians Daily Walke in Securitie and Peace* (1635), 665).

74 *the Angels carrying Lazarus into Abrahams bosom*: Luke 16: 22.

as if I had never seen or known them in my life: this appears to have been a frequent, though desolating, experience for Bunyan. See pp. 73, 74, 91, 92.

Heb. 12. 22, 23, 24: the words 'but ye are come unto mount Sion, and unto the city of the living God . . . and to Jesus . . .' seem to answer the voice's 'I must go to Jesus'. This triumphant moment is paralleled by the end of Christian's pilgrimage, when he arrives at the Celestial City (*PP* 130).

75 *that I might have imparted unto them what God had shewed me*: the communicative urge comes as a break-out from the solitary confinement of doubt and despair.

and helped: edition 5 (followed by Sharrock) adds 'my self' to 'helped'. This converts the passive locution into an active one and also runs against the usually consistent Calvinist denial of human agency in edition 1. It is clearly either a hurried revision by Bunyan or a printer's supply of what he thinks is an omission.

to speak a word of Exhortation unto them: the *Church Book* notes that 'Mr Bunyan began to preach some time in the year 1656' (p. 15); this presumably refers to his 'public preaching' (para. 221. [268.]). His 'word of Exhortation' to the faithful, 'in private' (para. 219. [266.]), probably dates from 1655. Bunyan's 'awakening', his startled reaction to the poor women of Bedford, could not have been earlier than 1650, when Gifford began his ministry.

76 *more particularly called forth*: the 'particular calling' could be any vocation to which one was summoned by God, complementing, and to some extent substantiating, the general calling as a Christian.

sorely afflicted . . . concerning my eternal state: this, presumably in 1656, suggests strongly that there was nothing permanent about Bunyan's spiritual breakthroughs; the reprobate paradigm was liable to be reactivated in his mind.

bury them in the earth: alluding to the parable of the talents, this is the defence of the 'mechanick' preacher against arguments based on fixed social hierarchy and formal educational qualifications.

77 *Fox Acts and Mon.*: John Foxe's *Acts and Monuments* (1563), or 'The Book of Martyrs' as it was popularly known since it emotively recorded the fates of the Marian martyrs, was a major influence in the ideological consolidation of the English Reformation. Bunyan had his own copy in prison.

bowels: the seat of deep feeling; compassion.

had owned in his Work such a foolish one as I: this is not as self-depreciating as it seems since it alludes to Paul's paradoxes on foolishness and wisdom (1 Cor. 1: 18–31), a key passage for Bunyan and other sectarian preachers who lacked a formal education.

78 *sence*: feeling.

I preached what I felt, what I smartingly did feel: elsewhere, so presumably here also, Bunyan uses 'smart' to refer to periods of acute fear that he was a reprobate. Compare p. 63.

crying out against mens sins . . . because of them: Bunyan's third publication, *A Few Sighs from Hell, or the Groans of a Damned Soul* (1658), is in this vein.

79 *where I have lain as long*: Bunyan was arrested at a meeting in a barn in Lower Samsell on 12 Nov. 1660. He here dates his writing at the end of 1665, shortly before publication. (The third edition has 'above as long again'.)

the Doctrine of Life by Christ, without Works: Luther's doctrine of salvation *sola fide* (by faith alone) was the doctrinal crux of the Reformation.

79 *the Doctors . . . did open wide against me*: even in the Commonwealth period
Bunyan faced hostility from the university-educated clergy. Most presbyterian clerics welcomed the Restoration.

carnal Professors: those who professed themselves Christians but self-
deludingly because their lives were really governed by the flesh rather
than the spirit. The term particularly indicated those who set store by
their own respectable appearances.

when they shall be for my hire before their face, Gen. 30. 33: Jacob was paid
in kind for his labour; Bunyan implies that God will reward him with
souls to his credit, while the established clergy have already, as hirelings,
received payment.

80 *as to other things . . . I saw they engendered strife*: in his parting letter of
1655 John Gifford had enjoined tolerance over what he called 'externalls'—organized practices, including baptism (*Church Book*, 3). Bunyan
did, however, enter the lists, not only to dispute with Quakers, whom he
regarded as heretics, but with 'Saints' on the question of whether baptism
should be a condition of church membership and on the permissibility
of women's prayer meetings: on the first he was liberal, on the second
conservative (see *A Confession of my Faith, and a Reason of my Practice*
(1672), *Differences in Judgment About Water-Baptism* (1673), *Peaceable
Principles and True* (1674), and *A Case of Conscience Resolved* (1683) in
MW iv).

awakening-Word: Sharrock deletes the hyphen, though the compound
conveys a nuance of nonconformist diction: see also, for example,
'converting-Work' (*GA* 81).

Gal. 1. 11, 12: 'But I certify you, brethren, that the gospel which was
preached of me is not after man. For I neither received it of man, neither
was I taught it, but by the revelation of Jesus Christ.'

81 *travelled*: travailed (as in labour).

83 *them who have Gifts, but want saving-Grace*: divines distinguished between
'common grace', which could visit the non-elect, and 'saving grace',
which was effectual for salvation.

a maul: a strong blow.

85 *It began therefore to be rumored . . . that I was a Witch*: Bunyan was not
above harbouring suspicion of others as witches: he encouraged a
woman who had a most improbable fantasy about a Quaker witch transforming her into a bay mare and riding her to a banquet to take her
case to court (see appendix to Tindall, 217–22; and Stachniewski,
174–5).

But that which was reported . . . two wives at once: Agnes Beaumont's
'Narrative' gives details of one such calumny (which may have prompted
the addition of these paragraphs). Sectaries were often the target of
smears of this kind. In 1649, Gerrard Winstanley had to write *A
Vindication* to defend the Diggers from charges of *Excessive Community*

of Women, Called Ranting. Ranterism far outlived its known activity (1649–52) as a politically useful caricature of sectarian behaviour.

I should want one sign . . . Mat. 5. 11: Bunyan registers the persisting Calvinist habit of collecting 'signs' of election. Persecution seemed to have a fortifying effect on his faith. This particular text was especially useful in enabling dissenters to align themselves with God's chosen in the Bible. Agnes Beaumont also avails herself of its comfort (p. 215).

that I have been naught: this is the term attributed to the slanderers in Agnes Beaumont's 'Narrative' (p. 214).

86 *if all the Fornicators . . . till they be dead*: legislation for the death penalty for fornication was introduced in 1657.

it is a rare thing to see me carry it pleasant towards a Woman: this is borne out by Bunyan's brusque initial refusal to carry Agnes Beaumant on his horse. Two-thirds of the members of Bunyan's church were women, so he would be particularly sensitive to the likelihood of malicious scrutiny of his relations with them.

the holy kiss: see Rom. 16: 16: 'Salute one another with a holy kiss.' Perhaps the 'holy kiss' had come under suspicion as a result of its over-enthusiastic use by Ranters. See Smith, 201.

baulks: oversights or exceptions (derived from leaving a furrow unploughed).

87 *apprehended at a Meeting of good People in the Countrey*: see note to p. 79.

a Justice: the justice was Francis Wingate of Harlington Hall, a Royalist whose family had been fined by Parliament.

not conforming to . . . the Church of England: Wingate had to invoke the Elizabethan Act against Conventicles (35 Elizabeth, c. 1), as a new one was not passed until 1662. In fact, prosecutions continued to be brought under this act (referred to by nonconformists as '35 Eliz.'), because the punishment (banishment on pain of death following failure to conform after three months' imprisonment) was more severe than those prescribed by Restoration legislation (see Keeble, 45).

sentenced to perpetual banishment because I refused to Conform: transportation for seven years was the punishment for a third offence (14 Car. 2, c. 2; *Statutes at Large*, (London, 1769), 218). Bunyan seems to have been in some uncertainty about the possible punishments he faced. See pp. 88–9, 91, and *A Relation*, 99.

above five year and a quarter: edition 3 alters this to 'compleat twelve years', dating Bunyan's revision to 1672. As the accusations concerning Agnes Beaumont, to which he later appears to reply, occurred in 1674, this undated edition presumably came out between 1672 and 1674.

87 *what man can do unto them*: see Heb. 13: 6.

88 *I have been able . . . to fear neither the Horse nor his Rider*: this could be an allusion either to Job 39: 18, implying insouciance, or to texts such as Exod. 15: 1, implying God's destruction of the persecutor.

O the mount Zion . . . and Jesus: Heb. 12: 22–4.

Before I came to Prison, I saw what was a coming: Bunyan had been indicted at the assizes for preaching at the village of Eaton Socon in February 1658 (Brown, 113; Hill, 106), so it was not hard to predict what the Restoration held in store for him.

89 *reckon my Self . . . as dead to them*: edition 5 adds: 'He that loveth father or mother, son or daughter, more than me, is not worthy of me, Matt. 10. 37.'

Thou art my Mother and Sister: see Job 17: 13–14.

my poor blind Child: Bunyan's first child, Mary, was born blind in 1650.

90 *Pray read it soberly, Psal. 109. 6, 7, 8, &c.*: Bunyan takes the Old Testament words of David and confidently ascribes them to Christ in a very specific context. This exemplifies the way in which puritan retrieval of Old Testament types could impart harsher colours to the picture people had of God, and even Christ.

91 *The Holy Ghost witnesseth . . . bonds and afflictions abide me*: Acts 20: 23.

my imprisonment might end at the Gallows for ought that I could tell: although a death sentence was a remote threat, which was prescribed in law for illegally returning transportees, it appears that Bunyan's captors exploited his ignorance of the law by intimidating him with it (see p. 111). In fact, twelve Aylesbury Baptists and a Bristol Quaker were sentenced to death, though the sentence was not carried out (see Keeble, 45).

92 *sink or swim, come heaven, come hell*: a similar climactic act of faith is dramatized, in *PP*, by Christian's passage over the River of Death (pp. 128–9).

Doth Job serve God for nought? . . . curse thee to thy face: see Job 1: 9–11.

Psa. 44. 12 &c.: Ps. 44: 12–26 is a plea of the persecuted faithful: 'Thou makest us a reproach to our neighbours, A scorn and a derision to them that are round about us . . . All this is come upon us; yet have we not forgotten thee . . . Arise for our help, And redeem us for thy mercies' sake.'

Conclusion

93 *what can the Righteous do?*: Ps. 11: 3.

With such strength and weight have both these been upon me: this pattern evidently continues at least until 1672, and even in 1680 there is no disavowal of the present tense confession.

94 *When I would do good, evil is present with me*: this alludes to Paul's lament in Rom. 7: 19.

A Relation of the Imprisonment [of Mr. John Bungan]

98 *as if we that was to meet . . . to the destruction of the country*: the Restoration government was inclined to equate conventicles (sectarian meetings) with seditious plotting. Recent scholarship has suggested that seditious intent was indeed widespread amongst dissenters, though execution of intent was enfeebled by the fragmentation of opposition groups (see R. L. Greaves, *Deliver Us from Evil: The Radical Underground in Britain, 1660–1663* (Oxford, 1986), and Hill, 111–18). There is, however, no evidence that Bunyan was a party to any plotting and no reason to question his clearly stated advocacy of passive resistance and opposition to insurrection (see p. 112 and n.; and R. L. Greaves, *John Bunyan and English Nonconformity* (London, 1992), 46–7).

afraid of me: afraid on my behalf.

After this I walked into the close: the farmyard (the meeting was to be held in the farmhouse).

99 *the forlorn hope*: a detachment of men to the front line to begin the attack.

in this country: county.

and so to the justice. Original note: Justice Wingate. These notes appear at the foot of the page in *A Relation of my Imprisonment* (1765). They were probably in Bunyan's manuscript, intended for the margin.

armour or not: military arms.

100 *follow my calling, and preach the word also*: Bunyan accepts the conservative premiss of the question, that the dutiful Christian should maintain his calling.

he. Original note: Ibid.

mittimus: a warrant committing a person to prison pending trial (or bail).

Dr. Lindale: vicar of Harlington.

Charging and condemning me . . . I could shew no warrant: this kind of hectoring helps to explain the allegorical use of a certificate in *The Pilgrim's Progress*: the assurance of salvation, regarded as objective validation from God of elect status, is the only true warrant for communicating the gospel.

taken the oaths: some Baptists, like all Quakers, refused to take oaths (of allegiance and supremacy) on principle (see Alfred Clair Underwood and James Henry Rushbrooke, *A History of the English Baptists* (London, 1956), 90–2). Bunyan's position is left unclear.

As every man hath received the gift, even so let him minister the same, &c.: 1 Pet. 4: 10.

101 *I*: aye.

You may all prophesy one by one: 1 Cor. 14: 31.

Alexander a Coppersmith: see 2 Tim. 4: 14.

to devour widows houses: see Matt. 23: 14; Mark 12: 40; Luke 20: 47.

101 *Answer not a fool according to his folly*: Prov. 26: 4.

Mr. Foster: William Foster was a Bedford lawyer who was active in prosecuting dissenters.

102 *who is there, John Bunyan?* Original note: A right Judas.

Their tongues are smoother than oil . . . Beware of men, &c.: Ps. 55: 21; Matt. 10: 17.

When I. Original note: Bunyan.

my brother: Justice Wingate was Foster's brother-in-law. The patronizing friendliness, backed up by the power of the law and the social hierarchy, anticipates Mr Worldly-Wiseman and Mr Legality's house on the hill which threatens to fall on Christian's head.

103 *He that believes shall be saved*: see Mark 16: 16.

God hides his things . . . reveals them to babes and sucklings: Matt. 11: 25; Luke 10: 21. These were texts much favoured by radical sectaries.

God had rejected the wise . . . and chosen the foolish, and the base: 1 Cor. 1: 26–9.

exhort one another daily, while it is called to day: Heb. 3: 13.

104 *Their*. Original note: Justice's servants.

at a point: intransigent, resolved.

Mr. Foster. Original note: This is the man that did at the first express so much love to me.

105 *Mr. Crumpton*: in 1672, following the Declaration of Indulgence, Mr Crompton sold an orchard and barn to Bunyan's church to be a licensed place of meeting (Brown, 230–1).

For he knew that for envy they had delivered him: Matt. 27: 18.

not one hair of my head can fall to the ground without the will of my Father: a slightly odd conflation of Matt. 10: 29–30 about the numbering of hairs and the fall of a sparrow.

we know all things shall work together for good to them that love God: Rom. 8: 28. The triumphant certainty with which this text is adduced is in marked contrast to its meaning for Bunyan when he was subject to feelings of *inner* persecution, p. 44. Compare Beaumont, p. 193.

Here is the Sum . . . Justice Snagg: Justice John Kelyng, chairman of the bench, was a leading Royalist who had been imprisoned in Windsor Castle from 1642 to 1660. He confronted Bunyan fresh from his prosecution of the regicides. Knighted shortly after Bunyan's trial, he became Chief Justice of the King's Bench in 1665. He acquired a reputation for bullying juries, and for severity towards nonconformists. He helped to draft a Bill for Religious Uniformity (passed on 3 July 1661). Like Kelyng, the other JPs were local landowners and Royalists who had been fined during the Interregnum. The prejudiced animosity Bunyan experiences here finds imaginative expression in the trial of Christian and Faithful conducted by Lord Hategood in Vanity Fair (*PP* 76–9).

106 *I said, but not by the Common Prayer-book*: Bunyan was soon to elaborate his arguments in favour of extempore prayer and against the set forms in the Book of Common Prayer in *I Will Pray with the Spirit* (*c.*1662) (see *MW* ii. 235–86).

107 *Faith comes by hearing*: Rom. 10: 17.

the spirit that must convince them. Original note: If any say that God useth means; I answer, but not the Common Prayer-book, for that is none of his institution, 'tis the spirit in the word that is Gods ordinance.

108 *or else.* Original note: see Heb. 4: 2.

It is the. Original note: John xv. 16.

and the. Original note: Matt. iii. 16–17.

set: nonplussed.

109 *that is.* Original note: It is not the spirit of a Christian to persecute any for their religion; but to pity them; and if they will turn, to instruct them.

they often said, that I was possessed . . . of the Devil: this was a stock charge against religious dissidents.

pedlers French: rogues' jargon.

we ought to exhort one another daily, while it is called today: Heb. 3: 13.

asked me where I had my authority: Bunyan instantly reaches for proof texts. 'The Bible,' says Christopher Hill, 'was the traditional counter-authority to the authority of the hierarchy' (*Society and Puritanism*, 159). Bunyan's calm derives from his superior biblical knowledge, which supports his positions with an authority his judges cannot deny.

110 *at a point*: see note to p. 104.

I could not tell what he said: presumably Bunyan recorded this inaudible rejoinder because it subsequently preyed on his mind (see. p. 111): perhaps he thought his declaration of intent placed his life in more immediate jeopardy.

he will give a mouth . . . or gainsay: Luke 21: 15.

111 *Mr. Cobb*: Paul Cobb, Clerk of the Peace, later became Mayor of Bedford.

or else worse than that: see *GA* 87 and note, and p. 91 and note.

112 *the late insurrection at London*: on 6 Jan. 1661, Thomas Venner's Fifth Monarchist congregation of about 50 people mounted an ill-judged rebellion (which they expected to be favoured with divine intervention). There was in fact a good deal of plotting at the time, in which Baptists were involved, so the rulers' fears were to some extent justified. Greaves points out, however, that in areas of the country where nonconformists were numerous, and therefore confident of their survival, passive resistance was the norm. Bedfordshire was such a county (Greaves, *John Bunyan and English Nonconformity* (1992), 58). Paradoxically, Venner's bloody rising (22 people were killed on each side) seems to have pushed many towards quietism: the Quakers only declared themselves pacifists after

this (see Hill, 105). But inevitably the event, after which over 4,000 Quakers and Baptists were put in gaol (Keeble, 29), did not improve Bunyan's chances of lenient treatment.

112 *I should willingly manifest my loyalty . . . by word and deed*: while it is true that Bunyan associated with some nonconformists who had more radical political views, and while it is also true that he entertained millenarian hopes, he saw it as no part of a Christian's remit to oppose the *de facto* monarch except by refusing to comply with orders which conflicted with God's. See Greaves's discussion in *John Bunyan and English Nonconformity*.

114 *We may all prophecy one by one, that all may learn.*: 1 Cor. 14: 31.

Wickliffe saith: Bunyan would have found this in his copy of Foxe's Book of Martyrs (John Foxe, *Acts and Monuments*, ed. S. R. Cattley (London, 1837) iii. 21). John Wycliffe (*c.* 1330–1384) contended that the Bible was the sole criterion of doctrine, overriding all ecclesiastical authority, and inspired its translation into English. His followers, the Lollards, in some ways anticipated puritanism, and especially congregational dissent like that of Bunyan's church.

115 *even the man Christ Jesus*: Gal. 3: 20; 1 Tim. 2: 5.

a compleat, or perfect, or able high-priest: probably a reference to Heb. 7: 26–8, though the word 'complete' is not used.

116 *the powers that are, are ordained of God*: Rom. 13: 1.

the time in which the King was to be crowned: 23 Apr. 1661.

117 *Judge Hales*: Sir Matthew Hale was unusual in having puritan sympathies (he was to draft legislation aimed at comprehending Presbyterians in the national church) and a lenient attitude toward dissenters.

Judge Twisdon: Sir Thomas Twisden, the other judge at the assizes, appears to have given considerate treatment to the Quaker Margaret Fell in 1664 (Keeble, 45). Elizabeth Bunyan may have caught him on a bad day.

High Sheriff: Edmund Wylde ('let us remember his name with honour,' says Brown, 'for he was the only man who spoke a word of cheer' (p. 157)).

as the poor widow did to the unjust Judge: Luke 18: 2–8.

Swan Chamber: the upper room of the Swan Inn, near the bridge over the Ouse.

118 *before there were any proclamation against the meetings*: as stated above (p. 112), the authorities had relied on an Elizabethan statute.

Lord Barkwood: the name is a puzzle. Sharrock suggests that the name intended may have been the Earl of Bedford, who had puritan sympathies; but it does not seem likely that the name Bedford would have been misconstrued.

119 *mother-in-law*: stepmother.

and because he is a Tinker . . . he is despised, and cannot have justice: Elizabeth's response confirms the social attitude to tinkers to which Bunyan himself reacts—for example when he describes his father's household as among the 'most despised of all the families in the Land' (*GA* 6). She is probably reacting to a general sneer conveyed by the eagerness of some standers-by to supply this information, and their choice of 'tinker' rather than the slightly more dignifying 'brazier'.

get a writ of error: lack of precision in an indictment or mittimus was the most common reason for the discharge of prisoners in the late seventeenth century.

120 *when they shall there answer . . . whether it be bad*: Elizabeth Bunyan's lofty response is remarkable testimony, in view of the social intimidation to which she had been subjected, to the liberating effects, perhaps especially for women, of puritan convictions. Compare Agnes Beaumont's concern for the soul of her persecutor, Mr Feery (p. 223).

how I had, by my Jailor, some liberty granted me: jailors had some discretion in the treatment of their prisoners, though Bunyan's was unusually liberal in allowing him to travel to London, as the sequel suggests.

121 *exhorting them to be stedfast in the faith of Jesus Christ*: there are entries in the Church Book, for late summer 1661, recording Bunyan's visits to backsliders to admonish them.

They charged me also . . . make insurrection: London was seen, especially after the Venner rising, as the most likely venue for conspiracy. Bunyan's church had close associations there with similar open-communion congregations—Southwark and All Hallows the Great.

Kalender: the list of prisoners to be tried at the assizes.

Richard Norwood, 'Confessions'

125 *Jesus Christ came into the world to save sinners of whom I am chief*: 1 Tim. 1: 15. Norwood's allusion to Paul is conventional, as is that in Bunyan's title. The fact that it is an allusion makes it self-evident that in one sense at least it is not to be taken literally. But it was an imperative step towards salvation that the sinner felt and believed him or herself to be 'chief of sinners'. Intensity rather than comparison is the point.

that mass of sin and folly which was bound up in my heart: Norwood's sense of himself as a child appears to have been strongly conditioned by the doctrine of Original Sin, which was given an even darker tone by the Calvinist emphasis on the total depravity of human beings. Children were assumed to be completely evil without external disciplinary restraint because, even if they were to turn out to be of the elect, they were not yet regenerate (had not yet received the divine grace which would enable them not to be evil).

accidence: elementary grammar.

125 *I was in danger to have bene drowned*: compare Bunyan's early providential rescue from drowning (*GA* 8). Such incidents gave reassurance that
God was protecting them because he had chosen them as later recipients
of grace.

126 *I acted a womans part in a stage play*: many puritans saw plays as morally
corrupting (William Prynne, William Perkins, and others wrote to
denounce them); enjoyment of the theatre later represents to Norwood
the rejection of godliness.

preserve me from the plague . . . at the next house: bubonic plague killed
33,000 people in 1603. It is not hard to see why ordinary people like
Norwood felt threatened by dark forces, on the one hand, and arbitrarily
spared on the other. This pattern of experience seems to correspond
to the terrible threat of reprobation and the extraordinary favour of
election.

*I thought it no small matter to be beloved of God . . . besides I knew my self
to be worse then they took me to be*: the early influence of Calvinist theology on the self-consciousness of the child is apparent here (compare
Crook, p. 159). The child knows that only his own conscience can judge
his spiritual state, and that there is a strong possibility of not being loved
by God. It seems very likely in the circumstances Norwood describes that
his severe treatment by authority figures fed this uncertainty.

affections: feelings.

127 *natural estate*: for the Calvinist/puritan the natural state was one of total
depravity.

catechise: the Church of England 'catechism' was a formal series of questions and answers on doctrine.

in a general and very confused and uncertain manner: Calvin declared that
'the reprobate do never conceive but a confused feelinge of grace'
(*Institutes*, 3. 2. 11).

Neither was it doubtless at best any more then moral: the term 'moral' was
generally used by puritans to indicate willed effort to obey religious pre-
cepts in contrast to the inward spiritual experience of grace, which alone
could enable virtue and promise salvation.

128 *he had very great losses in sheep and otherwise*: the period from 1590 to 1620
was one in which many farmers were forced by adverse economic conditions to sell up. See D. M. Palliser, *The Age of Elizabeth: England under
the Later Tudors 1547–1603* (London, 1983), 93–4.

latins: translation into Latin.

Naso: the family name of the poet Ovid; it was derisive because *nasus*
means 'nose'.

129 *Per fas aut nefas*: by fair means or foul.

sea-cows: aquatic mammals.

forsaken the calling wherein my parents had placed me: acceptance of parental choice of calling was regarded, especially by puritans, as an absolute filial imperative. See William Perkins, *Christian Oeconomie*, trans. T. Pickering (1609), 147; *Works*, 905, 910.

130 *Palmerin de Oliva, The Seaven Champions*: both popular romances, and typical reading for apprentices. (Bunyan had also read *Seven Champions* when young.)

131 *My heart after this grew more hardened*: the hardened heart was a dangerous spiritual condition in which one became impervious to religious and moral feeling. Calvinists regarded it as, often, a divine punishment on the reprobate, preventing the possibility of their repenting.

132 *nocturnal polutions*: nocturnal emissions (wet dreams).

133 *only I think once or twice . . . to settle my self I cared not in how mean a calling*: the Christian man, said Puritan John Cotton, 'should stoop to any work his calling led him to . . . if it appears to be his Calling, faith doth not picke and choose, as carnall reason will doe' (*The Puritans: A Sourcebook of their Writings*, ed. Perry Miller and Thomas H. Hudson (New York, 1963), i. 323).

134 *I read it again and again and was more and more affected.*: Emotional letters conveying advice of this kind seem to have been common in puritan culture.

135 *forsaking the calling . . . to their liking*: Mr Elton reinforces the orthodox view that Norwood's afflictions are divine punishments for forsaking his calling. See note to p. 129.

I apprehended my self . . . in a forlorn condition: this is a clear instance of the intersection of the discourses of religion and class. Norwood feels something of the social prejudice permeating theology which Bunyan too had to resist.

stomack: *OED* sb. 8c anger.

136 *I thought being in that poor condition . . . I should find no better success*: this is again indicative of how excluded the poor (such as Bunyan) felt from the established church.

Mr Topsall: Edward Topsell, a divine of puritan inclinations at St Botolphs, Aldersgate, published two zoological manuals, in addition to two books of biblical exposition. No doubt this indicates broader sympathies than in other divines Norwood encountered. He died a couple of years before Norwood is writing.

137 *for if we sin willingly after we have received etc. . . . that I should not persevere*: Heb. 10: 26–7: 'For if we sin wilfully after that we have received the knowledge of the truth, there remaineth no more sacrifice for sins, But a certain fearful looking for of judgement'. The doctrine that those who are truly elect necessarily persevere ('the final perseverance of the

saints') was an important Calvinist tenet. It posed a dark threat and
serious inhibition to Norwood and many others because an apparent conversion followed by relapse would indicate reprobation.

137 *corruptions of nature*: Norwood evidently doubts whether divine grace
could take complete control of deeply rooted and entirely corrupt natural
inclinations.

It had bene better . . . the holy commaundement etc.: 2 Pet. 2: 21.

138 *being enthralled unto sin and Satan*: Norwood's thinking is framed by
the Calvinist view of total human depravity: all that has tempered its
expression has been external restraint. This view rationalizes the
Calvinist/puritan stress on work; puritans believed literally that the devil
makes work for idle hands. Independent of external discipline—'myne
own man'—Norwood appears to be free; but, lacking the internal discipline of the regenerate, he is actually a slave to another master, the devil,
whose designs his corrupt nature cannot but obey. As for Bunyan, the idea
of real autonomy has no credibility.

stage plays: Norwood here encapsulates the puritan arguments against
plays (though, as Margot Heinemann has shown in *Puritanism and
Theatre: Thomas Middleton and the Opposition Drama under the Early
Stuarts* (Cambridge, 1980), not all puritans shared the disapproval). They
were a waste of precious time, a distraction from serious thoughts, deceiv-
ing (in the sense of fictitious), and spellbinding. All this adds up to thral-
dom to the devil.

fortune: the Fortune theatre in Golding Lane was, from 1602, the home
of the Admiral's company. Marlowe's *Doctor Faustus*, with Edward Alleyn
in the title role, was one of its achievements.

Mr. Phinehas Pett: Phineas Pett (1570–1647) was the royal shipwright and
a friend to the young Prince Henry.

139 *if I did diligently use the means*: this whole passage shows how closely
intertwined were socio-economic and religious experience. The phrase
'diligently use the means' refers at once to Norwood's studies, the instrument of his social betterment, and, because it was a puritan cliché, to the
means of his salvation (hence the 'glances towards heaven' of the next
line).

Limmington: Lymington, on the south coast opposite the Isle of
Wight.

140 *the light of the Gospel . . . flourishing there*: this was a period of Calvinist
domination of the national church, and puritan domination of City of
London government.

nor settle my self effectually: Norwood's inability to settle effectually
extends the social–spiritual parallelism: those not of the elect were often
recipients of an 'ineffectual calling'. His unresolved spiritual state continues to be reflected in a wanderlust.

frame: See *GA*, note to p. 11.

141 *but now I thought . . . deprived of human society*: Norwood's experiences inevitably evoke *Robinson Crusoe*. Donald Davie's question is worth repeating: 'Which is the more characteristically Calvinist response— Cowper's seeing the solitude of Alexander Selkirk as the worst of all possible privations, or Defoe's Crusoe exulting in it, as the condition of his autonomy?' (*A Gathered Church* (London, 1978), 9).

142 *I wished there were some midle estate between both*: other autobiographers longed to escape the extremes which Protestantism forced on the imagination: Lodowick Muggleton, for example, 'did not care whether I was Happy, so I might not go to Hell, but I could not be sure I should go to Heaven, nor certain I should escape Hell which was a great perplexity to my Mind, not knowing which way to help myself out of God's Hands' (*The Acts of the Witnesses* (1699), 25).

144 *the Holy Scriptures . . . of all other writings*: the very tediousness of religious exercises was a means of convicting people of their natural, and seemingly irremediable, badness (see *GA*, note to p. 73).

Who showeth mercy . . . he will have compassion: see Rom. 9: 15.

So as when I think upon it . . . by some suddayne stroke from heaven destroyed me: compare *GA* 7.

145 *even as a ship after a long voyage descovers the place whereunto she saileth*: Norwood gives a reprobatee application to the ship reaching its harbour, which traditionally referred to the soul attaining heaven. See Bunyan's Preface to *GA*.

147 *The Right Knowledge of Christ Crucified*: *A Declaration of the True Manner of Knowing Christ Crucified* (Cambridge, 1596).

errors . . . of an Arminian tincture: Arminians (after the Dutch theologian Jacobus Arminius (1560–1609)) sought to revise Calvinism, rejecting in particular the doctrine of perseverance. They thought it presumptuous to suppose that the elect could never fall away. Calvinists regarded this belief as a derogation from God's sovereignty, since it attributed to human beings the ability to resist God's grace. Archbishop Laud and his party came to be associated with Arminianism, which figured importantly among the divisions leading to Civil War.

assailed at certain times . . . by fits with dispair: the idea of despair as fitful is picked up in *PP*, where Giant Despair himself is subject to fits (pp. 94, 97).

It is hard to express . . . hanging on my cloak or gown: Norwood's experience of demonic interference was extreme, as the ensuing passages show, but compare *GA* 32 and note.

149 *But notwithstanding my secrecy . . . Satan perceived my drift*: the scene is perhaps reminiscent of Doctor Faustus turning the pages of his Bible, only to learn later that Mephistopholis had been there: 'I turned the pages and led thine eye' (Marlowe, *Doctor Faustus*, v. ii. 102–3).

149 *but then it pleased the Lord to bring it to my remembrance*: the passive phrasing here should be noted, especially as some commentators on Bunyan have tended to speak of puritan memory as a faculty of deliberate use. See Stachniewski, 198–206. See also the victimization of Milton's Satan by his uncontrolled memory, *Paradise Lost*, iv. 23–6, 37–8.

150 *murmurings took hold of me*: 'murmuring' against God's justice, usually prompted by the arbitrariness of the decrees of election and reprobation, is commonly reported in this period. Calvin attached significance to it as the first symptom of rebellion (see *Institutes* 3. 9. 4 and William Bouwsma, *John Calvin* (Oxford, 1988), 183).

check me inwardly for foolishnes . . . burnt with fire: the psychological pattern described here is virtually identical to that allegorized in Bunyan's Doubting Castle: the self-rebuke for foolishness and the sudden vanishing of what had seemed powerful bonds (*PP* 93–6).

lay at a catch: a colloquial phrase meaning 'lie in wait to catch out'.

151 *And Satan had power to overwhelm all . . . with a thick dark cloud*: clouds and darkness readily suggest themselves as metaphors for the doubting puritan. See, for example, *GA* 48.

captivate me in all the powers and faculties of mind and body: again, Calvinist theology—the devil's power to seize control, independently of human will—is psychologically attested.

152 *concealing my greatest greivances and fears . . . a man forsaken of God and given over unto Satan*: compare Bunyan's reluctance to disclose, and the cold comfort he received when he risked doing so (p. 51); also Crook (p. 162).

cast me off: the term 'cast off' is used by Norwood both of the attitude he imputes to his father and to God. The threat to 'cast off' children seems to have been not uncommon in this period. The similar concern about God's attitude may be related (see Stachniewski, 102).

lifted me up to make my fall the more terrible: such a possibility was provided for by the Calvinist category of 'ineffectual calling'—an apparent calling, effecting a temporary conversion, but revealed in the event of 'relapse' not to have represented saving faith (see Perkins's 'Table' prefixed to his *Works*).

put my mouth in the dust: Lam. 3: 29.

My son despise not thou . . . and scourgeth every son whom he receiveth, etc.: Heb. 12: 5–6.

I thought there was some other there present . . . to whom he did especially apply himself: compare Crook (pp. 162–3) and Bunyan (*GA* 10) for similar experiences of what Althusser was to call 'interpellation'.

153 *it is good for me that I have bene afflicted*: Ps. 119: 71. Compare Beaumont (p. 193).

prone to doubting distrusfulnes and qualms of despair: compare Bunyan's Conclusion: though relegated from the narrative, periods of loss of faith, and consequent despair, persist. Conversion is a less clean break than dogma requires.

154 *But it may be yea it is most likely*: Norwood exhibits a costly honesty in entertaining the possibility that his spiritual disease has *not* been for his good, since this allows for the shadow narrative: that his life obeys a reprobate teleology in which things work, providentially, against his good.

I rather thought her to be a hipocrite . . . by some greivous sin: Norwood's honesty gives a disturbing insight into a common response to misfortune, whether poverty or disease, in this period. R. H. Tawney wrote of the 'frigid scepticism' with which contemporaries responded to the view 'that distress was the result, not of personal deficiencies, but of economic causes . . . Like the friends of Job, [this society] saw in misfortune, not the chastisement of love, but the punishment of sin' (*Religion and the Rise of Capitalism* (London, 1922), 264–5).

Why then art thou cast down my soul . . . my present help and my God: Ps. 42: 11. The wording is close to the Geneva Bible version.

A Short History of the Life of John Crook

159 *Spiritual Travels*: Crook's editor, like the other autobiographers (except for Agnes Beaumont whose narrative is contracted to a particular episode and its aftermath), thinks of his spiritual development as a journey, as Crook himself does.

Breathings after God: OED (vb. sb. 5 'longing for') gives the first instance in 1652. It was a common puritan phrase verging on eroticism (compare Beaumont's 'fervent desires after Jesus Christ', p. 193). See Beek, 87.

some Corner or secret Place, and pray unto God: compare *GA*, Preface, and Beaumont, p. 194.

that they were in a better Condition . . . God was angry with me: compare Norwood, p. 126.

Openings: this is one of very few words used by Crook in this part of his autobiography which would suggest a distinctively Quaker retrospect: the word 'Openings' was favoured by Quakers because it suggested that the mind itself was capable of disclosing spiritual truths; the Inner Light had merely to be accessed.

160 *mind*: give any thought to.

went to be an Apprentice, about the 17th Year of my Age: boys were apprenticed to trades, usually around the age of 13, to serve for seven years. They were generally domiciled with their masters. London apprentices as a social group were a source of concern to the state: they were capable of rioting and of being politicized as militant Protestants.

in those Days called a Puritan: this is a characteristic way for 'puritans' of all sects to refer to a shared pre-Civil War experience, before most of them acquired a firm sectarian identity. Compare Clarkson p. 175.

160 *Lectures*: see Clarkson p. 174.

made me conclude, I was but an Hypocrite: compare Bunyan (p. 13), Norwood (p. 154), and Clarkson (p. 175).

become some eminent Spectacle of God's Displeasure: the haunting terror of exemplary providential judgment, the persecutory imagination, is common to many of the autobiographers (see Stachniewski, especially ch. 2).

and therefore concluded I was possessed with the Devil: this inference, culturally alien to us, is the only way, for Crook, as it was for Norwood, of making sense of the fact that he finds in himself some 'thing', some inner resistance, acting against his own perceived best interests. Contemporaries as sophisticated as John Donne were driven to the same conclusion (see Stachniewski, 269).

enquiring of Professors how it was with them: these anxious mutual interrogations, prompted by insecurity about assurance of salvation, were a staple part of puritan culture.

and how they understood . . . in Christ's time: this questioning of his condition closely resembles Bunyan's enquiry of an experienced Christian, from whom he receives cold comfort (*GA* 51).

161 *as if two had been striving in me for Victory*: the sense of passivity, so characteristic of Protestant spiritual experience, and related of course to belief in predestination, is counterparted by Bunyan (e.g. *GA* 46), but also, for example, by Doctor Faustus: 'Hell strives with grace for conquest in my breast' (Marlowe, *Plays*, ed. Steane, v. i. 70).

yet I durst not leave praying for all this: Bunyan (*GA* 32) and Norwood (p. 149) had still more vivid, even tactile, apprehensions of the devil's presence.

believed me to be a Child of God . . . I should deceive them: Compare Norwood's conviction of his fraudulence when others thought well of him (p. 134), and Clarkson's desperate pretence of extempore prayer (p. 175).

I should be made an Example to all Hypocrites: hypocrisy and expectation of judgment remain the preoccupations controlling consciousness.

for I was afraid . . . where I lay: the temptation to commit suicide is very commonly recorded by spiritual autobiographers, in spite of their belief that this would take them to hell.

162 *if [h]e were so . . . if he were not so*: Crook both generalizes informatively about the religious culture of London in the 1630s and exemplifies the way in which people were hooked on religion by this cunning emphasis on signs of election.

thus I was tossed up and down, from Hope to Despair: again, passivity is the striking characteristic of Crook's expression. The word 'tossed' occurs as readily to Bunyan: see *GA* 18, 26, 44, 53, 92.

and from a sign of Grace . . . to a sign of an Hypocrite and Reprobate: evidence gleaned from introspection was controlled by the two conflicting paradigms of election and reprobation which the puritan preachers constantly expounded.

tell me I was an Hypocrite: Norwood shares the trepidation about submitting himself to the judgment of a divine (p. 136); Clarkson abandons a letter he writes to famed divines (p. 175). The gnawing and irresolvable anxiety was, however, precisely what gave power to the 'physicians of the soul': it rendered the spiritual patient utterly supine to their authority.

exceeding afraid . . . Judgment of any other: compare pp. 50–1.

First Day: as a Quaker Crook desacralizes the Sabbath, denying that special significance inheres in a day of the week.

but only . . . as I should be led: compare Clarkson (p. 183).

it brought me into a Parish-Church (so called): as a Quaker, Crook does not accept the equation of the building with a 'church': see note on Bunyan's use of 'steeple house' (p. 13).

163 *as if he had known my condition . . . in particular*: the sermon presumes the anxiety over salvation which was so widespread (see, for example, Thomas Goodwin, *Childe of Light Walking in Darknes* (1636)).

and all these things were but to leave me without Excuse: Bunyan and Norwood are persistently prone to these desolating double-takes on past experience. Crook's suspicions here are akin to Norwood's that God had lured him into a conversion experience in order to make his fall more terrible.

in a better Condition than my self: as for Bunyan and Norwood, concern about his 'condition' is paramount, and 'condition' has interacting social and spiritual meanings.

the most contemptible Creature in the whole Creation: compare pp. 27, 31, and notes.

all which was heightened by Francis Spira's Book: compare p. 45 and note.

I cast it from me: compare pp. 58–9.

there sprang in me a Voice: the similarity to Bunyan in the verbalization of experience is uncanny, e.g. p. 48.

there shone such an Inward Light within me: here the distinctive emphasis of the Quaker is felt.

164 *which caused many of my Acquaintance to admire my Gift in Prayer*: compare Clarkson (p. 175), who is pressured into a false exhibition of this badge of spiritual status.

Ministers that came out of Holland: puritans who returned from Holland where they had ministered in exile exercised an important influence on the development of Independency. See, for example, the note on Sidrach Simpson (Clarkson, p. 178).

165 *a Volume of all Subjects within me . . . Scriptures without them*: this emphasis on 'experimental' religion, a linguistic style of personal testimony
and authentication, is probably the most reliable linking characteristic of
'puritans', especially in the pre-Civil War period. Compare Bunyan, e.g.
pp. 38, 80, and notes. But Crook is preparing his shift to an exclusive
emphasis on the Inner Light, the Spirit Within, by contrasting himself
with those who relied on the external authority of the Bible.

 as into an hidden Root: while Bunyan feels, at times, completely deserted
by God, Crook conveys the sense of a winter experience, the root of his
spirituality still secreted within him.

 Independancy: independents (who began to promote their position in
1641–2) believed that, rather than there being a national church, individual churches should be made up of members who gave public testimony to their conversion, and covenanted to join together in fellowship.
These churches would be self-governing societies. Bunyan's church was
Independent in organization and Baptist in doctrine.

 which frame of Spirit: see note on 'frame', p. 11.

166 *communicating our Experiences each to other*: Crook recognizes what
Bunyan found, that such oral integration of private experience into a
community of belief had a stabilizing effect on his sense of his own spiritual state.

 until it grew formal: puritans were vigilant of the risk of hardening practices into rituals so that the Holy Spirit, or the power of godliness, vacated
them. Quakers took this furthest by rejecting all ordinances, or pre-
arranged forms of worship, and by relativizing the authority of the Bible.

 Primitive Patterns: Crook signals again a strong shared motivation of those
called puritans: to restore the practices of the primitive church as revealed
in Scripture.

 shattered in our Minds and Judgments about it: Bunyan's church was divided
in this way, probably prompting John Gifford's valedictory appeal not to
fall out over 'externalls'. There were differences of view on the right to
baptize and how it was derived from the apostles; also over qualifications
to receive baptism. See *GA*, note on p. 80.

167 *keep me from those Principles . . . stirring in those Times*: Crook's account,
both of the succumbing of the godly to Ranterism and Atheism and
of the reason for his own escape, is remarkably similar to Bunyan's
(pp. 16–17).

 than either all my Notions . . . whatsoever: it is in passages such as this that
Crook moves further down the interiorizing path than Bunyan, for whom
the will of God in his conscience was always mediated by the objective
Word of God, or by some other external signifier such as a providential
event.

 the Twins in Rebekah's Womb: see Gen. 25: 21–4. The allusion suggests
that Crook's inner stirrings were pregnant with prophecy of a new division between the chosen and the rest.

as Philip did unto the Chariot of the Eunuch: see Acts 9: 26–39.

manifested plainly to whom the Living Child belonged: see 1 Kgs. 3: 16–28.

what was the Harlot: puritans regarded the Roman church as the Whore of Babylon, and the Pope as Antichrist; but they were also often prepared to believe that all churches other than their own would be leagued with them in the impending Final Days.

168 *with Jonathan*: see 1 Sam. 15: 29.

his sweet Refreshings in my wearied Pilgrimage: Crook does not turn his back on earlier spiritual experiences but regards them as part of his 'pilgrimage' to enlightenment. This was a common pattern, the general pre-Civil War puritan experiences—of lectures, signs of election, and so forth—preparing the ground for later conversions.

169 *William Dewsbury*: William Dewsbury (1621–88) passed through Presbyterianism, Independency, and Baptism to be 'convinced' by George Fox in Yorkshire in 1651. He became a vigorous evangelist.

like Children tossed to and fro: this sense of rudderlessness seems to have been widespread after the breakdown of ecclesiastical authority and the wider questioning of authority engendered by the wars. Jane Turner attributed antinomian excesses to this (see Introduction, p. xxxvii).

God within: one logical answer, after disappointment with all external sources of authority, was to look for an inner stability.

The Lost Sheep Found

173 *after many a sad and weary Journey through many Religious Countreys*: the individualistic quest for truth, imaged here, as in *The Pilgrim's Progress*, as a journey, emerges from a society in which monolithic religious authority has been fatally undermined. Increased geographical mobility, exemplified by the footloose Clarkson, is also a factor detaching the individual from a stable milieu and structure of social relationships in which values and beliefs are likely to be inherited rather than quested after.

reserved for eternal misery: this disturbing linkage of his own salvation with the damnation of others is a common pattern (see Introduction p. xxii).

may read in his Travels, their Portion after this Life: Clarkson here follows the tradition of the books of signs, where readers were mesmerized by the idea that their own fate could be read off by matching experience to the models of election and reprobation. To promise this distinctively puritan form of reader engagement was clearly a selling point.

yea a man of no mean parts nor Parentage in this Reasons kingdom: while appearing to reject 'Reason' entirely (associating it with the self-approving values of the propertied classes), Clarkson uses the social status of his sponsor to enhance his book's credibility.

that Soul as a brand be plucked out of the fire: see Zech. 3: 2.

174 *thou mayest in me read . . . Worship all along*: Clarkson seems to imitate the Calvinist technique of playing on the reader's fear of hypocrisy.

Mr. Hudson our Town-Lecturer: lecturers were usually appointed by parishes and supported by endowments, voluntary contributions or levies on parishioners. They were a means of securing preachers of puritan views, and were strongly resisted by anti-puritans such as Archbishops Bancroft and, especially, Laud.

I spared no pains . . . Godly Minister: the practice of 'gadding' to lectures, thus slighting the authority of the parish priest, was viewed by conservative elements in church and state (including many puritan clerics) as socially disruptive (see Zaret, *The Heavenly Contract*, 116–22).

an Order . . . Altar kneeling: in his Archiepiscopal Visitation of 1634, Laud ordered that altars should be returned to the east wall of churches and protected by a rail. To puritans the order, redolent of superstition and idolatry in its fetish for place and posture, also elevated priest above people, contradicting the Reformation principle of the priesthood of all believers.

did much incense our father . . . God before man: here we have the key to puritanism's revolutionary energies: the absolute emphasis on individual conscience relativized constituted authority, whether that of father, bishop, or king. Compare Agnes Beaumont's empowerment to defy her father.

Would force me to read over . . . Practice of Piety: puritans objected to the Book of Common Prayer because it represented the addition of human rites and ceremonies to God's Word (the Bible) and rigidified prayer, which they thought should be largely extempore (inspired by the Holy Spirit), into set forms of worship. Compare Bunyan's *Relation*, 106. It is interesting that Clarkson's resentment extends to Lewis Bayly's *The Practice of Piety* (1612): although it was written by a bishop, Bunyan speaks of it in *Grace Abounding* as an improving inheritance from his 'godly' father-in-law.

the next thing I scrupled, was asking my parents blessing: children were expected to kneel before their parents every morning to ask their blessing. Again puritanism is seen to pose a threat, legitimated by religious differences, to the authoritarian basis of seventeenth-century society.

175 *whether those things . . . was my own*: like Bunyan, Crook, and Norwood, Clarkson is impaled on the distinctively puritan rhetoric of introspection for signs, with the concomitant danger of inauthentic profession.

wanted parts: lacked abilities.

day of Humiliation: a day dedicated to humbling religious duties, especially meditation on the just punishments visited on the nation by divine providence.

the Puritans so called: this distancing from the term 'Puritans' is a common characteristic in the writing of what we would call puritan figures: for example, Crook: 'a Minister, who was in those Days called a Puritan' (p. 160). 'Puritan' was of course first used opprobriously.

came off like a hypocrite . . . damnation would be my portion: hypocrisy—inauthentic claim to the signs of election—was the abiding fear of those caught up in the puritan rhetoric. Clarkson, in general a less introspective figure than the others represented in this book, takes his hypocrisy into the public sphere (since he seems keener than the others on *social* recognition of his spiritual credentials).

whether such a soul as there related might be saved: this voluntary soul-baring is a typical testimony to the power of puritan ministers. It derived from their accredited expertise in spiritual diagnosis (see William Haller's first chapter, 'Physicians of the Soul', in *The Rise of Puritanism*).

176 *the Bishops began to totter and shake*: the period Clarkson refers to dates probably from the unpopular and humiliatingly unsuccessful 'Bishops' War' of 1639–40, which followed Charles's failed attempt to impose the Book of Common Prayer on the Scots.

the devil was a great Scar-croe . . . I thought was the devil: like Bunyan and Norwood, both of whom thought they were physically molested by the devil, Clarkson conveys the jumpiness this theological figment excited in people—though he prides himself on having developed a more spiritually mature understanding of the devil as internal to human beings (see *Look about You, for the Devil that You Fear Is in You* (1659)).

take heed lest ye fall: Clarkson's warning is given at the time of the Restoration, when an Episcopal Church of England is about to be re-established (by the Act of Uniformity of 1662).

burning Brick all the day: Pharaoh and his taskmasters forced the Israelites to make bricks (see Exod. 5: 6–19), so Clarkson is expressing his sense of spiritual slavery.

177 *So war being begun betwixt the Episcopal and the Presbyterian*: Presbyterianism was the system of church government most favoured by Parliament. The Episcopal system was finally abolished in 1646, having been effectively suspended since 1642. It is interesting that Clarkson characterizes the war, unproblematically, as a war of religion.

precise: London was dominated by puritans; 'precise' or 'precisian' was pejoratively applied to puritans, and referred especially to those who were strict in their own religious observance and in their censure of those who were not.

our Popish Country of Lancashire: Lancashire, a county dominated by Catholic aristocrats, was a stronghold of recusancy, though the bigger towns like Manchester and Liverpool were puritan strongholds (see map of England in 1660 in Hugh Barbour, *The Quakers in Puritan England* (New Haven, 1964), facing p. 42).

yet I was not clear but the Steeple was the house of God: see *GA*, note on p. 13.

177 *Calamy, Case, Brooks*: Edmund Calamy (1600–66) was a Puritan minister, polemical author, and preacher to the House of Commons. His popular sermon *Englands Looking-Glasse* (1642) advocated the burial of all superstitious ceremonies 'in the grave of oblivion'. Thomas Case got into trouble in Manchester for giving the sacrament to those who did not kneel. In 1641, he became a London lecturer, and in 1642 published *Gods Waiting to be Gracious*, in which he enumerated the church's 'idolatrous bowings, cringings, altars, crosses, and cursed ceremonies, false worship, false doctrine' (p. 68). Like Calamy he was a Presbyterian member of the Assembly of Divines. Thomas Brooks (1608–80) was an Independent minister who preached mainly in London from 1640 on. He gave the sermon at the funeral of the murdered Leveller Colonel Thomas Rainsborough in 1648.

assurance of Salvation: Clarkson shared with Beaumont, Bunyan, Crook, and Norwood the anxious quest for assurance which was central to Puritan experience.

Hooker had left several Books in print . . . I thought it unpossible to be saved: for a full list of Hooker's works, see Sargent Bush, Jr., *The Writings of Thomas Hooker: Spiritual Adventurer in Two Worlds* (Madison, Wis., 1980), 373–5. Hooker is one of the divines criticized by Giles Firmin, in *The Real Christian, Or a Treatise of Effectual Calling* (1670), for harshness of doctrine inducing despair.

help the Lord against the Mighty: this phrase became formulaic at this time. Clarkson seems from an early stage to have perceived the parliamentary side as social underdogs, anticipating the radicalization that accompanied the success of the New Model Army. The parliamentary leaders had in fact seen themselves as upholding traditional social hierarchy.

Covenant in their Hats: a reference to the Solemn League and Covenant between the English Parliament and the strictly Presbyterian rebel Scots in 1643.

the Second Commission: this refers to the New Testament spiritual covenant between God and mankind (or the elect) which should supersede God's Old Testament covenant with Israel to deliver her from her enemies. Clarkson's 'Muggletonian' beliefs enter in here: he believed that he was one of the Two Last Witnesses spoken of in Revelation as receiving God's final commission (see note to p. 182, below).

a great slaughter of the Protestants in Ireland: the Irish revolted in 1641, two years after the recall from Dublin of the brutally repressive Thomas Wentworth, who was created Earl of Strafford.

178 *Mr. Goodwin*: Thomas Goodwin was a leading Independent who opposed the Presbyterians in the Westminster Assembly of Divines (1643–9).

Doctor Crisp: Tobias Crisp (1600–43) came to be associated after his death with puritan Antinomianism, as a result of the publication of his sermons *Christ Alone Exalted* (1643).

Christ never died for all: Clarkson's scrutiny of the Scriptures seems to have been conditioned by the dominant Calvinist belief (actually that of Theodore Beza) that Christ died only for the elect.

yet I found Scriptures to the contrary: by supporting each soon-to-be-discarded position with scripture Clarkson progressively relativizes its authority (see Davis, *Fear, Myth and History*, 68), in contrast with Bunyan for whom the true meaning is absolute, though often wrongly taken.

Mr. Randel: Giles Randall (b. *c.* 1608), Antinomian and champion of religious toleration, had published a number of texts giving currency to the doctrine of the Spirit Within. Randall lived dangerously. In 1643, for example, he had been charged in Star Chamber with Anabaptism, Antinomianism, and Familism for a sermon preached at St Martin Orgar.

Mr. Simpson: Sidrach Simpson (*c.* 1600–55) was an Independent London lecturer and representative to the Westminster Assembly, whose ideas were formed by his ministry, from 1638, to an Independent church in Rotterdam. He advocated religious toleration and was one of fourteen ministers who were asked to draw up the 'Fundamentals' underpinning the religious settlement of the Protectorate.

179 *Paul Hobson*: as well as an army officer, Paul Hobson (d. 1666) was a leading London Particular Baptist and evangelist, who signed the 1644 and 1646 Confessions. He was a friend of the Leveller leader John Lilburne, unsuccessfully opposing Monck in 1659–60. He was suspected of plotting against the monarchy after the Restoration. Hobson adopted antinomian tenets and believed in universal salvation.

180 *to tell the people stories of other mens works*: one might think from terms like 'Priests', 'means provided for them', and 'tell the people stories', that Clarkson is implying retrospective distaste for a hireling clergy; but he is disarmingly honest, later on, about his own enjoyment of such privileges—always precarious on account of his lack of a university education.

Go ye teach all Nations . . . to the end of the world: Matt. 28: 19.

I loved her: Clarkson marries Frances Marchant.

181 *Dipping*: baptism by total immersion. In their 1644 Confession, Baptists declared that baptism should be given only to 'persons professing faith', and by 'dipping or plunging the whole body under water' as a sign of 'the washing of the whole soul in the blood of Christ'. The administrator of baptism must be a 'preaching disciple' (B. R. White, *The English Baptists of the Seventeenth Century* (London, 1983), 61–2. The Confession thus announced rejection of the authority of a state church and its system of licensed pastors.

got a Warrant from the Parliament: Clarkson is imprisoned in Bury St Edmunds for 'dipping' in 1645 until he becomes convinced that Baptist doctrine is mistaken, and so is set free in 1646. As a freelance baptizer by immersion who denied the validity of infant baptism, Clarkson fell foul of the Westminster Assembly's church discipline. Rumours, which Clarkson denied, of nude baptism also appear to have helped secure the warrant.

181 *Mr. Knowles*: Hanserd Knollys (*c.*1599–1691) was an influential Particular Baptist. He revised the Confession of 1646 which required that no one should be admitted to communion who had not been baptized as a believer.

and who was sufficient to publish the Contract as my self: Christopher Hill points out that church courts and JPs had little control over itinerants, so that '*de facto* marriage and divorce must have been common' (*WTUD* 320).

Mr. Sedgewick: William Sedgwick (*c.*1610–63) was a Bedfordshire-born Independent minister. A kind of Seeker, he was attracted by apocalyptic ideas and millenarian prophecy. He was drawn to John Reeve by 1652.

Mr. Erbury: William Erbury (1604–54) was a New Model chaplain and Seeker. He was alleged (around 1646–7) to be affirming universal redemption, and denying the deity of Christ and the existence of a true Christian ministry. He pressed Cromwell to tax the rich to create a 'treasury for the poor'. The collected edition of his writings was published by his disciple John Webster as *The Testimony* (1658).

no true Administrator: the Baptist Confession had denied that true baptism must await one 'extraordinarily sent'; but once again Clarkson uses scripture to free himself from his latest institutional authority, the Baptist creed. He is helped to his new view by William Erbury and William Sedgwick, who convince him that the validity of baptism ended with the Apostles. Erbury, known as a Seeker, believed that Christians should 'sit still, in submission and silence, waiting for the Lord to come and reveal himself to them' (quoted in *WTUD* 192; see also McGregor, 125). The beliefs that no church had legitimacy and that God would ordain new apostles and witnesses in his own time were the basis of the sect of Seekers (active from the early seventeenth century). If Clarkson was influenced by the second of these tenets (which was more distinctly held by the early Seekers), it may have prepared the way for his recognition of Reeve and Muggleton.

182 *preaching and prayer was to cease*: a Muggletonian tenet based on the belief that God's final revelation had been granted to the 'two witnesses', rendering preaching and prayer redundant.

Kiffin: William Kiffin was a well-known London Baptist and a signatory of the 1644 Confession (who also wrote an autobiography).

The pilgrimage of Saints . . . seeking truth: Clarkson's first publication was written, as the subtitle indicates, when he was a Seeker, in 1646. This tract, no longer extant, was quoted by the heresy-hunter, Thomas Edwards, to exemplify Seeker belief.

Thomas Gun: Gun was a figure of some significance in the London Baptist movement.

183 *some strange opinionated people in the town*: this can be taken as an indication of the marginal character of the more extravagant enthusiasts.

184 *Assembly of Divines*: the Westminster Assembly of Divines (1643–9) was the Synod appointed by the Long Parliament to reform the English Church. It was never formally dissolved, but was rendered ineffective by internal disputes.

My one flesh: an antinomian group with possible Ranter associations, though it appears from this account to have been Clarkson himself who enthused some of them with the idea of spiritual purity through sexual orgy.

Calvert: Giles Calvert (d. 1663) was a London publisher and bookseller who specialized in sectarian literature, including that of the Ranters and Quakers. He published the works of opponents of monarchy—some of Hugh Peter's works, and about half of Gerrard Winstanley's. He continued, after the Restoration, to publish material offensive to government, for which he was frequently in trouble.

185 *he was afraid I came to betray them . . . and satisfied I was a friend of theirs*: it was characteristic for sectaries, who at various times could be arrested on the basis of information received, to use this language-test on strangers. In *PP* a figure like Talkative is conversed with as a means of establishing that he is not one of the brethren (pp. 66–70).

receive an Angel: Heb. 13: 1–2: 'Be not forgetful to entertain strangers: for thereby some have entertained angels unawares.'

Mr. Copp: Abiezer Coppe is one of the best-known of the so-called Ranters, a loose group whose published works, while very different from each other, have in common a stylistic and doctrinal audacity and antinomian fervour. These works belong to the period 1649–51 (punitive new legislation having been directed at them and their authors in the summer of 1650). Coppe and Clarkson seem to have been at the practical end of the antinomian spectrum, both believing that their spiritual liberty should be demonstrated by 'sinning' without a sense of guilt. In Clarkson's case enactment of this principle seems to have taken a mainly sexual form. The Ranters' enduring achievement, however, lies in their extravagant language, their upending of religious and moral conventionalities with a mystical language energized by shocking paradox. They refused to be bound by any forms (social, linguistic, logical, or theological), as can be illustrated from *Single Eye*'s title page: 'Imprinted at LONDON, in the Yeer that the POWERS OF Heaven and Earth *Was*, *Is*, and *shall be* Shaken, yea Damned, till they be no more for EVER.'

there was no man could be free'd from sin . . . as no sin: this is virtually the only clearly owned statement of the practical Antinomianism with which 'Ranters' were associated by the authorities and the scandal-mongers. It is made, of course, ten years after the position has been discarded. The rarity of such explicitness may be owing either to risk of prosecution or to inaccurate caricature of what so-called Ranters believed and did. It does seem, however, from Clarkson's record, that he practised his liberating convictions with some gusto. He may have been untypical.

185 *for to the pure all things, yea all acts were pure*: Tit. 1: 15 'Unto the pure all things are pure: but unto them that are defiled and unbelieving is nothing pure'.

unfolding that was intended all acts, as well as meats and drinks: Clarkson's 'unfolding' of what Paul 'intended' (Rom. 14: 14) indicates the unlimited scope the Bible could offer the freelance interpreter.

now in Scripture I found a perfection spoken of: the idea of perfectibility supplied much of the utopian energy shared by the most radical sectarians and enthusiasts. (See Nigel Smith, *Perfection Proclaimed: Language and Literature in English Radical Religion, 1640–1660* (Oxford, 1989).)

186 *as I take it*: it is unclear what sort of qualification or safeguard is intended by this oddly repeated phrase.

The Single Eye: *A Single Eye All Light, no Darkness* (1650). This publication led to an order to search out the author, and helped to prompt the Blasphemy Act of 9 Aug. 1650 which introduced severe penalties for the denial of 'the necessity of Civil and Moral Righteousness amongst Men', and for other imputed Ranter opinions. The outcome of Clarkson's trial (of which he gives a brief account in *Lost Sheep Found*) was published on 27 Sept. by Parliament in a broadsheet which ordered the book's burning and announced the author's sentence to three months' imprisonment with labour, to be followed by banishment. In fact the sentence amounted to no more than one month in New Bridewell prison.

Captain of the Rant: again, one of the very rare avowals of Ranter identity.

but at last . . . height of this wickedness: Clarkson retains a sense of spiritual (and perhaps social) élitism, seeming to be put off his sexual demonstrations of purity by the riff-raff joining in just for fun.

Major Rainsborough: William Rainsborough (fl. 1638–73) was the younger brother of Colonel Thomas Rainsborough, the assassinated Leveller leader. William, also a Leveller, had asserted in the Putney debates that the end of government was to preserve persons as well as property. He was associated with Ranter principles, and was cited, and stripped of his office of JP, in the Commons on 27 Sept. 1650 under the new Act for the Punishment of Atheistical, Blasphemous, and Execrable Opinions for his approval of Clarkson's Ranter book *The Single Eye* (*BDBR*).

a God that was an infinite nothing: a typical Ranter paradox which achieved an effect of spiritual intensity while bucking the inhibitions imposed by the authoritarian, omnipresent deity in which Bunyan believed.

bringing us out of bondage, to the perfect liberty of the sons of God: Rom. 8: 21: 'The creature itself also shall be delivered from the bondage of corruption into the glorious liberty of the children of God.'

187 *Winstanley*: Gerrard Winstanley (1609–76) was the Digger leader and author who, in the spring of 1649, initiated, with John Everard, a demonstration of communist living by digging and manuring the common at St George's Hill, Walton-on-Thames, Surrey. He associated the Fall, or the curse, with property relations (the distinction between 'Mine and Thine'); the earth, he believed, was a 'common treasury' for all mankind.

Reason: 'Reason' was the term Winstanley preferred to God. Clarkson, who writes from the Muggletonian anti-rational perspective, sees his erstwhile attraction to Leveller and Digger ideas as mistaken. It had led him to a general religious disillusion and materialist pessimism. (See Barry Reay, 'Laurence Clarkson: An Artisan and the English Revolution', in Christopher Hill, Barry Reay, and William Lamont, *The World of the Muggletonians* (London, 1983), 162–86, p. 177).

Tithe-gatherer of propriety: shortly after the suppression of the Digger experiment Winstanley worked as a rent-collector for the aristocratic prophetess, Lady Eleanor Douglas.

I had as good cheat for something among them: the colony Winstanley established on St George's Hill was troubled by 'Ranters' like Clarkson, whose approach to communal living (feasting off the labour of others, spreading scandal and venereal disease through 'excessive community of women') was characterized by him as 'self-ended' (*WTUD* 229–30). Facing a Council of State inquiry and cruel persecution instigated by local landowners, the colony could ill afford bad publicity, as is evident from Winstanley's defensive *Vindication of Those Whose Endeavors Is Only To Make the Earth a Common Treasury, Called Diggers*, in *Works*, ed. G. Sabine (New York, 1941), 399–403). The site of the Digger colony, which had moved to neighbouring Cobham, was destroyed and its occupants driven off at Easter 1650.

not come under the lash of the Law: this reveals an intersection of the divine and secular law in Clarkson's antinomian thinking. He sees insouciant lawbreaking both as a liberation from the sense of sin under God's law and as the best way of lining his pockets so as to escape the penalties of secular laws against vagabonds.

188 *I had sometimes a relenting light . . . not be so*: this inability to shut out traditional thoughts of an afterlife bedevilled many heterodox thinkers of this period. Lodowick Muggleton flattered himself that he believed death meant extinction; but it was not long before his 'old Fears of Hell rose up in me, as it did formerly, when a Puritan' (*Acts of the Witnesses* (1699), 19).

Mary Midleton: Mary Middleton, whose husband's house was used for meetings of My One Flesh, appears in the derisive *The Routing of the Ranters* (1650), 4–5.

Doctor Wards and Woolerds Manuscripts: Woolerd has not been identified but Ward may be Samuel Ward, a Cambridge don who kept a spiritual diary and wrote *Magnetis Reductorum Tropologium* (1637), of which a translation was made in 1640 (Smith, 270).

189 *and the body rotted in the grave, and for ever so to remain*: Clarkson here expresses what was known as the heresy of mortalism. Christopher Hill observes that the idea of the 'drop into the ocean' 'picks up a long-standing radical metaphor' (McGregor, 202).

190 *Reeve*: John Reeve convinced Clarkson that he was one of the Two Last Witnesses of the Third Commission. One of the purposes of *The Lost Sheep Found* is, after Reeve's death, to bid for recognition as the other Witness, and thus as rightful successor to him as leader, by detailing his progress through and beyond all erroneous positions to enlightenment. The bid failed to displace Lodowick Muggleton, to whom Clarkson eventually made obeisance.

Look about you, for the devil that you fear is in you: First published 1659.

three Commissions upon this earth: Clarkson understands the Third Commission as the epoch of the Holy Spirit (that of the Father and the Son having passed).

the two Seeds: by these he means Faith (good) and Reason (bad).

my election and pardon of all my former transgressions: Clarkson, for all his heterodoxy, still adheres to the Calvinist idea of an elect few.

The Narrative of the Persecution of Agnes Beaumont

193 *Awakened*: used in a sense peculiar to puritans, it conflates the two phases of the conversion experience: the realization of sinfulness and the sense of new life bestowed by divine grace.

work together for good: Rom 8: 28. Compare pp. 43–4, 105.

it was good for me that I have been afflicted: Ps. 119: 71. Norwood also avails himself of this text in combination with Rom. 8: 28.

the more trouble . . . the more of gods presence: see *MW* x. 36: 'I have often thought that the best Christians are found in the worst of times'.

I have found trouble and sorrow, as David saith: Ps. 116: 3.

fiery darts . . . my soul hath been battred: Eph. 6: 16. The author mixes her metaphors (her soul battered with darts) in a way that suggests how familiar such phrases were: awareness of their literal sense was eroded with routine figurative use.

Oh, the great Consolations: this exclamatory euphoria seems to be a stylistic habit learned from Bunyan.

with fervent desires after Jesus Christ: compare Bunyan's Preface to *GA*: *Your hungerings and thirstings also after further acquaintance with the Father in his Son.*

some times one scripture . . . several days together: compare, for example, p. 40: 'the wicked suggestion still running in my mind'.

194 *taken me up into the mount*: the allusion is to the Transfiguration, when chosen disciples were granted a vision of Christ transfigured so that 'his

face did shine as the sun, and his raiment was white as the light'. It was read as a type for Christians' intense experience of Christ's presence and glory (Matt. 17: 1–8).

lead me into his banqueting house, and his banner over me was love: S. of S. 2: 4.

frame: see *GA*, note to p. 11.

fiery tryal: 1 Pet. 4: 12. This phrase assumed a special significance for Agnes Beaumont (see below, p. 216), which the biblical context helps to determine: 'If ye are reproached for the name of Christ, happy are ye; for the spirit of Glory and of God resteth upon you . . . But let none of you suffer as a murderer . . .' (1 Pet. 4: 14–15).

a Corner in the house, or Barns . . . my soul to god: compare Bunyan's Preface: *Have you forgot the Close, the Milk-house, the Stable, the Barn, and the like, where God did visit your Soul?* It was important to the puritan that prayer sanctified the most ordinary surroundings rather than being confined (idolatrously) to supposedly holy places.

195 *one promise to bear me up*: the spatial imagery—of sinking and being borne up—is familiar from *Grace Abounding* (and reappears in *PP*): for example, p. 55.

Call upon me in the time of trouble: Ps. 50: 15.

When thou goest through the fier . . . over flow thee: Isa. 43: 2.

And the many Dreams that I had . . . some of them was of God: dreams, like the premonitions delivered by Bible verses, both provide the narrative with a proleptic linking device and allow Agnes Beaumont to lay some modest claim to prophetic gifts. The dream of the old apple tree anticipates her description of her father's death.

my Brothers: John Beaumont (junior) owned the largest house in Edworth, suggesting that his father had already settled on him his share of the estate.

Gamgey: Gamlingay, Cambridgeshire, where there was a sister, or daughter, church to the Bedford meeting. The meeting Beaumont was desperate to attend took place on 13 Feb.

196 *Table*: the Communion table.

sealing ordinance: communion was referred to as an ordinance (in preference to 'sacrament': see *GA*, note to p. 31); properly experienced, it was a confirmation ('sealing') of faith.

197 *my way is hedged up with thorns*: Hos. 2: 6.

No not I, I will not Cary her: Bunyan's brusque refusal is consistent with his claim (p. 86) to have always been wary of intimacy with women.

198 *did raise a very wicked report of us . . . blessed be god*: Agnes Beaumont gives here a credible origin for one of the rumours to which Bunyan was responding in *Grace Abounding*. The Church of England clergy would

have been especially eager to discredit Bunyan at this time. Elected pastor of his church and licensed to preach in 1672 (after Charles II's Declaration of Indulgence), he was now building up a reputation as a preacher.

198   *a feast of fat things*: Isa. 25: 6.

   I sat under his Shadow, with great delight, and his fruit was pleasant to my tast: S. of S. 2: 3.

   the next way: the nearest way.

199   *pattings*: pattens (wooden soles strapped to shoe and foot to raise ordinary shoes above mud and puddles).

   some false reports that was raisd of him: we learn here that the ride on Bunyan's horse added fuel to existing rumours, as is suggested by Bunyan's generalized reply in 1680 (or before).

   he beleeved them because such persons affirmed it: Bunyan, like anyone else of his social status, had to battle against the strong ideological prejudice of his time that the respectable high-ups, clergymen, and the like, spoke with authority.

   So then I stood a while at the window silent . . . 'Depart from me I know yow not': see Luke 13: 27.

200   *Pray to thy father . . . shall reward thee openly*: Matt. 6: 6.

   Call upon me . . . thow knowest not: Jer. 33: 3.

   in a Chain: Jude 6. The bad angels are kept in chains.

   spread my Complaints before the Lord: see Isa. 37: 14.

   a blessed night to me; a Night to be remembered to my lifes End: compare p. 75: 'but that night was a good night to me, I never had but few better'.

   Beloved, thinck it not strange Concerning the fiery tryals that are to try yow: 1 Pet. 4: 12.

   Oh, this word (Beloved) made Such Melody in my heart: compare p. 28: 'the words began thus to kindle in my Spirit, *Thou art my Love, thou art my Love*, twenty times together'.

201   *I was greived to thinck I . . . Seek after Jesus Christ*: Agnes Beaumont's case exemplifies the cruel emotional and material sacrifices puritan faith could require. Bunyan was uncompromising in *A Few Sighs from Hell*: see *MW* i. 336.

   The father him self loveth yow: John 16: 27.

   do with me what seems good in thy sight: this loosely recalls Heb. 13: 21.

   as long as he lived: this phrase has an ominous persistence which adds to the sense of an overriding providence which nullifies John Beaumont's apparent power over his daughter.

   if yow Could stand in my steed . . . as well as other things: this, no doubt provokingly pious, statement exemplifies well the way in which puritan emphasis on individual conscience tended to subvert hierarchical order in English society.

202 *though when his Anger was over he was as good a natured man as lived*: Beaumont implies here both the fear of fathers and the proneness of fathers to violence which seem to have been fairly general in seventeenth-century England. See, for example, Thomas Ellwood's account of his father's near-lethal violence towards him in another instance where religious conviction prevailed over paternal authority (*The History of the Life* (1714), 49–57).

did not Leave me nor forsake me: see Heb. 13: 5.

203 *he would never give me a penny . . . Nor when he dyed*: the threat or deed of disowning children appears to have been fairly common in the seventeenth century (see Stachniewski, 102).

when my father and mother forsook me, then the Lord took me up: Ps. 27: 10.

who gave me hopes of an Eternal inheritance . . . a better portion then silver or gold: Beaumont follows Bunyan in setting a spiritual 'portion' against a material one, an eternal inheritance against the loss of a temporal one.

204 *soughly*: softly.

Call upon me . . . thou knowest not: Jer. 33: 3.

this scripture would often dart in upon my mind: see *GA*, note to p. 59.

205 *the Eyes of the lord . . . and his ears are open to their Cryes.*: Ps. 34: 15.

in all their afflictions he was afflicted: Isa. 63: 9.

But poor weak Creature . . . yow will hear afterwards: proleptic narrative technique controls alarm and insinuates providential oversight. Bunyan was followed by a voice calling 'Simon, Simon,' telling him that he was to be tried. Peter, in contrast to Judas, was a type of the forgiven traitor.

206 *hussif*: the meanings 'housewife' and 'hussy' were both available: either *OED* 1: the mistress of a household; a thrifty woman; or *OED* 3: a woman of low or improper behaviour. The 'hussif' is forced to be an obedient housewife—which confers a limited authority in the domestic arena, symbolized by the keys—in order to avoid being a hussy.

207 *not thinking what doler and misery I brought upon my self in so Doing*: Beaumont appears to be thinking of the torments of guilt she is bringing on herself. But there is also a sense in which the dolour and misery can be attached to her father's death. The magic of providence ensures that Beaumont is not kept from her spiritual obligations by exploiting her meaningly reiterated qualification '*as long as yow live*'.

They that deny me before men, them will I deny before my father and the Angels that are in heaven: Luke 12: 9 and Matt. 10: 33 are conflated.

he that forsaketh not father and mother and all that he hath, is not worthy of me: here Luke 14: 26 and 14: 33 are conflated.

208 *that word, Simon . . . I have prayed for thee*: Luke 22: 31.

   their shall be a way made for yow to Escape, that yow may be able to bear it: 1 Cor. 10: 13.

209 *I thinck my daughter will be distracted*: this was a common response to the emotional intensity of puritan religion, especially in relation to women (see, for example, Robert Bolton, *Instructions for a Right Comforting Afflicted Consciences* (1631), 199–200).

   These be they that lead silly women . . . make long prayers: effeminacy (such 'distractions', says Worldly-Wiseman, 'unman men' (*PP* 16)) and hypocrisy were stock smears against puritans. Two-thirds of the members of Bunyan's church were women.

   god brought me up out of this horrible pit . . . and set my feet upon a Rock: Ps. 40: 2.

210 *In six troubles . . . and in seaven I will not leave thee*: Job 5: 19.

   The Eternal god is thy Refuge, and underneath are the everlasting Arms: Deut. 33: 27.

   I could not tell what to make of these words, for they was very dark to me: like Bunyan (pp. 20–1), Beaumont is disconcerted when the words ('*the End is Come*') do not derive from a scriptural text.

   The set time is Come: Ps. 102: 13.

211 *And another thing*: the MS has 'Anothing'.

212 *lay not that sin to my Charge*: see Acts 7: 60 and 2 Tim. 4: 16.

   Fear not . . . I will up hold thee: Isa. 41: 10.

213 *the Angels of the Lord Incampeth round About them that fear him*: Ps. 34: 7.

214 *Lord, give me one seal more that I shall go to heaven*: this exemplifies the disturbing habit of self-reference produced by puritan anxiety over assurance of salvation. Compare the pilgrims' response when Vainconfidence falls into a pit: 'they heard a groaning. Then said *Hopeful*, Where are we now?' (*PP* 92).

   The Ransomed of the lord . . . fly away: Isa. 35: 10.

   mr fary: identified by Brown as Mr Farrow, a neighbouring lawyer.

   Caused it to work for good . . . afflicted: see note to p. 193 above.

   naught: an accusation of sexual misconduct (see note to p. 85).

215 *Blessed are ye . . . for my name sake*: Matt. 5: 11; see note to p. 85. It seems to have been characteristic for puritans to have greatest peace of mind when most persecuted. This text was a favourite support.

   yow are an officer in the town: Beaumont's brother John appears to have been a constable (though he and his wife Elizabeth were themselves fined in 1669 for not coming to the sacrament at Edworth parish church). This was a part-time civic responsibility.

216 *fiery tryal. I see my life lye at stake*: a fuller, more literal meaning of 'fiery tryal' begins to emerge, since, if convicted of parricide, Beaumont would burn at the stake.

217 *No weapon . . . thou shall Condemn*: Isa. 54: 17.

As many as are incensed Against thee shall be Ashamed: Isa. 41: 11.

petty Treason; She must be burned: the child stood in the same relation to the father as the subject to the monarch, as one to whom allegiance was owed. Hence parricide was treason. It appears that Mr Feery began to have cold feet about his allegation.

made a hand of: made away with (*OED* make v. 45b).

218 *brought before a Company of men . . . I should sinck before them*: Agnes Beaumont may be compared with Elizabeth Bunyan in her remarkable ability, sustained by the sense of righteousness, to withstand such intimidation.

ye righteous . . . shall grow stronger and stronger: Job 17: 9.

219 *Thow shall not return Again A shamed*: an allusion to Ps. 74: 21.

the Chariots of Aminnadab: see S. of S. 6: 12.

222 *have Another pull with me*: *OED* pull sb. 23: a turn or bout at pulling each other in wrestling or any struggle. Bunyan uses the metaphor for his tussles with the devil (p. 71).

but a shilling to Cut her off: the expression antedates *OED* cut v. 55i: To cut off with a shilling (Addison 1710).

brother: i.e. her brother-in-law.

224 *I was very chearful . . . that day*: Compare Vanity Fair, where Christian and Faithful 'look upwards, signifying that their Trade and Traffick was in heaven' (*PP* 74).

he will bring forth . . . as the noon day: Ps. 37: 6.